Praise for *The Dea*

"I loved *The Dead Take the A Train.*
with a horror bent."

—V. E. Schwab, #1 *New York Times* bestselling author

"An excellent grim and gory tale."

—*Library Journal* (starred review)

"An original, thought-provoking, and entertaining title that will call to readers from multiple dimensions."

—*Booklist* (starred review)

"Deliciously down and dirty . . . Khaw's and Kadrey's styles are a perfect match throughout. . . . Fans of urban fantasy, neo-noir, and pulp horror won't want to miss this raucous adventure."

—*Publishers Weekly* (starred review)

"Khaw and Kadrey are a powerful team of genre-blending mad geniuses, and *The Dead Take the A Train* is a gore-covered cake for horror lovers."

—*Reactor*

"An addictive, sprawling yarn. This city brims with underhanded dealings and odd magic, and every corner writhes with fresh horrors and delights."

—Hailey Piper, Bram Stoker Award–winning author of *The Worm and His Kings*

"*The Dead Take the A Train* packs a great concept and the combined talent of a horror super-team."

—*Paste*

"Everything old is new again in this comically horrific team-up. . . . An enchanting introduction to a magical bitch on wheels."

—*Kirkus Reviews*

"A bloody fantastic ride. Hop on this train now."

—Kevin Hearne, *New York Times* bestselling author

"Fun, thrilling, and compulsively readable."

—John Langan, author of *The Fisherman*

"A fast-paced madhouse of mayhem . . . *The Dead Take the A Train* is a blast and highly recommended for dark fantasy and horror fans looking for a good time."

—*Grimdark Magazine*

"Fast-paced and thoroughly entertaining!"

—Lucy A. Snyder, author of *Sister, Maiden, Monster*

"Eye-searing horror that's impossible to look away from."

—Kat Howard, author of the Unseen World duology

"Khaw and Kadrey have created a kaleidoscopic carnival of horrors and wonders."

—Matt Wallace, author of the Sin du Jour and Savage Rebellion series

ALSO BY **CASSANDRA KHAW**

The Salt Grows Heavy

Nothing But Blackened Teeth

A Song for Quiet

Hammers on Bone

"These Deathless Bones"

THE DEAD TAKE THE A TRAIN

CASSANDRA KHAW
& RICHARD KADREY

NIGHTFIRE
TOR PUBLISHING GROUP
NEW YORK

This is a work of fiction. All of the characters, organizations, and events portrayed in this novel are either products of the authors' imaginations or are used fictitiously.

THE DEAD TAKE THE A TRAIN

A Nightfire Book
Published by Tom Doherty Associates / Tor Publishing Group
120 Broadway
New York, NY 10271

www.torpublishinggroup.com

The Library of Congress has cataloged the hardcover edition as follows:

Names: Khaw, Cassandra, author. | Kadrey, Richard, author.
Title: The dead take the A Train / Cassandra Khaw & Richard Kadrey.
Description: First edition. | New York : Nightfire, Tor Publishing Group, 2023. | Series: Carrion City ; 1
Identifiers: LCCN 2023033063 (print) | LCCN 2023033064 (ebook) | ISBN 9781250867025 (hardcover) | ISBN 9781250867032 (ebook)
Subjects: LCGFT: Fantasy fiction. | Horror fiction. | Novels.
Classification: LCC PR9619.4.K49 D43 2023 (print) | LCC PR9619.4.K49 (ebook) | DDC 823.92—dc23
LC record available at https://lccn.loc.gov/2023033063
LC ebook record available at https://lccn.loc.gov/2023033064

ISBN 978-1-250-78930-3 (trade paperback)

First Nightfire Paperback Edition: 2024

Printed in the United States of America

0 9 8 7 6 5 4 3 2 1

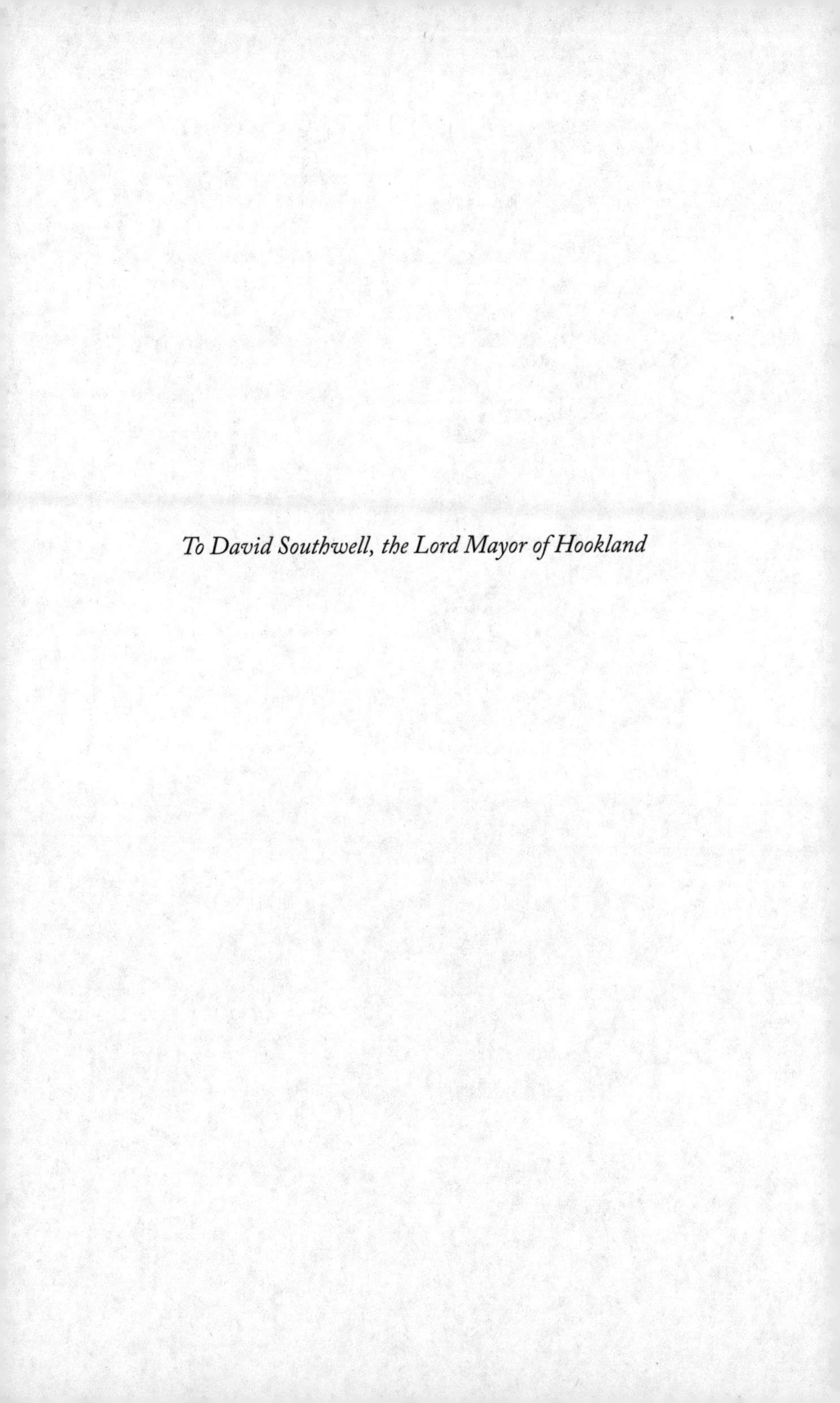

To David Southwell, the Lord Mayor of Hookland

CHAPTER ONE

There were few things in life Julie Crews enjoyed more than bachelorette parties. They were, by design, one of those rare events where women weren't just permitted but *encouraged* to throw off their inhibitions. No matter the amount of booze or the quantity of strippers, the drugs or the homoerotic shenanigans, the shrieking, the woo-girling, the balloon penises, the everything, it was all waved away as girls being girls, a bacchanal of the stupid, like oblations for a twenty-first-century neon Dionysus.

Julie *really* liked bachelorette parties, which, in part, was why she was so pissed.

"Okay. There are two ways we can do this. My way, or—"

"Please don't fucking say it," the *thing* slurred.

"—the wrong way."

Blood gouted from the stump of the bride-to-be's raised arm: a stinking ooze of red syrup, far thicker than it should have been, with fist-size clots and nearly black. The other reason all this needled Julie so much was she liked the NoMad speakeasy, liked its pressed tin ceiling, the expensive slouch of its furnishings, *loved* the gorgeous brass bathtub which stood as its marquee attraction and was now filling with the putrid slurry. Sure, this wasn't anywhere she had cause to visit save once an actual paycheck. But it was her spot for feigning any claim to pedigree.

And the demon was fucking it up.

And her toes, through the cut-out velveteen heels she'd borrowed from poor St. Joan—God rest their friendship—were getting *wet*.

No. Not wet, Julie corrected herself.

Sodden.

She was beginning to regret the emerald dress she'd chosen to wear instead of her usual jeans. In contrast to the elegant dress, her arms were a road map of deep scars, earned over years of work, threaded with what looked like barbed wire. On one arm was a rose tattoo, more thorns than blossoms.

From the bleeding stump, a cephalopodic eye glared at Julie and said, "I didn't do anything wrong."

Julie could see a tongue flicker in its oblong pupil and a rime of teeth inside the dark—teeth so small they looked like salt grains in the dim bronze lighting.

"You're in possession of a human body."

"I am borrowing it."

"Does she know she's on loan?"

The woman gibbered, eyes rolled back to the whites. Julie suspected she was beautiful when not drenched in gore, rictused face sheened in sweat, tongue lolling. She was runway-scrawny and cornfed-white. Legs for days. Delicate ankles, ankles now hooked around Julie's waist. Her knees banged on the rim of the bathtub. Taffeta was everywhere, soaked through with red. She—the *fuck* was her name? Ally? Alice? Some permutation of that, Julie was sure—moaned, soft and low and terrified.

"No," said the demon, sullen.

"In that case, it sounds like, what's the fucking word for it—?"

"Cohabitation?"

"Criminal possession."

"No. Wait. That's when you have something like—hold on." A frisson of tumors ran circuits under the skin of the bride's pale throat. Up and down. Up and down. Julie memorized the intervals, the specific count of the pebbling, not yet ready to commit to the prospect it might matter, but demons liked routines. It had to mean something. "No. I'm right. Criminal possession is when you are in possession of items or property prohibited by law."

"And the law says," Julie interrupted, "you don't fucking borrow a human body unless you have consent."

"Shit."

"So, what's it going to be, asshole? My way or the wrong way?"

There was no answer save for a wet *slorp* of tissue receding into muscle. The bride sagged, head ricocheting off the edge of the bathtub, the resulting clang eliciting from Julie both a wince and a muttered "*fuck*" as she fumbled for her oyster knife. It embarrassed Julie sometimes how makeshift her gear was, what with the armories at her peers' disposal. The stash her ex possessed—fucking Tyler, that charmed prick—had her wanting to pledge to God, *any* god, so long as it came with a blessing of arms.

But whatever got the job done.

The oyster knife was her latest acquisition: a pretty thing with a voluptuous ebony grip, impossible to differentiate from any other knife in its category save for the faint scabbing of rust along the blade. Under a microscope, the discoloration would be revealed as runic sigils, nothing ascribable to human invention, not unless they did business with Julie's very specific supplier.

She drove the blade hard into the bride's elbow and torqued downward, shearing a curl of flesh from the woman's forearm, hoping to spoon the demon out or, better yet, kill the fucker. (Her fee would require renegotiation, but convenience always came at a cost. Apartment hunting in Manhattan taught her that early.)

As her knife peeled flesh, the room erupted again in screams. Girls ran for the door, slamming into Julie's wards. Some slipped on the bodily fluids smeared over the floor as they went, and Julie heard people scrabbling to get up, trying, failing—nails and stiletto heels clacking on the tiles, unable to find purchase. She heard a few of the party girls throwing up *again*. Not that she blamed them. The bride-to-be's body held an absolute library of stenches and with half the speakeasy's guests dead, everyone was receiving an education in charnel perfumery.

Julie stared at the flayed tract of arm in her grip.

She'd missed the demon and found something else.

"Huh."

Eyes, heavily lashed, the same pastel blue as the bride's own irises, squinted up at her, neatly encysted amid the muscle fibers. They blinked in the glare of the club's lighting. Scrunching, visibly upset at their exposure.

"What the fuck?" Julie breathed.

Those were human eyes, nothing at all like the demon's, and there were hundreds of them. Julie wondered how many more laid hidden, asleep and dreaming, eggs in an egg carton. And she thought about the way the demon had traveled the bride's throat. Like a nervous tic. Like a squid moving along, fertilizing eggs as it went, and—

"What the fuck?" she said again, this time with a note of rising anger. "You turned her into a *nursery*?"

The eye hatched through the divot of the bride's right collar bone.

"I didn't start this."

"You're clearly a part of this."

"Yes, but I didn't *start* it."

"*Who cares?*" Julie hoisted up the bride's arm, stabbed a finger at the wound she'd cored out. "This is gross."

"It's part of our biological cycle."

"You're not biological!"

The screaming worsened. Julie shot a furious look behind her. "Shut. Up. I am *talking* here."

The clamor lowered to a few terrified whispers, then disappeared.

If any of Julie's youthful illusions had survived her twenties, they were gone now, eaten alive by the realization that in six months she'd be thirty, still with nothing to show but liver damage, debt, and frozen dinners in an icebox that worked only half the year. She knew what she excelled in and what she did not, and the former was a category that did not include getting a room of screaming, whimpering, gin-soaked girls to shut up with such force and completeness.

"What did you do to my daughter's *hand*?"

Julie turned to the source of the question. She was an older white woman, in her fifties, petite frame scaled in lace, with a pencil skirt slitting up to a hip bone. Leather gloves over thin hands, the material polished to a shine. She wore fishnets, stripper pumps, and to Julie's senses, she was a cut-out paper doll of nothing at all.

"What the hell?" said Julie.

Her hair was blond, brilliantined: a gamine look that flattered her softly creased features. Unlike Julie's, which was short, spiky, and black, always looking as though it'd been impatiently sawed into shape.

"You cut off her hand."

"I didn't." Julie had, in fact, not. "But what I want to know is who the fuck are you?" She frowned. "And more importantly, *what* the fuck are you?"

The woman sighed like someone used to sighing when she didn't get her way immediately. "My name is Marie Betancourt. I'm the mother of the bride."

Julie raked a look down the new arrival.

Had the woman been in the restroom? Ensconced in a booth with a much younger man? At the bar, commiserating with other grown-ups? Had Julie, doing lines with the bachelorette party, somehow failed to notice the woman? No. That didn't make sense. Not with that aura of Marie's, or rather the lack thereof, the physicality of said void possessing the same gravitational pull as the site of a missing tooth. No, no way some cheap drugs could occlude such weirdness from notice.

"Monster of the bride, you mean," said Julie.

Marie shrugged. Her accent was New England old money and a thread of something else, something she'd tried hard to gore out of her voice. "I don't care about your definitions. What I want to know is what you did to my daughter's hand."

"What your family hired me to do."

"We didn't hire you to disfigure my child."

"Sometimes," said Julie, wiping blood from her cheek with the back of her hand, "shit happens."

Julie gave the room a quick once-over, taking note of how the girls had clumped along one wall and the speakeasy staff were again in view, arrayed behind the bar. Each and every one of them had on the same posture, the same lights-on-but-no-one's-home stare. So, Marie worked magic too. But what kind? With the woman's old money pedigree, Julie's first guess was satanic. She rescinded the thought a moment later. The anarchic catechisms of the Church of Satan didn't seem like they'd fly with someone from the suburban oligarchy. Something darker, then. Much darker.

The woman said, "Whatever the case might be, get him out of my daughter and then we will *renegotiate* your fee. You did an ungodly amount of damage to my poor girl, and—"

"Wait, wait, wait. Let me get this straight. Did you say 'him'? Specifically?"

"I did," said Marie, crossing her arms.

"Just 'him'?" said Julie. "There are eggs in here, *Marie*."

Her voice was even. "Those are meant to be there."

"Like *fuck* they are."

Marie's expression creped. "Did you not read the contract you were sent? I thought it was very clear. We need him out. Just. Him. *Why* is that so hard to understand?"

"Because your daughter is infested with—with—I don't even know what the hell they are but I sure as hell know I'd dig them out with a garden trowel if they were inside me and I didn't have anything else to get them out with."

"For god's sake, do what you're paid to do and stop talking so much."

It hit her then. *Oh*, Julie thought, as the pieces mosaiced into place.

"It's like when the neighbor's shelter mutt won't stop trying to fuck your pedigree poodle, isn't it? You're pissed because *it's not the right dog.* You—you're breeding something in there. You're using your daughter as an incubator."

"*Perhaps.*" And there was the snap, the façade popped. "All right. Yes. One girl in every generation is honored as the Womb, and I'll be damned if my daughter will breed our family a litter of rejects."

"Hey," said the demon.

Both Julie and Marie ignored it.

"Is she going to survive this?" said Julie, suddenly tired.

Marie pinched the bridge of her nose.

"Survive what?"

"Being the goddamn Womb."

"Maybe," said Marie. "And if she doesn't, a part of her will live on in some way."

Julie stared down at the bride, coddled like an egg herself in the bathtub, limbs everywhere, and she felt pity: a sharp, wretched twang of sympathy. She'd been impressed with how hard the bride had gone, how much she'd drank, the way she kept up with Julie, snorting coke and dropping ecstasy, like it was nothing, like someone intent on living out her last day of being free.

"Jesus, you big money shits can't help being garbage, can you? She knew she wouldn't make it. Your daughter *knew.* That's why she went from zero to crazy the moment she got here." Julie smoothed the lank blond hair from the bride's face. Under her fingers, the woman's skin burned. "Did she even consent to this? Was she awake when you got her pregnant with . . . whatever the hell this is?"

"She consented to the rite," said Marie with care, the precision of her statement more telling than a confession. "As for the drugs, she'd always had a problem with them. It's why we were so pleased when she was made the new Womb. Finally, her useless existence was going to amount to something."

"This is your daughter you're talking about."

Marie shrugged. "And none of this is your problem. I—damnit, he's trying to find the rest of her eggs. Get rid of it *now*, or you're not getting paid."

The right thing to do, Julie knew, was to say no. The right thing was to tell Marie to fuck herself, save the girl, walk away, and burn the speakeasy down behind them. But the problem with the right thing was it didn't keep the lights on.

"Stay out of my way, old lady."

Julie spat a spell so filthy it leaked black ichor over her chin. Her jaw whined with the magic. It thumped through her skull, and up along every tooth, until Julie's head was a haze of shrapnel and static. Some people had it easy: they carried spells like a girl's trust in her mother, kept them chambered with no effort whatsoever. Julie wasn't one of them. She needed them stitched through the fatty part just under her skin. Otherwise, they washed away.

As the glyph-bindings snapped, one after another, wire fluttering from her wrists, Julie found her anger burning even hotter. She couldn't believe it. Here she was, unbuttoning the barbs of a spell from her skin and for what? The cable bill, last month's rent, a half-decent dinner if she skimmed from the first. Was she really stooping this fucking low?

The spell burrowed into the bride's shoulder, cauterizing the flesh as it wormed inside, leaving an inch-wide hole in its wake, and for a second, as the pain in her head blurred her vision into an oily smear, Julie thought she saw the meaty curl of a slug's tail flick and vanish into the wound. She knuckled the tears from her eyes, leaning back, tongue rinded with a sugar coating of something sour-sweet. As she did, the bride jackknifed up, as though impaled on a hook scythed through her diaphragm—and she banshee-screamed.

Loud enough to make Julie clap her hands over her ears. Hard enough that Julie heard the women's larynx tear: the screaming becoming graveled, turning wet. Her wailing didn't stop as convulsions billowed through her. The bride screamed and she would not stop.

Until, with a damp burst—

Her throat split. From the vulvic-like opening, the demon fell, splashing into the puddled gore at Julie's feet. It resembled a liver fringed with blue-red nerves and overgrown with tumors: little cauliflower protrusions, each of which, at its puckered heart, contained an eye gone dead and filmed with pus. The sight brought Julie no pleasure. At most, she felt an embarrassed relief. She was glad the awful affair was over and sorry about her involvement, and the fact she was both these things pissed her off.

The bride's throat closed and she swooned again, but this time, Julie caught her before her head could bounce on the tub's copper rim, held her suspended like the two were modeling for a painting: a hand under the small of the bride's back, the other beneath the bowl of her skull.

"I'm sorry," she whispered.

"Finally," said Marie. "You should have pulled that thing out when it started. If you had, we wouldn't have wasted so much time."

Julie set the bride down into the bathtub, arranging her arms so she looked like a saint laid out for display. Her expression was beatific, no longer strained. At rest, if not for long, not with her mother waiting.

"That spell cost way more than you were paying me."

"You should have negotiated your costs into your original fee, then."

"Yeah, yeah. Fucking pay me. A grand and not a penny less."

Marie tossed a handful of bills.

"The fuck. Was that. For."

Julie collected the money and counted the blood-stained bills, once and then again, irritation kindling. She had hoped for a different outcome but it was as she thought.

"This isn't what we agreed on."

It wasn't even close. Six hundred in soggy Franklins. Julie suspected Marie carried wads of fuck-you money, meant for use in these exact circumstances. Enough that she didn't look like a crook, but never enough to actually pay up. They were as much statement as her lacquered finger-wave hair, her carriage, her accent and the precision of her diction. Meant to show the gulf between Marie and the rest of the world. Here she stood on a rung next to the stairs and down below was everyone else, rutting in the mud.

"Be glad you're even getting paid. You fucking mutilated my girl."

Julie donned a sunny grin.

"Are you *sure* this is all you have for me?"

"It's more than you deserve."

Wiping her filthy hands on her jacket, Julie said, "You know, the problem with the service industry is you have to do everything you can to make sure the customers tip. No matter how screwed up they are, how much they fuck with you, how little they give a shit about your sense of basic human dignity, you have to smile and smile and make sure they have a good time."

She clambered out of the bathtub, wringing blood from the hem of her pretty, pale green satin slip. She wiped her fingers along the rumpled material, leaving streaks. Paused. In an afterthought, she removed her heels and strung them along the hook of two curved fingers. Briefly, Julie wondered how she looked in Marie's eyes: gore-splattered, her dress ruined, bare feet, rat-nest hair, a strappy little handbag made to resemble a child's idea of a stegosaurus.

Good.

"Here's the thing."

She approached Marie in a lazy slink, grin widening.

"I'm not your fucking waitress."

Julie popped open the latch of her handbag. Fingers—long, gray, with far too many knuckles—pushed out from the top, stretching out spider-like.

"You've got a nice face, Marie. A model's face. Cheekbones for days. Nice shoulders too. What do they call it? Fine-boned? Bird-boned? Something pretty like that."

She slowly approached the woman, holding the handbag just tightly enough that the fingers couldn't escape, but loose enough for them to grasp desperately at the air.

"You know, back in the Victorian days, some idiot rich bitches—like you—would have a couple of ribs removed so they'd fit their corsets better. Creepy, huh? Still. It was fashionable."

Julie kept approaching until Marie's back was pressed against a pillar at the side of the room.

"Of course, those Victorian surgeons were butchers. Amateurs at bone removal."

Julie held up her bag.

By then, Marie realized what was happening.

By then, it was too late.

"I always say, when you want to rip out a bone or two or a hundred, leave it to the professionals."

She opened her bag and something leapt out, all fingers and teeth and high-pitched screeches like a bat.

Julie took her lipstick from the bag and reapplied it where it had rubbed off, slowly, languidly.

Marie screamed and tried to run. Julie turned to leave, knowing that the woman didn't stand a chance.

She heard the first crunch just as she reached the door.

CHAPTER TWO

To blow off steam, Julie walked barefoot through the East Village all the way to Chinatown with St. Joan's ruined pumps dangling from one crooked finger. That sucked, she thought. She needed time to unwind. That *really* sucked, Julie thought, as she finished a cigarette, leaning against the wall of a head shop, careful to avoid the piss stain sprayed over one corner.

At a glance, Julie was mostly your stereotypical white girl: the oversized eyes made her resemble a knock-off Margot Robbie, but her features hinted at the Korean grandmother who she rarely saw now that she was an adult and could not be bodily dragged to church. Half because the old woman lived so far away, and half because—in her Catholic zeal—she never quite forgave Julie's mother for shacking up with the pretty blond piece of shit who took off shortly after Julie's birth.

She liked Chinatown. Most nights, it was more tourists than locals, the latter aware that if you wanted real Asian food you went to Flushing where the grandmothers held court, watched over by what few dragons survived their migration to America. But tourists—even if they walked too slow, even if they clogged the pavements and wore their fanny packs like an invitation—were as much New York as everyone who lived here. The city wouldn't be the same if there weren't people to scream *I'm walking here* at.

Cigarette pinched in the corner of a grimace, Julie flexed her left arm. There was a smiley face sloppily tattooed there, its lower half dissolving into industrial waste. It was ugly, but all her tattoos were ugly: the only tattoo artist she could afford to do spellwork for her also hated her. Not that it was Julie's fault. *She* had no idea the sunken-eyed guitarist she'd slept with was the woman's boyfriend.

People like Julie didn't get to be choosy. She winced as the spell began to work, the tattoo diluting, spreading over her skin until the entirety of her forearm was a palette of new bruises: yellow, with smudges of green and blue. It hurt, but this was how things went: a lesser agony paid for the removal of a worse one.

Julie gritted her teeth until she lost the urge to idly crush cars parked too near or too far from the curb or, better yet, to do it to their owners. She smoked and breathed and relaxed by degrees as blood pooled under St. Joan's sopping shoes.

When she felt somewhat human again, Julie joined the throng heading underground to the A line. At the turnstiles where commuters tapped their credit cards to get to the platform, Julie ran her nails over the reader and the bar unlocked for her. If anyone noticed, they kept their mouth shut. Likewise, no one met her eyes or said a word about the blood in her hair or the viscera caking her clothes during the half hour ride uptown. It might have been magic, but more likely it was New York indifference working in her favor. No one in the city gave a damn if you didn't give a shit yourself.

Up she went and out of the subway again, weaving between twentysomething tech workers still too broke for Williamsburg, a flotilla of exhausted moms and their kids; retail staff staggering home for a two-hour nap before their next shift; tourists intent on seeing the "real New York," gangbangers, middle-aged drunks, poets, actors, and hipsters looking to rent in what would hopefully be the next big thing.

Julie lived in a ramshackle four-story brownstone on 137th Street. Her apartment, at the far end of the hall on the first floor, was easy to spot for the delivery drivers who bought her food or—more often—the mind-obliterating drugs she loved so much. Her front door was slathered from top to bottom with a chaos of crosses, angelic and demonic sigils, gris-gris talismans, milagros, a vellum Seal of Solomon, tomb rubbings, and small idols of gods living, deceased, and mostly forgotten. Her neighbors seldom spoke to her, except for the meth head on the third floor who once tried selling her a bag of speed that was really baby laxative and strychnine. She didn't even bother using magic on him. She just pushed him down all three flights of stairs until one of his legs bent the wrong way. It was satisfying at the time, but not as satisfying as the speed would have been.

Inside her apartment, Julie slammed the door shut and stripped in the living room, the skylight more than enough illumination to stumble by. She stuffed her clothes into the special hamper reserved for anything that had been soiled or damaged during a job. It was St. Joan's suggestion. Something to do with accounting, depreciation, and taxes. Julie had never paid taxes but did what she was told because St. Joan was older, wiser, owned the building, and took Julie at her word when she said the rent was coming, just a little late.

Julie stepped into the shower and turned the water up until it was as hot—thank god for small blessings—as she could stand. She didn't bother washing at first. She stood under the steady, scalding stream, letting it carry away as much of the bachelorette party gore as was possible. Little red clots of *something* turned the water pink. Julie had a suspicion they'd result in a clog in the drain but that was tomorrow's problem. Today, she was too tired.

She reached behind the shampoo and conditioner—also St. Joan's, donated to Julie in the name of pity—for the pint bottle of vodka she kept there for shower "emergencies." She took swigs as she sponged and scrubbed until both she and the bottle were finished. A little tipsy, she stepped carefully from the tub into soft white slippers with rabbit ears on top. Wrapping herself in a fuzzy robe, she went back to the living room with every intention of lying down—until she got a look at the place.

The coffee table and floor were scattered with food cartons, dirty clothes, half-finished beer bottles, opened bags of potato chips, and drug paraphernalia.

"Fuck," said Julie. It seemed a good enough summary.

At times like this, she had a quick but thorough system for dealing. Julie grabbed a 30-gallon trash bag from the little kitchen and started throwing everything inside. Food wrappers, empty tins of THC edibles, liquor bottles, ripped bras. Anything she found offensive, anything that brought a frisson of self-loathing, no matter how small: it was gone, gone, fucking gone. It was a wasteful system, she knew—there was always a shortage of underwear—but it was simple and efficient, which is how she liked things.

Simple and efficient.

Not like how life was going to be for the bride.

The Womb, her mother had called her.

When she was done, Julie tossed the bag by the front door and stood there, shaking her head. Even clean and full of vodka, she could still hear the bride screaming as the thing *tunneled* inside her. She couldn't stop thinking of the woman and what might happen after, if her family would find her, would walk her right back into their ancestral home—it was always a manor, some fifteen-bedroom atrocity in the suburbs or, if she was really unlucky, somewhere on Long Island, which was *technically* New York but no one liked admitting such—where she'd have to sit in the dark and wait for the right demons to come breed inside her veins.

Julie exhaled.

It was going to take more than a couple of drinks to clear her head.

She flopped down onto her expensive designer sofa, a leftover from a bad affair she had with someone who thought he was too good for her. Surveilling her apartment, taking in the rank squalor, Julie wondered if he might have been right. Maybe she was trash.

Though she'd cleared away almost everything from the low coffee table, Julie had left the essentials: a bottle of really good vodka, her go-to vice when she was alone; the nearly empty mints tin that held her dwindling supply of cocaine; a plastic baggie with mushrooms and the stale pot brownie someone had left after a party; an empty pack of Sherman Fantasia cigarettes which held hits of molly and Norco.

And a small jade box filthy with dragons. Her most prized stash lived in here. These powders and pills weren't available on the street. You couldn't buy them for love or a fuck with every seraphim named in the good book. You had to know someone at Club La Pegre, the clandestine bar behind Billy Starkweather's bookstore in the Bowery. Julie poked a finger into the box, looking for her favorites. Hookland was an old standby: it gave you visions of all your possible deaths, letting you experience the end as many times as you wanted so you could puzzle out escape strategies. There were Power Puffs too, which turned the world rubbery and Technicolor and fun.

Tonight, though, was a night for a tab of Colors, which granted the user a powerful but temporary form of synesthesia. Julie washed the Colors down with vodka and a tiny line of coke and thought about food, hopeful the synesthesia would manifest as some gustatory malfunction. She was ravenous. Both for food and for some way to distract from the excitement of the day.

Usually, that meant stopping by the 24-hour deli down the street and filling a few cartons with goodies from the steam table. But that would involve getting up again and the food there bordered on healthy. No, she needed grease. She needed the kind of repast that would make cardiologists openly weep. She needed a soaked-in-yesterday's-frying-oil, each-bite-is-raw-cholesterol kind of meal. Before the drugs took hold, Julie got on the phone and ordered boneless fried chicken drowned in cheese, tteokbokki rice cakes, plum powder–dusted sweet potato fries, and some soju, from the Korean place around the corner.

When she was done, she put on Wolf Totem by The Hu, her favorite Mongolian metal band. With the Colors in her system, the music soon took on texture. *Actual* texture. It molded around her; a sensation like the scratch of good wool over her bare skin, like hands cupping her chin. What she loved best was the way the bass tolled through her; she felt like a cathedral bell, like a call to prayer, to war, to faith. Nothing human left to her, only sound and the sensation.

No memory of the Womb lolling in her arms, hoping she'd be dead of good cocaine before she was whisked away to the dark.

Powerful as that tab of Colors was, it wasn't potent enough to distract Julie from the fact that it was closing on the end of the month and there was rent she hadn't made. Thank all the demons in existence St. Joan was her landlord. Anyone else and Julie would have been out on the streets long ago.

St. Joan, as far as Julie was concerned, was better than any saint in any of the books, be it the Bible or its many torrid cousins. The previous tenant in Julie's apartment had been there since the fifties and thanks to rent control paid a paltry sum for her impressively spacious accommodations. When Julie asked to move in, St. Joan looked at her like a lost puppy and let her do so without a deposit. In the four years since then, the rent had stayed exactly the same. It was the only thing that allowed her to remain in New York.

It pissed Julie off that she couldn't just hand St. Joan her money every month on the first. It was, in fact, humiliating, which was the worst part. In a fair universe, fifties-era rent would have been easy. It would have been more than easy. It would have been reflexive. But she didn't live in that ideal world and since Marie had stiffed her a good portion of her fee, this was absolutely going to be one of those bad months.

Julie fumbled for her phone and ran through her voicemails, hoping for some job offers. But it was all bill collectors, telemarketers, and Dead Air wanting to play video games later that night.

No millionaires come courting. No exes hoping to win her back with a grand gesture. No shy widows hoping to speak to dead spouses, no soccer moms praying Julie could stop questions about why the walls sounded like Daddy begging for someone to let him out, *god please.*

Julie ran her tongue over chapped lips. Between the bachelorette party and the ridiculous hole she'd dug for her life, she felt herself beginning to spiral somewhere unpleasant. She couldn't let herself wallow, though. Not now. Not if she was going to make some calls and scare up work. She did a couple more small lines of coke—*you'd have money for rent if you weren't such an addict,* hissed her last reserves of common sense—and settled back into the music, letting it wash over and through her.

For a moment, she considered calling Tyler and begging him for a gig. He worked for Thorne & Dirk, which was technically a law firm, but that was just a minute part of their business. They were mainly an investment company like any other investment company on Wall Street, except for the fact that the majority of their fortune didn't come from cash or stocks, but from their more exotic investments: human souls, body parts, deals with preternatural gods, curses, the lifting of curses, demonic possessions, and murder of the human and inhuman variety.

Tyler had been the one who had given her the too-expensive sofa just before walking out and leaving her behind for Wall Street and the kind of money and life Julie didn't dare to even dream about.

No, begging Tyler for crumbs was too fucking depressing. Julie was lacking in options and shortchanged in the pride apartment, but she'd be damned if she'd go crawling to Tyler after what he did—taking credit for some of the hardest, most dangerous jobs she'd ever completed. Forget the assholery, the stringing-her-along, the abandonment. Those she could roll with. The credit thing, though? Hell no. Julie would never forgive him for that.

Or for leaving her behind.

Just one more piece of Manhattan trash waiting to be washed away in the next hard rain.

She thought, *I really have to turn my life around. And right away. Starting tomorrow, no more drinking or drugs. I'll go through my whole address book and call everyone. Someone will have something. Someone always has dirty work they don't want to do.*

There were always solutions. As she told herself this, the cocaine broke through her dread. Julie relaxed into her good mood. By the time her food arrived, she was almost happy. But her geniality was short-lived. As she closed the door on the delivery guy, her upstairs neighbors began their nightly theatrics. There was screaming and crying. The sound of furniture breaking. Crockery being shattered on the walls, the floor, anything with an edge hard enough to crack ceramic.

Every night was the same and every night Julie had to fight down the desire to fix the problem once and for all. Maybe get Kafka on their asses and turn them into roaches, except then the building would have bugs and St. Joan would hate that. For ethical reasons, murder was out of the question, but she often contemplated wrapping a binding spell around the whole apartment and translocating the building to another plane of existence. Only then there would be no more apartment and no tenants to pay their rent, something Julie suspected would upset St. Joan.

And that was the last thing she wanted to happen.

St. Joan was the closest thing to a mother she would admit to. So, she kept her magic to herself and ate her greasy food, sinking deeper into Tyler's sofa and the tactile pleasures of the music.

Her tab of Colors lasted longer than it usually did. Julie was still high at midnight. When her phone trilled, her world went velveteen and violet. Julie was stoned enough it took a minute for her to recognize the noise for it was: Dead Air's ringtone. Belly full and coming down from her chemical cocktail, Julie clawed off the sofa and went to her computer. She donned her headphones, tweaked her VPN, and fired up Burning Inside, the battle royale that Dead Air was currently obsessed with.

"Julie!" he shouted into her ears the moment she logged on. "Where the hell have you been? I had to solo my last few matches. You had me playing with pick-ups. Pick-ups!"

"Couldn't you get Them to play with you?" Julie drawled before she could catch herself.

She heard Dead Air suck in air between his teeth on the other end of the call. He was slightly younger than Julie, twenty-four or so, a Harvard dropout who lived alone in a shiny penthouse overlooking the New York Stock Exchange in the Financial District. When he and Julie first met, she had been convinced he was the scion of a billionaire magnate who'd decided poverty was a fashionable aesthetic.

Except surprisingly, he wasn't.

Dead Air belonged to what he would only call Them, a pantheon of nebulous *somethings* ruling over various microcosms of modern technology. Like gods but without an appetite for worship or any want for a clergy outside of Dead Air. To Julie, it had felt like a lot: one priest for a whole digital heaven. Dead Air didn't seem to mind and more importantly, seemed disinclined to dissect his relationship with Them. Given how hard it was for Julie to keep friends, she kept her mouth largely shut, and tried fastidiously to ignore how the light from his devices sometimes reflected faces in his dark hair.

"They don't play games," said Dead Air, sighing gustily. "I told you before. Come on, how many times do I have to explain it? They're Creator-level entities. They don't *do* games."

"But they can get pissed off at people."

"You said it wrong. It's *They*," corrected Dead Air. His avatar—a pink-stained knock-off Easter Bunny with a trail of blood wetting the right side of its grinning mouth—ran circles through the lobby as they waited for a new match to start.

"Okay. Geez."

Another sigh. "By the way, They said to tell you that you can automate your rent payment. You've been late—"

"I know how many times I've been late."

"St. Joan—"

"St. Joan will get her rent when I have her goddamned rent. Can we please not fucking talk about my *inadequacies*?"

Every character on-screen, NPC or otherwise, paused in their circuits to glare Julie. Even her own avatar gawked at her. Their accusation lanced through her screen. The hairs along Julie's arms and up the back of her neck rose under the attention. Julie had forgotten the first thing that Dead Air had taught about her about Them:

They were everywhere. Plus, she'd been rude. Mean and rude.

"Sorry, Dead Boy," said Julie. Had she been more sober and less exhausted by the world, she might have had a wisecrack to volley, but Julie was wrung dry, worn to the core of her marrow. She felt grayed out even with the cocaine incandescing through her veins: she felt unbearably mortal, frangible, and so very small. "It was a really hard day. I thought I had a little chaperoning job. But then there was blood and ancient family rituals and a fucking demon squid thing."

The tension wicked from Dead Air's voice as the game returned to normal, the characters jerkily easing into their animation loops. "Demon squid?"

"Yep," said Julie, attention moving to her loadout. Tonight felt like an evening for missile launchers. "It was polite, though. The host's mom, on the other hand, was a piece of work. She stiffed me on my fee."

The lobby filled with other players. "After making you go up against demon squid?"

"Yep," said Julie again, coercing a bravado she didn't feel into her voice. Demon squid was a funny phrase; it was easy to stitch into conversation, even easier to transform into a joke. So much better than the truth that the girl was probably sitting alone right now, waiting to be wedded to the dark. "Fucking demon squid."

"Wow. Did you kill the mom?"

Julie frowned a little, heat prickling across her skin. "Why would that be your first guess?"

"Because you're you."

"Hmm." It took her a minute but she realized then what that warmth was: embarrassment. Julie was embarrassed. Muddled by the cocaine and vodka, it took her slightly longer to establish why she was embarrassed and when she did, Julie couldn't help but choke out a bitter, entirely humorless laugh. Despite how she'd spent the last decade curating a reputation as a badass, Julie was ashamed that Dead Air thought of her as a killer first and foremost: someone who resorted to murder before any rational methods of resolution.

The problem was he wasn't entirely wrong and she wore the truth of this as endless scars. She was more keloid growth than skin. Her belly was cragged with deep slashes from when a pack of werewolves had torn at her, had dug and dug until the oily ropes of her guts went everywhere; her back somehow an even more impressive mess, mangled with bullet wounds and worse. There were places on her body so dense with cicatrices, the nerve damage so extensive, they could be burned until they were scorched and smoking without Julie feeling anything at all.

All of it was because Julie fought like a grenade blast, a last resort.

But she wasn't a killer, not in the way she knew Dead Air meant.

At least, she didn't think so.

She hoped not.

Quietly she said, "Maybe I need to change that. Soften my rep a little. Go more mainstream."

"Don't. I like you as you are." Dead Air gave a small whoop

as a match finally began, and then: "Did you kill her, though? Sounds like she deserved it."

Dead Air carried in him a very specific welter of bloodthirstiness at odds with the rest of his personality. He wasn't a gorehound, for which Julie would always be glad. She couldn't abide sadists, at least those who preferred their pain nonconsensually sourced: the other kind was more than fine (and, often, *fine* in the colloquial sense). Dead Air flinched from any detail of a violent situation, but he always wanted the abstract: the who, the how many, and the what was used.

"She did. But no."

"Aww."

She could hear his disappointment. "But I did leave her to dance with a hungry Verdigris. He probably did the job."

"Yeah," said Dead Air after a minute, slaked. "Good riddance."

The greasy food she'd hoovered up was beginning to make her head feel heavy. It was becoming hard to focus, hard to think about the symbiotic connection between fingers and keyboard and moving figures on the screen. Julie had to fight to remember she couldn't just *think* at her avatar to make it do what she wanted, the world unspooling into fleece.

After a couple of minutes, Dead Air said: "Julie? You there?"

She heard mumbling. Impossibly, there was a T-Rex in a biplane on a strafing run, gibbing the other players. The ground was a porridge of offal and disconnected limbs, and Julie almost wanted to laugh at how the latter had accumulated, a veritable cornfield of bloodied arms stretched to the indifferent sky. No one was running anymore. The chat was clogged with accusations of hacking and dismayed commands for whoever was doing this to stop. Dead Air's laughter rose over it all.

"Yo, Julie. Check out this dinosaur. You want a go next?"

Her tongue wouldn't move. It stayed wadded and heavy in her mouth.

"Please tell me you didn't fall asleep again."

Silence.

"Are you for real?" said Dead Air. "You owe me for this. If I go back down to Platinum, that T-Rex is eating you next time."

Julie staggered up and back to the sofa where she collapsed into immediate unconsciousness. She dreamed of punching Marie in the face. Instead of teeth falling from her mouth, each time she hit her, a wad of hundreds hit the floor. Julie slapped the Mother of the Year around all night long.

CHAPTER THREE

The floor of the rooftop meeting room was perpetually damp with a substance that the firm didn't want contaminating the rest of the building, although what that substance was exactly, no one in the company was able or willing to say. Anyone making use of the room was required to put disposable booties over their shoes and then deposit them in the incinerator chute on the way out.

Tyler Banks was Thorne & Dirk's head of Client Excisions, meaning he made problems disappear. Cut them entirely out of existence when necessary. However, he didn't like getting his hands dirty with the seriously dangerous jobs. That's what Julie was for—but she was the last thing on his mind as he stepped into the room.

Inside, the space smelled like the ocean at low tide: brine and sulfurous rot and things that did not belong on the shore. Bathyal things, deep water stuff, things Tyler desperately hoped would stay forever uninterested in the land.

He put on his booties and exchanged nods with the early arrivals.

There were old-fashioned fluorescent lights overhead, and something about their glow drained everything and everyone in the room of color, left them, if not exactly so, then very close to the warm infected white of a purulent wound. Occasionally, a bulb would pop, and the shadows rearranged themselves in unpleasant ways. The floor was tile and there were body-size refrigerator compartments lining the wall opposite where Tyler stood. No one at Tyler's pay grade knew what was in them.

Every surface was inscribed with ancient runes and symbols so obscure that only a few of the senior members of the firm could read them. The ceiling seethed with black chains. Large slaughterhouse hooks hung from the links at narrow intervals. Most of the time, they were there to hold various ceremonial vessels, but Tyler had seen them used for *different* purposes.

Considering its primary function, the room was tidy, which Tyler respected: the complete opposite of the other Shift Rooms and resurrection chambers in the building. There were no spooky candles or cobwebs. No altars heaped with human bones. This was a serious setting for serious people and—smell notwithstanding—Tyler quite liked the professionalism of the space.

He took his customary spot between Johnson Andrews from Recruiting and Annabeth Fall from Internal Security. Fall looked worse for wear: unsurprising, given how her department used its junior staff as living batteries. That Fall was still here, blanch-skinned and bruise-eyed, was testament to her strength. But she was human and Tyler estimated it would be another three months or so before a discreet ad looking for her replacement would begin circulating.

The last person to enter the room was Clarice Winterson from Surveillance. *Always Clarice,* he thought irritably. A century of employment didn't excuse her from basic courtesies like punctuality. Once inside, Clarice pulled the vault-like steel door closed and locked it. Then she and Alan Lansdale from Afflictions went in opposite directions to wheel two twelve-foot-tall Tesla coils to the center of the room, bookending a tall, baroque gold and glass vessel suspended from the ceiling. They fussily secured it to the floor, checking it over, clucking to themselves. Tyler shifted his weight from one foot to another, impatient, as the two traded places, inspecting the other's thoroughness at anchoring their respective devices.

When they finished, they went to stand at the tails of an Odal rune chiseled into the floor. Tyler and the other members of the meeting did the same, forming a knot of thirteen people.

Clarice looked around the group and said in her seismically low voice, "Put on your equipment."

Immediately, the assembled executives slipped on the heavy industrial earmuffs and tinted goggles they'd brought with them.

Except for Warren Brautigan from Contracts. He cursed and twisted at his ear cups.

"What's the problem?" said Clarice.

Brautigan swore again, his voice rising in pitch. "One of the damn side pieces came off my muffs and I can't get it back on straight. Can I go and get another pair?"

"No," said Clarice. "The meeting is about to start."

"It's going to ruin my hearing."

Tyler had to suppress a grin. Like everyone else in Contracts, Brautigan was reprehensibly handsome—radioactive blue eyes, cover-model haircut, a jaw square enough to plot on a graph—and unwholesomely aware of the fact: he was indolent in that way the very pretty always seemed to be, convinced he could be spared anything so long as he batted his eyes in the right direction. It brought Tyler a vicious pleasure to see Brautigan so frantic, his cheeks marred with high color. *You deserve this,* he thought with great satisfaction.

"Good," said Lansdale. "You *should* suffer for not checking your fucking gear before you got here. Now shut up and hold the damn things together with your hands."

Clarice took what resembled a chunky television remote from a jacket pocket and used it to turn off the overhead lights. Tyler knew what was coming. Discreetly, he checked to see if his earmuffs were on straight and waited for their visitor's big entrance.

After a moment of dead silence, the engines of the enormous Tesla coils droned to life and long million-volt purple arcs of electricity wound their way out from the summits of the two machines. When the edges of those arcs brushed the top of the aureate vessel hanging between them, the liquid inside began to swirl and darken, corkscrewing into a whirlpool, the violence of the momentum such that the container began to shake.

Though Tyler had the appropriate ear protection, the sound

remained deafening. His hair grew buoyant from the static, lifting straight out of its helmet of pomade. All the precautions in the world and the collateral effects still *hurt.* The ritual was always a reminder of what a helpless sack of meat he was and how the simplest mistake in the meeting room could snuff him out completely. The only thing that gave Tyler comfort was the pleasing spectacle of Brautigan cowering and squirming, hands clamped ineffectually to either side of his head, blood leaking in strands down the trunk of his throat, every vein in hard relief.

When the water had darkened to a lightless black, not so much a color as an eye-watering void, a tendril wormed into view. It bobbed thoughtfully for a few seconds, as if measuring a spread of options, a searing oxygenated *pink* against the jet-black nothing, like a good steak cooked to medium rareness, the incongruous vividity setting Tyler's teeth on edge. Then the tip curled, and it knocked thrice on the glass: an abashed-sounding *plink plink plink.* No one in the thirteen moved, or spoke, or breathed. Even Brautigan froze, his suffering overridden by a limbic certainty that attracting notice would mean immediate annihilation.

The tentacle made another attempt. When no one responded still, it seemed to wilt into the gloom. Tyler braced. He knew what would follow. In the next instant, dozens of tendrils whipped outward from an unseen radix, slamming into the glass, over and over, with increasing violence. Tyler had witnessed the process a hundred times. He knew the vessel wouldn't break; Thorne & Dirk prided itself on having top-shelf equipment. But still the sight filled him with a neolithic terror.

Soon, the vessel became overgrown with sucker-lined flesh, the tendrils flailing gracelessly over the rim of the glass: the motions of a newborn, disconnected from any experience of the physical world. Dark, now rancid, liquid sheeted onto the floor. Tyler checked that he'd pulled his booties up high enough to protect his expensive Italian loafers from the stuff. Brautigan, still in agony, resumed his tortured dance, soft shoeing a few steps back before slipping, turning almost a hundred and eighty degrees before finding his footing again.

He's going to wish he fell, thought Tyler. *Clarice is going to write him such a report.*

Then the creature birthed itself from that bloom of meat with a long, pleased groan of a sigh. Its body was a spiraling lattice of gristle, fervid with grape-like red tumors, some of which erupted as it moved, expelling phlegm and a cancer of stubby embryonic hands. The grasping neoplasms multiplied in number, until the thing was frilled with them, flower-like. At its crown was what resembled a horse's skull and that too was ravaged by malignancies, pebbly sarcomata fruiting through the joints, the eye sockets. It was the color of the light in the room, the same blighted white.

With the rite complete and their guest fully corporealized in its favorite habitat, the Tesla coils shut down and the fluorescent lights ticked back to life. Around the rune, people removed their earmuffs and goggles, exchanging surreptitious looks with one another: checking, perhaps, to see if any of them had been shaken and could be recategorized as prey. Clarice waited until the group was done with its cruel self-analysis. She raised her arms and everyone followed in an ostentatious bow to the creature before them.

Clarice said, "Welcome, Proctor. We're honored to have you with us."

The Proctor's head remained stationary, but its myriad hands—they were almost translucent, threaded with black capillaries—shivered and groped at the air in Clarice's direction. They beckoned at her but she stood her ground, her face unyielding. The thing laughed.

When it spoke, its jaws didn't move. Tyler, like the others, heard the Proctor's voice inside his head—a sensation he despised. It was such an intimate invasion. Another reminder of his helplessness in the presence of all this power.

"My children. Oh, my child—no, no we're not there yet, but

soon. Welcome, my colleagues then," said the Proctor in a curiously secretarial voice: pleasing, warm, deferential, female, utterly at odds with its appearance. "Your presence and obeisance fill me with joy."

"We are honored to have you with us and await whatever tasks you have for us," said Clarice.

"So many, many tasks. More than there are stars. But first: I ask a question."

"Yes, Your Grace?"

"Who among you turned their back on me as I arrived?"

All eyes went to Brautigan, and Tyler did not bury his grin.

"It was me, Proctor," Brautigan said, his voice barely above a whisper. "I'm terribly sorry."

"Your name, your name. We—I must have a name!"

"Brautigan from Contracts, Your Grace?"

"You gave such offense, Brautigan from Contracts." It clacked its jaws and Tyler wondered if it was trying to be *relatable,* if the sound was the Proctor trying to laugh. "You know the law, Brautigan from Contracts. You know what is right and what is *our right.*"

"I—I didn't mean to. You know I glory in your existence. You know my eyes are only for you. I am only for you. Please." Brautigan repeated the word in the hopeless whimper of a beaten child.

The Proctor said nothing at first and then: "What is the law, Brautigan?"

He dropped his gaze to the floor. The light was wrong. It reflected indigo on the skin though there wasn't a reason for there to be any purple in the room. Everyone looked necrotic, but Brautigan especially. He wasn't very pretty anymore. "That none may point a weapon or show disrespect to a Proctor."

"Then you admit to the offense?"

"Yes, but it wasn't my fault."

"Fault isn't the issue. The law is the issue. Thorne & Dirk is a law firm and the law must be obeyed. Otherwise, all is chaos. Do you understand? The law is the point. The law is everything."

"Y-Your Grace. Please."

"The law will be obeyed."

"*Please.*" It was a scream.

Something shot from the vessel—faster than any of Tyler's telemetric enchantments could record—and slammed into Brautigan's face, knocking him back several steps. A gelatinous mass of bloodshot flesh had welded itself to the man's face. As Tyler watched, the clot of meat feathered into a thousand delicate strands which in turn elongated: growing joints, spewing muscle, thickening until they became broad cables wrapped tight around Brautigan's head. In seconds, he was engulfed.

Brautigan gave a muffled scream.

He howled and torqued and stumbled and thrashed, clawing at his face. His nails found no purchase. They sank into the flesh glued to his own and *stuck* there, just for a moment each time, before he could wrench them free. Soon, his struggles began to weaken. It was clear to Tyler and every other witness in attendance that there were no openings in the mask: Brautigan was slowly asphyxiating.

Tyler couldn't look away.

Brautigan tottered a few steps to his right and then sank onto his knees. His chest heaved as he tried to draw in more air to scream, but the meaty lump only squeezed tighter. Soon, he dropped and lay silently on the wet floor. A hot tungsten light began to radiate through the fat-pocked tumor encysting Brautigan's head. Tyler thought he could see movement in the rime of tissue matter: something working itself into the man's mouth and nostrils.

The Proctor said, "Who here represents Afflictions?"

"Me, Your Grace," replied Lansdale.

Another moment and the Proctor said, "Do your duty, flenser."

"As you wish, Proctor."

Tyler's heart ratcheted in tempo but he kept his breathing even, made sure the burst of adrenaline didn't reflect in his expression. He knew exactly what the Proctor's decree meant: torture. The unending kind without even hope for death. Brautigan would only be released when the Proctor returned and pronounced the sentence complete, and who knew when that would be?

"The law has been served. Tasks must now be assigned. Who here represents Excisions?"

Tyler swallowed.

"That would be me, Your Grace," he said.

"Tyler. Your name is Tyler," it said, as though his name required memorization. "Yes?"

"Yes, Proctor."

He told himself this was a compliment, an enviable honor: such attention from the Proctor was rare and precious enough to be currency. Yet all he experienced was a bladder-emptying, sphincter-tightening dread.

"We have need of an extreme excision from the body of the firm's clients."

"Anything. I'll handle it personally."

"Good. Wise. You are cleverer than Brautigan from Contracts and we are proud of you, Tyler. Your name is beloved among us. You are loved," the Proctor crooned. "We have a problem with a foram anomalous. The rarest kind—a parasite that feeds on the dreams of its victims."

Tyler, already nervous, clenched his teeth so hard in the ensuing spike of anxiety he thought he felt his molars crack. He'd never faced a foram anomalous but had heard the gossip: they were reputed to be gleefully vicious and almost impossible to extricate once entrenched in a victim.

"Whether the parasite is here by mistake or by design does not matter," the Proctor went on. "Thorne & Dirk's clients are the most important mortals on Wall Street, and their dreams, good or bad, are proprietary business products."

The Proctor sang *proprietary business products* with the cadence of an ad executive, and Tyler fought down a shudder. His jaw was becoming dystonic. He sandwiched his tongue between his teeth so they wouldn't chatter, and his mouth filled with blood as he bit down.

"To remove such products without first a contract and proper remuneration is a violation of the law. Find the anomalous. Make it stop what it is doing."

Tyler searched his memory. There was something else he had heard about that phylum of horror. Some specific little nasty detail. What, though, Tyler couldn't remember.

"I will gladly do as you wish."

"You have two days. No more."

"Thank you, Proctor."

"We will not forget what you must do. I—" The Proctor said the word *I* like it was a laurel for Tyler to don. "—will not forget what you will do."

Oh shit.

The memory bubbled up then, exposed like a bloated corpse in the Gowanus Canal: to kill an anomalous, you had to let it inside you. To destroy it, you had to destroy yourself in the process.

How the fuck do you do that and survive?

The Proctor expected him to martyr himself for the firm, not out of malice but because no alternative had ever been recorded. Even company folklore was conspicuously bare of any accounts of someone surviving a rumble with an anomalous. What's more, every employee in the firm was required to sign a release form: in the event of a suicidal mandate, you were obliged to die for the betterment of the company. It was just business.

But Tyler had no intention of dying.

He had no plans of mutinying either, which left him one option: doing the impossible.

Tyler thought hard. He knew the corporate database kept comprehensive files on literally everything, but access was monitored by a rotation of strategically lobotomized personnel who never slept, never spoke, did nothing but watch until their handler—Yasmina, a Middle Eastern woman with the carved and coldly lovely face of a holy icon—wrung reports from them, which she did twice daily. It would be embarrassing—and potentially fatal—if anyone found him digging through the repository for an escape plan. No, he'd have to consult his library at home.

It was increasingly difficult to maintain his façade of milquetoast professionalism: he was swilling blood from his gnawed-through tongue. He was beginning to sweat through the suit. Showing weakness here though was more hazardous than engaging the anomalous. One would only kill him, the other could end in demotion. Or worse. Thorne & Dirk had an inventive Human Resources department.

The Proctor turned from him and began passing out assignments to the other department leads. On any other day, Tyler would have been listening intently, eager to diagnose any problem areas in his colleagues he could exploit, but he was preoccupied with his own future. He needed a way out. He needed a way to kill the anomalous without being devoured by it in return.

Can I just transfer it to another plane of reality? But then I'd be responsible for any damage it did there and the Proctor would be irritated if more regulations were broken. Maybe I can cram it into a subordinate and simply kill them both?

He throttled that thought too. That wasn't going to work. Employees were corporate property. He would need permission and that again was something that might be construed as weakness unless he could find a viable scapegoat.

Tyler kept thinking, feeling trapped.

He had no idea how much time had passed when Clarice droned: "Put on your equipment."

Everybody bowed to the Proctor and donned their earmuffs and goggles.

The Tesla coils whined again to life. Electricity burst across the room. The static glided over the sweat along Tyler's skin and this time, he didn't mind its presence.

Then the Proctor was gone. The various executives removed their protective equipment and began to file out of the room, their chatter already pivoted to banal topics: lunch, seating arrangements for the upcoming company dinner, the *commute* to lunch, and whether they could expense such to the firm and if they needed the justification of a client. If so, how many? And whose portfolio would be farmed for suitable companions? Almost no one paid any heed to Brautigan, stepping gracefully around—and in Johnson's case, over—him. In the time between the Proctor's sentence and the end of the meeting, all of Brautigan's visible skin had gained the pilled texture of an old sweater, an effect made especially horrendous by the honeycomb of lesions over every square inch of flesh.

He keened as each of them passed, the sound almost like the word *please*.

Lansdale and Tyler were the last to leave. The former briskly pulled on black gloves and dragged the moaning Brautigan to one of the refrigerated cabinets along the wall.

"We'll come back for you later, sweetheart," he said with a faint smile, patting Brautigan like a haunch of brisket prepped for the smoker.

Tyler wove past Lansdale. He dabbed the heel of a hand to the corners of his mouth, checking for blood. Nothing. Good. But as he flung his booties into the incinerator chute his hands shook slightly and he balled them into fists to force them to stop.

I'm fucked, he thought as he walked back to his office. *Finally, truly, and completely fucked. Plus, my tongue hurts.*

When he was back at his desk, Tyler poured himself a double shot of bourbon, but didn't touch it. He just stared at the glittering glass waiting and wanting to quietly and painlessly die.

CHAPTER FOUR

Julie wasn't sure what pissed her off more—that she was woken up by the one-eyed neighborhood tomcat who'd somehow slunk into her apartment, or that her phone was ringing at seven in the goddamn morning and the caller ID said *Fucking Dickbag.*

It was Tyler.

When he dumped her he was smiling like an angel as he explained she no longer fit his career trajectory. She was too entropic—whatever the hell *that* meant—for the workplace culture of his new company. That night, Julie had wrung the neighborhood dry of its cocaine and good vodka and drank and snorted until the world lost its hard edges. Then, she went through her address books and social media accounts, meticulously deleting their couple photos, and updating his contact information so it was more appropriate to her current sentiments about him.

The truth was that she didn't really care that he broke up with her. Relationships didn't always last. Sometimes, they fell apart for the pettiest reasons. Julie once walked away from a two-year relationship because she caught her then-boyfriend belting out Figaro while on the can. He hadn't been a bad singer, either. In fact, Julie remembered fondly how golden his voice had sounded, the acoustics of their closet-sized bathroom stripping away whatever imperfections there were, verdigrising his bright copper tenor. She just hated opera. If she could, perhaps rashly, abandon a relationship over one on-key incident, Tyler deserved the right to break up with her over whatever the hell he wanted.

It was just the way he *said* it.

The business jargon intermingled with his nice guy routine. His "it's not you, it's me, but also it's you not fulfilling all my needs" chicanery while he smiled and smiled, cupping her hands in his own, like this was some hideous labor he was undertaking for her sake and hers alone. His insistence they could maintain their professional connections, that they were good together as partners but not *partners*. And if Julie would deign to wear business attire while visiting Thorne & Dirk, that would be the icing on the top of this brand-new cake. It would all be great, Tyler insisted as Julie tried not to scream.

The phone rang. *Fucking Dickbag* again.

Any other day and she would have let his call go to voicemail, but Tyler was a good source of income. Shitty, soul-crushing income, but income nonetheless. He outsourced jobs to her that he was too chickenshit to do himself. Under the table, of course. Lousy gigs, sure. Lousy, dangerous, and obnoxiously intricate gigs. The kind that burned through whatever favors and resources you might have stockpiled. Assignments you didn't take unless you were desperate for rent or the approval of a panel of senior partners. But they were jobs, and Tyler paid mostly on time, even if he did garnish those hard-earned wages like a cook with a head cold.

The phone stopped ringing.

"Hell."

Julie swung her legs off the couch and eased onto her feet. She winced. A dull ache simmered where her spine met the base of her skull. Julie knew she wasn't old yet, but she was getting there. She needed to do something with her life, develop contingencies for when the clockwork of her telomeres began to die; find a spouse, maybe, a sugar person who liked going as hard as she did. Get a nest egg. Freeze her eggs. Could she pay a few months of rent by auctioning off her ovum? Study accounting. Learn about investments. Something.

Her phone began ringing again.

Julie grabbed it.

"What do you want, dickbag?"

If there was one thing she couldn't do with Tyler, it was play nice.

"Oh dear. You sound hungover again."

"Fuck you, Mr. Rogers." He wasn't wrong but it was the principle of the matter. "What do you want?"

"That street punk routine isn't aging well," said Tyler, tone soaked with pity. "It was cute when we were younger. But we're getting older now, Julie. Crow's feet and all that."

"I don't have goddamn crow's feet!"

"Soon though. You need a new act."

"Don't worry. I've been taking banjo lessons. Now, I'm going to ask just one more time: what the hell do you want?"

"For a start, for you to stop swearing at me so much."

"Fine, fuck boy."

Tyler spluttered a laugh, a totally insincere smile-for-the-camera laugh. "That isn't much of an improvement."

"Okay, cum stain."

The playfulness wicked from his voice. It never did take much to irritate him, and although Julie recognized her needling of the man was counterintuitive given her situation, she could not help herself. She hated the sheer privileged gall of him.

"Jesus," said Tyler. "Jesus Christ."

"Taking the Lord's name in vain. Isn't that against company policy?" Julie paced the length of her apartment. The cat was still there: muscular and gunmetal blue where the light had him in frame, his right eye cratered into slick pink tissue, a congenital anomaly as far as Julie could tell, not that she had any store of veterinary knowledge to extrapolate from. The cat yawned at her. The bastard was sunning himself on her windowsill like he hadn't just burgled her apartment and was looking for leftovers. He fixed her with an interrogative expression and Julie mouthed at him *absolutely fucking not*.

You allow one cuddle session, Julie thought.

"I can ask someone else," said Tyler coyly. "Maybe, the Barghest Sisters might—"

Julie sighed.

"What's the job?"

She could hear him grin.

"Formalus up in Midtown. It's been eating up banker dreams and the company is getting kinda antsy."

"Why? Bankers are a dime a dozen."

"Not the kind our, ah—" He laughed a little glass-bright laugh, a laugh that had never shaken hands with the idea of sincerity. A corporate laugh, soulless and pandering, and it made Julie want to punch him until he was all gums. "—*people* need."

"So the magic kind. Why the—you know what? You explained it to me once and I didn't care. I still don't care. And like, one way or another, Harvard shits those out like candy corn."

Of all the Ivy League institutions, it was Harvard alone that provided an off-the-books curriculum so shrouded in secrecy that none of the elite clubs—or, indeed, most of the faculty—knew about it. Partly through studying and partly through a few well-placed (metaphorical) stabs in the back, Tyler rose to the top of his class on handling the weird phenomena that prey on the high-profile cosmos of investment banking. Why the supernatural gravitated toward money men, though, Julie would never know. To Julie, everything in Midtown was drab, drab, drab: a soulless embankment of houndstooth suits and cut-glass vocal fry, cocktails that cost too much and lunch specials that included too little, people who preached and pontificated on the gospel of reuse and recycle, while buying up old tenements to carve out new homes for the gaudily wealthy. If there was a holy war for New York, those assholes would be on the side with the pitchforks and torches.

New York City might run on Dow Jones, lattes, dollar signs, and neon lies, but what beats in its breast is its people: its hip-hop, its bodegas, its art, its Union Square grifters, its subway mariachi, its two-jobs-and-night-school-thank-you-I'm-fine mothers, its daughters full of dreams of making it big, its multicolored sons and their hopes blazing bright as a meth tweaker's eyes.

That was the real New York to Julie, and those rich kids of Wall Street were a colonizing parasite.

So, fuck them, Julie thought but did not say.

Tyler said, "The problem is that the top-secret information they were carting around in their heads is being disseminated to rival corporations. It's making the whole industry very uneasy."

That didn't match up to what Julie knew of the entities but it didn't seem improbable. "What's the thing's exact classification?"

Tyler hesitated. The pause was so infinitesimal that Julie would have dismissed it were it not for the sudden klaxon shriek of her sixth sense. Questionable as some of the other components of her person might be, Julie knew she had good instincts and she knew they were good enough that it'd be suicide to ignore when her neocortex clutched at her frontal lobe, screaming *pay attention, goddamnit.* Julie narrowed her eyes, prickling with the increasing certainty that something was definitely, horrifically wrong.

"Standard-issue formalus, as far as the public knows."

"As far as the public knows? What about Thorne & Dirk? What's the real story?" said Julie. She wandered up to her kitchen and was simultaneously disappointed and unsurprised to find the pantry barren of grown-up essentials like coffee. There was instead a graveyard of paper cups, lids still on. Julie debated taking a swig at random but decided against it. Low as she had sunk, she still had standards, and playing tastebud roulette with spoiled caffeine felt like two steps too close to sitting out front with a Will Kill Demons For Food sign.

"Same thing," said Tyler breezily. "That's all the Analytics department knows too."

There, thought Julie, uncertain if she was more aggrieved or appalled by the transparency of Tyler's attempted nonchalance. Who the fuck did he think he was? And who did he think *she* was that he would try something so second rate?

"What about you?" said Julie softly. "What do *you* know?"

To her grim delight, Tyler went quiet.

"What the fuck is this thing's subspecies, Tyler?"

More silence.

"Come on, shitbird. What is it?"

And Tyler laughed the same way he always did: brightly, airily, brittle sitcom harmonics.

"Does it matter?" said Tyler.

"Of course, it fucking matters. You don't get a cardiologist to show up at someone's colonoscopy and not expect tears. I need to know what tools I gotta bring to the table here."

Julie's resolve was disintegrating. What was dignity in the wake of a hangover so vicious it colored her vision with the sting of bile? Gingerly, she sipped from the first cup in reach. It wasn't too bad, nearly lemony in flavor, the acidity a not-half-bad distraction from how the rest of it tasted. Stale cigarettes and sour but still a hundred times better than the backwash from last night's debauchery.

"Bring *everything*," said Tyler in lieu of an answer. "Then you take whatever intern you're fucking this week to the Arturia Estate and get rid of the thing."

"I don't like wasting my resources, Tyler. Tell me what you know."

"I know you like to get paid. It should be a quick job. You'll be in and out in twenty minutes. I can get you two grand."

Julie swallowed around a shiver of rage. She'd miscategorized Tyler's bullshit, it seemed. This wasn't an inept con. This was Tyler trying not to say the quiet part out loud, which was this job he was dangling at Julie most likely would cost an arm, a leg, and a few yards of intestines.

"Are you serious? Two fucking grand?"

"The outsourcing budget is tight this quarter. Take it or leave it."

Fuck, she thought. *Fuck fuck fucking fuck.*

"I'll take it, you bastard," said Julie quietly, not bothering to mask the bitterness in her voice.

"Super. Let me know when the job's done, yeah? Oh. And

bring me a piece of the thing. A tail or tooth or whatever. Something I can show management and put in our trophy case."

"You're goddamn kidding."

Julie ended the call before Tyler could say anything because she knew he wasn't kidding the least little bit.

CHAPTER FIVE

Julie's latest intern—Brad McWASPy or something—was a tall, pale slab of Midwestern beefsteak with a Clark Kent curl of dark hair over his forehead. He was good-looking: Abercrombie & Fitch catalog hunk-handsome but born too late to be its All-American centerfold. The kind of guy who'd have normally made Julie run away screaming in horror. However, a face that could move inventories worth of mass-produced capris and pastel cardigans had definite advantages. Brad got them into places that would have spat Julie out before her first hello.

In this case, the lobby of Midtown's austerely gorgeous Arturia Estate high rise, in which their quarry roosted. The doorman barely glanced at Brad but gave Julie a disdainful once over. Like Brad, he was white as could be. Early twenties and, from his carriage, supremely resentful of the cheap red velvet uniform and gold nametag labelled GREG he was required to wear while behind the black marble check-in desk in the lobby. Julie couldn't blame him. Those Grand Budapest Hotel vibes felt grotesquely servile, incongruent with modern values like basic respect for the working class.

After Brad explained that they had an appointment on the fortieth floor, Greg the doorman glanced back at Julie and said, "I don't know, man. The bosses are clear. You need an official appointment to go up there."

Brad gave him a sunny smile. "I understand completely. That's what we told them. I said, 'This is going to be a problem for Greg.' But our client, he doesn't want a paper trail."

Julie nodded, desperately wanting a cigarette and an extra hundred to bribe their haughty little gatekeep with. Right now, though, she was antonymous with the phrase "flushed with cash," so Brad was their best chance in. If he couldn't do it, they'd need to start kicking doors, the thought of doing such giving her cause to grin for the first time that day.

Brad leaned an elbow atop the gleaming counter and raised the wattage of his smile. Had Julie not known he was a *statistician* of the dark magic kind, dreaming of when he could domesticate the stock markets, make them bark and bellow at his behest, she'd have thought he was on the fast track to Congress. Or Hell. Either way, the smile found its mark. Greg the doorman would have needed to be dead and buried for it to miss.

"Help us out, okay?" said Brad quietly. "We promise it won't be more than half an hour."

Julie gnawed on her inner cheek. Half an hour wasn't enough time at all but the point was moot. If Greg came up while the formalus was still alive and kicking, he'd be a spray of red on the walls before anyone could shout him out the door. Whatever got them past the lobby, she thought and hoped she wouldn't have to eat her optimism.

Finally, Greg sighed, his starched posture crumbling. He mashed his palm into a cheek as he spoke. He looked agonizingly young in that instant, like a child braced for abuse. "Fine. Okay. Sure. But you break anything, it comes out of my paycheck, you know?"

"Why *your* paycheck?" said Julie.

Greg shrugged wretchedly. "Because rich assholes. Who the fuck knows?"

He jounced his chin in the direction of a vestibule softly lit in amber, its surfaces the same oiled-silk marble as the counter. Julie could see the bronze edge of the elevator frame, and a hint of the old-world curlicues rising like the tines of a crown or the villi of some deep-sea creature.

Greg said, "I've called the elevator down for you. Don't touch any buttons. If you do, you're going to get stuck, and then it's really my ass."

Julie nodded. "Hands off your ass. Got it."

Brad reached over the counter and fist-bumped Greg, who allowed the intimacy with another sigh. "Thanks, man."

Julie turned away so she could roll her eyes in private. Quickly after, the two filed into the elevator, its doors sliding noiselessly open for them. To Julie's relief, its interior was rather pedestrian: red carpet, taupe walls with their lower halves cladded in matte-dull aluminum. Tinkly bossa nova played as the elevator rose.

"Thank fuck," said Julie.

"What?"

"Thank fuck he listened to you. I was about to go Grizzly Adams on him," Julie mumbled.

"Who's Grizzly Adams?"

"You don't know about Grizzly Adams? I swear to god—" Julie stopped herself. "Never mind. You were probably out making touchdowns and banging cheerleaders. I'm just in a fucking mood. Ignore me."

"I didn't bang them. I was nice."

"Of course you were. Never mind. Point is I was going to make him cry."

Brad frowned. "You could have just messed with his memory."

"That's what I meant." Julie now wore a matching grimace. "I don't punch the help, Brad. I save that for the bosses. You know that."

Her intern said nothing.

Wow. Did you kill her?

Why would that be your first guess?

Because you're you.

Julie clenched her jaw against the memory of Dead Air's laughing explanation, the pitying caution glinting in Brad's expression, and fumbled for the cigarette packet squeezed into her right hip pocket.

Brad took a step back like Julie had pulled out a rattlesnake. "You can't smoke in here."

Julie sighed. "You know that with the kind of work we do, those jokers who hire us see us as just one or two steps above horse thieves, right?"

"Okay," said Brad uncertainly.

"So, outlaws like us, we don't follow their rules."

Brad's scowl deepened. "I get all that, but *smoking* . . ."

"Besides," Julie went on, raising the rotten tooth–yellow pack. "This box? You see the logo? You don't recognize it, do you? That's because it is older than the two of us combined. The company got cannibalized by its rivals way back in the day. Everyone who worked for the joint? Dead or brainwashed. Their enchantment, though. That still works."

"What's your point?"

"You kids today," said Julie, aware she was practically zygotic in the eyes of some of her peers. St. Joan would have guffawed at hearing Julie dismiss Brad as a child. "Have no patience. I'm getting to that. Back when the industry was trying to get everyone to ignore the fact that cigarettes are cancer, a marketing executive got it into his head to magic up their packaging so that any cigarette you put in there comes out smokeless."

"But," said Brad with care, "they didn't bother to make the cigarettes cancerless."

"What happens to the customer isn't their problem. Anyway, you're focusing on the wrong thing. If I were you, I'd be amazed at the artistry of a spell that was made to last decades."

"It's cool, I guess. But—"

"Damn right it's cool," said Julie, lighting up.

"The carcinogens," persisted Brad. "Don't you care about getting cancer?"

"Lungs are overrated and dying early is my retirement plan, Braddy boy."

"That's *dark*."

Julie shot him her most feral grin. "It's why I'm good at what

I do. Stick with me and maybe not giving so much of a shit will rub off."

"With all respect," said Brad in the exasperated tone of someone who was only paying lip service to the phrase. "I'm not really interested in that self-destructive stuff. I want to die at a hundred with everything still functioning."

"And if you want to live that long . . ." said Julie, taking a drag. As advertised, the cigarette produced no smoke but it did emit a smell of cinnamon, warm and familiar. "You're going to want to learn from me. This is a business with a high turnover rate."

"How high?" said Brad, coughing reflexively, fanning the air.

"Just a figure of speech. Don't worry about it."

"Really?"

"Sure."

"I think you're lying."

"Okay. You want the real story? I got into this line of work when I was nineteen. There was a whole community of baby monster hunters and what-have-yous. About thirty or forty of us distributed all over the state. Some of them were like you. College-educated, by-the-book gifted children. Good at what they did, but without that certain *something*."

Julie ashed her cigarette. "I'm the only one still alive."

"I—"

"Zombies got the last guy. You'd be amazed at how long it takes for someone to die when a necromancer tells their living dead not to go for the squishy bits. They ate him to the bone. It was ugly, Brad. A hundred mouths chewing away turns muscle into this slobbery paste. You ever seen like slightly stale Greek yogurt? When it gets weirdly thick? A little like that. Except red and a little yellow and—don't you dare throw up."

Her intern greened: the tributaries of his nervous system suddenly very visible, his eyes sunk into the deep pools of their sockets, the bags beneath them inflamed. Brad winced as their gazes met, his face churning through a complicated train of expressions before finally arriving on a puckered unhappiness like someone who'd eaten a rotten lemon.

"That was . . . graphic."

"Didn't anyone tell you what you were getting into?"

"At school—"

Julie barked a harsh laugh. "Do you really think they'd tell you the truth over there? The business needs bodies, Brad. They need to have fresh meat for the machine. If they tell you everything, we wouldn't have anyone new to work with and then where would we be, hm?"

"This is all coming a little fast."

"You'll get used to it," said Julie cheerily. "The nice thing about the job is that it's low on competition. Keep your head in the game and you'll do fine. But you've got to pull the stick out of your ass first."

Brad nodded, trying to look calm. "Remove stick from ass. Got it."

Julie puffed her cigarette again. "We cool?"

"Cool like rocky road."

"Awesome." It annoyed Julie to have to baby a full-grown man, but naive as he was, Brad remained the best intern she'd ever had. Her issues with his face aside, she didn't want to lose him. "We're almost at the top. Do you have any questions about the formalus?"

"Not really. I read up on them," Brad said. "They're pretty simple, right? Memetic infection. Anyone who thinks about them too hard risks opening themselves up as a habitat."

"Bingo. What else?"

"Let's see. They take over your dreams first and then your waking thoughts. When they've cleared out your brain, they eat the rest of you. Oh, and their young do that creepy thing where they can imitate the sounds made by the last thing their parents ate."

The queasiness in his expression was gone, substituted with a faraway stare as Brad combed his memory for information. Julie was impressed.

"I have a question, though," said Brad.

"What?"

"What is something like that doing here? They're usually rural threats. Formalus haunt quiet places. Wall Street is way too loud to be useful to them."

"This one has apparently been giving out the information from its victims' heads."

"That's impossible. Formalus are *barely* sentient."

Julie shrugged.

"There's nothing like that in the books," said Brad, with rising frustration.

"You're right. There's nothing like that in the books. There's nothing like that anywhere. They don't do this. Only this one does."

"Is it working for someone?"

Julie dropped her cigarette stub and ground it to ash beneath her heel. "Who knows?"

"But they don't *think*," said Brad, wholly absorbed now in the puzzle. He paced the elevator, hands at hip level, groping at nothing as if he could gouge an answer from the air. "It must be someone who set it loose. But why? For money?"

That shook out another laugh from Julie, this one unkind. "Why else does anybody use magic in New York? Someone is probably making bank off whatever the formalus has harvested. But that's not our business. We're here to kill it dead."

"I know why we're here," said Brad, stopped, the ghost of a pout weighing down his mouth.

"Then you know we're going to get paid American cash money for our work here. Long green. Keep your eye on the ball, champ. Stay calm—"

"I am calm."

"—and stop trying to think too much. Trust me. Trust yourself. And forget that Ivy League bullshit. This is brass knuckles time."

The elevator was nearing the fortieth floor. For a feature in such a classy building, it moved with geriatric speed, creaking and clanking through its exertions. Brad stared at Julie, something about his face irrevocably changed by their recent conversation: his expressions were starker, unsettlingly raw, as if he'd been denuded of skin and Julie could see the full theatre of his muscles at work. He looked feral and a little lost.

"What is it?"

Brad shook his head. "I don't know if I can do this."

Shit.

She *had* scared him. Bad.

"Brad," said Julie, wishing she could remember his full name, and settling instead for punching his arm fraternally. "Brad. Dude. What happened to you? Where's the guy who threw a touchdown from the free throw line—"

"That's not how football works—"

Julie clapped her hands around his upper arms as she'd seen coaches and Spartan warriors do and tried on an authoritative voice, anything to walk Brad from his metaphorical ledge. "Look, I'm not a hand-egg person, okay? You're focusing on the wrong thing here. Point is. You're brave. You've been through a lot."

This was patently untrue, but Julie long since learned if you talked fast enough, flattered hard enough, the particulars didn't matter. But Brad wasn't breathing right any longer: he gulped the air in jagged asthmatic bursts, hardly pausing to exhale.

"I don't want to die," he said in a bleak monotone.

Damn, thought Julie. They were almost there. If Brad lost it now, if he caved to his panic, the doors would open and he'd barrel straight into the formalus. She couldn't let it happen. Thank fuck for form over function. Julie gave hysterical praise to every deity she knew for the lionization of architectural features that should have long since been retired for the good for the world. Had the elevator been even halfway efficient, Brad's meltdown would have been a problem already. But she had time. Sort of.

Time enough for a single thought, one attempt at fixing the situation. Time that was sieving away, second by second, as Julie ransacked her brain for a strategy.

"Brad."

He shook his head so hard Julie worried it would disconnect from his neck.

"Brad."

"Yeah?"

"Look up."

When he turned his gaze to the ceiling of the elevator, Julie grabbed his arms and kneed him in the balls. Brad crumpled against the wall, his eyes wide.

"Jesus fuck, what the hell was that for?"

Julie patted him on the shoulder and pulled him back into a standing position. He wobbled like a newborn giraffe.

"You were being a big baby."

"I—" He scrunched his face, patting where Julie had socked him. "The fuck did I do?"

"You were being a big baby in a big baby panic spiral and needed to be shocked out of it. And it worked, didn't it?"

"Yeah, but—"

"Don't thank me. It's all part of the job."

Brad looked at her, more confused than hurt.

"Fuck—would it kill you to apologize?"

Julie thought about it.

"How about we go get drunk after this? We can find a classy bar with the good stuff. Top-shelf. My treat."

Brad raised his eyebrows at her. "That's your apology?"

"Pretty much."

"Okay, I guess. I mean, I suppose it worked. I'm more pissed than scared now."

"Pissed is always better than scared. That's lesson one."

"What's lesson two?"

"Always be prepared."

Julie snapped her fingers and a suitcase clattered onto the floor beside her: a vintage specimen with bronze caps and burgundy leather, scuffed-up, raked over with scratches, the lip gnarled with bitemarks.

Brad stared at it. "What's that for?"

"In case Tyler lied about the job and is out to fuck us."

"I should have stayed at Harvard."

"Nah. You're gonna love this."

The elevator dinged, saving Julie from further conversation.

"Showtime," she said, slinking out into the hall.

No one was there. The floor was pitch-black save for a hem of reflected neon along the windows where New York shone through. It smelled recently disinfected and heavily of Pine Sol, which suggested that the janitorial crew had already made their rounds. Julie exhaled. Good. Less chance of civilian casualties.

Because the formalus was *definitely* here. Antiseptic as the air smelled, its texture was anything but. It felt a little slick, almost membranous, as if all the oxygen had been supplanted by warm aspic. The first symptom of a formalus presence. Julie swallowed hard against her own revulsion. She really wished she had some vodka.

"You sense anything?" she whispered, eyes still straight ahead.

"You're the psychic. Not me," came the quiet reply.

"We'll work on that," Julie said half-heartedly, mostly relieved she wouldn't need to worry about Brad being overwhelmed by his environment.

Brad, either recovered from his meltdown or so traumatized he had emerged on the other side of his fear, stepped around Julie. "Let me take over this part. Okay? I checked out the building dimensions before we got here. The floor layouts are identical after the thirty-eighth floor, so if I run the numbers . . ."

He jabbered mathematical nonsense to himself as a crest of filamentous gray light billowed out from him, tinseling the furniture and the walls, mapping the space in a perspective grid.

Julie was impressed. The sophistication of his spell-working was beyond her. She could try for a lifetime and never come within range of anything so delicate. Her magic was as blunt as she was: like a nuke hidden in a birthday cake. Most days, she turned her nose up at magic that required more commitment than a decisive thought. Today she was jealous.

"How long did it take you to learn that?" she said.

Brad laughed tipsily, his eyes iridium, the silver running at the corners, dripping over his mouth and chin. "This? Since third grade, maybe? I was lost in an airport somewhere, and I knew I needed to find my mom. She told me about gate numbers, how airports were built, and I knew, I just knew, that if I broke the world down into precise little squares, I'd find her."

"You child geniuses drive me nuts, I swear."

"Shh. I need to concentrate."

The light kept spreading. Brad made a gesture: one of his hands rictused into a claw and then shot upward. The lathing grew more intricate, the lines more plentiful. Soon the office was modeled in fluorescent grayscale but there was no sign of the formalus. *It knows we're here,* Julie thought. *It's hiding.*

Julie sheared through the meat of her thumb with her teeth and let blood drip onto one of the glowing fibers emanating from Brad. Binocular vision flattened to something like sonar, something not quite real, Julie's awareness splintered along the striae of her intern's spell, searching. Her skin buzzed.

Nothing.

Mostly nothing.

Every few seconds, Julie could almost but not quite feel a skittering at the fringe of her awareness, like spider legs testing and then sharply withdrawing from a blaze. And the sensation of being smiled at, of being observed by the big idiot grin of a dog tortured into assuming human expression.

"How are we doing, Brad? Anything definite yet?"

"There's . . . something? I can sort of feel a weight on the grid."

"Describe it."

"Big. Multi-legged. But not quite corporeal. Like wet smoke."

"Sounds like our guy. Keep working at it, Brad. I have faith in you."

"Really?"

"You're the man, Brad," said Julie. "Find it and I'll buy you a balloon."

Before he could say anything else, the light abruptly converged into a single beam pointing at the far end of the room. The ray then shot along the ceiling toward them, speeding closer, accelerating with every inch. Almost at the same time, Julie heard mass and weight metastasize in the vents above the tiles, heard the metal creak as that unseen threat—*this isn't how it works,* babbled the last clot of good sense in Julie's head, and *fuck you, Tyler, fuck you*—filled more space than those shafts were ever meant to carry. It was beginning to shake apart and holy hell, Julie was glad she brought the suitcase.

What erupted from the vents—arms everywhere, human arms, so many of them, starved to sinew and wattled skin—definitely had familial ties with your basic formalus but it was *definitely* not typical, and what this job was was a mistake, and one way or another, this was not going to end well and Julie understood this before Brad even began to scream.

"Shit," said Julie as everything went to exactly that.

It had a guileless face, a glistening, peeled-grape face with the eyes too widely spaced and the mouth too big, and a smile like something it learned from a golden retriever. Julie knew she would never forget how happy it looked amid its writhing arms, which were coming down from the ceiling, holding it up, going everywhere, feeling their way along office chairs and cubicle dividers, knocking over snow globes, overturning fax machines. There was nothing like a skeleton behind the face, she realized. It was just skin, held there to the mass of limbs by a wreath of fingers, a discarded dollar-store Halloween mask on top of a true nightmare.

Julie screamed a single inchoate noise and a dozen of the creature's arms exploded clean off. All that did was buy her a moment of delusional hope as she lunged for Brad, hoping to grab the idiot.

The formalus got to him first.

Immediately, the creature swaddled him in its arms, fingers hooking into his ears and the nooks of his mouth, prying his jaws open. It palmed his brow, and gripped his hair, tugging in every direction until its hands were clutching sheafs of bloody blond follicles, bending his head back, his face stroked and cupped by a dozen hands. Julie howled another word of power, an old word, one of the last from a civilization eaten alive by a god equally forgotten by the modern age, a word that having now been spoken would forever be scoured from history, its existence undone by its very voicing. Another knot of limbs detonated, sleeting gore over the office. But it wasn't enough, wouldn't be enough even if Julie was exhausted of every option.

The arms—god, they were splitting along their tibias. From the grain of the revealed marrow came a forest of smaller arms, pale and thin as worms, and these were tendriling over Brad's eyes, nuzzling aside the organs; they were entering his nose, his mouth, spiraling into his ears. Brad had stopped screaming, as he was now choking on the formalus.

And the fucking thing was still smiling at her.

Brad went into seizures, his convulsions sending him sprawling backward atop a hallway table. Flowers gouted through the air as he thrashed over the gleaming wood. A crystal vase shattered on the carpet. Impossibly, the formalus was shrinking into him, thinning so it was as insubstantial as baby hair.

"Fuck you, Tyler," Julie whispered under her breath.

This was not normal. None of this was normal. This wasn't

even a routine shitty mission. This was worse. No part of her was shocked at Tyler's treachery but the depth of it surprised her. Up until this point she had assumed her longevity was of value to him even if her love was not. Had he found someone willing to do his dirty work for less? Was this what it is? Her being priced out of his garbage contracts? Him disposing of an obsolete instrument?

Or was Tyler just fucking stupid?

Brad went slack, a thin rill of drool snaking down his cheek.

There.

That was her window. Julie leapt forward. She slammed the suitcase down against the floor.

"I'm sorry, Brad, but this is really going to hurt."

Julie rolled up her sleeves and counted her way up thorns embedded in her forearms until she hit seven, then reached in and yanked. Barbed wire magic, in one form or another, had been around for centuries: a sacrosanct practice in its original form until kings and cartels realized pain didn't have to be holy, it merely needed to be obliterating.

She tore the barbed wire from her arm, blood and tattered muscle and strands of warm fat spraying the wall. Pain shot through her whole body, almost slippery, and she gasped as her vision burned to white along the rim. The world swam. She was drowning in the pain. But this was the price. She understood this was what she had to pay, and that in this world, nothing came for free. Especially not miracles.

Julie twitched the wrist of her uninjured arm and the barbed wire went rigid, thickening into a toothed obsidian blade. Without preamble, she brought it down on Brad's chest, the fabric of his shirt parting as easily as the bone of his sternum, calcium sluicing away like butter warmed on the stove.

Once it passed the bone and touched the substernal pillow of offal underneath, he woke up and screamed again.

Julie crawled onto the table, straddling her intern, both hands around the knife. She torqued it downward, cursing. Brad shrieked harder.

Where was it?

Where the fuck was the thing?

Julie, having no better recourse, plunged her hands into the opening she'd made, feeling through Brad's entrails: she probed beneath trembling lung and pounding heart, the latter practically vibrating, and for a second Julie wondered if it'd pop against the brush of her knuckles. Once or twice, her fingers bumped against the formalus, but the slickness of the abdominal captivity kept her from getting purchase.

"Come fucking out of there," Julie snarled to zero effect, hacking again at Brad, filleting him, splaying him like a book. She needed to be able to see more of him; she needed actual access.

When he was sufficiently gutted, Julie began spooning tangles of intestinal tract out, setting them in ropey piles to the right of her. She yanked out Brad's liver. The smooth pink steaks of his lungs. Stomach. Nothing, still nothing. At this rate, she would have to pull out everything and throw it on the floor, waiting for something to move.

Each organ she removed, she stabbed with a bowie knife—its only augmentation a curse that prevented any body it wounded to go into shock—she pulled from her boot. The innards did nothing but leak fluids, so Julie continued her excavation until Brad was almost scraped clean. Soon, there was only the heart left.

"No, no, no."

Then, for the first time in Julie's beleaguered life, luck decided to play nice. On the floor, a kidney rolled over, squirming with movement. Julie leapt from the table and grabbed the organ, squeezing like it was Tyler's throat in her hands.

Brad stopped moving.

Julie snarled over her shoulder, "Stay with me just a little longer, asshole!"

She looked back in time to see the kidney halve itself in her hands, its insides the red of a good expensive shiraz where it wasn't gummed with blood-streaked fat, and Julie, staring down at the organ in her hands and the fat polyps extending from the near-blackness of the winey tissue into the whey core, thought dementedly to herself, *this looks like two sleeping tardigrades.* The flat tapeworm ribbon of the ureter twitched once and flailed for Julie's throat, the pod-like nuggets in the kidney suppurating with comical speed, pus geysering, freeing a riot of prehensile veins. Where the ureter went for her neck, the flailing capillaries shot for her eyes, her ears. The formalus had lost all interest in Brad and was making a play for her. If she didn't stop it now, it would be in her brain.

"Julie. It hurts so much. Why did you cut me like that?" said the formalus in a breathy imitation of Brad's voice, its face protruding from new abscesses in the kidney, much smaller, much more numerous, but still with its recognizable smile.

"Shut up, fuck meat," she snapped back, grabbing at the profusion of blood vessels as if it were a ponytail, yanking the strands taut. She chewed her tongue bloody and licked the stretch of veins, trying the whole while not to think about what she was doing, or how bilious it tasted. She met the formalus' gaze with a red-stained sneer, a spell ready to go—

From what felt like a million miles away, strange thoughts and images slammed into her brain: a universe of numbers, assessments, invoices, bank statements, and more. All the dull machinations of business. It was the formalus injecting the financial information it had stolen from its victim straight into Julie's head. ("At least Tyler wasn't lying about that," Julie thought dazedly.) The projections and the spreadsheets meant nothing to her, someone who'd never even balanced a checkbook, but she couldn't help thinking that the creature was trying to bribe her.

Fat fucking chance, she thought. But there was one thing she glimpsed at the end. Something she could actually use. Nothing monetary: something far better. She couldn't wait to shout it into Tyler's face.

"Julie. You killed me. I trusted you," the thing said in Brad's voice, breaking her fugue. The formalus had doubled, tripled in size. Soon it would be unmanageable, impervious to her attacks. Soon, Julie would be dead. Soon, there'd be two bodies in a slaughterhouse of an office, and the NYPD would be trying vainly to profile a murderer, getting it all wrong, and St. Joan would be so mad once she understood Julie was dead, and it was this last thing that saved Julie from the impulse to let herself die.

"Julie. It hurts."

"Oh, fuck you."

A thought struck her as the formalus reached for her face, its own in bloom, her vision crowded with dozens of them, smiling moronically like it was their birthday. A last hurrah, a Hail Mary of a plan. Julie thrust her chin at the formalus and opened her mouth.

It leapt.

Barbed-wire magic was hungry as kings, and what it wanted most was its user's pain. If it found no pain, or worse, a stoic who thought themselves too clever for the warnings, the magic would do a horrible thing, which was to multiply its prongs and dig deeper, and deeper, until the user debased themselves with begging for an end. There were stories of how skeptics were found as bristly tumbleweeds of black iron, quivering in puddles of their own juiced insides.

The razor wire along her arms, the hollow between her ribs, tore from her and caught the formalus just as a single fingertip touched itself to Julie's mouth. She was rewarded by the thing's first change in expression: an infinitesimal raising of its brows. Then formalus met barbed wire and Julie heard a *crunch*.

It screamed one last time, "Mommy! It hurts!" and fell to the carpeted floor in an ever-shrinking, increasingly soggy ball. Arms were loped off as the wire tightened and squeezed, the formalus wailing incoherently still in Brad's voice. There was a chance it wouldn't die from this, but that was no one's problem but the creature's own.

Julie allotted herself an attosecond of triumph before she whirled around, grabbed the suitcase, and snapped it open.

Inside were glistening human organs so perfect, they'd make a thoracic surgeon swoon. Julie didn't waste time with niceties like sterilizing her hands or putting on a surgical mask, not with Brad already nine-tenths dead meat on the table. She just grabbed fistfuls of new organs and shoved them into Brad's empty gut. As she stuffed him like a Thanksgiving turkey, Julie suffered a moment of panic wondering if they'd all fit or if she'd have to leave something out—a thymus or a pancreas, something small and theoretically optional—but in the end, everything slid into place. She sewed Brad back together with what she was told was angel-gut thread. Whether or not it was true, each loop she stitched into Brad closed immediately and, in the end, there was barely even a scar.

Brad blinked a couple of times and Julie helped him sit up.

"What happened?" he mumbled.

"You killed it, kiddo. Well, we did, but you were a big help. I'll give you the details when we get out of here."

Julie stood and pulled Brad to his feet. He slumped against the wall for a moment and said, "You know what's weird? I feel kind of good. Like when I was a kid."

"Yeah. That's what having brand-new insides will do for you."

"What?"

"Later. Let's get out of here."

Julie draped Brad's arm over her shoulder and walked him to the elevator.

"Why the fuck are there so many arms?"

"Turns out you're a messy killer. Grab that one for me, will you?" said Julie, nodding at the limb flopped on a photocopier. She was so going to slap Tyler with the trophy he wanted, though he deserved a lot worse.

When they got in the elevator, it started down without either of them having to do anything. It was there, in those few moments of quiet, that Julie realized just how drenched the two of them were in effluvium. No cab in New York was going to pick them up. All-American good looks could only excuse so much. Exhausted as they were, it was subway time again. Could be worse, though, Julie decided. At least they wouldn't have to take the fucking G.

Fortunately, there was no one in the lobby but Greg. The doorman took one look at them and rushed over. "What the fuck happened up there?"

Julie shrugged. "We might have knocked over a table."

Greg covered his mouth with his hand. "Oh shit. Oh god. This is my job."

Brad swayed, a knee buckling like a clasp. Julie tipped sideways at the abrupt imposition of his weight, tottering until Greg provided support. Together, they maneuvered Brad to the reception desk, where they propped him against the counter.

"Not necessarily," said Julie, wiping at her face. It did nothing but smear more of her with blood.

"What is that you're covered in? Is that blood? Oh god, that is blood. What the fuck did you do?"

"Listen to me," said Julie. "Where do they keep the surveillance videos of the lobby?"

He pointed. "In the room over there."

Julie whispered some words and threw out her arm in that direction to less effect than she wanted: a quiet hiss came from behind the door, but nothing else.

Greg looked at her. "What did you just do?"

"I erased all of the surveillance footage. Don't thank me yet. Just listen. Me and my pal over there. We're just a couple of hooligans who broke in here and muscled you out of the way. There was nothing you could do about it. Got it?"

"I am so fired."

"There's just one more thing, and you have no idea how sorry I am about it."

"Oh god. What else is there?"

Julie pulled back her fist and punched Greg in the nose. He fell back and landed on his ass on the floor, so stunned that he didn't shout, didn't curse, didn't do more than blink rapid-fire at Julie as she helped him onto his feet.

"I'm so sorry. I never hit the help, but you needed something for the story to work."

"That really hurt," Greg said. A nostril dribbled red blood.

"I promise you a hundred percent that I'm going to make all of this up to you soon."

Greg stared at her.

"Please go away," said Greg, who looked at her with watery, disbelieving eyes. "Just go the fuck away."

Julie pulled Brad to the doors, saying, "I owe you."

"Go *away*!" shouted Greg.

So, she did.

❧

Back at Julie's place, she set Brad at one end of her good sofa and flopped onto its opposite, bottles of vodka for her and gin for Brad crowding the coffee table. She ordered takeout with the last of her cash and made sure that Brad was well-fed and utterly wasted before she explained what had happened on the fortieth floor of the Arturia Estate. To her relief, Brad laughed along with her and even pulled up his shirt to expose his belly so she could Sharpie where she'd cut him, stippling every place that should have borne a scar but was instead smooth skin. Tears streamed down Brad's face as she detailed how she had stabbed his innards and was almost murdered by his kidney.

Even a heavy-duty alcoholic like Julie had her limits. Around four in the morning, she closed her eyes. Just for a second. Thinking happy thoughts about the money Tyler would have to pay.

When she opened them again, it was half an hour to noon and Brad was gone.

There was a neatly folded piece of paper leaning against the empty vodka bottle. Julie opened it and once her eyes remembered how to focus, she saw the note was in Brad's handwriting. It said, very simply:

I'm going home to Texas to work at my dad's Toyota dealership. Fuck this magic shit. Good luck, Julie. Don't die, but also don't get anyone killed. Okay?

Best,
Brad

The vodka bottles were empty, so she picked up the lone surviving flask of gin and unscrewed the top.

"Shit."

CHAPTER SIX

Julie had been drinking for a solid hour and a half when came a light knocking at the door at two. She drained the remaining alcohol in her glass and dragged herself off the sofa, still in a foul mood because of what had gone down with Brad. Julie tried to recall if she had a meeting with a client or if any of the bill collectors might have her address. If it was the former, they seriously needed to fuck off and reschedule. If it was the latter, well, she would have to apologize to St. Joan for the mess she was about to make.

Almost to the doorway, Julie paused. Whether it was vanity or some relic of propriety, she didn't know, but she smoothed back her hair, straightened her wrinkled shirt, and spent a few seconds wishing she had a breath mint. Sure, Julie had a reputation, but there was no need to let whoever was on the opposite side of the door know she was actually three leprous raccoons in a human skin suit. Feeling minimally more presentable, Julie opened the door, a headache swelling behind her left eye, ready to chew out the idiot who dared to violate the safe space of her day drinking.

It was a woman, but not a client. She was prettily dressed in an ice cream–green Chanel suit and pearls. Perfect ballerina posture. Hair done up like she'd changed her mind and left before her Vogue cover shoot. Julie blinked, and then again, and then a third time, with the violence of someone in a dust storm, suddenly very unsure if she was awake, dreaming, or delirious from having finally succumbed to liver failure. The woman stood in the hall with her luggage, beaming timorously at Julie like she was sixteen still and afraid of what being beautiful would cost her.

"Surprise," the woman said quietly.

"Sarah?"

"Hi. I was in New York and thought I'd, well, surprise you."

Julie jabbed at Sarah's arm with a finger. When she was certain the other woman was either real or solid enough a hallucination to justify going all in, she threw her arms around her old friend. "You did surprise me. Come in!"

Sarah's smile teetered and she said, "You're sure it's alright?"

"Of course it is. Don't be silly."

"I was just worried showing up like this and not calling first and . . ."

"Come in," insisted Julie, pulling Sarah into the apartment. "You have . . . bags? One bag? Doesn't matter. Are the rest at a hotel? Are *you* in a hotel? You can crash here if you want."

"Could I?"

"Of course."

She hugged Julie. "Thank you so much."

Even through the burgeoning hangover, the hug struck Julie as a little weird. It was a little too tight. Maybe too grateful? Too relieved? Hard to say what it was exactly.

As Julie let Sarah inside, she felt a familiar spasm of embarrassment. "I'm sorry about the place being a wreck. We had a party last night."

"*We?* Should I come back later?"

"Nah. My intern is long gone." Julie forced a laugh and led Sarah to the sofa. "I think I broke him."

"I'm . . . sorry?" said Sarah with her usual compassion and her usual depth of warmth, the well of her empathy deep enough to drown in.

Realizing her joke had made things sound even more dire than they were, Julie slopped on a devil-may-care grin. "It's okay. He wasn't the first and he won't be the last. Not everyone is cut out for this life."

Sarah settled against the back of the sofa, head lolling sweetly onto Julie's shoulder, and let out a sigh. "You were always the brave one."

Julie laughed. "The stupid one, you mean."

"No, I'm serious. I always wanted to be as brave as you."

There it was again, Julie thought. That tone, that note, that gleam of something, like a sliver of bone in the mud. Sarah had a secret.

"How long can you stay?" Julie said.

Sarah gave her a shy smile. "How long can you stand me?"

"How long can you stand this total chaos?"

Looking around, Sarah said, "I think it's wonderful. The signs of an exciting life."

Julie found a clean glass amid the wreckage atop the coffee table and poured them both shots of the bottom-shelf gin. Though she had promised to ply Brad with the good stuff, in the end she'd opted for quantity over any semblance of quality. *Probably another reason he left,* hissed a voice in Julie's head. "To exciting lives."

"Yes. Always."

"Also, I kinda missed this," said Sarah before she added, "and you."

Julie drained hers in a gulp. Sarah took a modest sip and then cradled her glass on her lap, upright again: ramrod straight with her legs docilely crossed at the ankles.

"Don't get deceived by all the glamour," Julie said, unable and unwilling to contemplate the way Sarah had said "and you" so softly, like she was a prize. Like Julie was worth something. "Once you rescue people from demons or whatever, a lot of them forget to pay you."

Sarah raised a perfect brow. "That's so not fair."

"Some end up cursed for not upholding customer-seller etiquette so it's not all bad. That said, I can't turn everyone into a pillar of salt. If I did, I'd never get any money."

The bravado elicited an uncertain chuckle and Julie winced, chiding herself for rolling out the weird too quickly. She should have worked up to that. Spent some time assessing Sarah's openness to the topic. They'd played around with mall bookstore witchcraft when they were teenagers, but it was nothing serious. Ouija boards. Waxen hex dolls. Holding hands in darkened attics while doing seances that might, when she was honest with herself, have been more about holding hands than conjuring spirits. Half the people Julie had grown up with had converted to atheism, if their social media presence was any barometer of the subject. Maybe Sarah had too, and now she was regretting stepping into Julie's dilapidated excuse for a parlor. An awkward silence ballooned. It was Sarah who saved the day.

"Have you had breakfast?"

Julie, midway through pouring herself another glass of gin, said, "Good morning America."

"That's not breakfast."

"I'm a grown-up. Breakfast can be anything I want. Gin. Cake—"

"You know what I'm talking about: a real breakfast. With calories."

"This has calories."

"*Useful* calories."

"All calories are useful calories," said Julie.

"That's not true!"

"Don't be—" Julie paused. She wasn't ready to be clever this early into her day, but she was going to give it a shot. "—a calori-ist."

To Julie's absolute rapture, Sarah gained across the brief course of their banter a new vigor, mischief taking over from the Stepford vibes. She rolled her eyes at Julie, who wanted badly to do backflips at the sight. "You're an idiot, but I will excuse that. Back to the topic: have you had a real breakfast with nonliquid calories and—what's something that should be part of every meal—oh, I know. *Protein.* Have you had anything like that?"

"Not since I broke up with my last boyfriend."

"Julie."

"Fine," said Julie, lifting her gin to her mouth, only to have it taken away by Sarah. "The answer's no. And if it helps, I probably would have eaten something if there was actually . . . anything in the fridge."

The other woman let out an expansive groan.

"I don't know how you're alive."

"I don't know either, sometimes," said Julie, struck by a barrage of memories. The two of them had once run away together. During that time, it'd been Sarah who had made sure they ate, that they had more than cardboard-flavored ramen. Left to her own devices, Julie would have died of malnutrition. "Can I have my gin back?"

"No! We're getting takeout. My treat."

"I never refuse free food or doomed love affairs."

Sarah lost her smile for long enough that Julie's heart lurched, but it didn't stay gone, returning more incandescent than before. "Well, how about we start with breakfast for now and see how things go from there?"

❧

In the forty-five minutes it took for their food to arrive, Julie shoved everything but the gin and the glasses into a trash bag and dragged it into the kitchen. She kept trying to ask Sarah about her life, but her friend always eeled away from answering, turning every question into one for Julie, who answered truthfully because she just couldn't lie to Sarah: Were demons real? ("Totally.") What about tooth fairies? ("Sort of.") What was the consensus on Santa's existence? ("We try not to talk about him.") Did Julie have magic powers? ("Sure.") Could she show Sarah some tricks? ("Later. After breakfast. And maybe on the fire escape so we don't set fire to anything.") After Sarah's charming interrogation, Julie made it clear that to the world at large, neither she nor the kind of magical entities she dealt with existed. You had to be high up the New York financial food chain to know, or low enough that you'd probably fucked a few demons along the way. It was important that all the people who lived in the middle of those two extremes didn't know about magic, so she swore Sarah to secrecy about everything she'd revealed.

The food arrived, the delivery guy sixteen with marionette limbs he was still growing into. Sarah tipped him half the price of their order. It then became a game: laying out the pancakes, the breakfast sausages, the bacon, the eggs, the hash browns, the little coffees in their white insulated cups; the beans, the chutney, chimichurri, chili jam, and the rest of the weird condiments that Sarah insisted on rolling into their order because life was short, she said, and you didn't want to get old without trying all the new things. The food barely fit on the table, but they made it work with the help of a stool recovered from the closet. After Julie made sure there was no way the one-eyed tomcat could intrude on their breakfast, the two dove into their food.

Sure enough, Julie's hangover began to dissipate after two pancakes and far too many slices of crisped bacon. It was glorious. Glorious and restorative and precisely what she needed to finally ask the question she'd been putting off:

"How's Dan?"

Though she would never say it to Sarah's face, Julie disliked Dan. She remembered when the two started dating. Three years ago? Four? They'd been going out for around a month and about as far from exclusive as any couple could be. Dan had *insisted* that he didn't subscribe to the patriarchal norms. Monogamy was for people without imagination, or worse, people with no concept of passion. Then he found out that Julie had introduced Sarah to some of the local fetish clubs and sex dungeons and after establishing that Julie was in no way interested in threesomes—with him, at least—became furious at the pair's relationship. The truth was that as much as Sarah enjoyed the aesthetic, even the concept of kink, she was much too shy to do anything. Whenever they went, Sarah watched from the sidelines, while Julie played with a rotation of other perverts.

Not that it made any difference to Dan. He didn't believe Sarah when she said that she hadn't slept with Julie. Four months after that, he went on a long rant about how *he'd* been hurt by the two women. Julie rolled her eyes and Sarah tried to fix things. The week following the blow-up, Julie had sat confidently in the silence, waiting for the breakup to be announced and her friend to tell her what a mistake that asshole had been.

But it never happened.

Now on the sofa, Sarah quickly said, "He's great. We're great."

Julie didn't buy it.

Sarah went on. "He's stuck at work now, but we're going on a real vacation soon. To Bangkok."

Julie piled more bacon on her plate. "That sounds exciting. Why Bangkok?"

"I want to see the temples and Dan wants to get real Muay Thai training from real Muay Thai trainers." She laughed gauzily: a socialite laugh, ornamental. "He says the trainers in North America are a scam."

Julie thought, *I hope he gets his ass kicked,* but said, "That sounds like so much fun for everyone."

Sarah set down her food and flexed the fingers of her right hand several times.

"Something wrong?" said Julie.

"Oh, I hurt it in a door a while back and it still aches sometimes," Sarah said dismissively, and Julie might have said something were it not for the sudden excited light that lit up the other woman's face.

There she is, this is the Sarah I remember, thought Julie, hoping she'd stay.

"But I don't want to talk about my dull suburban life with its silly doors," continued Sarah. "Tell me about *yours.* I want tales of adventure, and monsters, and things that'd make me go *eep* in the night."

Julie finished her coffee and grinned at her friend, struck by the realization she'd do anything and everything she could to keep Sarah smiling like that, all bright and beautiful, electric with curiosity. "I've got a couple."

"Tell me. Please. Something wonderful."

"Something appropriate for a diner," said a new voice.

Julie and Sarah startled at the intrusion: Julie slightly less emphatically than her friend. The voice, though unexpected, was familiar.

"Hey, St. Joan."

A tall white woman swept into the apartment, barely sparing a look at the chaos. She was beautiful: shoulder-length hair precisely marcelled and as glossy as tumbled obsidian; a diamond froth of hanging earrings; a pewter silk blouse with its collar undone, men's slacks held by thin suspenders. Bacall's smolder and Vivien Leigh's rosebud mouth in a cherub's face too young for the kind of amusement in gray eyes. Her perfume seeped into the air: sandalwood and jasmine and blood.

She looked Sarah over, her expression inscrutable.

"Who is this?"

"I'm—I'm—" Was Sarah *blushing*?

"What did I tell you about overnight guests, Julie?"

Julie's attention ricocheted between the two women. This was too much, too early in the morning. Breakfast had helped but the hangover still hovered, only been made to lie down by the bacon: better but still a literal pain.

"Overnight guests?" Julie repeated, and was *appalled* when St. Joan waggled her eyebrows salaciously. "Jesus, J—you're messing with me."

"Of course. But it's your fault. Your first actual breakfast in a while and you didn't invite me to share."

"Should I go?" said Sarah, voice gone shrill with wide-eyed stress, her lilt recognizably that of someone desperately trying to wade out of an impending lovers' quarrel. "I can go if this is a bad time."

"Sarah, honey. No." Julie touched a hand to her friend's shoulder and was gratified to feel the tension ease immediately. "This is St. Joan, a good friend and my landlord."

Sarah looked between St. Joan and Julie, freezing up again.

"Should I go?" said Sarah, theatrically *sotto voce.*

The older woman said, "Only if you're coming with us for coffee."

Before Sarah could object, Julie said: "And we don't say no to St. Joan."

❧

Coffee was six blocks away at a stylish place called Ground to the Bone. The walk was pleasant, moving from the cracked sidewalks and semi-dying trees around Julie's building to a slowly gentrifying area with expensive shoe stores and cupcake shops.

St. Joan could entertain with the best of them. On their walk, she plied Sarah with compliments and stories of her own life, accounts of Julie's antics, observations about food trends. Briefly, as they crossed an intersection, the two went into a heated debate about couture. They talked about everything, their one conversational dead-end the topic of Sarah's existence. No matter how hard St. Joan tried, Sarah wouldn't say a word about herself.

The three took the counter facing the street, Sarah in the middle. St. Joan distributed the coffees, pastries, and cupcakes, keeping a glowingly bright key lime pie for herself.

"You were going to tell Sarah a story when I intruded—"

"Yes?" said Julie, sipping her coffee. It was good. No, it was excellent. Which made sense. St. Joan never paid for anything but great. "I guess I was."

"Will you tell me now?" said Sarah and then caught herself. "I mean, you don't have to. We're in the public . . ."

"This is New York, my dear," said St. Joan. "No one cares."

"She's right. You can put on a pink boa and run into the streets screaming, 'I am the God of Hellfire' and no one's going to give you a second look unless you get in their way. It's not back home where everyone was in everyone else's pockets," said Julie with a half grin.

"May none of us live in such a situation again," said St. Joan, hands steepled in mock prayer.

Sarah laughed. "Okay. Then tell me the best story you got."

"I don't know if this is the best story I've got but it's definitely the most recent. A few weeks ago, I was clearing a ghost out of like a billion-dollar flat on Central Park West. Massive goddamned place. Really old. Like, this was built before New York was really New York kind of old. You can imagine the ghost that would come with digs like that."

"Uh-huh," said Sarah.

St. Joan said nothing, preoccupied with sectioning her pie into bite-sized eighths.

"I managed to pry it out of the flat's walls but before I could finish the banishment, it speeds out of the house and zooms to the park where it jumps into a fucking horse."

"Oh no," said Sarah, rapt.

"Possessed livestock are the worst," St. Joan agreed. "No one thinks about how big they really are. You tell someone that there's something haunting a cow and everyone laughs until they're faced with the fact a cow can be two thousand pounds."

"Lots of muscle for stomping you flat," said Julie. "And let's not start on how terrifying it is when pigs are involved."

"Pigs?" said Sarah.

"Pigs," said Julie and St. Joan in unison, nodding.

"Anyway," said Julie after a pause. "The ghost jumped into this huge fucking gelding that was tethered to a hansom cab. Thank fuck no one was in it at the time. It sort of looked around, kicked through the cab, and then started running. I wasn't going to be able to keep up. So, I . . . borrowed another horse."

"You borrowed a horse?"

"Yeah. From a cop."

"Borrowed. A horse. From a cop."

"Yep."

Sarah cocked an eyebrow. "How exactly does someone borrow a horse from a cop?"

"I kind of put him to sleep before he said anything but I'm sure if he was awake, he would have been like," Julie lowered her voice into a god-awful attempt at tough-guy-from-Brooklyn. "'Well, Julie, you are helping me keep the peace so here you go, you may have my horse.'"

The laugh that it earned made Julie want to fight the world to hear it again.

"Anyway, *suddenly* it's the Wild West in the park and I'm trying to keep from falling off Black Beauty. The ghost horse gallops at full speed onto Fifth Avenue near The Met. I get up alongside the fucker and I realize, I realize I have no idea how the hell I'm supposed to do anything."

"So, what did you do?"

"Did I mention that I was on a lot of coke?"

"No, you didn't."

"Well, I was on a lot of coke. And the coke declared the thing to do was, you know, cowboy jump from my horse onto the other horse's back. You know. Like Roy Rogers or something. My quarry keeps going, obviously. Because unlike me, it's not all fucked up. It's just dead. As I hang on to the damn horse, it hits me that I don't have any way to stop it and the only thing I could do was perform an exorcism right there and then."

"On a haunted horse charging full-speed along Fifth Avenue."

"On a *goddamn* haunted horse charging full-speed along Fifth Avenue, yeah." A towheaded couple looked up as Julie roared her laughter then bent their attention back to their maps. *They'll fit right in,* Julie thought. "I start the ritual while clinging to its reins with one hand. And obviously, the ghost doesn't like that. The horse, at that point, is kind of pissed too. It grows fangs and tries to bite me."

"While you were on its back?"

"Yep."

"How?"

"By twisting its head a hundred and eighty degrees. You know, Linda Blair–style."

"Oh my god," gasped Sarah.

"The biting doesn't work, which pisses the horse off more, so it tries spiting acid at me."

"Acid!"

"You're the perfect audience, my dear," said St. Joan warmly, Julie's cupcake suddenly on her saucer along with a half-eaten key lime pie. "There are people who'd pay to hear you sigh at them like that."

"Mm-hmm," said Julie, ignoring St. Joan and her shameless theft. "But I get all the words out, reach in and drag the ghost out of the horse's eyes, jump off, *somehow* land without breaking every bone of my body, and slam-dunk the spirit into a manhole."

Sarah frowned slightly. "Wouldn't it just get away?"

"A little old lady gave me this cantrip that turns any opening into a hellmouth. I used one of those and sent the ghost straight into hell. Normally, I try to bottle them up and get them to the right people so they can be processed. But the asshole pissed me off so much, I just didn't care."

"Oh god."

Julie took a sip of coffee. "The best part was there was a crowd on the street by then and everyone applauded when I closed the manhole cover. They thought we were some kind of guerilla theatre show. I got fifty bucks out of the whole thing. Totally worth it."

"What about the people who hired you to clear out the flat?"

Of course, Sarah would take note of that little detail. Julie tried not to wince. Never had she been happier to have a cup in her hands. She stared into the unmarred abyss of it. The coffee really was very good: chocolaty with a hint of oat and barely any acidity. "They didn't want to pay me. I made too much of a *scene* or something. Threats were made, both mine and theirs—they had heavy connections I didn't know about, but I managed to get half my fee. But I was in a terminally shit mood after that and kind of blew it all on a weekend bender at the Plaza Hotel."

She couldn't raise her eyes. Not with St. Joan's gaze boring a hole into the side of her skull.

"Julie—"

"Your money's coming, St. Joan. I really really promise."

"Julie, it is the end-times for civilization. Ragnarok comes for our capitalist society. No one's making enough to do anything, least of all you—"

"I could get offended by that remark."

"What I'm trying to say," said St. Joan, reaching around Sarah to rest a cool pale hand atop Julie's own, "is that it's okay if you need another week. You don't have to be embarrassed. Completely unrelated to this, I am looking for a new superintendent. The fact you already live here is a huge bonus. I'd be willing to consider a mutually viable professional relationship."

"If you're any nicer to me, J, you'll have to start an actual charity to deal with how much you're wasting on me."

"Please. The apartment likes you."

"Not helping." Like Sarah, like everyone else who wafted into New York, St. Joan had secrets. Most of which had to do with the gorgeous, if somewhat rundown brownstone over which she presided. "Besides, I don't think it does."

"It's just offended at you making fun of the heating."

"Is the apartment building haunted?" asked Sarah with an odd note of hope. "It'd be kinda cool if it was."

"No," said St. Joan, retreating her hand. "Not *haunted*."

"Can I ask a possibly silly question?" said Sarah.

"Shoot."

"If you can do all this magic, why don't you just make people pay you? Or conjure money out of the air?"

Julie and St. Joan shook their heads at the same time.

"It's not a silly question," said Julie. "And, trust me, I wish I could just snap my fingers and call up a pot of gold. But magic doesn't work that way. At least in New York. Even those Wall Street wizards can't just make money appear. There are rules and the first is don't magic up money. And don't force people to give you money. Otherwise—"

"Otherwise what?"

"Powers greater than us make their displeasure known," said St. Joan. "Don't conjure money. Don't knowingly raise the dead—"

"To be fair," said Julie, "you could technically do it. You just—"

"Really should not. For your sake," said St. Joan. "As I said before, such acts can truly infuriate certain entities."

"Although I'd rather piss them off before I play Three Card Monte. So don't do that either. Not in this city," said Julie. Before Sarah could speak, Julie cleared her throat and got her phone out. "Speaking of money, it's time. Let's check with the bank to see how doomed I am."

"Oh, Julie. What did I just say?"

Julie didn't answer, mesmerized by the number in her checking balance. She clutched her phone with both hands, mouth ajar, too overwhelmed to say anything at first. Then: a loud whoop of joy that earned her a dirty look from a woman in a business suit and a warning from the barista. "Yes! I'm not going to be out on the street!"

"Someone paid you, I take it," said St. Joan.

"Yep. The ghost horse people. I guess me hinting that I could put the spook right back in the boudoir, angrier than ever, got to them in a big way."

Sarah said, "But you sent the ghost to Hell."

"First rule of the business: never tell anyone anything they don't need to know," said Julie, returning her phone to its place in her pocket. In her joy, she clasped both of Sarah's hands in her own and pressed them to her chest. "But it's you. This is all you, Sarah. You got me to tell you the story. You put them and me together in your head and bam, they realized what they had to do. They paid me. It was all you."

"I have no idea what you're trying to tell me but I'm really happy that they came through for you."

Julie threw her arms around Sarah, nearly sending them both toppling onto the floor. "You're my lucky charm. You're the absolute best."

"I don't hear that very often," said Sarah. "Say it again."

"You are the best person. You always were," Julie said, pulling back so she could stare into Sarah's eyes.

Silence, heavy with what-ifs and what-abouts.

"Ahem," said St. Joan.

The two jolted away from one another.

"Do you have plans for the rest of the day?" said Sarah.

St. Joan sighed and made short work of her remaining pie. The cupcake vanished with similar velocity. When she was done, she patted at the corners of her mouth, dainty as a pampered cat. "I have to go back to the apartment. The glamorous work of a landlady is never done."

"I have to go make a delivery to an asshole at a swanky bar uptown," said Julie, happy to not have to deal with her complicated emotions.

"I like swanky bars. Can I tag along?" asked Sarah.

"Of course. The drinks are on me tonight."

"But your rent—"

Julie flapped a hand. "Covered. I'm sending the money to St. Joan tonight. And we have enough extra to go paint the town red."

"You two should have fun," said St. Joan, impaling Sarah's untouched cupcake with a fork. She wagged the pastry at the other woman. "It's your first night in New York—"

"First night in New York ever," said Sarah.

"Yes. See? You must commemorate these things."

"Okay, fine. Julie, at least let me loan you one of the designer dresses Dan got me. We'll look fabulous together."

"I like looking fabulous," said Julie, though she hated the idea of touching anything Dan might have handled. But if that was what it took to get Sarah to a bar, get a few drinks in her, get her to talk more about her life, about what was going wrong and who else Julie needed to pulverize for her, it'd be worth it.

It was at least worth a try.

CHAPTER SEVEN

Julie wasn't sure when it was that New York fell in love again with speakeasies. One day, it was all about grungy dive bars with a slick of old beer along the floors and a dragon's hoard of pinball machines in the back. The next, it was all about the speakeasy life. Laundromat speakeasies. Speakeasies stashed behind coffee shop fronts. Speakeasies with passwords, speakeasies without passwords. Every door, no matter how plain, was suddenly at risk of being a portal to yet another one of those damn things.

Often, Julie missed when dive bars were the place to be. Today, however, she was glad to have somewhere glamorous to go.

The bar was in the basement of an old office building a short walk from the Wall Street subway station off Broadway. The outside was the blandly forgettable gray façade of a small bank that was under renovation. However, the renovations had been going on for fifty years or more, though most people never seemed to notice that the bank was never open. Wall Street magic. It kept the tourists away and provided investors with a tidy tax deduction. But mostly it was the tourists.

To get to the bar, customers had to first traverse an empty office space, lit eerily with a sickly tungsten glow, devoid of furniture save for clusters of rolling chairs huddled in seeming conspiracy. But down a flight of stairs at the back, there was a carved wooden door with the bar's name in demure gold letters at the top—The Morris Street Shoe Factory, a holdover from when the place had been a true speakeasy during Prohibition. You had to know the right passwords for access and rumor had it that some of the country's richest assholes were willing to pay thousands for the information. It wasn't that the Shoe Factory shunned assholes, but they had to be the right kind of assholes with the proper connections.

Julie never understood why.

Inside, the bar was pure Victoriana by way of Coney Island kitsch. You couldn't look in any direction without your eyeballs being assaulted by a hundred little details—carved oak chairs along the bar top; elaborate, wrought-iron tables in the middle of the room; faded, lion-colored photos of World War I pilots and unsmiling white women in drab kitchens; crystal chandeliers; mirrors on the walls at weird angles; and ornate columns bracketing the whiskey display behind the bar itself.

"It's like Charles Dickens dropped acid and went into the decorating business," said Julie.

Sarah quirked a smile. "I like it."

"So do I. Gotta wonder why Tyler chose this place, though. He's such a goddamn showoff. I thought he'd be hanging around one of those snootier Wall Street places where they drink thousand-dollar martinis and no one's shit stinks. This is way too . . . cute."

Julie set the small box she was carrying on their table as she and Sarah sat down. She was attired—after some cinching at the waist and careful application of a push-up bra Julie forgot she owned—in what Sarah had described as a bespoke Guo Pei. Julie had no idea who that designer was. What she did know was she'd never seen a dress more elaborate: a white slip, carefully tailored so that from the waist down it belled into what Julie had always imagined the Tower of Babel to look like, the fabric cunningly tailored so the folds fell like a madness of archways and stairwells haunted by ghostly figures: figures that could only be seen when the dress was in motion.

Sarah wore something more muted: a lapis Versace suit with no shirt underneath, only diamonds that seethed down her cleavage, and gold accents at the belt and the sleeves.

"So, what's in the box?" asked Sarah, tapping the top with a fingernail.

Julie shook her head, laughing. "You don't want to know what's in the box."

"But I do. It's part of your work, right? Is it something magic?"

"Yeah. But magic of the most fucked-up kind. No one needs to see this ugly little critter. *I* don't want to see this ugly little critter."

"Is it worse than a possessed horse?"

"A hundred times."

"But not a million times worse?"

"I was trying to play it down so you won't run scared."

"Okay. I won't beg for a peek."

"Clever girl."

Sarah replied with a velociraptor hiss, which had Julie laughing all over again. She recalled then with a certain vertiginous lurch an entire swath of memories she'd set aside ten plus years ago: Sarah and Julie in flannel pajamas together in a converted garage, a string of colored fairy lights staining their skin apricot and red; watching movies again and again until they could perform each scene from their nest of blankets. They'd been good together as friends. With time, without Dan, would they have been good as something else? Julie always wondered.

"That thing you said before about Tyler being a showoff, with all his friends in expensive suits. I hope you don't think *I'm* like that . . ."

Julie shook herself out of her reminiscing, alarmed.

"Wait. *What?*"

"I worry you think I'm trying to show off."

"First of all, no. You're nothing like those creeps. Secondly, *no.* Plus, the clothes are great. They have personality. Tyler's crowd has no personality and even less idea about what looks good. All that matters to them is the stupid price tag."

Sarah unclenched her shoulders—not by much but enough that Julie's heart no longer hurt from the sight. "That makes me feel better. Dan hates that I'm so interested in clothes. He thinks it's . . . frivolous. And you know? Sometimes, I think so too. The world is going through so many terrible things. And there's me, thinking about clothes."

"Fuck. That," Julie growled. "The world is always a wreck and life is an amusement park you only get to visit once. Clothes are your thing and that's okay. You get to like them. You can do that while worrying about the big stuff too. Anyway, Dan and anyone else who thinks otherwise can go get fucked."

Sarah bobbed her head, eyes downcast. "I'll try to remember that."

The waiter finally arrived and they put in their orders, with Julie insisting they get two rounds straight away so they wouldn't have to wait later.

"You always think ahead," said Sarah.

"Only when it comes to drinking."

When their drinks arrived—Manhattans for Sarah and straight vodka with an olive for Julie—they downed their first glasses quickly.

Sarah raised her eyebrows. "They make them strong here."

"As the good gods and the bad ones and the meh ones intended," said Julie. She propped an elbow up on the table, chin in the scoop of her palm. "I've talked about me and you've told me about Dan, but you still haven't told me about what you're doing with yourself."

Sarah waved a hand at her. "Oh, you know. I don't have a big career like you or anything . . ."

Julie laughed. "Big career. I can barely afford to feed the neighbor's cat."

"Cat? You have a cat?"

"You're changing the subject again—"

"I'm—all right, fine," said Sarah. "I am being serious. I don't do much. Some volunteering and part-time work at a little boutique at the mall. It's not, like, big or anything, but we get really great pieces from all over the world. Nothing from the *big*-big designers, mind you. But quality stuff from up-and-comers and avant-garde folk."

"Are you just doing the selling or do you help with the curation?"

Sarah dropped her eyes, cheeks pinking. "I help with the selection."

"Knew it," said Julie, leaning back, a glass brandished in a toast. "You always had an eye for this kind of thing. Without you, I would have spent my teenage years in nothing but army surplus pants and shitty band T-shirts."

"You did spend your adolescence in army pants and T-shirts."

"Yeah, but you always dressed me up like a person when I had to go to a funeral or a wedding or something."

Sarah sipped her second Manhattan. "You should have seen me at senior prom. I went a little overboard with crinoline."

"Yeah?"

"More than a little overboard. My date said I looked like a human cupcake."

"Fuck him," said Julie. Then, before she could stop herself: "If I'd known you were going as dessert, I might have gone to prom."

"My date that night was drunk by eleven and out cold by ten past. You and I should have gone together. You all scruffy and me looking like baked goods."

Julie was saved from having to respond—the words *I bet you looked good enough to eat* slouching unchivalrously on the tip of her tongue—by Sarah sitting bolt upright, a hand reached across the table to take Julie by the arm.

"Oh my god, Julie. Oh my god. Do you see her?"

"Who? What?" said Julie, still thinking alarming thoughts of Sarah frosted with cream, with sugar seed-pearls on her lips to be kissed away.

"There. Over at the bar."

Julie followed Sarah's gaze to where a cigarette-thin woman in a black dress sat lounging like she was Hollywood's best paid secret, mouth sheened with neon so that even from across the room, you knew which parts of her whisky glass to envy. "Uh-huh?"

"Isn't her outfit stunning?"

"Yeah?" Julie ventured, not so much treading water as she was fighting off drowning. "I think so? What am I looking for? Help me out. I'm less cultured than a raccoon."

Sarah gave a low laugh, fingers intertwining with Julie's hand before she gave it a squeeze. It was barely any pressure, but the bolt of electricity that ran up her arm made Julie's breath seize and her tongue lose function for a moment. "She's wearing a Yohji Yamamoto. I'm sure of it. He's one of my favorite designers. I mean, I love all the Japanese designers. And the street fashion they have there. God. Even the high schoolers have this talent for mixing and matching the wildest outfits you can imagine."

"Maybe you can go to Japan and look at clothes while Dan does his Muay Thai thing?" Julie was definitely not distracted by the fact Sarah was holding her hand.

At the mention of Dan's name, Sarah flexed her fingers and something in the machine of Julie's mind went *ding*. "Sure. Maybe."

"Hey. How'd you hurt your hand again?"

"Why?" asked Sarah, one of her overly sweet, nutritionally empty smiles pasted back on. "It's not a big deal."

"I just want to know what I gotta go chop up into firewood."

Sarah gave a little clattering shrug. "I smashed it against a dresser. And you can't chop that one up. It's from my grandmother."

Julie nodded. There it was: proof of the lie. Her injured hand. Julie would have wagered both kidneys it had something to do with Dan, who was problematic on his best days and someone she'd always seen as one bad idea away from being a danger. She didn't have a good way of saying she wanted to kick Dan down the stairwell in the Empire State Building, pick him up, and do it again. So, Julie ordered them two more rounds of drinks and two more after that.

A little over an hour later, they were quite drunk.

That was when she spotted Tyler and some of his Thorne & Dirk friends carousing in the VIP booth at the far end of the bar.

"Ugh," Julie said. "He's here."

Sarah looked around. "Tyler?"

"Yeah. Him and the Trust Fund Squad. I guess I should take him his damn present so I can get paid."

"It'll be okay," said Sarah. "I'll be with you."

Julie swallowed. "I'm really glad you surprised me today."

"Me too."

With a sigh, Julie picked up the box and slid from her chair. "Let's get this over with."

By now, the bar was nearly full and the crowd had lost its pretensions about being special. The clientele howled and jabbered at one another, whooped and cajoled and argued and flirted, their voices overpowering the music. Still Tyler, holding court with his little friends, managed to keep his voice above the din.

Loudmouth, thought Julie as she and Sarah approached. Julie had a script ready. She'd practiced in her head what she would say to Tyler, how she'd say it, the posture she would take, the way she'd gesture—staccato, indifferent—so Tyler wouldn't think she gave a shit. However, as they closed the distance, any thoughts of being strategic went out the window, chased to the pavement by her anger.

". . . so, I had the formalus cornered in the back room of the office, right? I'd beaten it up pretty well by then, but you know how a formalus is. Always dangerous, even when hurt. Anyway, as it's there cowering, I draw a circle on the floor and start a containment spell . . ."

"I would have been scared to death," said a voluptuous Scandinavian-looking woman seated directly across him.

Tyler faked a pious look, hands tented, eyes raised to pressed tin ceiling. "It was nothing really. Seriously, I don't know why people make such a big deal about them. I had it in the circle and bound less than a minute later."

"How did you kill it?" asked Julie, voice barely raised, but she didn't need to be loud to cut through the prattling, not with the rage balled in each syllable.

Tyler and his friends turned in her direction. His smile was grandiose when he saw the box Julie was carting, but it faded as Julie kept talking, her decorum sloughing away with every word she spat. "I mean, you have to tell me. Far as I know, there's no way to actually get at a formalus unless it's inside someone. So, you have to tell me how you did it. Was it you who took the formalus in like Jesus' cum? Or did you get someone else to host the little fucker for you? Because man, I'm going to have questions if you say the second. I know you pay worse than Fiverr."

"Well," he said. "Obviously, it was inside someone."

"Who?" said Julie and before Tyler could add another fucking lie, she added: "Actually, I'll tell you who. It was my intern Brad. He almost died because of you. We killed the formalus while you were home in Chelsea having wine and cheese."

But Tyler didn't break the way Julie wanted him to, didn't color with embarrassment, didn't stammer. He barely had any change in expression: an incremental raising of his brows, but otherwise nothing to say he'd been caught with stolen valor. His smile came back on, and he gestured in her direction. "This is Julie. You've all heard me talk about Julie. I don't think I need to make any introductions."

The looks she received ran from pity to disgust, and the kindest thing she could say about the group's appraisal was that they gave her the dignity of being halfway subtle about their scorn. Julie swallowed.

"Although her?" said Tyler, looking over her shoulder to Sarah. "I'd love introductions to. Is that Versace?"

"Leave her the fuck alone," said Julie, stepping between them.

"She's a grown woman. She can speak for herself."

"Leave me the fuck alone," said Sarah, and Julie could have howled in delight at the words.

"Whatever. Look, I know you love making a scene, but I'm here with actual grown-ups—" That elicited a round of chuckles. "—and we're trying to enjoy ourselves. How about you go home and we can pick up this discussion of your abandonment issues another day, huh?"

Without saying a word, Julie opened the box and emptied its contents atop the table. A pickle jar tumbled out, rolling to a stop a half-inch from the edge. Inside was a hand: gray, bloated, abscessed with the offspring of the formalus. Little larval Brads with none of the bones or any of the torso, like maggots wearing miniature masks. Exposed to the light, they began writhing in earnest, eager to bed down in a proper host. Had they not been encased in glass, had the jar broken on the floor, the formalus would have turned the bar into an incubator. "Thought I'd drop this off while I was here. A little take-me-back gift, *huh*? Doesn't it move your cold, lying heart?"

"Close that shit up."

Julie thrust the box at Tyler. "You do it."

The crowd didn't say a word, but their gaze shuttled between Julie and Tyler and the box and back. To his credit, Tyler manned up enough to grab the bottle and return it to its cardboard prison.

"I can't believe you're doing this, Julie. I kill the formalus and ask you to hold this for me, and you come here and risk everyone?" Tyler handed the box to the Scandinavian woman, his smile less a smile than a warning show of teeth. "I just needed you to take care of it until the firm's new containment facility is up and running, and this is what you do?"

Johnson Andrews from the firm's Recruiting department said, "When did we get a new containment facility?"

"Shut up, Johnny," snapped Tyler. He turned to Julie. "You know, I'm just sad for you."

He shook his head and continued. "It's always about making a scene with you. How many jobs have you lost because you need to be so dramatic all the damn time? How many interns have walked out on you in the past year alone? I've been helping you for so many years, but I'm done. I'm done with your crazy. Find another guardian angel."

Guardian angel.

Julie stiffened. "I knew you were an asshole, but I didn't realize you were a prick too. And such a little one."

She'd called him guardian angel once. All through the first three years of their relationship, Julie had told him he was her guardian angel, that she was glad for him, blessed to be watched over by someone so meticulous, so good at maneuvering through the bureaucracy of social interactions.

Tyler kept going. "And I'm personally offended that you'd try to take credit for my kill. Here in front of my friends."

Julie had no idea she'd taken a step toward Tyler until she felt a tug on her arm, Sarah clinging to her, shaking her head.

"He's not worth it," she whispered urgently.

"He isn't," said Julie, allowing herself to be led away. "You ought to know something, Tyler. Before it died, the formalus showed me something: it was an inside job. Someone from your firm did it. And I'm going to make sure everyone knows."

Neither Tyler nor his friends said anything after that, at least nothing that Julie could hear because Sarah had pulled her away from them and out of the bar.

On the street, both women stopped to catch their breath.

"What the hell was all that?" said Sarah.

"When we were dating, he was always the face guy. He did our negotiations. I was better than him at the actual magic stuff and well, as you might have guessed, shit at the niceness thing. Then he got a job with this place called Thorne & Dirk . . . and my luck in life got worse. He badmouthed me around town, until old clients stopped calling and new ones ran away screaming. I started having to take small jobs for crap money. And Tyler started taking the credit for them. He told me he'd keep giving me work if I kept my mouth shut, so I did. But then tonight happened. After what went down there, he's . . ."

"Maybe we should go back to your place so you can relax." Sarah put a hand on her shoulder.

"Or I could go back inside and set Tyler on fire."

"I think willful immolation is technically murder."

"You call it willful immolation. I call it—"

"Pest control," said Sarah, grinning. "You haven't changed."

Julie fought down the urge to stare at her feet.

"Yeah, pest control," she said, clearing her throat. Then, warming to the topic, she added, "The judges will agree with me. Tyler's *vermin*."

"Let's save that for another night. Okay?"

Julie took a few steadying breaths. "You're a good friend."

They walked arm in arm toward the subway for a few minutes before Julie stopped and said, "You definitely need to go to Japan. I know Dan wants you with him, but fuck that. Don't let men do that to you or you're going to end up screaming at bastards in bars and wondering if you have any future at all."

All Sarah said was, "Come on. Let's go get drunk. Drunker."

When they got to the subway entrance, Julie said, "I hope Tyler spends his life stepping on Legos."

"Legos?"

"I meant broken glass and barbed wire but I didn't want to sound too harsh." Julie managed a half-hearted grin.

"Fuck men," said Julie.

"Yes," said Sarah quietly. "Fuck them."

CHAPTER EIGHT

On the way home, and despite Sarah's protests, Julie bought two bottles of Tito's vodka. Four hours later, she'd finished off the last of the cocaine in the house and was pondering whether she should crack open the second bottle.

She and Sarah were on the sofa, Julie with her head on her friend's lap, Sarah stroking Julie's hair, like she was trying to calm a scared child or a grieving animal. From time to time, Julie woozily asked if Sarah was hydrating, and Sarah would say *yes, now your turn,* to little avail.

"I'm so stupid. I'm so fucked," Julie said for the tenth or eleventh time that night. Sarah had lost count.

"You never know," Sarah said. "Some of Tyler's friends, they seemed to be listening to you. A couple of them looked pretty skeptical of his story."

Julie fumbled upright. The world swayed to the left and stayed that way, slanted at an eyewatering angle. Her alcohol tolerance wasn't what it used to be. Another sign her life was fucked, Julie decided bleakly. "You don't get it. Tyler has all the power in that bunch. That's why he was yammering on like that—lording his position over his underlings. Even if they wanted to go against him, they're shit out of luck."

"I see," said Sarah soothingly. "One way or another, I think maybe you've had enough to drink tonight."

"You think so? Where's my glass?"

"You don't have a glass. You've been drinking out of the bottle."

"Huh. I don't remember that."

Sarah gently took the vodka from Julie's hand and placed it on the table. Julie glanced at the pitted surface. The topcoat was mostly gone, eaten through by years of spilled alcohol. "Maybe this is a good time to take a break. I can make us some coffee."

"There isn't any coffee. I was going to go shopping tomorrow."

"It's New York. A few cafés must still be open."

"Hang on a minute," said Julie, tonguing her inner cheek. "Let me check something."

She opened a badly battered but ornate art deco cabinet in the far corner of the room. "This is where I keep all my spooky magic stuff. Sometimes when I've been drinking, I get mixed up and put the coffee in here and the henbane in the kitchen. Which I don't recommend."

"Ooo. Can I see?" said Sarah.

"Come over to Halloween Town."

They peered into the cabinet together, Sarah's expression one of mild horror. *She always preferred neatness,* Julie thought, a little self-consciously, hoping at the same time that the carnival of magic items might make up for the mess. It was a chaos of faded labels and smoked bottles of varying sizes and hues, mineral chunks, some polished and others not, sprigs of herbs trussed up in string, pickled vermin and their skeletonized twins, jeweled fluids in pipettes and test tubes.

The light caught on a shadowed thing in the very back. "What's that?"

"Wolfsilver," said Julie, inching aside to give Sarah room. "And that's blue amber and that's red mercury. Some of this stuff is kind of rare, so I try to take care of it, but you know. Please don't ask me what any of this is used for. Some of it's kind of gross."

"No, that thing," said Sarah, reaching into the cabinet before she caught herself. She pointed at a dusty, wizened bundle that seemed mostly desiccated muscle and mummified skin. It looked older than the rest of Julie's collection. "What the hell is that?"

Julie's smile went mischievous and she grabbed the curio to rattle it at Sarah. "That's a bona fide monkey's paw."

Sarah leaned away reflexively. "Eww. I can't believe someone'd do that to a poor—wait. A monkey's paw as in the W.W. Jacobs story? I thought that was fiction."

"Fiction is the lens through which humanity makes sense of the mystical."

"What?"

"Yeah. Exactly like that. It allegedly grants three wishes but for some reason, possibly because some fucker cut off the paw from the original monkey, those wishes are always twisted horribly. You got to be careful if you want to use one of these—or desperate."

"Careful how?"

"Like don't wish for a million dollars because you might end up pulped by a million dollars in pennies raining down from the Empire State Building. Or with everyone you know and love dead as a doorknob in a freak accident and you discovering you're the sole benefactor in their wills. You never know. I think it kind of has a sense of humor about these things."

Sarah touched a single finger to the withered paw. "Have you ever used it?"

"Nah," said Julie. "This one came used and it only has one wish left. I'm saving it for a special occasion."

"Like what?"

"I have no fucking idea. Wait, no. I do have an idea," said Julie, brightening. "What if I wish Tyler—"

Sarah interrupted her. "Stay on topic. We're looking for coffee. And I don't think you have any in there."

"I'm afraid you're right. To the apps!"

While Sarah called up an assortment of food delivery apps on her phone, switching between them to see which had the best deals and the lowest delivery rates, Julie emptied the last of her vodka. When she was done, she said: "Fuck Tyler in the eye socket. Why did he have to be such a dick? How are some guys like that?"

Sarah flexed the fingers on one hand and the other. Julie took note of which of them moved stiffer than the rest, and thought of new tortures to inflict on Dan. "I don't know. Some men are just built like that. Coffee and food are on the way, in case you're interested."

Julie made a face. "Please tell me it's not health food."

"Depends. Is bacon and sausage and fried eggs and toast health food?"

"In a perfect world, yes. But because we're in this crappy timeline, I'll concede they're not, but only because you're you."

Sarah performed a seated curtsy and, putting on a creakily sartorial English accent, her voice made nasal and aged thirty years, said: "You honor me."

We're good together, Julie thought with sudden dizzying clarity. She could see with the prescience of the drunk what kind of life they might cobble from this mess if Sarah stayed. Even if they stayed platonic, even if Sarah was nothing more than a flatmate, it could be good. Would be good. Julie, who had never even thought of growing old, wanted badly then to be old with Sarah in whatever way her friend would have her.

Except people like Sarah never wanted anything to do with fuck-ups like Julie.

"Drinking is my retirement plan. I'm letting liver failure take me out," said Julie, forcing a smile. Then, "I'm sorry for everything. Being so drunk and angry at the stupid bar. Tyler's right. I fuck up everything I touch. Can't even show my oldest and bestest friend a good night out on the town. I fucked up your first memory of New York's nightlife. I'm a fucking waste of skin."

Taking her hand, Sarah said, "It's okay. Life happens at the weirdest moments. There's nothing we can do about it."

"My life," said Julie, "has always been weird. Has always been messed up. And I just made it worse tonight by pissing off my most reliable income stream—before he even paid me! I'm never going to work again."

"You'll figure something out. And I'll help. I'll stay until we figure out a plan."

Julie's heart skipped not just one beat but a succession of them. "Where are you going to stay?"

"I have money. I'll figure out something. Hey, I can even sleep on your couch."

"I don't deserve you," blurted Julie, unable to stop, guiltily relieved to be subsumed by self-flagellation, and glad, so very glad her stream of self-pitying blather didn't include anything like *there's one bed but we can share it* and *I am scared of the fact I am thinking of stuff like that last sentence.* "You're too good for this world. You've always just been so kind. You give without asking. You even showed up here in New York, while I was wallowing in my darkest moment. And you brought me luck. You kept me from having a fistfight in the stupid bar. You—"

When Julie looked back to her friend, she was startled to find tears in Sarah's eyes, and the whole of the taller woman's breath quavering with barely suppressed sobs. Her horror must have shown, as Sarah yipped when they made eye contact, jamming a fist against her mouth.

"What's wrong?" asked Julie, too afraid to reach for Sarah.

"I'm not a good friend," Sarah said. "I lied to you earlier."

"About what?"

Sarah looked around the room and gathered both hands in her lap. "I didn't just drop in because I happened to be in New York. I came here because I wanted something from you. Which makes me exactly like all these other people who use you." A ragged, in-drawn breath before: "No, I'm worse."

Julie scooted closer. "Hey, hey. It's okay. Everything's fine. You're not like them at all. You're my friend. I'm here for you until the end."

"I'm good at making people give me what I want. I smile and bat my lashes and coo over their stories—"

See? hissed that vicious little voice in Julie's head. *She didn't care. She was just telling you what you wanted to hear.*

"—I did like your stories, to be clear. I always have. But I . . . I am still a manipulative piece of shit," said Sarah, a little damply. She honked her nose. "I could have been direct."

"Could be, schmood be. You don't have to be Little Miss Perfect."

"Tell that to my mother."

"I already did," said Julie. "Remember? When we were fourteen. I thought she was going to run me over with her car."

At that, Sarah laughed and Julie's heart did a backflip at the sound.

"I remember. I just—thank you. I needed to hear that."

"Now what was it you wanted? You name it and you got it," Julie said. But to her dismay, Sarah erupted into actual wailing sobs.

"Please—"

Sob.

"—don't—"

A snuffling whine.

"—throw me—"

Another cascade of whimpers.

"—out!"

"I would never—I would—Sarah, what are you even talking about? Why would you even think that? Tell me what's wrong!"

Clear mucus seeped from both of Sarah's nostrils. She'd never been a pretty crier. Wetly musical, yes, but not pretty. She went both soggy and swollen in her grief. She held Julie with a flayed, desperate, very puffy-eyed stare as she mopped ineffectively at her face with her hands, took a rattling breath, closed her eyes. Calmer now, she said, "It's Dan."

This surprised Julie not at all.

"What about him?"

Sarah took another longer breath. "I want him to disappear."

"Define 'disappear' for me."

"I want him gone. Forever," said Sarah, her voice sounding

far-off and wretched. Julie remembered now. Where she turned to rage in her pain, Sarah turned inward, crawling as far into the illusion of the Little Miss Perfect as she could go. "I'm not—I'm not asking you to *kill* him but can you send him away somewhere? Somewhere so far away he can never come back and find me?"

It took Julie a minute to understand what Sarah was saying. Still drunk, she ran the words over in her head to make sure she'd heard them right. But she already knew she had. She already had her suspicions about Dan but this confirmed her worst fears. She said, "Where's Dan now?"

"Home," said Sarah, flinching, as if the word was barbed. "Unless he's figured out that I've left. Which he probably has. I'm an idiot. I shouldn't have taken anything. I should have left everything and just run."

Run.

The word was a bullet to Julie's belly, and she could not breathe around the pain of what it implied. One innocuous little word shouldn't have been able to do so much, but it did. Julie's world stove like wrist bones cracked by a door pushing down.

Men like Dan and Tyler—how did they get away with existing? So fetid, so full of themselves. Practically sloshing with the filth of their natures, getting it on anything they touched. The more she thought of Dan, the more she pictured Tyler. Those two could have been twins: same smirk, same hair, same masturbatory interest in their own well-being and no one else's. Convinced that they were the main characters, and everyone else was set decoration. Anything they didn't like, couldn't break down to serviceable components, they shot and buried far, far away from their sight.

Julie wondered what she'd be like now if she'd been able to transform for Tyler as he began his climb up Wall Street. She pictured herself as the perfect hostess: a pretty little Stepford wife with a pastel wardrobe and her mouth scoured of opinions. Julie knew she was lucky that Tyler had walked out. The breakup had practically atomized her. If he'd given her the choice of coming with him, offered his arm—there was a version of Julie that would have said . . .

"I'll do it."

Sarah blinked in rapid succession. "You will?"

"Of course."

"But I'm asking you—"

"You're asking me nothing that I haven't been asked before. Plus, I like making douchebags piss their pants."

"But I lied to you."

"Would it make you feel better if I said I was mad at—*joke!* I was making a joke. Sarah. Please don't cry. Oh my god, I'm so sorry. I will never make a joke again."

After Sarah could speak again, she said, "I was so scared you'd throw me out."

"Man, he really did a number on you."

"He really did."

"I wouldn't throw you out for the world. Not for money, or love, or God."

"What about Lana from senior year?"

The name called up a faded memory of high ponytails and rainbow scrunchies, but little else. Still, Julie said: "Not even for her."

"You had the worst crush on her."

Not as bad as the one I had on you, thought Julie.

What she said was:

"But back to the topic. Let me be clear. I'm not going to disappear Dan. Not as a first resort. Guys like that, the world notices when they vanish. If he winks out of existence, there's going to be a target painted on your back. You're going to be Suspect Number One. Especially after people start realizing he was a jerk to you."

"It's always the abused wife who turns out to be the killer," muttered Sarah.

"What?"

"I'm big into true crime series where the woman kills the man.

God knows why." Sarah managed a Pyrrhic smile. In her exhaustion, Julie could see the ghost of the old woman her friend would be one day: the faint cicatricial lines that despair had carved around her mouth, but also the first feathering of wrinkles from her smiles, her easy laughter. She was going to stay gorgeous her whole life.

"Seems like a strange thing for a woman in a happy relationship to be obsessed with."

"You know me, I'm a weirdo."

"So am I."

Again, that heated pressurized silence, full of portents, of waiting: a stillness, like the air before a thunderstorm. Julie cleared her throat, inexplicably shy.

"Anyway," she said. "Let me deal with him in my own way. I'll start with a serious chat and if I have to escalate from there, well, let's see how far he forces me to go. He might still get poofed into a hellmouth."

Sarah flung her arms around Julie but this Julie could deal with, not least because even unrequited infatuation faltered when assaulted with half-dried snot. "Thank you. Thank you. Thank you."

Julie felt depressingly sober. She had no real idea what she was going to do with Dan, but with luck, he wouldn't fuck around too much so she wouldn't have to find out how far she'd go. *Just enough,* she begged whatever divinity might be eavesdropping. To have an excuse to squeal and beg for mercy. No need for disappearing him. She wasn't in the market for reasons to do a murder. All Julie wanted was to visit abject terror, tears, and a hefty dry-cleaning bill on Dan.

"We'll let him make the first move," Julie said when Sarah loosened her stranglehold. "Make him worry a little about whether you've gone to the media or something. The moment he realizes you're gone, he'll start getting in touch with your friends, I'm sure. And at some point, he find his way down the food chain to me."

"And then the talk?" asked Sarah.

"Then the talk," nodded Julie. "And everything else that follows if he persists on being a little shit."

Leaning her head on the back of the sofa, Sarah said, "All of a sudden, I'm exhausted."

"Why don't you take the bed? I have a couple of things I need to do before I crash for the night."

"Absolutely not," insisted Sarah. The words came slurred. What fight she had, what remnant of pep she thought still twitched in her veins, was all gone. Her body was done with its cortisol binge. "I'm the one crowding you. I'll be fine here on the sofa."

"You sure?"

"Definitely."

"Let me get you some covers and a pillow."

"Only if they're not the ones you were going to use."

They were, but Julie wasn't going to tell her that. "I'll find you something that wasn't at imminent risk of being used."

"Promise?"

"Yes. Now go the hell to sleep."

By the time Julie settled into bed, she was tired and depressed. The scene with Tyler and what it meant for her future haunted her. And now knowing about Sarah's situation, well, that just compounded the shitshow, didn't it? She would never confess as much to Sarah—glass would break with less ease than her poor friend right now—but she regretted not decking Tyler, if for no other reason than to see the look on his face and maybe, if she was lucky, hear a jingle of teeth landing on the floor. That would have definitely cost her more than the stunt she pulled, but what a sight it would have been.

Still, there was Dan to look forward to, an opportunity that buoyed her spirits for a good minute until her phone buzzed on her bedside table. The bank had sent a message. The client she'd been counting on had been arrested for tax evasion and all their funds were frozen. There was more to the message, but her eyes glazed over and she couldn't read it.

She set her phone down instead and said quietly to the darkness:

"I can't do this anymore."

I can't go on like this. My friends are great, but how many times can I go to St. Joan, Dead Air, or the others begging for help? And I can't ask Sarah. She's here to be helped. I hope she has cash with her because if Dan knows she's gone, I bet he's cut off her credit cards. No. Fuck. This has to end.

But how, she wondered.

Julie racked her brain for insight, some clue or a thing like hope, a lead on how to turn her life around, but she turned up empty as her checking account. She was out of luck, out of resources, out of favors to call in. She looked around for something she might be able to sell, but the only things she had of any value were her magic supplies and those were off-limits. So, she thought harder. Until she was sure her brain would ooze out of an ear. Then she remembered what Tyler had said to her:

"Find a new guardian angel."

Fuck.

Yes.

Recent years had seen an increasing exodus from formalized religion, particularly those that maimed their scriptures for the sake of—Julie had no idea what, honestly. "Love your neighbor as yourself" seemed a straightforward enough directive. But then again, she'd kicked being Catholic before she picked up her first cigarette. Either way, from what she'd been told, the angelic were shortchanged on people to watch over. An apostate like her would be of interest. Although she had no idea as to how to flag one down for a heart-to-heart. But she knew someone who might: Billy Starkweather of Esoteric Unlimited, the magical-est fucking bookstore on the island.

Tomorrow bright and early—or as early as her hungover ass

could manage—she and Sarah were going shopping. Billy would have the answers she needed.

He had to.

❧

Esoteric Unlimited stood on Bowery between East First and East Second Street. From the outside, it was a drab-looking place: low-roofed with walls the color of loam, an air of dust and deep time. A place that sometimes seemed, especially in the late light, less a shop than the throat of a cave. Had it been any normal business, the landlord would have long since pulled the lease so the corpse of the place could be rented out for ten times the money, but that wasn't going to happen. Esoteric Unlimited had occupied its spot in lower Manhattan for fifty years, and if Billy Starkweather had anything to say about things (which he always did), it would continue standing for a hundred more. There were rumors that Billy paid no rent at all: gossip he loudly decried whenever it surfaced in his presence. While he believed in very little, Billy did believe that nothing in the world should come for free.

Outside the bookstore, around noon, Sarah looked through the smudged windows and frowned, just a little.

"This is it?"

Julie grinned. "Everyone says that the first time they see the place. But trust me. Things get more interesting inside."

"I hope they have what you're looking for."

"They always do."

Sarah cocked her head. "Always, huh? Bold remark there."

"Alllwaaaays," said Julie, drawing out the word. She held the door open, and they went inside.

Sarah did a 360-degree turn.

"Okay, what am I missing? It still looks like a bookstore," said Sarah after she'd acclimatized to the murk. Billy kept it dark in Esoteric Unlimited, much to the dismay of his customers and the relief of his products. "Even if it smells like a museum."

"See? You're getting it. Give it a bit and all shall be—oh, hey, Eric."

Julie waved to a young man slouched behind the counter, his sneakered feet kicked up onto its planked top. He was thin, pale, and dressed in a red Pendleton shirt with the sleeves rolled up. His arms were honeycombed with tattoos—eyes in every configuration with every variation of pupil in the animal kingdom; eyes of varying detail: grisaille masterwork and graffitied symbols; eyes with irises that festered with infant versions of themselves, as if something had laid eggs there; eyes that, from the right angle, seemed to move and blink and rearrange themselves. Hard to tell how many they were, packed as they were on his skin, like lotus pod seeds or lesions.

"Hi Julie," said Eric brightly. He set down his magazine and bounced onto his feet. Behind him was a massive glass cabinet covered in wards in which were a myriad of dusty tomes: Billy's most precious and dangerous titles. "How are you doing? We haven't seen you in a while."

Julie rubbed the back of her neck, sheepish. "Yeah. You know, money, et cetera, et cetera."

Eric folded his arms. "You know Billy always lets you buy on credit. It might take a while, but he knows you're good for it."

"I do my best," she said, unsettled by the reminder she was never punctual with her money. Julie dressed her face in its most charming smile, changed tack, and gestured. "By the way, Sarah here is a friend and knows the score. You can drop the look."

Eric sagged with relief. "Thank god. This silly glamour was giving me a migraine."

The skin along Eric's arms drew inward as short insectile spines burst through the top layer of flesh. He blinked several times as his eyes morphed from an ordinary brown to silvery and black compound structures. His lips drew back into a smile revealing rows of very small, very sharp teeth. He shuddered once as his hands were replaced with the type of complex grippers a fly might use to trap its prey. With a happy sigh, the young man stretched both arms above him, finally relaxed.

"Shit, that feels much better. I—uh, Julie, I think your friend is about to have a litter of puppies."

Julie glanced behind her. Sarah had taken several steps back away from the counter and while she didn't look *scared* per se, she did however bear the vacant expression of someone who wasn't sure they were awake or dreaming.

Julie put a hand on Sarah's shoulder and said, "It's okay. You're awake. Everything is fine. This is real. Eric is mostly teeth—"

"Hey."

"—and heart—"

"Thanks. Much better."

"—and we're good friends. You can also stop gawping now."

Sarah shut her jaw with a theatrical *clack*, blinking at Eric still, her brows furrowed so hard they almost touched.

"You told me that things get weird—"

"Be careful who you call weird," said Eric, shaking his head. "I like it. But not everyone does."

"Sorry," said Sarah, mortified.

"It's fine." Eric grinned wide enough for them both to see the innumerable molars now studding his jaw.

"Yeah. So," began Julie. "Civilians tend to think of magic as this invisible thing that's—what is the analogy I'm looking for, Eric?"

"Electricity?"

"That works. Media tends to make magic sound like electricity. You can manipulate it. You can make it light up rooms. But it's generally this invisible force, you know?"

Sarah bobbed her head, her frown beginning to loosen. "I think so?"

"But magic is also people like Eric."

Sighing, the aforementioned added, "Unfortunately, magic like me doesn't always jibe with the tourists so we keep a lid on things. Sorry for scaring you."

"No, I—this is amazing. I promise," said Sarah.

"You haven't seen anything yet," said Eric. His inhuman eyes flicked between the subjects of his attention. Had Julie been less familiar with Eric, more like Sarah, she might have bolted under the scrutiny. Eric was stage fright on two legs. "Are you taking her to the thing at the place?"

"In a few minutes," said Julie. "But first I need a very specific book."

"All of our books are very specific. Which one were you looking for?"

"A Bellocq grimoire."

Eric beamed at Julie. "A Bellocq grimoire, huh? Are we trying to make up with the big Sky Daddy?"

"He wishes," said Julie. "Please, please tell me you have one."

"Who's Bellocq?"

"Ah!" said Eric, with a clearing of his throat. He had a good voice in his human disguise, and a brilliantly oratorial one without its restrictions. "I'm so happy that you asked."

"Here it comes," muttered Julie to Sarah, who hushed her.

"Bellocq was a fourteenth-century French theologian who was convinced that something was badly wrong with heaven, that there was something that had the angels there running scared. He wrote hundreds of books on the subject, and then on ways humanity could help the angels escape whatever it was they were fleeing."

"The Church did not like him," noted Julie.

"Not in the slightest," said Eric.

"But what led to that?" said Sarah.

"You heard of the term musical universalis?" asked Eric.

"Yes," said Sarah promptly. "That's the music of the spheres. It was a Greek philosophical concept that describes the movements of celestial bodies as a form of music."

Eric nodded.

"Bellocq believed that that music was actually the angels screaming."

"Oh."

Julie cleared her throat. She had heard the apocrypha a thousand times before, in a hundred forms: each of them positing different theories about who Bellocq was, and why he might think such appalling things about those on high. Whatever the truth was, Julie could only guess. Bellocq's texts were infamously obtuse, labyrinthian to the point of incoherence, each one contradicting the last. The only element that was ever consistent was his fear: Bellocq was terrified for the angels.

"So . . . book?"

"Yes, of course. Let me go get it." Eric went from the counter to one of the many bookcases lining the store, shimmying up a ladder to rummage through one of the uppermost shelves.

"Yes!" Julie said, throwing a fist into the air. She beamed at Sarah, the latter only beginning to regain her composure. "You continue to be my good luck charm. Thank you."

"Sure, thank *Sarah* for getting the book. Don't thank the guy trying to find it."

"Thank you, Eric!" Julie sang out gaily, earning her an amused snort.

"I don't really like taking credit for something I didn't do," protested Sarah.

"Oh, I like this one," said Eric as he came down, book in gripper.

He set the tome on the counter. It was very old, its pages smudged from hard use. The rotting bookcloth cover was still a brilliant emerald green, ornated with gold stamping: vegetal patterns growing out of closed-eyed, smiling death masks. Julie made note to keep Sarah from the grimoire. She recognized the color of it for what it was: a sign of arsenic in the pigment.

"This looks nineteenth-century," said Julie after a moment.

"Sixteenth-century, actually." Eric corrected as he wiped the cover with an oiled cloth. "A very good translation."

"I don't get originals anymore? The horror. Oh, the horror."

Eric fixed her with a stare from his enormous eyes.

"Tu parles le français, Julie? Étrange que tu n'aies rien dit?"

Julie stuck her tongue out at Eric and instead of answering said: "How much?"

"You don't even want to know. Just go ahead and take it. You and Billy can work out the payment details on your own."

Julie forced herself not to worry about how she'd accrued yet another debt. She had a plan. The angel, when she had it on her side, would help with that—the details eluded her then, but she was certain that it would be solvable by a representative of the god in some fashion. If not, she had worse problems than another bill. Julie bounced on her heels as Eric swaddled the book in brown butcher paper, occasionally and discreetly licking his green-stained grippers.

"You look really excited," said Sarah.

"More relieved. More . . . I don't know. I could be excited. I mean, I definitely am excited about maybe getting a drink with you in that place if Eric—"

"Oh, go right ahead," said Eric. "Just keep her close. We've got some real hungry ones tonight."

"Point taken. We'll be careful. Right, Sarah?"

Sarah looked from Eric to Julie as the latter hooked an arm through Sarah's own. "Excuse me? Did you say 'hungry ones'? Because that sounds really ominous."

Eric pressed a button under the counter and the wall at the back of the store *changed.* Between one blink and the next, it went from flaking plasterboard to an L-shaped corridor leading into blue-tinged violet light. Faint music, and the smell of cooked meat, incense, and cigarette smoke, drifted out. Julie gave Sarah a tug.

"Have fun," said Eric as he closed the bookshelf behind them. "Don't get eaten."

❧

The club behind Esoteric Unlimited was never empty. Though it was only early afternoon, it was crowded with people and what looked almost like people if the observer was willing to forgive a few inconsistences. The low ceiling was the pressed tin common throughout New York, except a reflective black. Every surface, from table to stool to walls and carpet, was black.

They moved unhurriedly through the throng, which paid them less attention than Julie was concerned they would: mostly, the clientele busied themselves with their own fun. A tattoo artist—her skin entirely translucent, revealing underneath a wealth of organs that were mostly tubing—did her work in one corner, encircled by a queue of waiting customers. On the opposite end stood an enormous aquarium in which swam what resembled copies of the tattoo artist—save these were without torsos, only heads appended to loops of mauve intestine.

As Julie and Sarah passed a group of ordinary-seeming teenagers, Sarah leaned over.

"Shouldn't they be in school?"

Julie glanced at the lanky pack. "Yeah, but vampires are kind of jerks, especially the new ones. You can't tell them anything."

The kids—nothing about them said "vampire," nor would until they were ready to feed—were watching *Lost Boys* on a big-screen TV, the brightness turned high enough to bleed all definition from their skin. They were sharing an enormous bucket of popcorn, and laughed hysterically at every other interaction between the actors.

"Vampires? *Really.*"

"Perfectly harmless unless you're a dentist."

Finally at the bar, the two sat down. Julie called over the bartender, while Sarah did her best to ignore the mass of squid arms comprising their server's lower half.

"A Dark and Stormy, right?" said Julie, placing their orders.

"You remembered!" exclaimed Sarah, more delighted than Julie would have liked. It was one thing to be appreciated, another to be adored because the bar was low enough to be subterranean. Sarah was owed more than the meager courtesy of being treated like a person. It genuinely *hurt* Julie to see Sarah elated by this scrap of thoughtfulness. Maybe she *would* make Dan vanish into a puff of gore. Just for kicks.

"Why wouldn't I?"

"Dan—"

Julie shook her head. "You know what? We don't need to bring him up. This is an asshole-free zone tonight."

"And every night," said the bartender as he returned. "Which is why I'm surprised Billy lets you visit."

"There's a difference between an asshole and an entertaining loser."

"A rose by any other name."

"Shut up, Jeremiah."

Whatever comeback the bartender had planned was interrupted by the arrival of a familiar woman in a floor-length red dress. Unlike Julie and Sarah, the club noticed her. They stared at her with expressions that ranged from worship to naked hostility. But the woman ignored them as she emerged from the press of bodies, straight-backed, the carved statue of a goddess brought to haughty animation.

"Joan," said Julie in way of greeting, patting the stool beside her.

She pecked Sarah and then Julie on the cheek, her lips cold. The beveled purplish light from above the bar made her seem strange, less three-dimensional than she appeared in daylight. "How lovely to see you here."

Julie beamed at her. "You really get around."

"Not like I used to," said St. Joan. "No one wants to have absinthe and threesomes these days."

"Hey, speak for yourself—"

This comment earned Julie the sight of Sarah downing half her cocktail in one go.

"This is good. Holy shit, this might be the best Dark and Stormy I've ever had." Sarah took another more modest sip. "Yeah, definitely the best."

"Jeremiah is good at what he does," said St. Joan before she looked back to Julie. "We had better dancing too. Although I'm glad that we now live in a time and age when people like Gene Kelly wouldn't be tolerated."

Sarah rucked her brow. "Gene Kelly? Like, the *Singing in the Rain* star? I used to love him when I was a kid."

"Was he how you got into ballet?"

"How'd you know I did ballet?"

"Your lines," said St. Joan, raising her chin at Jeremiah, who showed then that he could be deferential, just never with people like Julie. The bartender, who had not been given an actual drink order, moved away nonetheless with the purpose of a zealot. "You move like you did ballet. You carry yourself like you did ballet."

"Fifteen years," said Sarah with embarrassed pride. "But Dame Margot Fonteyn, actually. Now, she had beautiful lines."

"She did. Lovely person too," said St. Joan, and before Sarah could ask the obvious question, her attention went to Julie. "And why are you at Billy's place of business today?"

Julie held up her book.

St. Joan gave her a devilish grin. "A *Bellocq*? How lovely. People said the cruelest things about him, but he was such a dear man."

Julie scooted eagerly forward on her stool, so she balanced almost on the edge. "Wait. You never told me you knew Bellocq. When was this?"

In answer, St. Joan fluttered a hand. "Oh, who remembers these things? He must have been about five hundred or so when I met him, and so devilishly gorgeous even despite his inane ramblings. Gorgeous enough to drag me away from a party at Louise Brooks's bungalow."

"Louise Brooks? Like, the silent movie star?" said Sarah.

Julie could see Sarah doing the arithmetic in her head. "St. Joan doesn't talk about it much, but she made some movies back in the day."

The older woman's expression turned unconvincingly demure. "Hush, you. I had my Hollywood fun, but I was never *star* material like Brooksie. I was always too busy with other things."

"Like charming people out of realty."

"More like into real estate, sometimes," murmured St. Joan.

Sarah, having finally arrived at the impossible, cocked her head and said, not with awe, but the wariness of someone confronted with not one but an entire herd of gift horses. "But Louise Brooks made movies in the *twenties*."

"Brooksie worked well into the thirties."

"Does that mean you're a god or something?"

At this, St. Joan erupted into guffaws. "You can keep this one, Julie. I like her."

"You only like her because she recognizes you for what you are."

"*Wait,* does that mean I'm right? You're a *god,* Joan? I—"

"No," chuckled St. Joan. "Not a god. Though I wish sometimes I were. It'd be easier than this middling life."

"But—"

Julie put a hand on Sarah's arm.

"But you're divine in our eyes." Sarah amended with enough bombast to set off St. Joan's laughter again.

She's learning, Julie thought with exultant pride.

When she could function again, St. Joan took an exploratory sip of her cocktail, glanced at the men's Rolex strapped to her right wrist, and let out a defeated sigh. "But I might be going a little senile in my old age. I forgot entirely about the time. This is silly. I have to go."

"Another romance with a . . . whatever Bellocq was?" said Julie, wiggling entreating fingers at St. Joan's drink.

"If only," said St. Joan, sliding her glass over. Its contents were iridescent, starry with particulates that Julie hoped vehemently were edible, although it wouldn't have stopped Julie if they weren't. She had a policy of not turning down free booze, especially when it originated from people like St. Joan, who had such refined tastes. "I just have a beef bourguignon in the oven. If I leave it in there any longer, none of us will have a place to live. Bye, girls."

As St. Joan vanished back into the crowd, two women approached Julie and Sarah from opposite sides of the room. They both had dark, shaggy hair and muscles enough to make Schwarzenegger renounce any claim of ever having been a bodybuilder, the kind of muscle that came footnoted with disclaimers like "not to be attempted if you're not similarly genetically blessed." Big as they were, they moved like their weight meant nothing to their bones, with the impossible animal poetry of wolves on the hunt.

Julie frowned a little and said, "Sarah, meet the Barghest Sisters."

"Hello ladies," said the sister on the right. Her eyes were chips of unflecked amber, and in the dim of the club, they had no scleral white: only wasp colors, like a warning.

"Who's your friend, Julie?" said the one on the left.

Once, several years ago, during a particularly boring swatch of months, Julie had tried to teach herself the subtleties between the two. An inch or two of height or shoulder broadness? But she quickly gave up because they and their creepy-twins act bored her. They were just more cheap bullies in a city of cheap bullies and not worth another second of her time.

Julie said, "This is my friend Sarah. Say hi."

"Hi."

"She's a civilian," said the leftward sister. If the thrum in her voice wasn't *exactly* a growl, it was, at the minimum, immediate cousins with the noise.

"That she is," Julie said. "She's with me. And Eric let us through."

"Eric?" said the sister on the right, lifting the corner of her upper lip to flash white teeth. "It's not Eric's club. It's Billy's."

"Gosh, is it? I'll have to jot that in my little notebook of fuck off, both of you. We have permission and we're staying."

Now they were *smiling,* which was much worse a sight than the reverse. There was enough of the obligate carnivore to their grim, square faces to incite apprehension. "That's good. Because it's our job to keep out riffraff. Eric said we can do anything we want to the people who don't belong."

The right sister said, "We wouldn't want any virgins devoured on club grounds. It's bad for business."

Sarah looked at Julie, no longer able to disguise her worry. "That's the second time someone said I'm going to get eaten."

"Relax," drawled Julie, forcing her face into a shit-eating grin as she slouched back, arms spread and strewn over the bar, her chin raised just so: a challenge offered in the way she crossed her ankle over her knee. "Everything's cool because it's the Sisters' job to make sure it stays that way. Right, ladies? They're only joking about the virgin thing. I know this because if they're really truly only interested in protecting those who haven't enjoyed the delight of being a beast with two backs, well, it'll mean they have to compromise the safety of—"

Julie pretended to count on her fingers.

"—about maybe three fourths of the clientele? Which would be bad because Billy would then throw them out and they'd have to work at Dunkin' Donuts."

By some sleight of light, the Barghests, who'd never been good about spatial constancy, seemed then to grow to fill the club, their silhouettes distending: mouth, shoulders, the thick ropes of their spines. Until they were as big as worlds, as wolves waiting for the end of the end of everything. Julie smelled damp fur and deep woods and dried gore. Sarah gave a tiny shudder.

"Don't be bullies," said Julie. "I'll tell on you to HR."

"Julie, can you *not.*"

"We don't have a HR department."

"I'll tell Billy."

"He won't give a shit," growled one of the Barghests. Julie couldn't tell which.

"Maybe," said Julie. "Maybe not. But I don't think you're willing to take that risk."

If they were, she'd be fucked. Julie just about kept her breathing even and her smile insouciant, her nerves wound so tight they could have cut straight through a throat. In a feat of willpower, she managed to raise her chin slightly to a taunting angle.

The Barghest on the right let out a sound that was definitely a growl, the percussions juddering through Julie's bones, and to her relief, that was the worst it got. The sister on the left said in a quiet voice: "We have our eyes on both of you. Any trouble at all and you're out of here and barred from the place. Permanently."

Julie had won.

Barely.

"Shouldn't you be shaking down those vampire kids for their lunch money or something?"

The twins proved classier than Julie, meeting her comment with cool, deprecating expressions. The purplish light soaked them in neon and when they turned to leave, that brilliance ran like lightning across the silked black of their leather jackets, catching strangely at their wrists and the tuck of their elbows, along their triceps where muscle strained at the sleeve, and on the matching grins they bared at Julie.

"*Permanent* ban, Julie. Don't fuck with us."

Julie put a hand to her ear. "Say that louder. I couldn't hear over the sound of you leaving."

When they were gone, Sarah said:

"That wasn't terrifying."

"Don't let them bother you. They're all bark and no bite."

"I'm not sure about that . . ."

"There's also this." Julie joggled the brown-wrapped grimoire at Sarah. "Billy is going to be pissed if they kill us—"

"I'm sorry, did you say *kill*?"

"—before I pay up, and we all know that so it's fine."

"Couldn't he just take the book back and resell it?" said Sarah, fidgeting with the dregs of her cocktail. "Jesus, what the fuck? Should we leave?"

"Do you want to?"

"No . . ." said Sarah as she looked over the bar, her voice gaining conviction with every word though it never raised in volume. "I think I like the idea of them grumbling in the corner, wishing they could get rid of us but not being able to."

"Fuck them," said Julie, raising her glass at what she was sure was a Barghest but wouldn't have been surprised to discover was a large fridge in a shadowed alcove. "Fun's just getting started. Time to show everyone how to really party."

Out front in the bookshop, Eric was making a phone call. A part of him wondered if he was a hypocrite. He liked Julie. Had said as much to her on multiple occasions. Even gone carousing with her on those increasingly rare nights when Billy wanted to get his hands dirty with actual retail work.

What he was going to do wasn't personal, though.

It was just business.

"Hello, this Tyler?" said Eric.

"Yes, it is. So, Eric. Did she come by?"

He hesitated. He liked the new girl. What was her name? Sarah. Yeah, that. She was pretty and she was cordial without being ingratiating, charmingly bewildered without being ignorant. Sarah radiated small-town pageant girl vibes through her well-ironed veneer, something Eric would have ordinarily been repelled by were it not for the air of melancholia tying it all together. There was a pleasing misery to Sarah: it showed in the impressive shadow of her eye sockets, the infinitesimal flinch before every smile.

Eric wondered if Julie recognized it too.

"Yeah. Just a few minutes ago."

Tyler audibly *nodded*. How, Eric had no idea.

"And you gave her a book?" said Tyler, shuffling papers, typing, his disinterested fidgeting mirroring the blandness in his voice.

"Yeah. Just like you said."

"Which one?"

Eric licked his lips. It felt reckless discussing the parameters of his betrayal here in Billy's shop, in earshot of his books.

"Angel," he said curtly, wishing they'd come up with code names.

"The fake Bellocq?" When Eric would only commit to a grave silence, Tyler sighed in what sounded like clear relief. "God, she's so predictable. What a stupid little girl."

Eric, who knew enough about Julie to not want to go on record as having defamed her, only said: "So, about the cash?"

"I'll send your money by courier later today."

With Tyler's payment, Eric could finally think about transitioning into home ownership. He was bored sick of the climbing rents in New York and of the city itself, and he was tired of Billy's so-called subsidies, how his employer nickel-and-dimed worse than the meanest insurance broker. Co-pays and deductibles for existential shit like having a reflection at four in the afternoon. Billy Starkweather lived for the fine print. "Okay, cool. Also: We're not going to tell You Know Who about this, right? He likes his inventory perfect."

"That you fucked around with his stock? No. Of course not. Not unless Billy asks."

"Hey—"

"I made you an offer. You could have said no. Don't ever forget that."

The darkening westerly sun made orange syrup of the light in the bookstore. Eric went cold. "Sure thing, Tyler. How could I forget?"

"I'm glad to hear it. The money should be there in an hour. I even threw in a little because it's your lucky day. I was dying for Julie to pick up the fake Bellocq. Buy yourself something pretty."

"Tyler—" Eric began, but the other man had already hung up.

CHAPTER NINE

Dan liked his world neat. It wasn't because, as some people thought, he had obsessive compulsions—he didn't—or that he was a control freak. Dan didn't *need* his world neat, he simply preferred it that way. He'd learned early on there was a specific kind of power to being ruthlessly organized. Knowing where everything was meant he could access it when it was needed. It also meant that people knew to rely on him and being depended upon meant power. Systems existed for a reason, as did the fulcrums around which they turned. A clock was nothing but a dial of printed numbers without its hands.

But then Sarah had to go and break the fucking machine.

He leaned back in his seat on the flight from LA. Of all the places she could go, Sarah chose New York. Why couldn't she have fled to Paris? Or Milan? Somewhere accessible by a decent airline. Domestic first class inevitably sucked no matter which company he chose. If she'd gone overseas, Dan would at least have had the pleasure of enjoying respectable service. But no, it had to be New York. New York and its rats and its dreamers and its shitty bodegas though you'd think the last was a gift from Prometheus from the way the natives crowed about how there was nowhere else in the country where you could buy *this one particular* unsalted butter.

Fucking New York.

How he loathed the city. He understood why it appealed to a certain low-minded demographic, how it could engender the foolish hope that tomorrow was when the casting director would call, when the agent would say yes, when Times Square would spell out your name in ten-foot lights. Dan knew the truth, though. New

York was nothing but a glittering conman, barely able to choke out its own lies anymore. Anyone with half a clod of brain tissue knew that. Which was, in part, why Sarah's exodus to the city appalled him so much. He had thought she knew better.

"Champagne?"

He looked up as the flight attendant extended the bottle for his inspection. Champagne his ass. It was sparkling wine. The label didn't even *say* champagne. Fortunately for the attendant, Dan understood the way the world was meant to work. He *knew* it wasn't her fault that he was being offered knock-off alcohol. Someone told her to hawk it to all first-class customers. She didn't choose to do this. Maybe she resented being a liar too.

"Sure," said Dan.

He held out his plastic cup and smiled winningly as the woman poured out a generous measure. It slopped over the rim, beading Dan's fingers with a pale residue, which he licked clean as he looked her over. The flight attendant—MINDY, said a nametag pinned to her sagging chest—must have been beautiful once. Middle age, however, had come for her *hard*. Dan could see the fault lines under the careful makeup, the puddling of skin along her neck, a growing leatheriness from too much sun. *Poor thing*, Dan thought and wondered how many years she had left before she was replaced by a younger, prettier, less used-up version of her.

"So, New York, huh? Big business trip or something?"

"No," said Dan, lapping at his thumb. "I'm going there to see a girl."

"A girl? Oh, I hope she knows how lucky she is. I can barely get my boyfriend to leave New Jersey."

Dan shrugged.

"Sadly, she isn't the appreciative sort. I try, but she just keeps being—" Dan bit back the first word to leap to his tongue. Mindy looked like the sort who would take umbrage. "—difficult."

Mindy regarded him with a thoughtful silence, blue eyes unreadable. The smile slid from her, replaced by something more formal, less friendly. There was brain under the frizzy hair, more perspicacity than he had expected of her, and he pitied her then for her acumen: she might be smart enough to recognize her slide into obsolescence, and what despair that must be.

"She probably has her reasons."

"Mm."

"And remember, it's okay for people to not want the same things. Sometimes, that's just how it is. Some people don't click together all the time."

Was she trying to *lecture* him? Dan stared at her, filled with sudden revulsion as the epiphany sank into his bones, this horrified understanding that yes, she *was* presuming she had the authority to chastise *him*.

How fucking dare she.

"And some people need to learn how to shut up."

"*Excuse* me—"

"*I'm* not the one who offered unsolicited advice." He ran his eyes up to the cascade of her chins and down to the little bit of pudge welling from under her belt. "And with respect, *Mindy*, I really don't think you should be giving life advice given the fact you're still here in a dead-end job with no husband and no future."

There. He said it.

"Sir," said Mindy. Then again, in a more strangled whisper. "Sir."

"Thanks for the wine. Now get the fuck out of my sight."

With great deliberateness, he turned his attention to the window, sipping from the cup. Dan heard what he hoped was a muffled sob and the woman shambling away. By and large, he wasn't someone who enjoyed hurting people but he understood that agony, whether emotional or otherwise, had its place in the modern man's toolbox. Sometimes, no number of carrots was enough to convince the horse to move. Sometimes, you just needed to beat the animal for its own good. With luck, this encounter with Dan would ensure that Mindy never forwent professionalism again.

Dan sighed and drew a long breath, recentering himself.

Focus. He had to focus. He wasn't going to waste energy on a fucking nobody, not when he had such a serious task ahead of him. There were so many moving parts to keep track of, and god knew if it'd be possible to stay on top of it all in a city like New York.

Dan ran through his mental to-do list. First things first, he would go to his hotel, check in, make sure the package he'd sent himself had arrived intact. It was risky, of course. New York allowed for firearms but he knew from experience that the locals were squeamish about the topic. Dan wouldn't put it past the hotel staff to raise a fuss over what was a perfectly legal possession.

He frowned at his reflection in the darkened glass. Down below, a dot matrix map of light: the city. Maybe he'd call his lawyer first instead, make sure the man knew Dan needed him to be glued to his phone, ready to provide legal assistance should any problems arise. Under other circumstances, Dan might have thought about risking it. After all, there were places in New York where someone with the proper influence could easily acquire new munitions. Unfortunately, this time around, Dan lacked that luxury.

Dan knew Sarah as a creature of sentiment. She gravitated to places that had made her happy in the past, places she had visited with people that she loved. And if Dan was right about this, and he was rarely wrong about such things, there was a strong chance he would run into her immediately. Given that, he needed his gun to be there.

Just in case.

Absently, he pulled out his phone and studied the inactive device. Of course this goddamned flight wouldn't have decent Wi-Fi. Dan would have traded his life savings for an internet connection. If he had Wi-Fi, he would have been able to continue keeping track of Sarah's whereabouts. He comforted himself with the knowledge that Sarah wasn't savvy enough to realize he'd installed stalkerware in her phone. She was offensively naïve: a trait he'd encouraged when they'd been younger and he too had been less formed, more like clay before its time in the kiln. Part of Dan always wondered if it'd been his fault she emerged into adulthood this way, but no one's trajectory was static. He grew up, became wiser to the world.

Why hadn't she?

Had Sarah asked him, he would have collaborated with her on a self-improvement plan, held her hand while she did that grim work. But she hadn't. Sarah stagnated while Dan continued to evolve. A gulf had expanded between them because of her inaction and Dan, he—how could she have done that to him when he had invested so much in her?

How could she go to New York? What was she *thinking*?

He recognized his spiraling for what it was and purged it with a surgeon's efficiency, drawing another steadying breath as he sipped from his knock-off champagne. It tasted sour and faintly of plastic. Dan leaned his head back against the faux leather of his headrest, tried to relax. No point in agitating himself. He had a plan. He knew what he'd do. And for all of New York's immensity, it was easy enough to navigate. Wherever Sarah was, he would be able to find her.

And then, they'd have a nice long talk.

CHAPTER TEN

I'm summoning an angel, Julie thought and wondered what her grandmother, rest her argumentative soul, would have said about the situation. It wouldn't have been anything polite, Julie decided. The old Korean woman was aggressively, relentlessly Catholic. She treated Sunday Mass like a war to be won and made sure that ten-year-old Julie could recite her prayers with the diction of an accent tutor. There was no reality where she'd have thought kindly of Julie forcing an angel into a compact. The divine was to be coddled, plied with prayer. Not stuffed into a cage and prodded with a stick.

"Guess there was a reason I was never your favorite grandkid, huh, halmoni?" Julie muttered to herself, running her penknife over the back of her forearm. She never understood why Hollywood horror movies always insisted on having people cut their palms when a blood sacrifice was needed. It was so impractical. Magic required manual dexterity and finesse, and manual dexterity and finesse often required full use of one's dominant hand. Julie knew professional ritualists who even went as far as to only take blood from their buttocks, although how they avoided laughing themselves to death was something that mystified her.

Julie's blood sheeted onto the center of the summoning circle, thinning quickly to strands.

She exhaled, flashing the door a guilty look. Sarah was still asleep. Though they'd talked about Julie's intent, had, in fact, dissected it thoroughly on the cab ride back to the apartment, even enumerated the possibilities—what Julie would do with angelic favor, grading her asks and rating them by their usefulness—she didn't want Sarah bearing witness to the summoning. Julie didn't want Sarah anywhere close to the angel.

And she didn't quite know why.

It didn't make sense. Not once had Sarah balked or retreated from the grotesqueries she'd seen. If Sarah was going to be a liability, she'd have demonstrated it already, but all she had displayed in the time since she arrived on Julie's doorstep was a fascination with Julie's world and a savant-like intuition for when to sit very quietly.

So, why was Julie hiding away like an addict on their umpteenth relapse?

The air sharpened with the stink of brine. Julie ran her tongue over her upper lip, suddenly focused again, glad to be wrenched from her introspection. Overthinking was hazardous in her field of work. It led too often to things like contemplating how her peers seldom lived past the age of thirty-five.

The odor was becoming unbearable. Julie wanted to throw up, but she knew from other people's experiences what happened if a summoning circle wasn't kept in sterile conditions. You died. Horribly, wetly, often with your ribs greedily unbuckled from their sheath of skin and eaten, along with everything else you were: slurped down into a gullet where you don't die but linger as ingredient for something else. *Weird how heavy magic always smells of low tide,* Julie thought as a little bubble of vomit soured on her tongue. Weirder still was how even heaven had the same miasmic sillage.

A hand—a disembodied Barbie doll appendage, slightly too attenuated, poreless and cold as polished enamel—rose from the summoning circle, its fingers threading through the rivulets of Julie's blood like they were an offering of ribbons. *Or rope,* Julie thought, as her wrist felt the abrupt weight of a corporeal body. Julie grunted, lurching back before she could be dragged face-first into her runes.

Julie began inchworming backward away from the summoning circle and nearly yelped when the angel's fingers spasmed shut around her wrist. She'd expected its touch to be cool. Not *freezing.* Not this dry-ice burn that left her immediately dazed from the pain. As Julie processed this development, a second hand emerged from the knotwork of sigils, its fingers outstretched as though imploring Julie to take hold. Before Julie could make any decisions, before she could even let go of that ragged breath she'd swallowed at first contact, she was speared by a consuming horror, a sense that the world was both less and more than she'd thought it was.

That—

—it was the black of old rot, the black of the sea, of its underbelly, of the bathyal places where nothing but the thalassic dead will go. Here in this darkness, here where there needed to be new words to describe this absence of luminance, there were things anomalous to reality, fetid and hungry, so abhorrent to the cosmos that the mind skids away from any description of them.

What a pity—

—Julie ricocheted back into herself, a headache churning between furrowed brows. What the fuck was that? *What a pity,* echoed the thought again. *What a pity, what a pity, what a pity.* Each time it repeated, Julie caught again a glimpse of that oilshine emptiness, and with every repetition, she thought she saw more things in the umbra. Bodies, writhing. Luminous muscle engorged with an overgrowth of mouths. Julie thought too she sensed a choral elation, the pathogenic joy of parturition.

What even was that, *seriously*? An omen? The fuck did she just see?

"Julie Crews."

All thought stopped at the sound of her name. In the angel's mouth, it was made holy, and Julie nearly wept at the uncomplicated relief flooding through her. All they said in their silvered voices was her name but Julie knew, just from that alone, that god—*what god, which god*, asked a voice that was hers, she was sure was hers, small as it was in the face of the divine, small and filthy and shameful in its humanness, its worthless mortality—would forgive everything. She only needed to ask.

She cleared her throat, sitting upright.

"Hey."

"I am Akrasiel," said the angel in madrigal, each of their voices a different octave, ungendered and harmonious. "Archangel of Justice."

They cocked their head, expectant. The angel—*archangel,* Julie corrected herself with heady glee—was beautiful. Everything Julie had pictured. They were cassocked in ivory, their feet invisible beneath the frothing silk. Dusky golden ringlets of hair framed a countenance gorgeous as worship, its bones and its shadows like something painted by a master's hand. Looking at the archangel was like looking at a stolen da Vinci stashed in a dirty room, which was not far from the truth: compared to the room, the building, herself, its colors were glossier, its shadows bluer, almost velvet. In its presence, Julie felt cheap and shabby, a feeling she might have resented if it wasn't so familiar.

The archangel towered a full head above Julie and as they settled into the material plane, they tented their hands, magnificent pale wings unfolding so the tips crumpled against nicotine-caked walls. Julie stared for a minute and then guffawed despite herself.

"Fuck. Point to the Christians, I guess."

The archangel stayed silent.

"I mean," said Julie, abruptly embarrassed. "Thank you for answering my summons. I imagine you're busy fighting . . . underwater kaiju or whatever it is that angels do."

Akrasiel bent their head the other way.

"I saw . . ." Julie swallowed. "When you touched me. I saw things. A watery abyss. I guess that's what hell is like? Does that mean there is a hell? Shit. I gotta ask. Is it just one hell? And if so, does it have to be underwater? Fire, I can handle. I can't drown for an eternity."

"Hell does not await you, Julie Crews. There are no ledgers there with your name."

"Oh." Julie said nothing else for a little while, the words lost to her.

Then, "Wait. I thought the spell was for summoning a guardian angel. How the hell did I get an archangel?"

"I am the one who the Lord bade to keep the dark in check. I am the one who the Lord gave scale and quill and told to weigh the hearts of men. I am the watcher, and I have watched this world for millennia, and I have seen what you have done to keep the dark at bay, and I am here. For what is a shepherd who does not come when their flock calls for them?"

And a tiny seditious molecule of Julie, the one straggler in a body atomized by reverence, thought sullenly, *Wrong mythology.*

"You are worthy, Julie Crews," they whispered.

Worthy.

"Worthy," Julie repeated, as if testing the weight of the word. "First time anyone said that."

And it was then that the archangel set their hands upon her shoulders, and this time, their touch did not freeze. This time, it warmed her. Whatever doubt Julie had possessed before, whatever fear she'd nursed, all of it withered under that numinous heat spreading through marrow and sinew. Julie felt buoyant, frictionless, the crash of her heart lulled to a steady hum: a hymn taken up by every cell in her animal body. She wondered if this was what her grandmother had felt in church, if that was why she insisted on going year after year, day after day, even after she became tethered to an oxygen tank and could barely stand long enough to take communion. This ineffable sweetness, this grace.

This *love.*

"Why have you called me here, Julie Crews?"

"I need help," Julie croaked, face wet, voice hoarse from awe. "I need someone to throw me a line. Things have been so fucking hard lately. I try, and I try, and it feels like all I'm doing is digging a deeper hole for myself. Something needs to give because I'm going to break. I just want things to go right for once."

The archangel stroked a palm over Julie's cheek. "It shall be as you asked."

"Thank you, thank, thank you."

"Is there anything else you desire?"

"If anyone ever asks, tell them I absolutely did not fucking cry."

Julie woke up entombed in a duvet she did not recognize and on sheets she was certain she did not own. She scowled at the ceiling. Where the hell was she? And why the fuck was she so *cozy*? Her one-night stands rarely included waking up nice and tucked. Groaning, she pinched the bridge of her nose, let her thoughts drift. Her memories of last night were clear up until just after the point where she told the archangel—*I summoned a fucking archangel*, she thought with an electric thrill—what she'd needed. After that?

Nothing.

Nothing at all.

Which was strange to her as she'd always prided herself on her inability to black out. Even when coked out of her mind, Julie could always at least remember impressions of her debauchery. Had she gone on a bender with the angel? What the fuck happened after the summoning?

And whose fucking sheets were these?

Slowly, Julie came to realize that she was, in fact, in her own bedroom. There was the familiar dingy light radiating from her pigeon shit–encrusted window. Here was the sound of Harlem waking up, shouting at itself in five languages and a hundred accents, already rancorous with pedestrians. This was home.

But this was absolutely not her bedding.

And the smell wafting from her kitchen? Not native to her apartment either.

Julie sat up, stretching her arms high above her head, and took inventory of her surroundings. Some psychopath had snuck into her bedroom and tidied it up. Her laundry was put away, her bookshelf neatened. They'd even polished the crappy armoire opposite her bed. The wood *shone* with the bright patina of professional attention.

Did I ask the angel for sheets and a fucking cleaning service? Or am I just going crazy?

"Julie? Are you awake?"

Right.

"Yeah, I'm awake. What are you making?"

Sarah laughed. "I've got coffee, grapefruit juice—"

"Long Island Iced Tea?"

"No!" Sarah made a comical face. "This isn't a weekend."

"I'm not a corporate drone," said Julie, clambering onto her feet. She staggered to her dresser where she picked out an oversized shirt and gym shorts, marveling the whole while at how even her socks had been triaged and sorted. "I don't need weekends as an excuse to drink. What time is it?"

"It's a little after ten, I guess?"

Not enough time for Sarah to have snuck into her room to straighten it out, and hadn't it been about eleven when she called up Akrasiel? None of this added up.

"How do you feel about bacon and maple beans?"

"Depends on the sausage situation."

"Good. I found maple sausage at the bodega—"

"You're really big on this maple thing, huh? I thought you were the clean eater of the family." Of the family, she said. Like she and Sarah were already a unit. Any other day and Julie might have brooded over her faux pas, but her head was still unsettlingly porous.

"I guess it was because we went up to Montreal last year and did the cabane a sucre," said Sarah, her Québécois as French as the American pronunciation of croissant. "It was great. I'm not sure I'd do it again. But the food was interesting."

"So you're going to inflict it on me?" Julie checked her face in the small mirror she'd hung beside her bed. A little smudge of last night's eyeliner, leftover lipstick bleeding from the corner of her mouth. That at least was just like she expected.

"Yes?" said Sarah, after a moment. "I mean, if you don't want to, it's okay. I can go down and get something else. We don't have to—"

Julie grimaced. She could hear where Dan had wounded Sarah as clearly as if it had been air whistling through great holes gouged into her oldest, dearest friend. Whatever other thoughts she had were gone, engulfed by her fury. In a just universe, the perfect hate Julie felt toward him would have made Dan combust where he stood wherever he was, but it wasn't a fair cosmos so Julie thought up more torments for the man instead.

Maybe she'd ask her new archangel friend if they made house calls.

"Maple sausages sounds great. Bring on the sugar."

Julie had no idea what Sarah intended to do after her Dan problem was dealt with, no clue as to where she wanted to go, where she'd stay, what plans she had for jigsawing her life back together. But she knew two things. One was that unless Julie was obliterated in such a fashion that not even her spirit could claw spitefully back to its purpose, Dan would not come within ten blocks of Sarah ever again.

And two was Julie would eat nails before she let Sarah stay sad on her watch.

The call came as Julie and Sarah were finishing breakfast.

"Hello?" said Julie through her last mouthful of shakshuka. Sarah, despite her modest objections, proved an exhilaratingly talented cook. Julie, who could barely string a sandwich together, had stood and watched in open and fervent wonder as Sarah lined the kitchen in food. There'd been maple sausages as she had promised; bacon that she crisped, and also caramelized, and stuffed into a waffle she made with a waffle maker Julie didn't even know she owned; baked beans made from *scratch*; but also the shakshuka, and roti crammed with spiced potatoes, and noodles stir-fried with spam, and slices of spam on beds of rice ribboned with seaweed and garnished with teriyaki sauce. It was all good, and it was a Lot: the dizzying industry of a trapped animal finally let off-leash. There'd be leftovers for days.

"Julie Crews?"

Her surprise was so profound it took Julie an entire thirty seconds and the voice on the other end of the line repeating her name to register the identity of the caller: it was Marie, the mother of the Womb who'd tried to kill herself on her bachelorette party so she wouldn't be married to the dark.

"I know the right thing to say is that I'm glad you're still alive and kicking but Jesus fuck, I was hoping that little critter I left you with would have eaten all of you."

Across the table, Sarah's face went ashen and worried.

"Yes," said the woman. Something was strange about her enunciation. Every word she spoke sounded like it required careful strategy before it could be birthed and there was a clumsiness to her vowels like her tongue was too thick or she'd stuffed her mouth with cotton. "I thought you might say that."

"Why did you call?"

"I wasn't—" A beat. "—fair to you before. I want to make it up to you. I want to give you the money I owed you. And I'd like to hire you for another job."

"You couldn't afford me."

The woman named a sum with more zeroes than Julie could ever dream onto a check. Her fork clattered away from nerveless fingers. Julie whistled. She couldn't help herself. It was more than a year's worth of rent. It was fuck-you money on a scale Julie hadn't the vocabulary for. Sarah raised her eyebrows at Julie who responded by mouthing an empathic *holy shit,* which wasn't sufficient an answer, Julie knew, but she was still processing the concept of being financially solvent. But then she remembered who she was talking to.

"No."

"Fine. I'll double the fee. But you have to come here tonight."

Julie's insides ached at the thought of having so much money in the bank at once. She thought of St. Joan and how pleased she would be that Julie was finally making good business decisions and paying rent. Still—

"No."

There was a pause on the line. When Betancourt came back her voice was breathy and rushed, like she was scared.

"How much more do you want? I'll pay you anything."

Julie sighed, feeling the money drain away.

"I don't want anything from you. You sold out your own daughter to monsters. In my book that makes you a monster of the lowest, lowest kind. And if you'd sell out your own kid, I can't imagine what kind of mess you want me to clean up for you. So, fuck you very much, but no."

"Please. I—"

"Goodbye."

Julie thumbed the phone off and set it down.

Sarah looked at her.

"What was that all about?"

"Nothing," said Julie. "No one. Absolutely no one at all."

Marie set the phone down with care.

"There. I tried," said Marie. Half her face bulged with bandages. The stitching along her jaw, what little could be seen in the room with the curtains pulled so tightly shut, was inflamed, the skin a torrid unhealthy carmine. "The little bitch wouldn't listen to reason."

The creature opposite her at the desk did not move.

"I'm disappointed."

"Please. I did you want you wanted. Will you leave me alone now?"

The creature set a nearly fleshless hand on the desk and loomed over Marie.

"Soon," it said. "But having failed, I feel it fitting to amuse myself with your flesh before moving on."

"No. Please—" Marie choked on the words.

"Do go on," said the creature. "Nothing tastes better than your pleas."

"Oh god."

The next afternoon, Julie sat with Sarah and Dead Air at Max Brenner's on Broadway eating chocolate s'mores sundaes.

Dead Air did not look like much out in the real world: a standard-issue Chinese guy in his late twenties, with lank hair desperate for a stylist's attention and a face that wasn't so much angles as it was an excess of jaw. He was very thin and enormously focused on something.

"So, are you Julie's girlfriend?" said Dead Air.

Sarah coughed twice, choking a little on her ice cream. As Julie slapped her on the back to help dislodge whatever was in her throat Sarah shook her head.

"We're just good friends," she croaked.

Dead Air arched a brow. "You two don't act like good friends."

"Rude," said Julie.

"Good friends," said Dead Air, gaze shuttling between the two, "don't spend all their time blushing at the sight of each other."

"I'm not—"

"—blushing," said Julie and Sarah in the same tone and with the same cadence. When the pair realized what they'd done, they both blushed to varying degrees: Sarah growing pink enough that even her eyebrows went rosy around the edges.

"And They know all about your porn searches," Dead Air taunted.

To Julie's surprise, Sarah was laconic. "Do it. Tell Julie about my porn searches. Tell the restaurant. I don't care."

Two tables down, a tired-looking Asian woman who'd been stewarding a cluster of young children peered in their direction, brows ratcheted up to her hairline. Sarah took no notice, but Julie flashed a reassuring grin. It did nothing to assuage the middle-aged woman, of course, but it did make her snort and avert her attention.

"Are you sure?" Julie asked.

"I'm not ashamed of the fact I have a specific type."

"Annnd . . ." said Dead Air, lacing his fingers and setting his chin on them, a lopsided smirk on his face.

"And that Julie fits that type. She's pretty. Nothing wrong with that at all."

Dead Air laughed. Julie looked every which way except at Sarah, stupefied by the revelation. The thought that Sarah might have had impure daydreams about her was enough to overheat her brain. There was no way. They'd spent years together and Sarah had only ever described them as friends, had only ever treated her as one. She glanced at her friend and was pinned to her seat by Sarah's gaze. The words poured out of Julie's skull, replaced instead by warmth.

"I—" she began.

"You," said Sarah.

Dead Air saved the day by clearing his throat. "Should I go?"

His question broke whatever damnable spell had spooled around Julie and Sarah, the latter's intensity evanescing away, replaced instead by horror. "No! No, no. Stay. I want to get to know you. Please."

Dead Air cocked his head one way and then another before he said, "Well, They said it'd be another hour before They need me so, sure. But we're getting a chocolate fondue for the table and you're helping."

"Done," said Sarah with great satisfaction. "I have to catch up on all the sugar I wasn't allowed to eat."

Julie was giggling at them—it was good to see the two of them getting along—when her phone pinged with a text message. Then another. Jobs. People were leaving texts and voicemails about jobs. Big money jobs, but easy jobs. The kind she could pull off between lunch and dinner. She texted back "Yes" to everything, counting in her head how much money she was coming into. There didn't seem to be a ceiling.

She looked around smiling, not quite able to speak yet, when through the front window she saw Akrasiel standing outside looking at her. Julie gave her guardian angel a small wave.

Thank you, Akrasiel, you big, weird looking, spooky bastard. You've saved me.

She glanced back at her friends and was about to point Akrasiel out to them, but when she looked back the angel was gone.

CHAPTER ELEVEN

Tyler sat in his office with a hot cappuccino on the desk, feeling pleased and almost entirely content with the world. Despite the mishap at the speakeasy, things were going well. The infant formalus was in Thorne & Dirk's trophy case, literally riveted to its plaque. Tyler had gone over the Julie situation with his coworkers, subtly reworking the details of the altercation and making it clear in his recitation that *this* was the way it all really went down and anyone who had questions could ask them while being dangled off the roof by one leg. The money he made at Thorne & Dirk and the power it gave him were delightful things, but sometimes they paled in comparison with simply being able to scare the shit out of everyone who wasn't a department lead. He knew it was a childish impulse, but it just felt so damn good. Like a deep tissue massage after arranging for the murder of an acquaintance at a rival firm.

As for Julie, well, it pained him a bit to think she might be maligned as a "crazy woman" by his colleagues, but really, what kind of feminist would he be if he didn't put the safety of his female coworkers first? Though he had made adjustments to their shared narrative, none of these edits were outside the realm of truth. Amplifications, yes. But not lies. None of what he said was invented. Julie was absolutely Chernobyl in a woman-suit. She was radioactive, poison to anything that got too close.

Tyler sipped his cappuccino. A thick dusting of cinnamon sugar softened the intensity of the drink: it was good. Everything was good. He'd solved the problem the Proctor had given him without losing a scintilla of skin and he'd impressed Upper Management with his conquest of the formalus. Things were looking good. Still, he couldn't dislodge that vague sense of dread lurking around the back of his mind. Julie had said a thing that night as her pretty friend dragged her away: *It was an inside job. Someone from your firm did it. And I'm going to make sure everyone knows.*

If it was true, it would mean the death of Thorne & Dirk. Their literal death. Wall Street wouldn't forgive such a slight. For all the politics, the backstabbing, the interfirm cannibalism, the Financial District was very clear that such butchery was reserved for the companies and not their affiliates. Certainly not a law firm retained to keep things nice.

Could it be that Julie was just fucking with him? Tyler wasn't sure if she had a capacity for such sophistry, but he'd been surprised before. He set his mug down. It was the one gift he'd retained from his time with her: a wide-lipped, gaudy, Christmas-palette nightmare with the words "King of the World" ballooning from its side. Julie had made it for him. Rust splotched a corner of the pale ceramic, marking where she'd cut herself during the process.

No, Julie wasn't messing with him. Whatever else she was, she wasn't a liar. If she as much as said there was a conspiracy within Thorne & Dirk, she meant it. And that meant when Excisions heard, they'd be coming after him first. The firm didn't do internal investigations. It simply made people go away.

But who had it out for him? Tyler ran through a list of his current enemies. It was longer than made him comfortable, consisting not only of rival department leads but interns he'd humiliated out of the field. A hot ball of anger knotted in his stomach. At least he had no adversarial relationships with Upper Management. If he did, he'd be well and truly fucked as opposed to only imminently screwed over.

There was a light knock on his office door and it opened just wide enough for someone to step halfway into the room. It was Phoebe Garland from HR. She was a pleasant enough middle-aged white woman, belling out at the hips as they always seemed to do, a paunch beginning to show even through the careful rucking of her skirts. Little about her wasn't a placid, soporific beige—her complexion, her clothes, even her shoes were always variations of that same dull shade of dun.

The overall effect made her seem a bit blowsy and forgettable, like some half-recalled memory of a sixth grade English teacher. And she almost—almost!—pulled off the act, Tyler thought admiringly. Despite all her efforts at looking innocuous, she couldn't fix her eyes. They were blue and soft in color, like leftover paint in a glass of water a kid had used to clean their brushes, and they were cold as a knife in one's gut. Sharks had a kinder gaze. Chimpanzees had sweeter regards. Garland was an apex predator in Lane Bryant Outlet camouflage and she was one of the last people Tyler wanted popping into his office unannounced.

"Good morning, Tyler. Do you have time for a quick chat?" Every sentence was spoken with the same drowsy melody, the cadence mild, the pace slightly too slow.

"I always have time for you, Phoebe. Come in," said Tyler, forcing a sunny grin to his face. Whatever crap this was, he wanted to get it dealt with quick.

It wasn't until Garland stepped fully into the room that he realized she wasn't alone. His throat tightened when he saw she was accompanied by Todd Cranston from Upper Management. Cranston was white-haired with papery white skin so translucent it was almost blue from the veins beneath and he wore a tailored suit that did strange things to the light around him. Tyler kept his face neutral and extended a hand to the two chairs facing his deck.

"Two guests? What an embarrassment of riches. Please sit down. Make yourselves comfortable," said Tyler, his pleasant smile rictused into place, knowing that meetings with HR seldom ended without someone being fired, demoted, or sent on an "important errand" to one of the "secure records rooms" where no one would ever find any trace of them again, at least after the walls had been pressure washed clean.

Garland kept her eyes focused on Tyler while Cranston looked around the room at anything that wasn't their equally resentful host, giving off the air of a man who'd rather be eating lunch in a blast furnace than be stuck *here,* with the cannon fodder. When he had exhausted his surroundings of tchotchkes to study, Cranston, with a drawn-out sigh, turned his attention to Tyler and offered the half-hearted beginning of a smile, only for his will to peter out as if he'd lost interest. The man's face emptied into impatient boredom.

Thumbing through a stack of folders—these too were the same dilute fawn as the rest of her—resting on her knees, Garland spoke first. "I just wanted a quick chat with you about the upcoming celebration around . . . the event."

"What event?" said Tyler, suddenly afraid that he'd forgotten an important birthday or beheading.

Garland let loose a tiny gurgling laugh. "I keep forgetting you were newly appointed to your current role. It takes so long to process clearance for people. Sorry about that. I thought I'd set you up but I guess I'd forgotten about you. You have that kind of face."

Tyler didn't take the bait. "I still don't know what event you're talking about."

"Of course. You see, after a century or so of dormancy, the sentience of The Mother Who Eats is finally returning to the firm from the Outer Realms. It's time for her to meet her current mate, and for us to prepare for what comes after."

Tyler stared at Garland and her yogurty face and her vague, front-desk smile, wondering if she was trying to fuck with him. The name rang no bells whatsoever. Had it been just Garland, he would have instantly demanded clarification. But Cranston was sitting right fucking *there,* his fingers tented beneath his chin. Someone like Cranston wouldn't appreciate him showing ignorance, but if he was caught lying—

He did not want to think about what would happen if he was caught fibbing to Upper Management and its proxies.

So, Tyler raised the wattage of his smile and said, “I’m sorry, but what?”

Cranston chuckled to himself. Seated this close, Tyler could see every detail of the man’s skin: the widow’s peak brindled with age spots; the horrendously lineated jowls. The old man said in a pallid voice, “Don’t feel too bad. We really try not to brief people about what’s coming.”

Garland said, “It keeps people from panicking.”

At this Tyler felt a sudden wash of terror. “I don’t quite follow—”

“Garland, I’m bored with this already. It doesn’t matter if he knows about the upcoming ritual so long as he can do his job. Let’s give him his briefing and be done with this idiot.”

“Protocol must be followed,” said Garland and had Tyler not been so preoccupied with being scared out of his mind, he might have erupted into stunned applause. No one talked back to the Upper Management.

No one but Garland, it seemed.

“Protocol is cutting into my lunch,” said Cranston petulantly. He scratched at his neck, digging gray furrows into his skin. His nail beds filled with tooth-colored powder. “I’m serious, Garland—”

“Five minutes.”

Cranston sighed again. “Fine.”

“The Mother Who Eats,” said Garland, her attention wholly on Tyler again. The whites of her eyes were very red: a blood sea that darkened to indigo as the blue of her irises seeped outward, intermingling with the crimson. “She is us. She is this building. She is that which Thorne & Dirk was and is and will be from now to the death of days. We are her children. We are her children’s feast.”

For the second time that night, Tyler said, “I’m sorry, but *what*?”

“The building,” said Cranston. “Every key personnel—even

your fucking desk—are parts of The Mother Who Eats. These are her bones and her gristle."

"Alright, thank you, but that part isn't what's bothering me. What did Garland mean by her children's *feast*?"

In the voice and tone a kindergarten teacher might have used on a moronic parent, Garland said, "You see, Tyler, once The Mother Who Eats mates, we remove her eggs from the incubation chamber in the sub-basement so her mate—"

"The Proctor," said Cranston.

"You know what they say about men with lots of hands," said Tyler for lack of anything useful to add and for want of doing something with his voice that wasn't a scream.

"Oh, for fuck's sake, shut up." Cranston drew a squiggle into the air with a finger. Almost immediately, Tyler felt his cheeks deliquesce to a toffee-like consistency and drip, the melted flesh trammeling his mouth, sealing it shut.

"—can fertilize them. Once he's done that, the eggs will soon hatch and the offspring will, as young creatures often do, go looking for sustenance. In this case, the current employees of Thorne & Dirk."

"Upper Management is exempt, of course," Cranston said. "Got to have teachers for the little ones. Besides, the babies don't like what we've got in our heads."

Garland nodded at the old man. "Upper Management has responsibilities to other . . . *life*."

"Ravenous chimerical life," said Cranston with great satisfaction. "After a few thousand years, we grow up into, well, I suppose you'd call us gods."

Tyler pointed to his face and Cranston, with a sigh, squiggled his finger in the air again. Instantly, Tyler felt his mouth reappear.

He said, "Out of curiosity, is there a name for these chimerical beauties?"

Cranston raised a bushy white brow.

"*Le Parasite Glorieux*," he said. "That's what the Mother and the others call themselves. Why do you ask, Tyler? You going to look for one of your own?"

"Wouldn't think of it. But it doesn't hurt to know the names of your betters."

"Tyler, we'd like you to coordinate with Annabeth Fall in Security to make sure there's no risk of any little rebellions while we're preparing for the event."

Garland smiled. Her eyes were gravity wells from which no light could escape: a cruel and starless black, the color at the end of everything.

"Is that clear?" said Garland.

"Like crystal," said Tyler with feverish brightness. Realizing he couldn't leave it at that, he added: "Won't people notice if the entire staff goes missing?"

"Not at all," said Garland, shuffling her papers. "The offspring won't eat *you*. Well, they will. But also, they'll cannibalize your knowledge and attributes. No one will be able to tell the difference. Consider it a form of immortality. It's a great honor when you think about it."

"It's a hell of an event," said Cranston.

Tyler forced a small smile. "It sounds delightful."

He was simultaneously nauseous, dizzy, and frightened passive by the deluge of revelations. Cranston was on his *phone,* tapping at what looked like an ancient Tetris game. Garland, on the other hand, was still staring at Tyler, her eyelids absorbed into whatever had turned her gaze abyssal.

"It is. It so is. I've watched the process so many times now, and it never fails to fill my heart with joy," said Garland piously. "To be ritually consumed. Immortalized in the gut of those born of The Mother Who Eats. I can't think of a greater destiny."

"Then why aren't you signing up to be turned into pod people?" The words came out before Tyler lined up his thoughts about their presence.

"I'm going to shut him up again—" said Cranston. At the word *up,* Tyler's flesh sizzled.

"Please, Mr. Cranston. Let me handle this," said Garland gently. "Because it was our turn already. Mine, at any rate. I am a child of The Mother Who Eats. I am born of her and of the lovely little woman who gave me her name. One lives in my thoughts," said Garland, touching a knuckle to her temple. "And one lives in my heart. I can hear her screams every day."

Tyler had never been ashamed of his dearth of empathy, but it wasn't a quality he was necessarily grateful to possess, not until today. The thought that there was a real Phoebe Garland, alive inside this dead-eyed copy, begging for what Tyler could only assume was the relief of death, turned his stomach, but only mildly in a "better her than me" way.

"I see," said Tyler.

"Who knows? You might be lucky. Perhaps you too will enjoy such a relationship someday. You have the real potential."

Never had Tyler been prouder of himself than he was in that moment, under Garland's relentless gaze and Cranston's amused regard. That he held his expression static. That he kept smiling, if a little effortfully. That he was sitting here despite a churning limbic system, flushed with so much adrenaline his mouth tasted of tin. That he wasn't screaming in immediate idiot repudiation of the thought of being parasitized and then trapped inside his own skin *forever.* No, Tyler was sure he'd peaked with this demonstration of will.

"If I may be so lucky," said Tyler, and if his remark wasn't as wishful or as bloody with hope as it could have been, no one commented. "We should all be thrilled at the chance for corporate immortality."

"Anyway," said Garland, sliding a thin sheaf of carefully clipped documents out from her folder. "These are your official marching orders—"

"And if you're thinking of getting the fuck out of Dodge," drawled Cranston, his eyes a grayed milk, cataracted with the faintest hint of algae, "don't. The Mother will know. And so will we. Besides, you can't."

"Can't?"

"Didn't you read your contract when you joined the firm? Along with your office, salary, and benefits you received a little brain—we like to call it—upgrade. Step too far out of line, run too far from home, and *poof,* no more brains. No more Tyler. It's a standard Wall Street clause. Check with legal if you like. They'll explain it to you."

"No need," said Tyler before Garland brought the full power of her stare on him, and he wilted to moronic submission. "I understand perfectly."

"There you go, Banks," chortled the old man. "That's the spirit. Now, sign these so the rest of us can get on with our day. Next time we have a meeting, we're removing the witness clause."

Garland heaped a ziggurat of blank forms atop Tyler's desk.

"What are these?" he said.

The dumpy, still-smiling Garland handed him a gorgeous fountain pen—onyx cabochon, streaked with opal—and a straight pin. She said, "Just standard Subsumation permits, release forms absolving Thorne & Dirk of any responsibility to immediate family, and a few silly other things."

Those silly other things were nondisclosure agreements that would have him bound from now until time itself became old. Under Garland's unblinking instruction, Tyler scrawled his name and initialed all the forms, knowing he didn't mean a word of it, but also that it didn't matter. He bled for every page. By the time Garland was satisfied, his fingers were raw meat and little of him was left that didn't belong to the firm.

Garland gathered up the signed forms and replaced them in her folder. Cranston stood with her, head bobbing like a balloon being bounced on its string. "We'll be in touch in a week, closer to the time of the actual ritual. Until then, please keep an eye on things and, of course, mum's the word."

Tyler grinned at her and mimed locking his lips with a key.

On her way out, Garland said, "Have a lovely day."

"You too," he called as she pulled the office door closed.

Fuck fuck fuck fuck fucking fuck.

To Tyler's shame, the first person he thought of after his breathing had regulated was Julie. She was always good in a crisis for all that she often was the reason they were happening. Nothing fazed her. Tyler couldn't imagine this exciting more than raised eyebrows and a thoughtful expression.

But what was it that they said about a jilted woman? Hell hath no fury—and that was prescriptive of a normal specimen. Julie was as far from the normal specimen as you could get and still remain a mammal.

How badly had he burned that bridge? Tyler briefly toyed with the possibility of getting Julie back, only to conclude she'd laugh in his face if he tried. No, he'd incinerated any hope for reconciliation.

Maybe I can set up a blind through another client? he thought. *Fuck you, Julie. Where are you when I really need you?*

Tyler's office door opened again, and Annabeth Fall from Security came in. She looked unusually vigorous. There was actual color to a mouth often bloodless from fatigue, a blush of life in the high cheekbones. Like most of the senior staff, she dressed exclusively in crisp monochrome, a piano wire tautness to every line.

"Go away," he said.

In answer, Fall just hooked a thumb over her shoulder and said, "Meeting. Rooftop."

"When?" said Tyler.

"Now."

This had started as a good day, portentous of better things to come. He rubbed his aching temples.

"I have things to do and there's nothing about a meeting on my schedule," said Tyler, aware he was whining but too tired and too sick of existence to adequately care.

Fall set both hands on Tyler's desk and leaned forward, her voice dropped to a slow growl. "Fuck your schedule and fuck you. Rooftop. Now."

He followed Fall upstairs where they stiffly put on disposable booties before entering the rooftop office. With only Fall for companionship, the room seemed much larger—especially in its corners which seemed to lengthen and thin the longer they were observed. Fall locked the door behind and turned to face Tyler, palms behind her as she laid back against the foot-thick metal.

Tyler looked at her. "Where's everyone else?"

"This is it," said Fall. "Just you and me, sweetheart."

He wasn't a bad fighter, Tyler. Before his big job with Thorne & Dirk, he'd had one-on-ones with more than a few demons and madmen, and while he had relied on Julie to handle the worst of it, he couldn't have survived the career without skills of his own. But Internal Security was something else.

Even their greenest intern, their freshest and most damp-behind-the-ears hire, could end Tyler while pouring their morning coffee. Internal Security had a rancid gift—and appetite—for corporate wetwork, and Tyler had seen enough of their business to know none of their reputation was hyperbole. If Fall wanted him dead, he was fucked.

On the bright side, Tyler thought morosely, at least he was becoming numb to the prospect now.

"Should I be praying or getting out my checkbook?"

Fall rolled her eyes. She was, Tyler realized with a jolt of surprise, much younger than he was: palpably in her early twenties. "Calm down, asshole. I didn't bring you here to kill you."

"Then why are we here?"

"Because it's private and no one can monitor us here," said Fall.

"What's so special that you're afraid of being monitored?"

"I take it that you got your paperwork? The special kind?"

Tyler shook his head, hoping there was a way to worm his way out of working with Fall. "I don't know what you're talking about."

"Oh, please." Another extended eyeroll. Tyler wondered then if she was a teenaged savant, preternaturally aged by her employment here. "It's all over your face. You look like you're about to cry."

"Be that as it may, what's it to you?"

"I got the same forms today too."

"Congratulations."

"You fucking idiot," said Fall, enunciating every syllable with a pubescent, waspish impatience. "Ask me the right questions."

"I have had a long fucking day so how about you tell me what I'm supposed to ask you?" Tyler crossed his arms.

Fall pushed away from the door and strode up to him, jabbing him in the chest with a finger. She could have been beautiful if she didn't look so tired all the time. Like Julie, she seemed to abhor makeup, appearing "fresh-faced" at every meeting, skull-like with the sleepless pits under her eyes.

"Hey, watch it—" He shoved at her. Fall didn't so much as wobble.

"Or what? *I'm* Internal Security."

"I still outrank you."

Fall bared her teeth. "Oh? Well, I'm the only friend you have in the whole fucking world."

"Friend? When have we ever been friends?" Tyler withdrew by several long steps and adjusted his stance, keeping his weight on his back foot. Sure, Fall *said* this wouldn't be a murder attempt but he had every reason to distrust her.

"When it comes down to who dies around here and who doesn't."

"You mean mommy dearest's ritual?"

"Damn right."

Tyler inflected a hand, palm turned up like he was extending an invitation to dance. "What do you propose to do about her?"

"It might be all my department training talking, but I have a few thoughts on the subject involving murder."

"Murder?" said Tyler. He looked around. "From what they said, The Mother Who Eats is an entire building. How the fuck do you plan to murder architecture?"

Fall shook her head. "Not mom, you waste of space. The eggs. I was talking about the eggs. I want you to help me kill the eggs."

"Why the fuck would I do that?"

"You can't afford to be this thick," mumbled Fall. "Because if all the eggs hatch, we're all doomed. But if only some of them hatch, at the right place and at the time of our choosing, we might be able to engineer it so we're running this place."

And Tyler, only thirty-four but already feeling growingly outclassed by the next generation, aware the next word would damn him as a member of a senescent demographic, could only, against his will, grind out:

"What?"

"You imbecile," said Fall, panting with venom. "You—you—if you weren't the only person I could use, I'd feed you to the eggs myself. How do I make this any clearer? I need you to help me—" She spoke each word like he was an infant with a concussion, pantomiming with her hands. "—kill—" Fall pretended to stab the air. "—some members of—" She pointed up. "—the Upper Management so we can take over."

"Yeah," said Tyler, more to be a problem than anything else. "Still don't get it."

Her answering shriek was guttural and everything Tyler could have asked for. Fall balled her hands to fists and thumped her skull with the heel of one. She breathed in so deeply Tyler wondered if her lungs would give out. Then she exhaled angrily, as a bull might, and glowered at Tyler with eyes gone black as cinders. Wreaths of inky smoke leaked from where he assumed her tear ducts were.

"You're *fucking* with me," said Fall in an arctic voice.

"A little bit."

For whatever reason, his confession seemed to appease Fall. Between one shallow breath and its successor, Fall regained her composure, eyes losing their abyssal tinting, becoming again a mild and pleasant brown.

"Why me, though?" said Tyler, as if it mattered.

"I saw your name on the list," said Fall. "You're one of the people in the know. Excisions gets full run of the building, which Internal Security doesn't."

Tyler, who had not seen the list, said: "That's because Excisions is discreet, while Internal Security is like an elephant on roller skates—very noticeable. So, if you want me to help you, you've got to tell me why you asked me and not someone else."

"Fine," said Fall. "It's because you're the next youngest person in this stupid company who is in any position of power."

This was not the answer Tyler had been anticipating.

"What?"

"Is that the only word in your fucking vocabulary?"

"Right now, yeah," said Tyler, his astonishment so paralytical, it suspended any instinctive urge to be churlish or witty. His dumbfounded honesty drew a laugh from Fall.

"I don't want to die, Tyler. I don't want to fucking stand there like a lobotomized nitwit while something crawls inside me and wears me like a hat. All this work, all the shit I've done to get to where I am, and I'm supposed to be applesauce to some holy maggots? Fuck. *That.*" Fall lowered her voice to a discontented mumble.

Occam's razor, thought Tyler to himself. Always the simplest answer. It was fear motivating Fall. Not ambition, not want for a better life, not lust for dominion over anyone and everything who'd ever bullied her.

Tyler could use this.

"And you thought I could understand?"

"I would certainly fucking hope so," she snapped. "I don't want to have to kill you and start this goddamned process again."

"One problem," said Tyler.

"What now?"

He pointed at his head. "They stuck something inside my head to make sure I don't fuck anything up, and I think your plan is going to result in my gray matter being eaten."

"Oh," said Fall, striding closer. Something was happening to her right hand: the pores were extruding cheese-like filaments, which cobwebbed together as soon as they touched air. They wrapped about her fingers, capping each finger with six inches of white razor. "That's easy. What's your pain tolerance like?"

"High. What are you—"

Fall didn't wait for his answer. She lunged: a single, gorgeously economical thrust of the arm that punched the sharpened tip of her index finger straight into Tyler's right ear. He didn't feel it. Not at first. But eardrums inevitably took notice of their perforation and an exquisite pain geysered through him, traveling straight down and out through his mouth where it tore free as a shriek. Tyler's knees started to buckle.

"Don't move," said Fall distractedly. "I'm not going to be able to fix this if you move."

Somehow, Tyler kept himself standing. He screamed until he ran out of strength for such at which point his body went on to produce a low keening that didn't seem to require air or input from him. His eyes wept from the sustained agony; he wanted to die. Every nerve felt irresponsibly alive, fatally aware of Fall trepanning him. It hurt so much Tyler worried he'd piss himself.

Then:

"There we go." Fall retracted her hand and let it fall.

Tyler turned in time to see the spike Fall had used to puncture his brainpan draped with what appeared at first to be jelly and then, when one lobe of mucus winked, a string of dimming eyes.

"I don't understand why they keep using these. They're so easy to kill."

"I can hear," said Tyler, taking audit of his condition. "Why can I still hear?"

"I'm good at what I do," said Fall flatly.

He looked to her. "No shit. You know what? Fuck it. I'm in."

"Good. I didn't want to have to wash your brains off my shoes."

"Funny. I was thinking the same thing about you."

Fall laughed. The last few minutes hadn't been without cost; she was soaked through with sweat, and there was blood coming out of both nostrils. She flicked away the remnants of what she had extracted from Tyler's brain. It made an undignified splat. "Next thing we need is a scapegoat. Just in case I'm wrong. Someone we can pin this on if anything goes wrong. I'm thinking about Clarice from Surveillance. No one will miss that little bitch looking over their shoulder."

"No. We might be able to use Clarice for something," Tyler said, moving to the small, writhing parasite. He knelt down and bagged it like it was a heap of dog turds. "I have a much better idea."

CHAPTER TWELVE

For the hell of it, Julie and Sarah decided they would have Thai that night. Not the kind cooked up by gnarled old ladies in the street stalls of Bangkok. No, the Thai food the two women wanted was suburban soccer mom fodder. Crab rangoon. Pad thai with sauce sourced from a supermarket bottle. Treacle-thick massaman curry, drowned in too much coconut milk, so sweet it left a rind along their teeth. Spring rolls. Fried rice that was mostly corn oil. That sort of shit. Because it felt correct, somehow. Like the perfect fuck-you with which to send off Sarah's relationship with Dan.

"Dan would lose his mind at the amount of spring rolls we're ordering."

Julie, barely listening, said: "They have prawn toast too."

"In a Thai restaurant?" said Sarah, mock aghast.

"And sushi," said Julie, her smile like a scalpel. Though sober as a fresh nun, Julie felt reckless, feral, practically effervescent with an inexplicable pleasure. Maybe the anti-drugs ads were right. Maybe you didn't need drugs to be happy. You just needed to find God or Buddha or whatever it was your subconscious categorized as a higher power. Like love or love for your fellow man or an archangel in a back pocket.

"Oh god. I don't know if I can do bad sushi."

"They have fried chicken hosomaki," said Julie, slinging a glance back at where Sarah sprawled over the sofa in an oversized band shirt, her hair undone and a beautiful mess. An old rom-com—*Loving,* from the seventies—was playing on the TV. For some reason, Sarah was *obsessed* with finding movies of that genre that involved the Grand Central clock, but Julie wasn't ready to ask those big questions yet.

Sarah sat upright. "Like, karaage hosomaki?"

"What's the difference?"

"Karaage, you season the meat. Fried chicken's more—"

"Would karaage come slathered in cream cheese?"

"Probably not."

"Okay, so this hosomaki can come smothered in cheese—"

"Oh my god."

"Is that a good 'oh my god' or a *how dare you suggest that* 'oh my god'?"

"Good. So good."

Sarah padded over on pink-slippered feet. Dan had made her a no-shoes-indoors type of girl, but Julie's floors had seen neither broom nor mop since the day she moved in. So, she bought Sarah slippers: big, slouchy things with smiling unicorns stitched into the toe box. When Sarah saw them, she squealed and Julie would have bought her ten more on the spot if she asked.

"See?" said Julie, beaming at her friend. "Fried chicken hosomaki."

"You weren't kidding, oh my god."

"I don't joke about these kinds of things."

"Let's get two," said Sarah.

"You're the boss."

Playing house with Sarah the last couple of weeks was a revelation: Julie didn't actually hate living with other people. As the winter snow gave way to rain, she realized that she'd just been living with the wrong ones. For most of her life, Julie sneered at anyone who went on about community, about how no man was an island and the point of life was to be of service to the species. Julie's stance on that was simple: no fucks would be given unless preceded by payment.

Yet here she was, in awe of this frictionless happiness, the ease of it.

"Is that . . . uni?" said Sarah, trailing a finger down the glass of the monitor.

"Uh, I don't know. I don't even know what uni is."

"Sea urchin gonads," said Sarah and laughed as Julie gagged reflexively. "You've stuck worse in your mouth."

"Only because they let me spank them later."

Another bright trill of laughter. Julie wondered if she could convince Sarah to stay permanently in New York, with the two of them going halfsies on a bigger place in that liminal trim between the suburbs and the city proper. Somewhere not too far from the action but far enough that they could be seriously involved with the twin luxuries of "actual food in the pantry" and "rent paid on time."

Could they get a dog, maybe? A little Pomeranian—

Julie shook her head of daydreams.

"You want anything else?"

"A Coke," said Sarah, nodding to herself. "Dan hates soda."

"What I'm hearing is we need to order like a whole pallet."

"Stop!" Sarah, so near to Julie the latter could smell her perfume: a murmur of roses and leather, intimate. "You're ridiculous. And that's more food than we can finish."

"We can freeze the rest."

"Okay. If you insist. If we run out of freezer space, it's your fault."

We. Julie liked hearing her say the word. Before she could process how much she liked it, there were fingers on the nape of her neck, a thumb on the soft jut of a vertebrate, and then in her hair, sifting through the matted strands. Julie leaned back into the touch and tried not to purr.

"When was the last time you got your hair done?"

Julie hesitated. "Way, way too long."

"I think you'd look good as a blonde," said Sarah, sudden. Just as quickly, she followed up, voice dovetailing into a sheepish whisper, with: "Not that you don't look great now. I mean, you're gorgeous—"

Gorgeous. She called her gorgeous. Female friends called

other female friends gorgeous all the time. Surely, it was out of sororal affection. She wasn't going to think too hard on this, but Sarah was so close and she was so hot.

And she did say that you're her type.

"—but I've been hearing about how people with round faces can really pull off light colors? I could see you with this rose-gold hair."

"I have a round face?" said Julie.

"More heart-shaped, but—"

Sarah cupped Julie's jaw, thumbs rested on the widest points of her cheekbones. It was becoming progressively more difficult to breathe, and harder still to convince herself not to blush.

"See? It is wide here. And then it curves into your chin."

"Are you saying I have no chin?" She didn't care about whether her face was round, oblong, or trapezoidal. What she did care about was Sarah being in such close contact and how she could ethically motivate her to continue being in such luxurious proximity.

"No! Geez. I'm just saying you have a round face."

Sarah moved her hands from Julie's face to teasing out the mats in her hair. Short as she kept it, it still frizzed and tangled with a dedication that, in a living thing, would have definitely been called spite.

"You haven't told me if that is a bad thing."

"Depends on what you think of Ginnifer Goodwin, I guess?"

She thought on this. "She's hot."

"Good. So, we're clear on this now? You having a round face doesn't mean you're not hot—"

Is being told "it doesn't mean you're not hot" the same as being told you're hot? wondered a desperately juvenile part of Julie, while the rest of her tried to stop her heart from bursting into pleased glitter.

"Uh-huh," Julie managed intelligently.

"—and in fact, just means you might look really good with rose-gold hair. Something to think about, I guess?"

"I'm not really big into sitting in a salon for hours reading shitty magazines, though."

"Fair. But what if I do it for you? I just need to get out and buy some supplies."

Julie closed a hand gently—fingers grazing over hers, charting the words suspended between them, unsaid still but maybe soon—over Sarah's knuckles.

"In that case, let's go for gold."

❧

The color was pinker than the box suggested: a cotton candy champagne, with just enough gold to keep its marketing brochure from being a lie. Sarah was aghast.

"It's great," said Julie, laughing, as Sarah loudly bemoaned her failure again. "I swear. I really like it."

"But it doesn't look like it should."

"Who cares? It looks awesome." Julie twirled glass noodles around her fork. Years ago, a friend had explained to her that the ubiquity of chopsticks in Southeast Asian–American restaurants was a lie, a concession to racist presumptions. White people expected chopsticks everywhere, so the proprietors made sure to have a surfeit of cheap wooden eating sticks. No reason to argue cultural accuracy when pad thai was verging on too exotic for the clientele. Since then, Julie had gone with what felt the most natural: in this case, a solitary fork.

"But I did it all wrong!"

"Did you?"

"Your hair is *pink*."

"Only in certain lights."

"It's *pink*, Julie!"

"Who caaaares?" said Julie, jokingly drawing out the words. "All that counts is that you did it and I like it."

"Are you sure?"

"Yes," said Julie, exasperated, looking over their spread. Only half had arrived and part of the half was someone else's order, someone with less sacrilegious wants. "One of us should probably go figure out where the rest of our order is."

"I'll do it," said Sarah, already on her feet. "You're busy eating."

"I can also just as easily be not busy eating, you know?"

"Well, I have shoes on."

"Those shoes are house slippers."

"Just let me be nice to you. *God.*"

Julie scanned her apartment. A laundry hamper now sat beside the door to the bathroom. There was food in the fridge. Real food rather than half-eaten, mostly forgotten takeout. Food like apples, like fresh blueberries. Butter for the long-neglected butter dish. Spices in the pantry. When the jobs and the money started rolling in from Julie's lucky guardian angel, Sarah had insisted they go hard on quality ingredients. Last night, a *cake*—topped after with canned frosting, but who was counting?—had been baked.

"You've already been nice to me."

"Yeah," said Sarah, pulling on sweatpants, one sneaker on, the other still en route to being laced up. "And now I'm going to keep being nice to you."

She jingled the keys at Julie.

"Love you, bye," said Sarah, blowing a kiss and shutting the door behind her.

Julie regarded the space where her friend had stood.

"Huh," she said to the emptiness, not scared but not happy either, thoroughly unsettled by the flutter in her stomach, unable and unwilling to mine her psyche to put a name to what she was feeling. Though it rose to the roof of her mouth, craning for release, Julie refused. She would not say it aloud.

Besides, in what universe would Sarah want to be with a gremlin like Julie?

Depressed by the thought, Julie went to search for her last reserves of cocaine, only to decide it wouldn't be what Sarah wanted. Maybe she'd clean instead. Sarah liked things neat. And there was, she decided, a certain joy in being of service. So, Julie went for the trash bags and began her usual routine, disposing of the worst of the mess. Then, she continued her assault with broom and mop, and the battered vacuum Sarah had recovered from god knows where. The exercise wasn't as fun as cocaine, but each time Julie's enthusiasm faltered, she thought of how delighted Sarah would be, and that drove her to another circuit.

As she was gingerly doing the dishes, someone knocked on the apartment door. Julie immediately clocked the noise as unusual. Like bad news waiting politely to be admitted, shirt tucked, face somber; unhurried, as disasters often were. Julie squinted at the door.

Nah.

"I'm coming, I'm coming," Julie said, collecting herself from the sofa, a hand raked through her newly pale hair.

Who the hell could it be? Not Sarah, not unless she lost the house keys. But she had Julie's number, didn't she? St. Joan never knocked; she didn't need to. Her subtle psychic connection to the building meant her tenants always knew when she was at their doorstep. Dead Air would blow up her computer. Tyler, well—nice as it was to think he might come crawling for the sacrament of forgiveness, Julie had gutted him publicly. There was no way.

A client? Julie thought as she set her fingers on the doorknob. No, the knocking felt too insistent. This wasn't a nervous atheist professor of archeology, bewildered by how his artifacts wouldn't stop trying to go home; not the knocking of a housewife gone insomniac from the corpses purring in her walls; not the cheerleader who couldn't stop seeing visions of the friend everyone said died of an accident but whose slit throat spelled something worse; not the old widow still haunted by a bad husband; not them, not anything Julie knew.

Don't, said her lizard brain, but the curiosity was louder and anyway, wasn't Akrasiel in her life now? Julie's blood fizzed with optimism. Maybe this was what happened when your client base levelled up. They have esteem you can hear through the rata-rata-thump of their knuckles.

Julie opened the door.

"Julie Crews! It's so good to see you. How many years has it been? I love the hair. Really updated that rocker-chick look. I approve," said Dan, enfolding Julie into a Hollywood-guy hug that she did not return. "Say, is my Sarah with you?"

The next words from Julie's mouth were purely reflex, spoken without referral from her higher mind, which was still processing Dan's appearance at her door, acting like they weren't just friends but friends who went on vacation together.

"Why the fuck are you here?"

Dan frowned at her. He was prettier than she remembered. Julie would give him that. A mustachioed Rhett Butler in black suede, even if he did come with a side order of being inestimably punchable. The privilege, my god. He reeked of the good life. Julie wanted him to die—or at the bare minimum, fall out of a window.

"I really need to talk to Sarah," said Dan, still with that smile cocked, still with that look that said *I belong here.*

"She isn't here."

"Are you sure? You two were—"

"I said she's not here."

"—so close back then. I'd have thought you'd be the first person she'd reach out to."

"Well, you guessed wrong. She ain't here, so fuck off."

Then he proceeded to *walk into her apartment* without so much as a cursory look at Julie. The brazenness was so profound, so flagrant, it almost worked. Poleaxed by his audacity, Julie stood immobile as Dan strolled past her. It wasn't until he looked back and patted her on the shoulder, like she was a child, or a small stupid animal that had finally learned not to pee indoors, that Julie snapped out of it, grabbing him by the back of his sweater and flinging him out of the door.

"Do that again and I'm going to break your arm."

The congeniality evaporated.

"This doesn't need to be difficult, *Julie.* I just want to talk to Sarah."

"I told you, asshole. She isn't here. Also, she told me everything so like hell I'm going to tell you where she is."

The color in Dan's face drained to wherever his warmth had gone, leaving him with only a garish, pasted-on smile. Julie noticed as he adjusted the balance of his weight, a foot moving slightly behind the other: a pugilist's stance. He was spoiling for a fight.

Good.

So am I, Julie thought.

"You're talking about the door incident with her hand," said Dan quietly.

"Yeah." Julie straightened. Pity that Sarah had made her vow not to kill Dan. Otherwise, there'd be brain matter in Dan's carefully pomaded hair, brain matter on the floor, brain everywhere that wasn't otherwise the mess she'd make of his fucking face. Never had she so badly wanted to kill someone dead.

"It was all a big mistake. A comedy of unfortunate circumstances, honestly."

"A comedy?" Julie bared her teeth. "Oh well, then I guess everything is cool. Sure, come in."

Dan tried again to enter and Julie shoulder-checked him straight back into the hallway.

She said, "You childish fuck. You dickless coward. I should rip out your guts and feed them to a sewer rat."

"This isn't any of your business," said Dan.

"This is absolutely my business. Sarah is my friend."

"And she won't fuck you no matter what you do."

Julie half-laughed. "Is that all guys like you think about? Whether someone's going to fuck you or not? Jesus, if that's the yardstick you use, stick it up your fucking ass."

"I'm not going to ask again. Where's Sarah?"

"Fuck. You. Dan."

He moved but Julie moved faster. She slammed the door in his face and heard, to her absolute ecstasy: a wet, unhappy howl. Julie could only hope she'd made a ruin of his nose. Her triumph did not last as the realities of her situation asserted itself. She had a problem: namely, that Sarah was coming home at any minute. Dan, who Julie was sure was guilty of many inadequacies, didn't appear to be an idiot. It would cost him nothing to wait out the possibility of Julie lying.

Julie ran through escape plans, contingencies, a checklist of options, beginning with what if she went back out and beat Dan into the carpet. Part of her really, really wanted to go with Plan A. If she could hurt the bastard enough, she might be able to scare him off. But she had no frame of reference for what might happen if Sarah found Julie elbow-deep in her ex-boyfriend's corpse.

So, what now? First, she needed to call Sarah. Let her know who'd found his way to their door. Sarah could take the train to Forty-Second Street and get lost in the Times Square crowd. Julie would need to let Dead Air know to rescue Sarah but that was easy: a quick text message.

What about St. Joan?

Subsumed by her worries, Julie didn't hear the ratcheting sound of a bullet sliding into the pistol's chamber, or the shuffling two-step of Dan maneuvering into position. She was just stepping away from the door when the wood shattered as two bullets punched through. Only when she began to crumple did Julie's awareness finally, *finally* lock in on her situation and the heat boiling from her belly. She touched a hand to her abdomen, her palm coming away wet, red.

"Shit," Julie mumbled, looking muzzily back to the ruin of her door, head lolling forward on her chest.

A vision came to her then, as if the door to her apartment had dematerialized. She could see straight through into the familiar hallway, with its stucco pillaring and its incarnadine carpet, the defunct chandelier that St. Joan swore she would fix up. But what she saw at the end wasn't what she was expecting at all. Instead of Dan, it was Akrasiel standing there, but something was wrong with the archangel.

"Akrasiel," Julie said, more to herself than the world, the margins of her vision filling up with shadow. "Why is your head the wrong way?"

Consciousness slipped away from Julie before she could register Akrasiel's reply, a blackness mercifully deep, and cold, and sharp-scented as a body rotted to salt.

CHAPTER THIRTEEN

Dan leaned against the fire escape door, panting with exhilaration. In the past, he'd dreamt bashfully about gunning down the unworthy, the waste elements of the population, those useless wretches who chipped daily at the declining reservoir of the planet's resources, never giving anything back, only taking and taking to fuel their brief and meaningless lives. A younger Dan nursed those fantasies with caution, knowing he'd be rebuked for them. For some people, for empty-headed idealists like Sarah, all lives were equally entitled to their full lengths.

But he proved her wrong. He finally did it.

He was uncertain whether he'd actually killed Julie, but the angle and the height of the shots were such that Dan was certain he had at least inflicted a severe wound. And that was alright too. He could live with not killing her. This could be her come-to-Jesus moment, the instant when she finally commited to bettering herself for the species. And wouldn't that be great? No more of that pathological irresponsibility. She might finally get a real job, get married, have kids. Become a real person.

Maybe then, Sarah would stop fucking talking about her so much.

Dan sank down into a squat, the Glock dangling on the hook of his thumb. All he could think was how he wished he had X-ray vision so that he could have seen the impact of the bullets—Julie rocked back, her head snapped forward, her body twisting as she lost all motor control and collapsed onto the floor. Years ago, one of Dan's bosses invited him to a big game hunt in Nairobi—a very discreet and illegal one. He'd made the mistake of letting Sarah know and she threw such a fuss that Dan was compelled to refuse the invitation. Dan had been glad for the excuse then, glad he could blame someone instead of admitting he might be a coward. Back then, he hadn't been sure if he could handle being a killer. What if all the societal indoctrination and millennial pacifism had him dry-heaving into a bucket in front of his employers?

Now, he knew.

He wouldn't throw up. He liked it. He enjoyed the power, the unassailable potency of knowing that if he so chose to do so again, he could end someone and remain on his feet. The act felt like a demarcation, a severance from the mundane. Dan was different now. Uplifted. Better because he could stomach being one of the elites who cleaned the streets of trash when others wouldn't.

As he wiped sweat from his forehead, he giggled, the sound higher in pitch than anything he remembered himself making. The noise became a full-on guffaw, then, as the seconds passed, climbed again to a hysterical pitch. In desperation, Dan jammed his forearm between his teeth and bit down. The cotton was brined in his sweat. He was drenched, he realized. His shirt clung slickly to his armpits, the prow of his breastbone.

Deep breaths, he told himself.

Dan stood up, embarrassingly aware now of how he shook, the tremors in his ankles and the joints of his wrists. He was cold. He was so fucking cold. Dan's teeth chattered like he was a wind-up toy grown absurdly large. Adrenaline, he assured himself. He'd just done something herculean, after all.

Then why was he so *scared*?

The hallway stood empty. No one had come to investigate the gunshot. This being New York, he couldn't foresee anyone caring. There were places to be, things to do, dreams to chase down the myriad alleys. No time to squander on neighbors. Keep your eyes down and your mouth shut. Dan took in the tired glamour of the building, assuring himself again that this would be no consequence.

This place might have been pretty once.

Though corroded by the decades, Dan could still see a gleam of pseudo-Hollywood glitziness. It was a shoddy wax cast of his memory of some hotels in Los Angeles: step tray plaster ceilings and the sporadic chandelier, reeded walls, dark wooden flooring overlaid with red Persian rugs. Except scuffed, ill-maintained.

Still Dan could picture starlets eeling sleekly between the apartments, laughing, slightly desaturated because it was the past, and everything there is washed in sepia. Though why anyone could come here when Hollywood itself stood in the desert, he would never understand. Dan—

Motion twitched at the corner of his vision. Dan panicked, nearly dropping the Glock. He heard the sharp intake of a breath and for a second convinced himself it was Julie, a towel pressed over a flesh wound, come to seek revenge.

"Please," said a man's voice, lushly accented, Slavic. "I don't want trouble."

Dan blinked out of his fugue.

In front of him stood an old white man with a prodigious gray beard, stooped, with a gold-topped cane, no hair, barely anything but bone in crinkled wads of skin. He was dressed like the apartment: shabbily appointed in a paisley silk button-up that might have been gorgeous once, faded slacks meant for a bigger man, leather shoes that had seen no polish for years and years.

"Please," he said again. A laurel of liver spots wreathed the crown of his bald head. The old man was shaking too, although not as much as Dan, who didn't know what to do with his hands. God, he was still shaking. "I don't want trouble. I was only going to the pharmacy."

"What did you see?"

The words startled him. What Dan meant to say was anything but that.

"I saw nothing. Just you: Julie's new boyfriend coming out for groceries. A nice man. A friendly man. Not that I saw your face. No. Not that."

Julie.

The man knew Julie.

Something in his expression must have changed for the man was talking faster and faster, the acceleration fraying what little American there was to his voice.

"—or maybe, you are not boyfriend? Hook-up. Friends with benefit. I don't know what you young Americans say anymore. Please. Take no offense. I am old and know nothing."

Dan swallowed.

"You heard us."

"Not a thing. My hearing aid broke a few days ago. You could fire gun next door, and I'd still sleep—"

The words emptied into a terrified silence. There was a stricken regret in his face that Dan knew was mirrored in his own, a soft and terrible horror of what would come next.

When he spoke again, the old man was practically sobbing.

"I have grandchildren," he said, every pretense shed. He tugged at the overstuffed black wallet jammed into his front pocket. "Seven of them. The seventh was born two days ago. A little girl, who look so much like her mother. I have not seen her yet. Only through the phone. But I cannot wait to hold her. Tomorrow, I visit her. Tomorrow, I hold her. Please. You are good man. *Не убивайте.* Please. Let me see my family tomorrow."

Dan raised the gun and pulled the trigger.

The entrance wound was perfect: a neat black circle through which seeped a tiny rivulet of blood and brain matter, the fattiness of the latter lending a greasy shine to the effluvium. The old man's brow rucked. His eyes rolled up, showing just the whites, as if he was struggling to assess the damage. Behind him: a fine red mist as the bullet made its exit, physics mashing living tissue into pulp. Aerosolized brain went everywhere. The air became soupy with gore, with the hot metallic reek of gunpowder and blood.

The old man dropped.

But he wasn't dead. Not yet.

He lay on the ground. Humming. Despite the smoldering tunnel through the center of his skull, he still hummed an inchoate, off-key little tune: a lullaby, something sweet and simple. He stared up at Dan, haloed by a widening puddle of blood, and he smiled moronically. Blood filmed his teeth.

Dan backed away.

"Shit, shit, shit."

The old man kept humming. The same three bars on a growingly erratic loop. Likely the lights upstairs turning off one after another. Yet somehow despite this, the old man found enough strength to raise one stubby finger and sway it through the air, marking the pulse of the damn song. *There's a fucking hole in your head, old man,* Dan thought. *Let go. Just let go. Stop humming!*

Almost without thinking, Dan pumped another bullet into the old man. It sheared along a rib before it found his gut. Dan heard bone crackle, maybe break. He wasn't sure. The man stopped his humming. He began to cry instead at a volume that should have been impossible with most of his brain matter freckling the hallway, and a bullet lodged god-knows-where in his lower abdomen. He wailed like he was being born until his sobs ran wet.

Dan backed way. No one told him any of this. Not this smell. Not the backwash of ammonia as the old man's bladder slackened. Not how this charnel reek would assault his nostrils, his tongue. Dan could taste it. He was practically gagging on the old man's death.

"Shit," Dan said again.

A door at the far end of the hallway creaked open, and Dan heard a woman's hushed warning, caught the flash of a child's wide-eyed face before it was yanked inside. Muttering as the door slammed decisively shut. Muttering that spread between apartments until the corridor roiled with sound.

They had all seen it and if not, they were surely texting one another about the carnage, asking *did you see the corpse on the floor?* Like a fucking idiot, Dan was just standing there. The weight of his actions crashed into him. Gone was the initial flush of excitement, its substitute far less pleasant. Dan's stomach torqued as he took a couple of unsteady steps to one side and then another, hardly able to think.

This was empirically, undeniably, indelibly bad. If he was caught, if the police found him here, it'd be all over.

He stumbled toward the stairs, no longer concerned about stealth. It was too late. If he was to be saved, he needed to move quickly. His life, every dream he had queued up from now to his distant deathbed, would be obliterated if he was caught. He had to get out of here before anyone could transcribe him to memory.

Don't run, he told himself. Walk with purpose. Look concerned as you pass by the tenants of the lower floors: answer if they ask, tell them you're getting help. Be unobtrusive, Dan repeated as more and more of the building's residents came out of their apartments, rushing up the stairs to see what he had done.

Don't run, he said again and again and again until the mantra decoupled from meaning, became instead a soothing nonsense as Dan exited the apartment and vanished into the bustling streets of that awful, indifferent city.

❧

Back in his hotel room, Dan was angry that his gun hand wouldn't stop shaking. He'd left Julie's apartment building and jumped into the first taxi he saw, paying the driver three times his fee in exchange for him promising he wouldn't tell a soul about Dan. The man—older by a few years but poorer kept—looked him over and said, "Who you talking about?" in a treacly Brooklyn accent which Dan decided was his method of saying yes.

The drive was uneventful. Dan paid him with a crumpled roll of fifties, which the cabbie pocketed without so much as a change in expression. Then, once deposited on the stoop of his hotel, Dan took the elevator to his room, arms crossed and hands pinned under his pits, and shut the door.

It didn't help. He was still shaking. Dan paced the small, well-appointed suite, stalked by the certainty a camera had caught him and that a video of his crime was everywhere now, making rounds on social media, passed between his relatives as evidence that Dan had always been a bad apple rotting on their family tree. His boss probably already knew. His coworkers. Sarah's milquetoast little family.

Dan marched another circuit through his room.

He could turn on the TV to see if his catastrophizing was valid but that would involve dealing with what-ifs potentially transmuting to fact, and he wasn't ready for that. All his notifications were off. They would stay that way for now. He cupped his throat with a palm and scratched at the skin, feeling the haptic phantom of a noose tightening there, pushing on his Adam's apple.

Would they hang him or put him in the electric chair?

Would it be the injection instead?

Dan coughed once and became aware of just how parched he was. He stopped his listless orbit to rummage through the minibar where he found a tiny bottle of vodka and a marginally larger juice box. Both of these were slopped into a dirty cup, its rim scalloped with coffee stains.

It was too hot, too musty. The hotel smelled, as did all of New York, a kind of willful neglect. He drained his makeshift cocktail in a single gulp, and then made himself another and was halfway through that before the air frissoned, the stale heat and the mildewed stench vanishing. In its place: an abject chill, a cold like an ending, worse still than the grave. It had a pang of salt to it, an abrasiveness, like a jaguar's tongue rasping the ligament from a knob of bone; it left Dan's throat dry and him gasping. He turned, drawn to a thundering of wings.

There, about a foot behind him, stood an image from a hymn book he remembered vaguely from his childhood. Its face was gorgeously carnal, the carved image of the ecstatic martyr: rolled back eyes, drawn back lips, the nub of its tongue clenched between its teeth. Its hair was gold. It wore robes that were the same incorruptible nuclear white as its feathers. It was beautiful and it was awe-inducing and at the sight of it, Dan hoped, although he did not know why then, fervently to die before it ever touched him.

"Daniel Alastair Jones," said a triptych of voices in disjointed chorus. "When you were thirteen, you allowed your neighbor's young daughter—Rosie, they called her that because her mother loved the flower more than she loved anything else—to die. You saw the truck coming. You said nothing. You watched as she burst under the fenders of the vehicle."

Dan froze, cup still in his hand. He'd told no one. He recalled the incident with searing vividity: the *pop* of the girl's head as the pressure exerted by the two-ton vehicle did its work, an eye leaping out of its socket, the orbital nerve like a coil of silly string. Whenever asked, however, he always said he had no such memory, pleading trauma, the protective amnesia of a charitable brain.

The angel bent its head. It had *so* much hair, golden ringlets spilling over the valleys of its collarbones, down its robes, down, down, down, crawling over the pea-green carpet, its gleam like a ransom enough to buy the soul of every dead king that ever was.

"You were so . . ." A euphoric sigh. ". . . *happy*."

"Who are you?"

"The patient hunger of the protozoa. I am the want of worms. I am what waits when the coffin lid shuts and there is nothing but the dark and the flesh cooling in its heart." It laughed with girlish modesty, as if being prompted to discuss an old and mostly forgotten act of valor. The shyness was performative, however. Nothing in its approach hinted at abashment. The angel—angel-*thing,* amended Dan's terrified subconscious, putting emphasis on the suffix—advanced with a terrible eagerness, its voices rising in volume. The angel began to advance, eagerness in its voices. "And I need you."

Dan said nothing as whatever inner strength or flaring panic had carried him thus far finally died the quiet death Dan envied.

"We can *use* each other," it said, dragging out the word *use.*

"I don't understand—"

"I can help you kill Sarah. After that, I can kill Julie. So long as I am the one to kill her, the Door is safe and I can't be sent back. The ritual is complete. And once we are done there, who knows? Who knows," it said, and it was clear that it certainly knew, that it didn't only know who else to take to the charnel house but also how it intended to do it and what it would do with the resultant detritus.

Its feathers were of every color and pattern configuration, an encyclopedic representation of the world's population of birds: pigeon, brilliantly rubied cardinal, vulture, peacock, tufted titmouse with its softly blue-gray plumage, condor, and more, so much more, enough that even an ornithologist might need years to taxonomize the chaos.

But hadn't those feathers been *white* before?

And hadn't they been without *eyes*?

For each and every feather now had a lidless human eye inlaid impossibly in the barbules, and every one of those eyes was staring at Dan. He backed away another step, tripping over his suitcase.

He gulped air. "Actually—"

"You have one more chance to offer the right answer."

It was so close to him now, too close, much too close, stinking of the sea and of docks overgrown with mold and barnacle. Close enough for him to see the scintillant rime of salt grown over the edges of its face and to understand, yes, it was wearing an almost unnoticeable mask, and that under the expertly made, exquisitely fitted enamel was something Dan did not ever want to see.

He needed an excuse to make it stop moving. Thinking hard, he said, with clearly no interest in the answer, only hope it would give his guest reason to literally pause and think, "I mean, that depends. I . . . what do I get out of it?"

It laughed. "What a question to ask in the face of the divine."

Out of nowhere came a bolt of misplaced rage, a reactive and useless fury. How dare it *patronize* him? He clung to the emotion, recognizing it as absurd but also relieved by its familiarity. Being angry was at least a change from being terrified out of his mind. Dan let it ripple over him. He let it build until he was brazen with wrath.

Dan took a long breath and looked coldly at the thing that wasn't an angel. "I'm an atheist, motherfucker."

It laughed, louder this time than the last.

"If only that meant anything."

He degenerated into instinct. Dan felt through his pocket for his gun even as the little clot of his brain still capable of reason bayed impotently: *how the fuck do you think that's going to help?* But as his hand slipped around the Glock's grip, the thing's mask raised, as though an invisible hand had gently hooked a finger under its chin and lifted, and underneath—

Underneath—

His mind receded into a memory: Dan was eight and sitting beside his father, the man inexplicably gargantuan in his recollections, but otherwise winnowed of any distinguishing features or smells. He was laughing at a glossy photo of a puzzled sunfish in the ocean, lampreys trailing from its body like the streamers from his birthday party. The sunfish had looked so *puzzled.* Dan remembered being fascinated by the close-up of a lamprey's mouth, the rings of teeth, the paradox of those idiot eyes atop its innocuous face, so *ridiculous* in comparison to its dentition. There'd been something in the middle of the teeth too. He'd told his father it looked like a bunny.

What silly things those lampreys were.

How much less silly they looked as they fountained from the beautiful stem of the angel-thing's neck, darkly mottled olive bodies sheened with a milky film. One turned to regard Dan and before he could scream it was already burrowing into his throat, chewing through esophageal tissue, through larynx and trachea. Dan choked as it tunneled down, writhed deeper. And it hurt, and it hurt, and he could not breathe, and—

It took a long, long time for Daniel Alastair Jones to die.

CHAPTER FOURTEEN

The joke Julie liked to tell people at parties was that she had a one-way relationship with drugs. She loved them. They only ever wanted to leave. Julie had a supernal gift for metabolizing whatever she took. Whether it was molly or mushrooms or weed, it burned through her system in a fraction of the time it would have taken to exit another person. Nothing ever stuck around long enough for her liking.

Including anesthesia.

She woke, she knew, too early for her own good. Julie winced as the world strobed and ran to white along the shifting margins of her vision, the inconstancy leaving her queasy. People, faces diluted to smudges, circled her. She felt fingers threaded through her own: a familiar grip. Sarah? Julie didn't realize she'd said her friend's name until Sarah answered, voice unraveled to a whisper.

"I'm here. I'm here, Julie. Don't leave me."

"They told me the moment someone made the report. I should have gotten here sooner. I'm so sorry. We're going to try everything." Dead Air's voice, mixing with Sarah's.

Julie raised a hand to palm Sarah's cheek, marveling at the tenderness she heard. "I'm not going anywhere."

Her fingers met air.

"Shit, she's awake. Someone up her dose—"

"Can't. We've already given her the max."

"Ma'am, you have to stay down."

Julie furrowed her brow and tried hard to focus through the pain. "Where's Sarah? Dead Boy? Where are they?"

"Who—"

"I think that's her girlfriend. Ma'am, your girlfriend is in the waiting room. We need you to stay calm."

"Who the hell is Dead Boy?"

"No fucking clue. Jesus, keep her calm."

Someone took her hand and set it down on the operating table.

"It's cold," croaked Julie.

"I'm sorry, ma'am. Surgery rooms are like that."

Julie frowned as she said, "Who's in surgery?"

The world diffused: cotton candy in cool water. She was on the floor of her apartment again, the nub of her shoulder wedged against the door hinge. Julie had intended to crawl to her phone, to do something, find her reagents, enact revenge, be anything but a useless heap, but it was hard, so fucking hard, to think much less do anything with this much blood coming out of her.

The crack of another gunshot.

Screaming.

There was the slam of a door. A scrabble of heels on the linoleum. People in her apartment. Sirens, and the world bruised red and blue.

"Oh my god, Julie. Oh my god, oh my god, oh my god. What happened? Oh my god, you're bleeding so much. Stay with us. Stay with us." Sarah. Was that Sarah? She wasn't sure. So many people were talking all at once.

She wanted so much to tell Sarah to be careful, for someone to pass the word to Sarah, but her tongue weighed too much and the words wouldn't stay, draining between her fingers along with everything else.

Julie ricocheted back to the present, gasping. She realized she was no longer on a first-name basis with temporality, although it was anyone's guess as to why. Dan had shot her in the gut. Had she hit her head on the way down onto the floor? Or was this what dying was like?

Don't leave me.

"I'm not going anywhere," Julie whispered. "Not again. I shouldn't have left you to that fucker in the first place."

"Ma'am, you need to calm down—Jesus, can we get her a sedative?"

"It's okay," she said. "I just need to focus."

Julie was always good at pain. She learned the trick of it from being broke as a teenager and desperate to impress the older kids with how hard she was. Over the years, she got better. Julie worked hard on making pain her *bitch*. She taught herself how to isolate it and how to drive it where she needed it to go. Julie excelled so terrifyingly at this, she could make a battery of her pain, keep it banked and accruing momentum in the back of her head until it was time to let loose.

Even with all that in the background, this hurt.

They were stitching her up. There were hands reaching inside of her, sifting through organ meat, and Julie understood dimly that it was only by the grace of modern medicine that she wasn't screaming her fucking head off. The pain stalked her through her head, bigger than worlds. It was in every room in her mind palace. She couldn't escape it.

"Am I dying? It's okay if I'm dying. But you have to be gentle when you tell Sarah. She's going to be so mad at me. And sad—god, she's going to be so sad. Tell her I'll miss her and I'm sorry . . ."

Whispers, pitched too low for her to glean any information.

"Ma'am, please. You need to stay calm."

"I'm trying here." Her mouth rusted with blood. It was all she could taste. "Honest."

Julie heard a sigh and what sounded like the start of a sentence, but unconsciousness took her before she could parse out the rest.

Julie dreamt of a man being eaten alive. He sat in a squat fauteuil that might have been emerald once before the pilled fabric was worn to an exhausted colorlessness, his arms dangled between spread legs, his back drooped, his chin rested on the divide between his collarbones: the picture of an abjectly fatigued man. The man did not move even as he was hollowed out to an onion-skin thinness, and Julie could see right through him, into the mass of worms silhouetted inside, each of them crowned inexplicably with broad human grins that were all molars and several inches of inflamed gum. They were straining for her, as if magnetized in the very technical sense of the word, and thank god she woke when she did because she was sure they were about to speak her name.

"Welcome back to the land of the living."

St. Joan.

"Hi, Mom."

The shudder in St. Joan's voice was palpable. "Two years younger than you, Julie. I am two years younger than you."

"More like—"

"Two years younger than you," St. Joan repeated in a theatrically strangled voice before she sighed and muttered almost below range of hearing. "For all eternity, but who's counting?"

"Me," said Julie, awake for all of five seconds and already itching to cause problems on purpose.

"Hush," said St. Joan, who knew her too well to take the bait.

Dirty apricot light sifted from a curtained window on the right wall. To Julie's surprise there were no other beds in the room, which was a shock considering she had no insurance and expected to awaken in a dank Bedlam cell on a pile of dirty straw.

"What the hell? You didn't pay for this, did you? I mean I have money in the bank now, but no one's rich enough to have a comfortable time in the American health care system," said Julie, propping herself up on a trembling elbow. An IV line ribboned from her left arm. Monitors sat atop rolling stainless steel trolleys of varying height, telling anyone who knew how to read them the embarrassing particulars of Julie's health.

"I didn't pay for the room." St. Joan wore a dazzlingly sequined chiffon dress, white where it wasn't peacock rhinestones. It should have been gaudy: an outfit like that in a place as grim as a hospital. But, as with almost everything, St. Joan made it work.

"Then who did?"

"There was an absolute queue for it. Sarah initially wanted to do it, but as it turned out, none of her good credit cards work any longer," said St. Joan, uncrossing and recrossing her legs as she tried to get comfortable in her hardback chair. "So, Dead Air . . . fixed things."

"Fixed things, huh?"

"Mhm. As it turns out, you're actually on a very good insurance plan. An amazing one, come to think about it. No deductibles whatsoever and a *stipend* too. The hospital was very impressed. Just took Dead Air's help with the forms."

"I fucking love that guy." Julie ran her tongue over chapped lips. ". . . how's Sarah?"

"Asleep. Finally. She stayed up all night through your operation."

"That's my Sarah, alright. Ride or die forever," said Julie.

The smile St. Joan flashed chased a bloom of heat to Julie's cheeks.

"*Your* Sarah, huh?"

"Don't start."

St. Joan in close-up sometimes unsettled Julie. Just slightly. From afar, it was easy to buy into the fiction of the woman: that she was an eccentric with archaeological preferences in fashion. Nothing more, nothing less. Take away that distance and it became impossible to ignore how St. Joan was limned with silver, like the cathode glare of a black-and-white television. It was similarly difficult to overlook the *texture* of her skin, how it shimmered like static on a screen. Sometimes, when St. Joan wasn't paying enough attention, she desaturated.

"Anyway, yes, it's all dealt with. You don't have to worry about becoming a pauper by this little visit."

Julie scratched at the back of her head. "But I worry all the time these days, mostly about Sarah. Honestly, she needs to learn how to care a little less. She's going to get herself hurt, the way she runs around, giving a shit about everything."

"I don't miss being young."

"Keep talking like that and people are going to realize you're actually a billion years old, and not the ingenue you pass yourself as."

"Touché," said St. Joan. She looked as if she might have more to say but the door banged open, and Sarah and Dead Air were suddenly there. "Oh, look. The kids are here."

"You're awake. Oh, thank fucking god," said Sarah. The relief in her tired gaze woke a sweet guilty ache in Julie's chest. She was somehow gaunter than Julie remembered, hunted-seeming, haunted around the eyes.

"Hey, guys," said Julie.

"I tried to tell her she needed more than two hours of sleep, but Sarah just stole my can of Monster, and—" Dead Air stuffed both hands into the pockets of his cargos, shrugged, his expression curtained by hair. "Here we are."

Sarah inched uneasily toward Julie, moving a step back for every two she took forward, hand balled so tightly at her chest her knuckles stood out white. It was only when Julie motioned her closer that Sarah lost her hesitance, bounding forward to scoop Julie's left hand into her own.

"Careful. Ow, ow. Easy."

Sarah let go as though singed. "I'm sorry."

"It's fine," said Julie, even though it wasn't completely true. Sarah's grip having jostled the angle of the needle, Julie could feel where it was pricking the ligature between her metacarpals, but she would set herself on fire before admitting any discomfort to Sarah. She'd already put her through so much.

The lie worked. Sarah relaxed, her expression losing its friable quality, gentling into something Julie wasn't prepared to name. As if in a trance, Sarah skated her fingers over Julie's arm, tracing the knuckle-deep ruts where coils of barbed wire had previously been, the myriad scars now on lurid display. Julie wondered how she looked to Sarah, relaxed like this, bare of anything but old wounds.

And she had her answer in the smile on Sarah's face, a smile both girlish and ancient in its exhaustion, a smile like the sun waking over a morning everyone was sure wouldn't come.

"Hi," said Sarah, very softly.

"Hi," Julie said in return.

The two said nothing else for a minute, for a lifetime, until St. Joan drawled loudly, "Oh, just fucking kiss already."

At that, Sarah recoiled from Julie. "We're just friends!"

Julie tried not to wince, thankful for the cover of St. Joan's chortling. Though they'd been acquainted for years, St. Joan's laughter—the real one, not what she wheeled out for clients or marks or people she didn't give a shit about—always surprised Julie with its unruliness. It made her wonder who St. Joan had been before she only answered to St. Joan, but friends didn't ask friends questions like that.

Chagrined by the situation, by the pain in her abdomen, by the fact Sarah had been so blatantly horrified at the idea of kissing her, and the fact that someone as pathetically mundane as Dan had gotten the jump on her, Julie changed the topic.

"Thanks for bailing me out, Dead Air."

The scrawny Chinese boy, clearly discomfited by being out in the open, shrugged, gaze fixed on the hallway outside the hospital room door. "Yeah, well. I didn't really do anything. Just had a chat with the hospital computer system."

"You came to rescue me, too."

"They told me where to go. If it weren't for Them, I'd still be at home playing video games. I really should have known. I'm so fucking sorry."

"Thank you, Dead Air. It means the fucking world."

Dead Air scrunched his nose and his pupils illuminated for a second by pinpricks of cathode green. "If you wanna thank anyone, you can tell Them you're grateful."

"Thank you, strange and all-powerful electronic gods."

"They said you're an idiot." He paused. "Me too, apparently. But eh."

"I'll take it," said Julie, to which Dead Air said nothing but smiled, a little embarrassed about being the center of attention.

A small television was mounted on the wall opposite Julie's bed. On screen was an excessively Brylcreemed newscaster, his hair nearly a wax monument, talking about an incident at a local hotel, but Julie couldn't focus enough to make sense of the details. She couldn't focus on anything: she was tired. Julie wanted sleep like a pilgrim wanted God, the voracity of her longing so intense, it made her fret again about whether she was dying and didn't know it.

"Drink this," said St. Joan, pressing a sleek vial into Julie's unoccupied hand.

The shock of the chill glass cauterized her exhaustion. New York was still recovering from the recent winter so everything was tinged with an unexpected frost, but this was outside the bounds of normal: it was like being handed a paring of dry ice. Julie raised the vial for inspection. Inside: a phosphorescent blue grease, which was a matte sapphire from one angle, eye-wateringly coruscant from another. A faint scent emanated from the corked top: cigar smoke and jasmine soaked in rainwater.

"What—"

"Oh, my curious cat. It's something old. Something Babylonian. So, drink it and ask silly questions later."

That was good enough for Julie. She had a love for everything pharmaceutically intriguing and complete trust in St. Joan. She drank it down. Her attention sharpened but her pain did not: though the latter didn't go away, it was defanged and stuffed with a pleasant downiness, so it felt temporarily like someone else's cotton, stoppered and separate from the rest of Julie.

"Mmm," said Julie.

"You're welcome."

Julie would have been happy to float in that fugue for the rest of her life, her closest friends around her, the sunlight warming to orange as the day nodded off into night. She didn't need much, she realized. She didn't want fame. Fortune would be nice, but she would feel guilty if there was too much of it and very much like she would go crazy surrounded by too many rich people things.

Then, Dead Air spoke up.

"So, what exactly happened here? Your neighbors said they found you in the apartment, trying to die of a gunshot. And there was an old man in the corridor? I'd have checked the cameras but someone doesn't like tech in her building."

St. Joan lifted a cool stare at him. "I had enough of cameras years ago in Hollywood. These new ones can keep their voyeurism away from what is mine."

Dead Air rolled his eyes.

"I checked the apartment," said Sarah. "No one tried to take anything. Was it an enemy? A client?"

"It was . . . Dan."

The room went quiet.

Dead Air steepled his hands over his nose and mouth, thumbs anchored under his jaw. "That fucker. See, this is why I say murder always should be the first option."

"You don't say that," muttered St. Joan, sotto voce. "You can barely look at a steak without getting woozy."

"My Dan?" said Sarah.

"I'm sorry," said Julie and Sarah said nothing, her color gone and her grip on Julie clammy with sweat. "I should have checked your phone for stalkerware. He came to the apartment looking for you—"

"This is my fault," said Sarah, cutting her off. "If I hadn't come here, Dan wouldn't have—"

"He'd have kept *beating* you until you were dead and don't you fucking start. I'd rather get shot again than let that happen," said Julie. "Anyway, I'm the idiot. I should have just exploded him over the carpet."

"Oh, all of you. Just. *Stop*," said St. Joan, temples pinched between her index finger and thumb. "No more of that competitive flagellation, please. It serves no one and also, it is giving me a headache."

She paused. "Also, I will remind you that I have a strict *no gore on my fucking carpets* policy, thank you. I *will* charge you a cleaning fee."

Sarah laced her fingers through Julie's own and—carefully, this time—squeezed. Julie reciprocated. Dead Air deigned to slink inside from the hall, coming to stand next to the diagnostics machinery. Satisfied there would be no more self-castigation, St. Joan turned her attention to the television.

"Lurid," said St. Joan, switching channels just as the camera cut away to footage of the NYPD swarming a hotel room. Costumed puppies bounded onto the screen instead, and Julie swallowed back a laugh as a dalmatian in a fireman outfit joined the rest.

"Would it help if I left?" said Sarah.

"And go where?" said Dead Air.

"For what reason?" said St. Joan as she removed from a pale clutch a vintage Zippo lighter, an engraved cigarette case, and its matching holder.

"Away," said Sarah. "To keep him from coming after Julie again. He's after me. Not her. If I'd been in the apartment, none of this would have happened."

"*You* might have been the one getting shot instead," said St. Joan, setting a cigarette in the holder. The flame that leapt up from the lighter was pale and oily, as was the odorless smoke that rose from the cigarette: less a color than a placeholder, less a thing than the idea of it.

"He wouldn't have. Dan cares about his *property*."

Sarah said "property" with the affectless tones of someone reading off a grocery list.

"He broke your wrist," said Julie. "If he cared about his property—" She spat the word, hating it, hating Dan. "—then he wouldn't have done that, would he?"

Julie might as well have been jabbering into a vacuum for all the reaction it got. Sarah's expression bore the leaden, far-off quality of someone who had recited their cancer diagnosis ten times in one hour and was more tired of being pitied than the terminal nature of their condition.

"I know how to handle Dan," said Sarah with a terrible dignity.

"He'll kill you," said Dead Air. "Telling us he thinks you're property is not the reassuring line you think it is. They showed me his text messages. They told me what he's like."

"You say it like he didn't read those messages out to me," said Sarah, still with that affectless tone.

"One way or another," said Julie, thinking anew of ways she'd make Dan fucking pay. "You can't just hang around while I'm recovering from this fucking gutshot. I've got a friend up in Vermont with a safe house who owes me a favor."

"Yvonne?" said Dead Air.

"Yeah. Remember the man-eating washing machine?"

Dead Air shuddered. "A blasphemous abomination."

"Also hella weird," said Julie. "But she'd take Sarah in. That's the important part. You should go hide up there until I've fixed everything."

"Fixed everything how?" said Sarah, her fingers threaded still with Julie's.

"I'm going to make sure that Dan doesn't fuck with you ever again," said Julie, a proclamation that might have had more impact were she not bedridden and swaddled in bandages, but she tried regardless. Sometimes, it was the thought that counted.

"In that case, no," said Sarah.

"No?"

"If you're going to hunt him down, I'm staying here."

"I—*excuse* me?" Julie spluttered. "Did we just not have an entire conversation about how you're in danger?"

In answer to that, Sarah cast a strange look at Julie: a dangerously animalic stare, with pupils blown out. The look of a trapped wolf with nowhere to go but through.

"Like I said, Dan cares about what is his. Whatever else he might do to me, he's not going to shoot me, and if I'm here with you, he's not going to take the risk."

"What if you're wrong about Dan?"

"Then I die with you."

Without thinking, Julie brushed her lips over the knuckles of Sarah's right hand, with the solemn and tender courtliness of a revenant come home one last time, her eyes never leaving Sarah's own. What other objections Julie might have raised, what argument or scant logic she might have mustered in her already embattled condition, died. The enormity of the words left Julie overwhelmed and if Sarah had asked her then to take a leap from the hospital roof, Julie would have thrown herself into the sky with no thought of how badly she'd splatter on the pavement below.

"You're the best friend a girl could ever ask for," said Julie, thoroughly ruining the moment.

"I don't say this lightly," said St. Joan. "But you are an absolute and complete idiot."

"Don't know what you're talking about," mumbled Julie, who absolutely did and would to her deathbed pretend otherwise.

Sarah, flushed and disarrayed in a way that Julie, had she more ego and less dearth of self-esteem, might have read as terror at having overshared grievously.

"It's like they're *trying* to be stupid," said St. Joan in an awful stage whisper.

"I know," said Dead Air before his face softened. "But we probably should let them be stupid in peace."

"I agree. Let's go. We can see what hospital food is like. Grotesque or merely awful," said St. Joan, rising to her feet with a diamanté swish.

Neither Julie nor Sarah spoke until the door clicked shut behind Dead Air. The light had deepened. It bronzed some of the flyaway threads of Sarah's hair, gilded others. Julie thought again of poets and their work and wondered if there was a word for the perfect arc of a perfect cheek and if there wasn't, what it would cost to have one invented.

"Go to the safe house," said Julie, because the silence had to be broken and she sure as hell wouldn't let the first words out of her mouth be something as maudlin as *you make me wish I could paint.*

"No."

"Why?"

"Because I—" Sarah thinned her mouth to a hairline, her breath snagged on a consonant, on the corner of a word Julie was sure Sarah wasn't about to say, was sure she *didn't* want Sarah to say, mostly because Julie wouldn't know what to do if she did. Never mind that it seemed both an improbable idea and a fantastically narcissistic concern given their upcoming woes.

"I care about you," said Sarah.

"I care about you too. That's why you should go."

Before Julie's heart could finish breaking, Sarah added: "I've been living the wrong story. I made a mistake all that time ago. Choosing Dan over us. I left you. Then I left you to Dan—"

"You didn't, though."

"I won't do that for the third time. I won't ever leave you alone again."

Julie couldn't speak for fear she would fuck up, as she often did, no, *always* did, the trainwreck of her life being proof she'd never made a choice a normal person wouldn't regret. No, better to be silent and to keep Sarah's hand sleeved in her fingers than risk shattering the fragile enormous thing that now hung between them.

"Was that too much? I'm sorry. I didn't mean to," said Sarah, her voice cracking on sorry, like the word had never been enough in the past. "I got—"

"Right story," said Julie throatily. "Bad chapter. We all have a few."

"How many have you had?"

"All the ones except this one."

And it wasn't the best answer, but it was good enough.

CHAPTER FIFTEEN

Tyler sat in his office watching his coffee get cold. He was losing what quaint excuse for a mind he still had left. A light on his desk phone blinked, reminding him that voicemails were piling up. At the end of every extension was another client waiting to complain about a stubbed toe and could Tyler come over, *please,* because the injury definitely presents as symptomatic of a bogeyman.

Fuck 'em all, he thought.

"Fuck 'em," he said aloud as if that would help the cortisol bath he was having.

The magical scuttlebutt on the street said that Julie was in the hospital. By all accounts, she was near death too, having spent hours in surgery while surgeons frantically crocheted her organs back together. A lesser being would have died on the operating table, leaving a truly bizarre corpse to be interrogated. But Julie was alive, and the people caring for her were thankfully Samaritans more preoccupied with her continued survival than the science behind it. Thank fuck for that. If Julie had died, there would have been Questions.

Still, he worried.

After the incident at the speakeasy, it was public knowledge just how much he resented Julie. He had a reputation, Tyler knew, for being fastidious about said reputation—and Julie had humiliated him. Even if she was alive and contentiously well, she had been subjected to targeted violence, and it would make sense to frame Tyler as the primary suspect. He would blame him too.

Tyler didn't care, of course, about being accused of something as pedestrian as an attempted assassination. That he would have happily been tried for. What unnerved him was the possibility that some friend pawing through Julie's possessions postmortem would recognize the fake Bellocq. Because of the things Tyler needed right now, Billy Starkweather's ire was at the absolute bottom of that list.

Sure, he was just some shitheel with a seedy little bookstore, but Billy famously took umbrage at people messing with his merchandise and he had friends in low, low places he could and often would call when he lost his temper.

Like the Barghest Sisters.

Tyler did *not* want those terrors on his ass.

Worse than the thought of pissing off Starkweather was the risk of having his access to the club revoked. Billy's establishment was where you went if you wanted goods moved and careers shaken up: it wasn't like New York was shortchanged on places to congregate, but something about the place made it so everywhere else felt like a pitiful bootleg. It'd be embarrassing to be banned from the club and Tyler was fucking done with being made a fool of.

Tyler took a sip of his tepid coffee. There was one more aspect to Julie's accident that bothered him. What the *hell* did her in? If he hadn't been the one responsible for the fake Bellocq, he might have guessed that. But Tyler knew the grimoire. He'd had it created in Thorne & Dirk's own Document Forgery department. It didn't seem like a big deal at the time. He'd created a lot of cursed documents over the years (both for personal and professional reasons), and the Bellocq should have been just one more. It was designed to encourage misfortune: constant, unyielding, relentless deluges of bad luck, but bad luck the victim always survived. The point was sustained misery.

So, what the hell happened? Maybe he'd been a little too insistent on the depth of misery he wished on Julie when he was having the book put together. He just wanted to teach her a lesson, right? *Right?* There weren't supposed to be any terminal outcomes for her or anyone else. Just a twist on a good luck charm. A nice angel to sing her to sleep. Did the twist get too twisted—?

He sipped again at his coffee. Neither it nor his mood improved.

Before being aware he was doing it, Tyler had taken his phone out and was dialing Eric's number. He answered on the second ring.

"Hi—"

"Don't you dare say my name."

"Right, right," said Eric. "Tick a lock."

"Are you at the bookstore?" said Tyler, marveling over the anachronism. Eric *almost* got being a youngish millennial right. His antiquated style could be blamed on a thrift store fetish, and his love for absolutely prehistoric comics could be attributed to weird parents.

"Where else would I be?" said Eric. "Ask me how much a bookstore clerk in New York makes an hour. We can have some fun figuring out just how much money I have to spend on shit like not working."

Eric sounded just a little hysterical and Tyler didn't like it one bit.

"Honestly, I couldn't care less," said Tyler, wondering if Eric had heard of Julie's situation and was similarly affrighted by the possible ramifications.

"Wow. Thank you very fucking much. What do you want?"

"The Bellocq," said Tyler quietly. The evening had worn the sunlight down to a rich terracotta, which had the effect of making the pitted wood of his desk look more expensive and everything else like a murder scene. "Do you still have it?"

"The original? Sure. Why?"

"Destroy it."

A sharply in-drawn breath. Then: "I don't know if that's such a good idea."

"Are you fucking with me?"

"Not at all. If things go to Hell, as long as I have the real book, I can stick it back on the shelf like nothing happened."

"I'm not sure you heard me," said Tyler, trying to keep his voice level and baritone. "Burn it. Shred it. Eat it. I don't care. Just make it gone."

"The thing is that as much as you scare me, Billy scares me more. If he finds out I'm messing with his inventory, he's going to pull my guts out—"

"Or I'll do it myself."

"Trust me," said Eric evenly. "If I go down, I'm absolutely making sure you land right next to me."

The discussion was beginning to erode what patience Tyler had. He rummaged one-handed through the file cabinet to the right of him, slamming through drawers until he found what he needed.

"I only agreed to equal responsibility on any goods you sell," said Tyler, unfolding a badly creased printout he'd finally fished from a biscuit tin.

Eric's voice turned guarded. "Say that again?"

"I only agreed to equal responsibility on any goods you succeed in selling. All unsold inventory remain—" Tyler tapped at a clause with the nail of his index finger. "—the sole responsibility of the vendor, i.e., you. If you try to snitch to Billy, you're going to have to do it with your mandible on the literal fucking floor."

He didn't have to wait long for Eric to say, "You fucking asshole."

"Always read the fine print, man," said Tyler, leaning back in his chair. It was, to be fair, a dirty trick: an aged cliché so tired he should have been ashamed to leaven it into his contract with Eric. But Tyler was nothing if not petty. Petty and careful. "First rule of business."

"You suck."

"And I still need you to burn that book."

"No," said Eric, rallying heroically. "To hell with that. I'm still taking my chances with Billy. Maybe he'll let me off with a mild dismemberment if I tell him I was *coerced* into messing with his inventory."

Tyler wanted to reach through the phone and strangle Eric.

"Eric," he said.

"I'm serious, Tyler," said Eric. His voice had the frantic animation of a drunk about to throw down behind the dive bar: he hyperventilated through every word, half-giggling. "I'll do it. You try anything and I'll make sure you get double."

Tyler seethed. As much as he hated to lower himself to Eric's level, the man—or whatever he was—had a point. He couldn't fuck over Eric without inserting his head into a woodchipper. So finally, Tyler gnashed out, "How much?"

"To destroy the book?"

"No, to paint my garage. What do you think?"

"A fucking lot," said Eric.

"Ten thousand dollars."

"Ten thousand? It might have been ten thousand before you threatened to snitch on me, you *dick*."

"Twenty."

"I once saw Billy turn a guy inside out just for dog-earing a page in Gilles de Rais's day planner. I mean, intestines and spleen juice everywhere. Twenty wouldn't cover that risk."

"What the fuck do you want, then?" said Tyler.

"A hundred and fifty thousand."

Tyler stopped cold. "You're a fucking prick."

"Last time I checked, so were you. How's it feel, big shot?"

Tyler said nothing for a moment, gathering his composure. "Fine. You win. When the job is done, send me a photo at this number and I'll wire the money to your account."

"Do you think I'm stupid? Send the money and then I'll send you the goddamned photo."

Eric hung up before Tyler could reply, leaving the latter so congested with fury, he threw his coffee mug across the room where it shattered against a side table. Tyler had the resources to fulfill the stupid bargain: a house in Long Beach he could easily mortgage. But he didn't want to. He *hated* knowing Eric held the upper hand, and that there was nothing he could do except wire one hundred and fifty thousand dollars to an idiot who'd probably waste it on one weekend in Vegas.

Still, expensive as the solution was, it was one problem solved.

He needed now to deal with the optics of his situation with Julie. Tyler ran through his options. It had to be something public, indisputably magnanimous, even sentimental. Twee might work well for him here. He had to show contrition but not too much, nothing that could be misread as guilt. Maybe flowers? A drift of yellow roses messengered to her hospital room. Something gaudy enough to be memorable. Sure, Julie would immediately trash them, but people would see the gesture. He'd make sure of that.

Tyler had only just raised his phone to his ear when Annabeth Fall prowled into his office, draping over the chair opposite him—a leg over an armrest, an arm slouched over the back—with a queen's haughtiness and a killer's nonchalance. Before he could say anything, she nodded at his coffee mug shards. "You seem to have lost your coffee."

"It's against the wall. Do you want me to order more? Maybe have them bring up some petit fours and ice cream?"

"Depends," said Fall. She only ever answered to Fall. Any variation of Annabeth was met with an arctic stare until a correction was made. "Does it come with a side of you being competent?"

Halfway through devising a comeback, Tyler gave up, too spent on all the other piling bullshit to engage in a snark-off with an actual child. "What is it you want? I'm busy."

Fall planted both feet on the gray carpet and set elbows on her knees. The half grin she raised came from somewhere other than a human heart, a cold and carnivorous facsimile. "It's the end of the fiscal quarter and everyone's either in meetings or gone home to nurse a headache."

"So what?"

"So?"

"I thought today would be good day to take you on a tour of the forbidden zone."

Tyler glared dully. He wasn't in the mood for any more games. "The what now?"

"Someone shoot me before I can get old," sighed Fall. "The egg chamber. The mating amphitheater. Where the eldritch intend to get down and dirty."

The idea of traveling to some secret subbasement with Fall made Tyler uneasy, and the phrase "egg chamber" left him a little squeamish. But he couldn't say no. Though he *could* prevaricate.

"First thing you do after a promotion is bring a boy to work? Sorry, Fall. You're a little too young for me."

According to office gossip, two years earlier, Fall had enacted a one-woman coup after her boss mistook her for a willing sacrifice. His endeavor to drain her dry left *him* a desiccated husk on the floor instead. Fall then purportedly offed four of her colleagues in the ensuing chaos before the rest fell meekly into line, crowning her as their new lead of Internal Security.

She stared at him, her little half grin unseaming. The flinty boreal gaze went hot with hate.

"Do not," said Fall, "try me."

Fall had a way of looking at people, an intense scrutiny that belied her youth: it scraped skin from muscle, gouged tendon from rib, dug and dug, until there was nothing but the wet and quivering heart of her attention's recipient, bare and vulnerable to analysis. She shifted forward in her seat. Tyler held his breath, belatedly anxious he'd gone too far. He still had the advantage: every atom of the office was booby-trapped with preventives, some of them his work, others the firm's. Any attempt to kill him would have Fall reduced to a clotty spray on his walls before it could happen.

Maybe.

Hopefully.

He glanced with feigned boredom at his computer monitor.

"Well, I guess I don't have any appointments for a while. Yeah. Sure. Why not? Let's go see where management is storing our betters."

Fall leered wolfishly. "*Our betters.* I like that. Let's go."

Without another word, Fall got up and headed for the door, so that Tyler had to trot a couple of steps to catch up with her. He had about a foot of height on her, but it wasn't enough to counter the impatient speed of her loping walk. At the elevator at the corridor outside the directors' bracket of offices, Fall pushed a button for the basement and the two rode down without conversation as the machinery outside sobbed and whined. It only took thirty seconds or so to reach the basement, but when the doors slid open and Tyler stepped forward, Fall placed an arm over his chest like a crossbar.

"Not there yet," said Fall, hitting the close button. After the doors had shut, she used a chunky brass key to open the button panel. Inside, amidst the jumble of wires and connectors, was a single ludicrously red button.

"Push it," she said.

Though he was still suspicious of her, Tyler didn't hesitate. There came a blunt *thunk* of a sound and the elevator took a rattling breath before the back wall screeched upward, revealing a dingily lit service corridor. A wide-set row of halogen lights ran down the curved slate ceiling, like spokes on an alien spine. Staring down the hallway, Tyler wondered if it'd been gored from a single wedge of concrete: nothing delineated wall from floor and floor from ceiling. Fall strode out and jauntily crooked a finger at Tyler to follow.

They took a second elevator—one whose walls were lined with five-inch-thick heavily cavitied gray foam and whose floor was scarred with the marks of metal wheels and heavy objects dragged in and out—to an even lower level in the building—the subbasement. Though as the seconds ticked by and they continued to descend, Tyler began having doubts as to whether they were still on the property. It had been—he checked his Blancpain, just to be sure—six minutes since they entered the second elevator.

"You didn't tell me we were going to Australia," he said.

Fall glanced sidelong at him through lidded eyes. He could see Julie in her expressions: not Julie as she was now, weighted with cynicism, but Julie as she was when he met her those years ago. She had been unbelievably, unconscionably angry then. Julie had blazed, mad as a saint, with outrage at the world and a nuclear want to carve some of that good life for her own. Tyler thought it was the hottest thing he'd ever seen. Not so with Fall.

The elevator stopped.

"We're here."

Tyler followed Fall out of the elevator into a knot of corridors that were much like the elevator—worn and not very clean. There were ducts overhead and dendritic nests of electrical cables along the ceiling. The hallways branched periodically into rooms swaddled in tarpaulin, the material mottled with stains. The lights buzzed in a way that made the inside of Tyler's skin itch.

Fall led him down several flights of concrete stairs where the levels were marked with symbols Tyler couldn't decipher. The katabasis continued until they arrived at an innocuous fire door at the terminus of a very long and claustrophobically narrow passage. It wasn't anything special, but it was violently illuminated by a halo of tungsten bulbs.

"The fuck is this?" said Tyler, shading his eyes with a hand.

"They don't like the light," said Fall.

She opened the door. The insides were not what Tyler had expected. For one, the space was massive: at least fifty yards in length and almost as wide, with groin vaulted ceilings that held a sky of faceless angels. Serried rows of banquet tables, each swathed in indigo satin and mounted with golden candelabras, covered the floor. The air sweltered: it dripped with the stink of lilacs, a perfumed heat that coated Tyler's tongue.

"Weird-ass place," said Tyler.

"You have no idea."

In the middle of the room was a raised circular dais. It was shallow enough that Tyler could see a pressed-tin syllabary of runes tiling the very center of the platform. Above it was a dense curtain of wrought-iron chains and vicious-looking S hooks, not unlike what fell from the ceiling of the rooftop meeting atop the Thorne & Dirk offices.

"Sorry. It's just . . ." Tyler hesitated. "What the hell is that place?"

"It's the mating amphitheater."

"What about all those dining tables?"

"Upper Management are all voyeurs," said Fall with a minute shrug. "It's going to be a whole thing, apparently. They're going to eat and chat as the happy bride and groom get it on."

"Eat *what*?"

Fall laughed. It wasn't a pleasant noise. In lieu of explaining, she jabbed at the room with her chin. "You want to take a closer look?"

Tyler eyed her warily. "Depends. You coming with me?"

His tacit accusation drew out what had to be the first real smile Tyler had ever seen dawn on her face, briefly rendering Fall beautiful.

"Smart guy. That's an extradimensional crosscut into spacetime. Without the proper sanctions, you'd get sucked into an entropic pocket dimension that makes Hell look like your junior prom."

There was something unsettlingly like saudade in her tone.

"Would you have let me walk in there?"

"Definitely. No offense." The smile vanished. In its place was her familiar indolent cruelty. "I just want it to be clear: I don't actively want you to die."

"What about passively?" said Tyler, unable to stop himself.

Fall ignored the question. "I needed to see what kind of person you are. If you're the type of idiot who'd have waltzed into that room, you're no good to me."

"Because I'd be dumb dead," he muttered.

"Not dead," said Fall with an infinitesimal raise of a corner of her lips. "Dumb yes. But also in eternal torment. So, nothing personal. I just had to make sure you were smarter than you looked."

Tyler mulled it over as Fall shut the door and led them down yet another industrial passage. They mounted a spiral of steel and cable stairs into what resembled a warehouse space, this split by a mezzanine held up by abnormally thick pillars, the landing itself barely a rusted wafer. The air there was cooler, if with the aridness of chemical refrigeration. Tyler decided as his heel went *clang* on the uppermost rung of what he hoped would be the last flight of stairs he climbed today that he couldn't fault the cold logic of Fall's methodology, or her pragmatism. Even if he was annoyed at being tested like some summer intern who didn't know his ass from an athame.

On top of the entresol was an empty platform with a quilt of square lights and a bank vault door at the opposite end.

Fall said nothing as she went up to the combination lock panel and keyed in the sequence. What unsettled Tyler was that she made no attempt to obscure the code: she stood in a way that almost invited him to snoop, but after what had happened at the amphitheater, Tyler kept his eyes elsewhere.

He heard a slightly muffled beep and then the whoosh of steam being released as unseen mechanisms cranked apart, turned, let go. Then a protracted groan followed by a nails-on-chalkboard screech before Fall yanked at the lever. The smell that wafted out was sickening: a damp, sweetly fecal mustiness, like dying roses, complicated by the stink of rotting meat. A metal walkway shot from the door into a lightless gloom.

Tyler said, "Another prom night portal?"

Fall shook her head. "No. This is what it looks like: a storage facility."

"You mean the eggs?"

"That's exactly what I mean."

He stuck his head beyond the vault door, still apprehensive. Tyler regretted, not for the first time and certainly not for the last, his spontaneity: he could hold his own with preparation, but like this, he was a sitting duck. There was no turning back, however—Fall had made it clear what she'd do if he exposed any inadequacies she didn't like, which he suspected were arbitrary and myriad. So, he forced himself onto the catwalk, squinting. Nothing happened. It was just a metal walkway. Fall pushed past him and went into the dark, so Tyler followed, less out of allegiance and more out of oversized fear of what might happen if he was caught here alone.

"Behold our betters," Fall said.

At first, Tyler couldn't see anything. Then his eyes adjusted, and he came to realize there was a lusterless glow there, a light that didn't so much illuminate but texturize the darkness, providing a gray-green shape to what laid below. He'd expected something more orderly—clean chicken eggs in neat rows like they were laid out for the world's biggest frittata. Instead, what he found was a sprawling jumble of soft-shelled monstrosities: squat, wet eggs of uneven dimensions, each about the length of his spread arms. They sat in a few inches of a mealy, weakly lambent fluid, which Tyler took to be the source of the stink burning his nostrils.

"How long has all this been down here?"

Fall shrugged. "Decades? Centuries? Ask Upper Management."

"No thank you."

"Exactly."

He said nothing for a long while after that, overcome by the magnitude of the grotesquerie, the sheer fecund breadth of it. There was something primordial to the sight, a beauty that wasn't articulatable, not with his deficient tongue and menial brain.

Tyler was certain if he just gutted himself of those useless implements, he might—

"Easy," said Fall with one hand set warningly on his shoulder.

Tyler ricocheted back into himself. He started to speak a couple of times, stopped, then frowned at Fall, who'd come to stand beside him, her cool amusement a welcome anchor in his sudden confused state.

"They do that," said Fall. "First time I came in here, I wanted to spoon out my eyes and offer them in tribute. It makes things easier when no one wants to fight them."

He blinked drowsily at Fall. It felt like coming out of anesthesia: he was woozy and encumbered by the aftereffects of what had happened, every thought coming apart under their cottony weight. Tyler sharpened up, however, after Fall slapped him.

"Thanks," he said, his jaw cracking as he worked it.

"Stay alert, you useless shit," said Fall as she peered over the rail. "And tell me what you see."

Tyler counted the eggs. When he reached one hundred, he stopped and looked over to Fall. "Way too many fucking eggs for the firm. Thorne & Dirk's a couple hundred people, at best. Maybe a hundred more if you include the satellite offices. There are thousands of those things down there."

Fall chuckled lowly. "Thousands? There's a lot more than that down there."

"What are the extras for?"

"Everyone else, I imagine. Everyone and everything in the world. The Mother Who Eats wants to replace the universe with her offspring."

"What the hell is she going to eat then?" said Tyler, less because he cared and more because it was something to focus on that wasn't the understanding that he'd nearly disemboweled himself for some zygotic horrors. "Her kids?"

Fall shrugged. With all their recent exertions, her hair now stuck to her pale skin in slick ringlets, like curlicues on fresh plaster. Three of the topmost buttons of her shirt were undone, and Tyler could see a froth of embroidered lace. To his surprise, Fall had a killer rack.

"I guess if hamsters will eat their babies . . ." said Tyler, scooting his gaze from her cleavage to her face. If Fall had noticed his perversity, she made no indication, her attention held by the ocean of gametes below.

"I brought you here so that you understand the scope of what we're facing. There's no fighting our way out of it. But if we're smart enough, we might be able to get The Mother Who Eats to decide this is no place for her young to be."

"What would that do?"

"Buy us a few hundred years if we're lucky."

"And if we're not?"

"If we're not, we should, if everything goes to plan, be sitting pretty as new members of Upper Management. Which conveys a certain privilege of Not Being Turned Into Skinsuits."

"You'd fit the role perfectly," said Tyler, sidling up beside Fall.

"What?"

"You're good at sitting prettily."

The profound disgust on Fall's countenance delighted Tyler. It meant she was human, fallible: something less than the perfect apparatus of Internal Security, something he could manipulate. "Are you *flirting* with me?"

"Do you want me to be?"

Tyler wasn't as pretty as Brautigan or the rest of the beauty pageant rejects in Contracts, but he was good-looking: thick-haired and thick-lashed, with the sunken cheeks of a runway model and olive-green eyes stained gold around the pupils, like light through a strange forest. His thirties had softened him, though not enough that it could be seen through the layers of his suit.

"Fuck that," said Fall. "No. You're way *old*."

She pushed away from the rail and stalked out of the vault, her stilettos clicking over the metal panels. Tyler grinned at her retreating back. Fall would not look at him as she locked up behind them, and would not look at him throughout their walk to the service elevator, his every attempt at small talk met with an increasing air of hostility. So preoccupied was Fall in ignoring him, and so focused was Tyler in needling her, neither noticed the ping of a second service elevator arriving until Brautigan shambled out.

"What are you doing down here?" Fall said.

Brautigan didn't flinch. "I was about to ask you the same thing."

"We run security around here."

Fall looked furious. Brautigan—who Tyler last saw being dragged away for torture after he annoyed the Proctor—looked better than Tyler would have expected him to. True, he resembled an animal fed through a meat grinder then put together by someone with neither interest in nor talent for the process. But he was standing and he was walking and when he spoke, the lisp was slight enough to be inconsequential. It was more than Tyler could say for most of Lansdale's victims.

The Contracts director stared at them.

"You might be security," said Brautigan before he jabbed a finger at Tyler. "But he's Excisions. What the fuck is Excisions doing down here?"

"What the fuck do you care, you stitched-up Frankenstein piece of shit?" said Tyler.

"I wasn't talking to you." The nail on Brautigan's finger sloughed off and fell. "Annabeth—"

"Do not call me that."

"—is the one who needs to explain." Brautigan showed his teeth. "What is Excisions doing here?"

"Apologize," said Fall through gritted teeth.

Tyler glanced at his companion. She was thrumming so hard he wondered for a single wild moment if she would vibrate apart. A rill of blood ran down the right corner of her mouth. The tendons of her jaw stood in such vicious relief; he could have flossed with them.

"For what?" demanded Brautigan.

Fall grabbed his collar and yanked. Brautigan was a big man. Easily seventy pounds heavier than the chief of Internal Security and four inches taller. Yet when Fall pulled, he went down like he was so much man-shaped gauze, dragged to eye-level as Fall began to weep black smoke. She fisted both hands in his shirt, snarled:

"Apologize for using *that* name."

"Did you know she ate her mother?" said Brautigan, flicking a glance at Tyler. His eyes no longer matched: one its old radioactive blue, the other a large mauve button.

"Shut. Up."

"She's from a family of cultural cannibals. The oldest inherits the mother's gift by eating her on her sixtieth birthday, taking her name and everything else. But Fall was the middle child, weren't you? Destined to be a nothing. She took matters into her own hands and she ambushed her mother the night before that fateful birthday, and—*gurk*!?"

Of the sounds Tyler would have expected from a dying man, *gurk* wasn't one of them. Then again, he'd never been this up close and personal with a kill—especially not one so imminently mortal. Tyler adjusted his grip on the hilt of his knife and pressed his weight down, while Brautigan gurgled like he was being drowned in custard.

Tyler saw Fall let go and when she did, so did he, allowing gravity to do the rest of his murderous work. Though he kept his expression neutral, he felt cold inside. As many times as he'd fantasized about killing an enemy in such an intimate manner, Tyler had never found the nerve to do so, outsourcing it to those with stronger stomachs. Whenever he was directly responsible for someone else's death, it was still through the proxy of a complicated spell.

Never once had he done anything like *this.*

Brautigan pitched forward onto his knees and stayed there, knelt like a penitent waiting for a god who would never come. The sight made Tyler a little sick and inexplicably sad. For all that he had hated Brautigan, here was a person who must have had friends once. A family. Maybe, a dog or—who knew?—a little hamster in a big plastic aquarium. Tyler wiped his hands on his slacks.

"You didn't deserve that," said Tyler calmly to himself and it surprised him to discover some of it was sincere.

"I could have handled that," said Fall.

"I know," said Tyler. "But he still didn't deserve that."

The tiniest corner of Fall's mouth lifted in reply. He could tell she trusted him as far as she could physically toss him, but it looked as if he was being reassessed, elevated through the categories.

"Anyway, what are we going to do about the security cameras?" said Tyler and if his voice was hoarser, if it broke after every fifth syllable, Fall was decorous enough not to comment.

"I had already set them on a loop when we came down here. No one saw a thing," said Fall. Her gaze fluttered down to the sad mountain of Brautigan's corpse: it was sagging very gradually to the right, what tension that held it upright for those initial moments leeching away with brain activity.

It, thought Tyler, mulling over the pronoun shift. How quickly a person became meat.

"And the body?"

"Easy. We strip him and dump his ass into one of the nutrient vats in the next corridor. That pool you saw in the egg chamber didn't show up out of nowhere."

"What about his clothes?"

"Garbage chute."

"Impressive," said Tyler. "You thought of everything."

His head still swam with the adrenaline of the past twenty minutes, which was impossibly still not the most exciting thing he'd endured in the recent week even if it was the most personally edifying. His pity for Brautigan was mostly gone now, eclipsed by dawning self-pride.

"I've done this once or twice." She reached down, careful throughout to avoid coming into contact with any of the byproducts of the man's demise, to grasp Brautigan by an arm. With both hands around the wrist, shoulders rounded in preparation for a monumental pull, Fall then looked exasperatedly at Tyler.

"Help me?" said Fall.

"Only if you say please."

In a just universe, her magma stare would have steamed the meat from his bones, but all it did was make him laugh softly, pleased anew by the fact he could now, on command, agitate a reaction from her. Tyler sloped up beside Fall, taking Brautigan's other arm. Together, they began dragging his carcass down the hall.

"By the way," said Fall as they turned a corridor. "Julie was shot."

"You don't say."

"Like you wouldn't know. Aren't you her ex?"

He suppressed a grimace. Tyler wasn't surprised even if he had hoped the gossip would have dissipated by now, especially given the care he put into impressing upon his coworkers that Julie wasn't a former lover but an aborted, ill-considered fling. But that version of the story was hardly as titillating as the truth.

"We only keep in contact on a professional level," said Tyler. "And I try not to think about her. She's a welter of bad memories."

"Sure, okay," scoffed Fall.

"Why'd you bring her up?" asked Tyler after they'd hustled Brautigan down a flight of stairs, losing grip at one point, and then having to hurry down to the toppled and slippery mess on the landing, the corpse's inventory of intact bones greatly diminished by its fall.

Fall squatted beside Brautigan, raising his slack face to the halogen light. His right cheekbone was stoved in so far, the eyeball wobbled precariously on the brink of lolling out. Whatever she saw must have satisfied her as she stood up and took hold of an arm again, gesturing at Tyler to do the same.

"Because I somehow doubt we can use a patsy that's laid up in the hospital."

"Oh," said Tyler. "Fair. I guess we'll need to find someone else. Who do you hate most around here?"

Again, the air rang with Fall's unlovely laugh. "You don't have time for that list."

Eventually, they arrived at the mouth of an enormous, gray-paneled chute. Without delay, the pair set upon Brautigan, stripping him with no small effort, his clothes gummed up by the gore from his murder and then all his posthumous injuries. Tyler averted his eyes when Fall rolled down Brautigan's briefs, earning him a scoffing, under-the-breath "prude" from his co-conspirator. He did not, however, shy from manhandling him down the trough, thoughtful as Brautigan's pasty, shit-splattered ass descended into the murk.

"What about Phoebe Garland?" said Tyler. "Everybody hates HR."

"Hmm," said Fall, fussily collecting Brautigan's effects. Somehow, the veritable trail they'd left behind mattered less than his socks. "Not a bad idea. You know what? Yeah. Fuck Phoebe. Let's feed her to the sharks."

Tyler smiled, but only on the inside. Though Fall was way ahead of him on so many of the firm's machinations, Tyler still had his own resources and he'd managed to take some classified documents about the Proctor back to his apartment. Now all he needed was a little time to see if he was as smart and devious as Fall. It bothered him that he wasn't sure, but he'd know for certain soon. Either he'd be dead or, well—On some level the good possibilities scared him as much as the bad ones. But not being dead was a good baseline to work from. He'd hit the books again when he got home. The Proctor had to be good for something besides scaring the shit out of everyone.

CHAPTER SIXTEEN

Sebastian had big dreams. Yes, the Hunter Hotel in Lenox Hill was beautiful, but he wanted a hotel of his own one day: a boutique establishment with complicatedly chamfered ceilings; mahogany and polished steel everywhere, everything sharply angled, sleek as the suit he'd wear as he promenaded from restaurant to lobby to rooftop pool. His guests would be as rarified as the decor: no reality stars, no third-rate moguls. One day, it would happen.

His parents had promised.

That they insisted he first work like the everyman was no problem at all. A few years at the bottom? They'd feel like nothing at all when juxtaposed against his shining future. Besides, he knew his parents had his best intentions at heart. They wanted him humble, they desired him attuned to the needs of the working man so he would be prepared for the egos and the upsets of a staff.

And Sebastian appreciated them for that.

Unlike so many of his peers, he understood the responsibilities of being heir to an unbelievable fortune. Noblesse oblige: a vital lesson. His parents had made amply clear how much the adage mattered: they were new money, not old, blue-collar billionaires who would not see their son forget their modest roots.

He had to admit it helped that he worked *here* instead of a grease-encrusted fast-food restaurant. The hotel teetered on shabbiness: an old bank building resurrected by six friends pooling their fortunes. They kept the original moldings, its Brascolite pendants, the stained glass, the vitrified ceramic tiling, but, thank god, brought in a better class of furniture. The place was elegant, if not to Sebastian's exact taste, and the benefits were superb. Even if he had no actual need for such, the thought was what counted.

Sebastian leaned down to inspect his reflection in the silver cloche. He straightened his tie, licked the corner of his thumb before smoothing the digit over a runaway cowlick. Though only twenty-four, he could already see where and how middle age would transform him, and while Sebastian would miss his hair, he was grateful for everything else. The cheekbones he'd acquired from his mother, his father's imposing jawline. His height. His green eyes. Life was good for Sebastian Hunter and he knew it.

The elevator *ding*ed quietly, announcing his arrival on the fifth floor. He mouthed a thank you—Sebastian took an animistic view of the city around him; it was hard not to. New York felt too alive and impatient to be miscategorized as mere architecture—to the cabin and wheeled his trolley out, the assemblage of plates rattling as he went down the corridor.

He wondered if the guest in Room 248 was throwing a party.

The last few meals he had brought up were relatively minimalist affairs: grilled salmon (with asparagus, steamed), salads (Caesar, dressing on the side), overnight oats (always with sliced fruit but nothing else) and a gleaming carafe of black coffee, never with any sugar, only occasionally with a side order of milk. The repasts of a man invested in his health, who viewed food as metabolic fuel and nothing else.

Today was different.

Room 248 had, quite literally, ordered one of everything—including drinks. There were so many items, in fact, the kitchen couldn't fit it all into a single trolley. While two other servers were en route with food carts of their own, Sebastian went on ahead because he'd been taught to be eager, to lead by example. The common man lurked, awaiting instruction. The elite did not.

An unpleasant odor permeated the corridor, a stink reminiscent of a lake Sebastian had once visited, the water so strangled by algae it no longer had any oxygen, could only produce methane and ammonia. Everything save for the algae was dead and Sebastian recalled thinking it was obscene how green the lake still smelled, how cloyingly *alive,* even with the carrion bubbling under the surface. The pungency in the corridor reminded Sebastian of that, only more expansive, richer, salt-tinged, and old, so very old.

The blond hairs along his forearms stood on the end, the skin beneath pimpled. He realized he was somehow being unnerved by the starched texture of his sleeves, by the sweat beading his collar; that he was, truth be said, not actually unnerved but outright *frightened,* although he couldn't, not for the life of him, pinpoint what it was exactly that spooked him so hard.

He wanted to run.

He wanted desperately to be anywhere else, or at least, his skeleton did: it felt like his bones were agitating to emancipate and escape down the corridor. Flustered, Sebastian nearly marched himself past Room 248, but then he caught himself in time and stopped.

He drew in a breath and counted to eight before he exhaled in a long whistle. *There we go,* he thought to himself. He was calm again. He was all right. In the middle of his affirmations, it dawned on Sebastian that he was trembling too. He looked back toward the elevator, struck by the alarming certainty he should wait for backup, that it wasn't safe to go into the room alone, not for him, not for anyone, and if he knocked now, without other people in accompaniment, it would be the last thing he ever did. He stared at the door.

"This is ridiculous," said Sebastian under his breath before raising his voice. "Room service."

"Ah! Coming," said a muffled voice from inside, and again Sebastian felt himself bludgeoned by terror, his lizard brain no longer subtle about its misgivings. It screamed at him. Every synapse wailed in chorus, every sinew went taut with the urge to run, the impulse so overwhelming, Sebastian nearly succumbed to its entreaty. *Run,* begged his limbic system. *Run now. Run fast.*

Sebastian clenched his jaw. He was a Hunter. While his family didn't espouse unnecessary stoicism, they weren't old money either, and they still remembered what it was like to fight for the wealth they amassed. If Sebastian caved now, he would be an embarrassment to that hardworking legacy.

So, he didn't. He stood his ground.

The door opened. The man inside the room was tallish, six feet or so, maybe half an inch under. He was older than Sebastian by at least ten years, judging from the soft creping at his eyes and the ashing of silver in his hairline. Sebastian wasn't sure. What Sebastian was sure of was that the man was ill. He radiated a feverish heat: a hellish, unhealthy warmth so intense its presence drove Sebastian back a step.

And his eyes, thought Sebastian. Something was very unwell about the guest's eyes.

"Hello," said the man, face spasming into a broad grin. "Come in. Come in."

His voice warbled. He gurgled like an old smoker holding court at his deathbed. Sebastian was suddenly glad for the trolley, glad for the barrier it presented, glad for the chill of the stainless-steel handles under his fingers. It felt like the only real thing in a reality gone abruptly wobbly. He rolled the trolley into the room and said, "How are you doing today, sir?"

"The skin itches. It's dry, this place. The air doesn't agree with me. I don't like it. But it is a body and I am," he cocked his head, as if listening to a radio Sebastian could not hear, "*happy.*"

Sebastian forced a smile to surface, his jabber patched straight from some atavistic corner of him that was committed eternally to professionalism and would have, even in the apocalypse, been able to read out the day's special with sunny kindness. Thank god for its existence, as the rest of Sebastian had crawled far, far into itself to hide. "It might have something to do with the radiator in your room. It dries out the air sometimes. If you like, I can see if we have a different heater—"

The words faded.

Something was happening to the older man's left eye. It was

receding into its socket, moving inward as if dragged into the skull by the optic nerve, and at such a glacial speed that Sebastian couldn't help but think that whatever was responsible for this phenomenon wanted as much of his horrified attention as it could command.

Well, it had it.

Sebastian couldn't look away, couldn't do anything other than marvel at the impossibility of what he was witnessing. His understanding of the human anatomy wasn't comprehensive, but he knew enough to know that what he was witnessing wasn't at all biologically plausible.

I should have run, came the stark and miserable thought.

Deeper went the eye until it was swallowed by glistening pink tissue, slick and shiny as a burn scar.

"Sir," he found himself saying in a faint, dazed voice. "You don't look well. I can go down to reception and have them call you an ambulance."

"No," said the other man, beaming. "No, I'm fine."

Before Sebastian could answer, the emptied socket began to wetly foam with what looked like slugs, like maggots nurtured to an unsettling immensity. Jellied white bodies, smooth as the surface of an egg. They wriggled over themselves, crowding the cavity until it became too cramped to house them, before spilling across the man's face, over his nose, up into his nostrils, burrowing under the lid of his other eye, their writhing forms causing the flap of skin to bulge obscenely.

"Sir, I really think I should go call an ambulance for you . . ."

"No, no. That's fine," the man said. "We are very fine."

No, thought Sebastian, correcting himself. The *man* said nothing. It was the worms who spoke. They smiled at him from the glistening mass now entombing the man's face, each of them crowned now with human mouths, with gums and with molars that did not quite fit. They spoke in unison and with such synchronicity, Sebastian nearly mistook them for a singular voice.

"Sir—"

"No. We think not," said the worms, matching their cadence to his, the Midwestern lilt they'd stolen from the man giving way to Sebastian's New England diction and somehow, that—not the low tide-stink in the air, not the man's manic expression, not the worms saturating his face—was what broke the soap bubble of Sebastian's composure and he heard himself scream, a girlishly shrill shriek that went on even after he'd exhausted himself of breath, becoming at that point a terrified wheeze. His throat burned but he couldn't stop himself. All Sebastian could do was inhale and try to scream again.

Midway through the second attempt, the worms were on him.

"Christ, we need to send someone up there," said Veronica. She was forty-two, a dark-skinned Dominican woman with a cut-glass upper crust accent and manners to match. Only once had she ever copped to taking accent classes to rinse the Bronx from her voice, describing it as an unfortunate evil, the consequence of working in an environment where people insisted on typecasting the boroughs. Her concession to white people's ignorance paid off. Within six months of her graduation, Veronica had been promoted to front desk manager. "That's the third person who called to complain."

The exhausted Chinese woman working reception with her looked over and sighed. "I don't understand. Security said the surveillance cameras picked up nothing weird."

Veronica shrugged. She understood her coworker's frustration. The rich fucks who made up the hotel's primary clientele were often unrepentant divas, eternally outraged by how they weren't being treated with sufficient obsequiousness when any other respectable hotel would have jumped to provide them with towel chinchillas and chocolates filled with caramels, not mint, god fucking shit, didn't they know how to treat their guests right?

Nine times out of ten, their concerns were entirely petty. Just insecure socialites and overpaid techbros wanting to feel important.

That said, three complaints were three complaints and there was protocol to be followed.

"No weird sounds either?"

"Nope. Nada. It's been peaceful all night."

Veronica glanced surreptitiously at the other woman's badge. There were so many hires as of late, too many for her to keep track of. The hotel seemed to hemorrhage staff. Something about the establishment being haunted by violent specters: crying women who wept black ichor as they stampeded after the cleaning staff, headless children in the elevators and the supply closets. Things like that. The stories were bad enough that Veronica, pushed to the end of her wits, had given up and hired an exorcist from Craigslist, a foul-mouthed woman who stomped through the hotel for two hours and then declared the hotel ghost-free.

Worst two hundred dollars of her own money Veronica ever spent. Two weeks after the so-called exorcism, three of their bellhops quit, citing what-ifs, what if the hauntings come back.

Bertha. The Chinese woman's name was Bertha.

"I don't understand. The CCTV should have picked up something. That was the third guest who called up to complain about screaming."

"Maybe it's just someone having really loud sex?" Bertha shook her head. "I don't fucking know."

"Maybe," said Veronica.

Up until his death four years ago, Veronica's father claimed to see visions: premonitions of disasters, mostly. Veronica had not believed any of it but when she turned twenty-two, her father begged her to leave her boyfriend at the time, a well-spoken Ivy League white boy who volunteered at soup kitchens on the weekends. The request was so strange, so uncharacteristic of a man who had made it his life's goal to ensure his daughters understood that their needs should never be subsumed by male wants, that

Veronica had acquiesced. A year later, her ex was charged with the murder of his new girlfriend and their six-month-old. The police said it was a "racially motivated crime."

She wondered what her father would have said about this evening, the guests calling up to say they heard a scream that the CCTVs should have recorded, a scream that all three parties insisted lasted seven minutes exactly. Something was wrong but Veronica wasn't sure what, and it scared her, which did not happen often these days.

"I'm going up to check."

Bertha, who didn't look anything like a Bertha, far too gaunt and hollow-eyed for her country girl name, tilted her head. "Do you have to?"

Veronica paused. Despite the oddness with her father, she wasn't a particularly superstitious woman. In her heart of hearts, she was sure she was an atheist, a conviction she wouldn't ever admit to the rest of her family. But something about tonight, something about how the very last guest had whimpered into the phone, had Veronica convinced she needed to check on the fifth floor or more people would die.

More people would die?

The last part of that thought, its groundlessness, startled Veronica, but not as much as her certainty that this was a true thing, and that someone on the fifth floor was dead in one of the rooms. She briefly contemplated passing the responsibility to someone else and having them check if her hunch was right, but even as the idea flitted through her head, she was overwhelmed by the wrongness of it. It had to be her or she would come to regret this night forever.

"Yeah," said Veronica, coercing herself to smile. "It won't take long. You can handle the front desk on your own, right?"

Bertha winked. "Like I handle my husband's dick."

Veronica laughed, thankful for her crudeness and how the tension broke under their laughter, even if only for a second.

"I'll be back soon," said Veronica and hoped what she would find wouldn't make a liar of her.

❧

Veronica went first to check in on the guests who had complained. Two couldn't remember calling the front desk; one was midway through a threeway and more eager to entice Veronica to join in than she was to discuss what she'd previously heard, another shouted at her from behind a panopticon of laptop screens.

The third guest was different.

"It was the Devil," said the old French woman. She—Honorine—was a frequent guest at the hotel, and one of the few regulars who wasn't an asshole. No one knew very much about her, only that she was a widow and that she made a habit of coming to the hotel twice a year and that, most importantly, she tipped better than her wealthier counterparts, of which there were vanishingly few.

"The Devil, ma'am?" said Veronica politely. "I am going to need more context."

Honorine pulled a long drag from her vape stick, the blue indicator light further harshening a face mostly angles of bone and hachuring. "I know it is hard to believe, but I meant exactly what I said: it was the Devil. The Devil took him."

"Took who, ma'am?"

The woman sighed. "I'm not senile."

"I never said that, ma'am."

"But you are thinking it. Here is an old woman, mythologizing her trauma, making it so she doesn't have to think about how humans can be monsters to each other."

Veronica said nothing.

"I wish you were right," said Honorine, exhaling. The air sweetened with the smell of kush. "It would be easier if I was one of those bible-thumping Baptist grandmothers from the South. But the French, we gave up on God a long time ago. I wouldn't know how to lie to myself like that."

Veronica nodded carefully. Honorine's accent reminded of her of her own: artificial, meticulously cultivated. Under different circumstances, she might have asked her to a platonic coffee so as to find out if the other woman had scoured her voice of its original accent for the same reason Veronica divorced from her own.

"So, when I tell you that the Devil was here, I mean it." Her voice quieted. "I wish I wasn't. That poor boy."

"What poor boy, ma'am?"

"The server," said the old woman, offering the vape stick to Veronica. "The overeager one. Sebastian. The Devil made him scream for a long time."

Shock rippled through Veronica. She'd forgotten about Sebastian, who'd gone up to Room 248 and never come back. Memories flooded her, water swirling into a cistern. Sebastian from a hundred casual interactions at the hotel: at work, sauntering to lunch, talking to the bellhops, interrogating the managers, smiling, obnoxiously aware of the privilege he had; he had big dreams, dreams he never tired of telling everyone, dreams he wanted them all to be a part of because it takes a village to do anything of value. So many memories of him returned with the invocation of his name.

But what the fuck stole them from her in the first place?"

"The Devil is as powerful as God," said Honorine softly, as if answering Veronica's musings. "It's why God drove him away."

"Sebastian," began Veronica. "When you say the Devil made him scream—"

Honorine nodded. Her eyes, which Veronica had originally thought were red from the weed, were bloodshot from crying, the effects of which were mostly camouflaged by matte brown shadow and navy liner.

"For seven minutes. I counted," she said.

"How did you know it was Sebastian?" said Veronica.

Another toke from the vape stick. Honorine folded an arm under herself, queenly in her elegance, the archetypal French woman in her gray silks and black slacks. But now that Veronica knew to look, she saw the flippancy for what it was: Honorine armoring herself against her fear.

When Honorine finally answered, she spoke so quietly, with so little inflection, with the flatness and chill of a mirror forgotten in the winter, that Veronica almost didn't hear, distracted by the low roar of her own pulse.

"I heard him beg."

Veronica knew better than to do what she did next, knew so because she had trained countless hires to treat the guests worshipfully, to put them first, to never question any requests the guests made of them, and to save any disgruntlement they felt for when they were alone and could *safely* gossip about how stupid this or the other guest was. She knew, knew it in her marrow, that what she was going to say was absolutely going to be a faux pas.

But she said it anyway.

"Why didn't you go help him then?"

Honorine studied Veronica with the cool, thoughtless directness of the aged. As she did, a tiny smile curved her thin mouth, an expression that had very little to do with humor. It held a bitterness that Veronica didn't understand and wasn't sure she wanted to. The woman ashed her vape stick, a pointless motion, but she did so with a deliberateness that made Veronica second-guess herself. Maybe there was a point. To this. To the banality of existence. To every question Veronica ever asked herself but never thought to seek answers for.

Veronica squeezed her eyes shut. A dull pulsing ache was growing under the left brow bone. She had migraines, sometimes, mostly the sort which rendered her vision prismatic, but this felt different. Her father had talked about headaches that left him nauseous for days, and Veronica wondered if this birthright had finally caught up to her. The world swam.

"I'm old," said Honorine with frigid contempt. "But I'm not stupid."

She shut the door on Veronica. The corridor seemed enormous in the renewed silence, hostile even. Veronica felt herself watched, studied by something she could not see, a sated predator still deciding if it was in the mood for a possible snack. Quick as it came, the feeling abated. Whatever had been studying her was either gone or distracted by more interesting prey.

The headache worsened as Veronica turned to Room 248. Her eyes watered; the pain was so bad she couldn't draw breath without agony. The air smelled of the sea: kelp and salt and dead things rotting on the shore. She wanted so much to leave, but she'd committed to this. She would see this to the end. Wincing, she took out her key card and touched it to the lock, nearly doubling over, nearly blacking out as her vision flared white. Veronica persisted, clinging to the door handle with both hands, and it took all of her to not collapse, to use her weight as counterbalance so as to swing the door open.

The stench of a slaughterhouse boiled over Veronica. The horrid drone of flies.

Burst intestines. Fecal matter warming on old carpet. Piss and blood, so much blood it almost blunted the sourness of spilled stomach acid. Veronica sank her face into her elbow, gagging. She squinted at the inside of the room, unable to process what she saw, her mind mutinying against the macabre task she demanded of it. Eventually, want supplanted self-preservation and the tableau revealed itself, one detail at a time.

Her eyes went first to the crude door painted over the floor-to-ceiling windows opposite her, a churlish childish effort like a kindergartener's first foray into art. It had a handprint for a doorknob, handprints for hinges; handprints daisy-chained into a winding path to yet another door, this one much smaller and positioned above the shattered flat-screen TV. Veronica ran her gaze up to the ceiling: there were doors there too, a swarm of them, drawn with far less precision, and she couldn't shake the feeling they were meant to depict a feeding frenzy, the doors cannibalizing each other—although it was lost upon her what *that* was meant to represent.

Focus on the doors, Veronica willed herself. *Don't look at anything else.*

If she did, she wouldn't have to look at the bed, wouldn't have to think about the flies jewelling the gore heaped atop the sheets, the hummadruz of their patient feeding drowning the gurgle of the radiator. If Veronica just kept herself focused on the doors, there wouldn't be a need to linger on the little wire frame house someone had made of Sebastian's bones, gristle ribboning from the joints. Or the skin of his face, stretched over the entrance, positioned so the sockets rested where twin doorknobs would have been.

Look at the walls, Veronica told herself. *Count the doors. Think about what you'd have to do to deal with all these flies. Figure out what to say to the hygiene inspector. Think up the email you will draft. Do anything else.*

She inhaled shakily.

Her gaze went anyway to a message scrawled on the ceiling, written in block letters, in pre-colonic detritus, not yet drained of its water:

THANK YOU
FOR OPENING
THIS WORLD

CHAPTER SEVENTEEN

"I've never seen anything like this," said Dr. Kalpakian. He might have been Frunzik Mkrtchyan's perfect doppelganger, with his basset-hound eyes and gloriously Armenian nose, if the actor was a head and a half taller. "You took *multiple* gunshot wounds. The severity of your abdominal trauma made an EMT sick."

"Do I get a medal for that?"

The physician lifted an eyebrow. "No, but I kind of wish I could give you a medal for the speed at which you've healed. We've run X-rays, MRIs, ultrasounds—"

"Yeah, I was there for all of them," said Julie. Though repeatedly assured that Dead Air's machinations had taken care of everything, she maintained a very working-class terror of doctors: one errant diagnosis, and she'd be chased by bills to her deathbed and beyond.

Kalpakian kept leafing through the brick of papers appended to his clipboard, rifling back to the first page when he was done, his expression one of poleaxed wonder. "—and they all show the same thing: you're basically *completely* healed."

"Does that mean I can go home?"

Sarah laid a gentle hand on Julie's arm. Dr. Kalpakian blinked at them twice through half-moon glasses, squinted, and then blinked again, though this third time it was with the rigor of a man hoping to squeeze a migraine out through his tear ducts. With his eyes still closed, he said, "I don't know. I'd like to keep you under observation for a few more days. I mean, your recovery was . . ."

"Magical?" said Julie with schoolgirl brightness.

Kalpakian thumbed through his documents. "That's not a bad word for it."

Thank you, St. Joan, Julie thought. She was sick of being bedridden, bored ill of her confinement. Three days of listlessly switching between the same four channels, breathing hospital air, eating hospital food, was more than Julie could deal with. It was time to go. That or she would be causing problems with considerable purpose. Wiggling into an upright position, Julie beamed at Sarah before she pointed an even sunnier smile at her doctor, who was enraptured by his umpteenth study of Julie's records. "Really, if I'm doing that well, I'd like to go home and finish up the recovery process there."

The doctor removed his glasses and, with a hinge pinched delicately between two neat-nailed fingers, knuckled at an eye. "If that's what you want, I can't stop you. But I *really* would prefer it if you gave us a couple more days."

"Just give us her medications. I'll make sure she takes them," said Sarah.

"Plenty of painkillers, doc," said Julie, increasing the voltage of her smile. "I'm still a weak, fragile thing. Every breath is torment. Every movement is torture, and I tremble in horror at the thought of going to the bathroom."

When the doctor left, Julie turned to Sarah, ready to go with a joke or two about abusing all the Norco she could get, but that went away as she took in how very bruised and tired the other woman's eyes were.

"When's the last time you slept?" she whispered.

"Let's worry about you for now. I'm fine."

"I'll make you a deal."

Sarah crossed her arms, suspicious. "What kind of deal?"

"I'll let you take care of me if you let me take care of you."

"What's the catch?"

"No catch. You just have to do as I say, and I'll do the same for you."

"Does doing what you say involve shit like 'drink vodka and watch cartoons while stoned'? Because if so, I want no part of this game."

Julie erupted into quickly halted guffaws, St. Joan's healing potions apparently having forgotten what web of ligaments surrounded the muscles that allowed human laughter. She winced through a tremble of spearing pain, then smiled wanly at Sarah.

"No tricks," said Julie. "I swear."

"Fine."

"Good. The first thing you're going to do when we get home is take a long fucking nap."

"But I was going to start some soup for dinner."

"A long fucking nap. New York is full of soup that people will bring to us."

"But I'm out of cash and Dan's canceled all my credit cards."

"For once in my life, I have actual money in the bank. I can be soup daddy for now."

And Sarah laughed, sterling and sweet, a sound Julie would have jarred and kept next to her heart for the rest of her life. "You win. Knowing you, we'll be ordering in cheese soup. Or vodka chowder."

"I would absolutely do vodka chowder," said Julie. "Also, have I mentioned that you're absolutely no fun?"

"Once or twice. Let's get you dressed and out of here."

"Yes, Mom."

They arrived at Julie's apartment a little after five and she all but harangued Sarah into the bedroom for a nap. Despite her objections, and several attempts to crawl out of the bed, once Julie convinced her to lie down Sarah was dead to the world in seconds, snoring quietly into the pillows.

In the living room, Julie took her antibiotics with a swallow of ice-cold vodka and laid down on the sofa. It'd be a lie to say she felt safe here, what with everything that had happened, but alone with the noises of her apartment, she felt, at least, on level ground, stable enough to mentally run through the shooting.

There were still holes in the door, but they'd been duct-taped over on both sides, which didn't really do anything, but Julie couldn't fault the gesture. On the floor was the barest stain where Julie had collapsed and then crawled from. She had a fever dream–memory of the police questioning her in the hospital—standard procedure after a shooting, they explained. Even deeply drugged, Julie didn't trust cops, so she played the innocent moron during her interrogation. *Did she know the shooter?* No. *Did she have any enemies?* No, she lied again. *What about money? Do you owe anyone cash?* No, she said, perjuring herself but almost laughing. Did she know the old man who'd also been shot? Nope—another fib, the only one that repulsed her.

I was too easy on Dan, Julie thought. She should have taken him more seriously, should have ignored Sarah's plea to do anything except kill the fucker. What was the line? Forgiveness was easier to seek than permission?

The gloves are off now, rich boy. I'll see you in a vat of boiling shit with little devils flossing your taint with razor wire.

She wasn't sure what she would say to Sarah if asked what her plans were, but that was future Julie's problem. Present Julie was in the unenviable position of dealing with the rippling pain of her injuries. Pity she didn't have the wherewithal to ask Sarah for a preemptive Norco. No way she would wake her to request one now.

But there was some coke still on the table, the barest dusting, which she carded into a line and snorted. Her nerves ignited and the pain burned down to a simmer. Better than nothing. She closed her eyes. Julie ran fingers over the scars zippering her skin, hoping there was a spell still briared in her flesh, but found none. Tomorrow, she would need to find someone who still liked her enough to refresh her inventory. Julie fell asleep pondering who that could be, and her dreams were all about drowning in rivers of blood and someone holding her down with a boot on the back of her head.

St. Joan and Dead Air came over around eight when the two women were awake again. Julie had talked Sarah out of a painkiller and had pinky-swore not to have any more cocaine until she was properly healed. It hurt but a promise was a promise.

Meekly suckling on yet another of St. Joan's concoctions, this one contained in an equine-patterned sippy cup, Julie said: "This actually doesn't taste like dog puke and holy hell, is there cocaine in this? Because I feel great."

"No," said St. Joan with a long-suffering sigh. "No cocaine."

"Could it have some cocaine? I could see that working really well for certain demographics."

"No."

"Fine," said Julie, popping the lid so she could empty it in a gulp. "Will I live forever now?"

Lighting a cigarette, St. Joan said, "Don't make foolish wishes."

She was dressed down for once, comfortably attired in a silk blouse with black slacks, a kitten-bow wreathing the long pale stem of her throat and ballet flats topped with beige flowers. Dead Air sat to her right, dressed in his usual uniform: massive T-shirt and cargo pants, painfully thin under the tents of cotton.

"I have a present too," said Dead Air shyly, as Sarah slid an ashtray meaningfully under the red sun of St. Joan's cigarette.

"What's that, Dead Boy?" said Julie.

"While you were in the—" An agonized terror flashed across his expression. "—while you were out of commission," corrected Dead Air, mumbling, "I had a talk with Them about the situation. Now that They have Dan in Their crosshairs, it became pretty simple. We managed to trace his credit cards to his current location."

"Wait, wait. Do you know exactly where Dan is right now?"

"I don't know if he's there at this exact second," said Dead Air, reddening. "But I do know where his hotel is and I know for a fact he hasn't checked out."

Julie launched out of her thoroughly beaten and grossly understuffed armchair, the floral print so jaundiced from yearslong exposure to its owner's nicotine dependence it was impossible to say what color the fabric might once have been. She was so utterly happy to have somewhere to go and even if Dan wouldn't be right the fuck there the minute they arrived, she was ready to camp out until he rolled into her homicidal arms.

"Someone bring me pants," she demanded grandly. "I'm going to kill a motherfucker."

"Julie, wait," said Sarah.

Julie did not, in fact, wait. She pogoed one-legged to the bedroom, enthusiastically attempting to kick off her sweatpants as she went, buoyed throughout by murderous intent, while St. Joan sank her face into a hand, groaning something about idiot children. Dead Air, for his part, had gone completely scarlet with embarrassment.

"*Julie,*" Sarah tried again, and her friend whirled to face her.

"Dan tried to kill me. Dan clearly is going to try to kill you, Hell, did you forget that he killed poor Mr. Eliava? *Mr. Eliava,*" roared Julie, as if by shouting his name she could impress on Sarah and more importantly, the city, that the old man had been kind, and that he had mattered, and it was a sorry thing he laid now in a coroner's freezer, never to hold his grandchildren again. "Richie Rich has nothing more to lose. He's absolutely going to try to kill you."

"And what about you?" demanded Sarah. "Isn't he immediately going to try to shoot you in the face too?"

"Yes," said Julie, bouncing from foot to foot, like a boxer on Adderall. "But this time, I am ready for him and I am going to turn him into so much chopped brisket before he can pull up the gun."

"Please do not rush into this."

"Texas Chainsawing the motherfucker," said Julie. "I'm going to make his ass into a throw pillow."

"Please!"

St. Joan sharply cut in. "There is a simple compromise."

"What?" said Julie.

"You miraculously regain your knowledge of who shot you, and we hand Dan to the police. Let them deal with the scum."

Sarah studied St. Joan.

"We can't," said Sarah.

"We damn well cannot," said Julie, pantless, a fist propped on a narrow triangle of hip. "Handing him to the cops just means he's going to get a million-dollar-an-hour lawyer who'll plead 'self-defense and, by the way, the bitch he shot was trying to steal my client's wife.' Is that what you want?"

"You do have a point," said St. Joan, adding to the nicotine staining of the apartment with her aggressive smoking. Fragrant plumes of smoke cinctured her head, her eyes flashing silver through the gray haze. "I know you're angry, but don't let your emotions turn you into someone you'll hate."

"I have self-loathing to spare. A little more won't hurt."

"We're trying to help," said Dead Air, eyes still on the undecorated wall. "You're way too shoot-and-ask-questions-later."

"See, that's where you're wrong," said Julie, sidling into the bedroom. She fished the least filthy pair of jeans from the laundry basket and squirmed into them. To her astonishment, it took effort. Recent hospitalization notwithstanding, Julie had filled out under Sarah's tending, sleek where before she'd been mostly ambulatory bone and perpetual hangover. She pinched the flesh along her midriff and marveled at how there was something to knead between her fingers.

Emerging again, she said to the group, "I'm not going to shoot. I'm going to feed him his own entrails."

"But how will Sarah feel watching you turn into a murderer?"

"He doesn't have to *die*."

St. Joan, merciless in her reason, said: "Ask her if she'd be alright with that as an alternative."

"But—"

"Because I know I won't be."

That stopped her in her place. Every atom of Julie sang with a furious want for Dan's suffering. She didn't want him dead but dying for as many hours as she could unstring from the body she'd open from throat to groin. She wanted his tears, wanted him to beg and blubber, as she read him his sins, removing his entrails one after another until he was as hollow as the wretched parody he called a heart. Julie had thought she knew what it meant to hate people, but no, nothing came close to this fire-white, annihilating loathing that blazed through her.

But she knew what it would cost.

Julie stood at the doorway to her bedroom for a minute, nursing a kaleidoscope of violent fantasies, and she resented, truly and unconditionally, how each of them ended with her friendless, alone save for her myriad addictions.

"Shit," said Julie, unwilling to look at Sarah. No doubt her face bore an expression twin to the pitying looks Dead Air and St. Joan were wearing. "No torture and no death. But I'm not calling the cops or anyone else until I have some up close and personal time with the prick first."

"There's my smart Julie," said St. Joan.

"Come on. Let's pay Dan a house call."

❧

The hotel surprised Julie.

"I thought he'd go somewhere . . ." She ransacked her brain for diplomacy as they filed out of the giant SUV, the driver clutching at the nape of St. Joan's sleeve, until she kissed his brow, a benediction that left him weeping. "Less *boring*."

"The insides are much better," said Dead Air. "Or worse, depending on how you feel about goblincore."

"I am the embodiment of goblincore," said Julie, winking.

"More like a gremlin," said Dead Air.

"Dan likes boutique hotels," said Sarah, as way of contextualization, her hand stretched out for Julie's, who twined their fingers like they'd been doing it their whole lives. "He always wants to be the first to try new things. Dan lives for those days he can say, 'I knew about it before the media did.'"

"What a douchebag," said Dead Air. He paused, then added: "He would have absolutely loved this place."

Together, they went inside, with Dead Air at the head of their party. True enough, its interior was grander than its weathered façade, and even if the décor had a whiff of colonizer to it, she had to admit the furnishings had a certain awful moneyed gloss.

Passing the front desk to the gold-doored elevators in the rear of the hotel, Julie braced for someone to shoo them away, but all that happened was an exchange of nods between Dead Air and the managerial-looking woman working the phones.

"The fuck," whispered Julie admiringly to Dead Air, bumping shoulders with her friend, "did you *do*?"

"I fiddled with some public records. Everyone thinks we're the insurance company come to audit the situation."

"We really don't look like we work at an insurance company, though."

"No one fucks with auditors."

Julie couldn't argue with that.

Into the elevators they squeezed and then up to the fifth floor where they stepped out into a flood of low marmalade light. Though hotel corridors weren't typically epicenters of human activity, the long passage up to Room 248 felt eerily quiet, like the held breath of a sky right before a storm. The air smelled rancid with bleach, a stink that grew stronger as they closed on their destination. The door stood faintly ajar. Police tape could be seen through the gap.

"Oh my god," said Sarah at the threshold, her eyes very wide and very carefully bereft of emotion. "Do you think he . . . ?"

"Killed himself?" said Julie as Dead Air pulled a knife from god-knows-where, given his nerd uniform. It went *shwink* out of its hidden sheath, and was very impressive indeed: slim, denticulated along one edge, long as Julie's arm, with the silked burnish of something pathologically waxed. "He's not the type. It might mess up his hair."

"Then why would the police have come here?"

"We'll know in a second," sad Dead Air.

He went inside first, then St. Joan, both flattening themselves against the door frame so they broadened the opening. Julie stepped carefully over the pool of yellow tape, and hesitated. She looked back at Sarah. A stranger might have mistaken her measured expression for calm, but Julie knew it was abject terror wrestled into something polite.

"Sarah?" said Julie, blocking entry to the room with her body. "Maybe you should stay in the hall as watch."

"What's in there?" Sarah said, and Julie was overcome with pride at the steadiness of the other woman's voice, her determined gaze. Sarah might be terrified but she sure as hell was making fear her bitch.

Julie thought on this.

After a moment, she settled on a wary, "Nothing good."

"I'm coming in."

Julie held her hands up in front of her.

"Listen to me, you come inside and you're going to be changed. There's no going back to who you were." At Sarah's darkening expression, Julie paused again, wishing badly for the right words. But it was *so* hard. Ignoring the decreasingly complicated things—this simplification, Julie knew, would be a problem soon, but it was a problem for tomorrow's Julie—she felt for Sarah, Julie remained unused to moving in a pack. Caring for others. Communicating without backchat.

The look Sarah shot her could have cut granite. "I don't care.

Dan was here. He shot you. There's no going back to who I was regardless. I'm going to walk around forever with the knowledge I was the reason you got shot. I—"

"Do not take the blame for that fucker."

"Let me finish," Sarah snapped, actually *snapped,* and Julie would have been lying if she said she wasn't a little turned on by the tigerish gleam of her eyes. "If he's still in there, I want to see it. I am seeing this through to the end, one way or another. I know you think I'm weak and innocent, but I'll handle it."

"I've never thought of you as weak," said Julie, stiffly.

"Good. Then let me in."

To Sarah's credit and Julie's unending admiration of her, she held true to her statement. Sarah did *not* scream, even though her eyes bugged a little, as she made a stumbling pirouette, taking in the charnel that soaked the room. She thrust a knuckle in her mouth and bit down, all the color gone from her face.

Julie followed the orbit of Sarah's gaze, taking in the hallucination of bloody doors scrawled on the ceiling and the walls, so densely congregated in places they weren't recognizably doors any longer, but a muddy splash of dried blood.

Nearby, a couple of chairs were overturned on the floor. A small table near the larger chair had splintered against the wall during the struggle. Beside an astonishingly gorgeous smoke-colored sofa in the middle of the room sat a larger table, its glass top smashed into thousands of glittering shards. Blood splatter painted stripes across the ruins of the table, caking a portion of the shattered glass.

There was so much blood.

More of it than Julie could imagine coming out of a single person. Blood doused every piece of furniture, every corner. Handprints trailed over the sofa, onto the floor, in a sinuous circuit, like the victim was being wielded like a cumbersome paintbrush. Here and there, Julie could see where they'd grabbed at a table leg, or the corner of a pillar, or in a desperate instance, the cable to the now-broken television, in vain hope of escape. It didn't work. The blood stains wended all the way to the bedroom.

Something white was embedded in the corner of the glass-top table, a jarring hyphen of ivory amid all the carnage.

"What's that?" said Sarah, a little weakly.

Dead Air pried the object from the table with his black-gloved fingers. Turning it over in his hand, he made a face, and passed it to Julie.

"What is it?" Sarah repeated.

St. Joan, peering over Julie's shoulder, said:

"It's a tooth."

"Oh god," said Sarah.

Julie flipped one of the chairs upright and sat an unresisting Sarah down onto it. Sarah was breathing hard: panting through gritted teeth, both arms around herself.

"Do you think it's Dan's?" she said.

Julie shrugged.

"Hard to say offhand. We need to keep looking."

With Sarah distracted, Julie snuck into the bedroom. Once, it must have been a gorgeous suite, with its frescoed ceiling, the subtle navy damask on the walls. The bed: canopied with taffeta, mountainous with pillows, a California king that could have fit four Julies with room for tomfoolery.

But as with the living area, the bedroom was gore-stained, soaked to the mattress with the myriad liquids a vandalized body can produce when it has endured sufficient and relentless trauma.

"How many people do you think it would take to make a mess like this?" said Dead Air, craning his head in.

"I don't know," said Julie. "Depends on how talented the person responsible is."

St. Joan looked up from where she knelt, wafting a bottle of vapors under Sarah's nose. "So, Dan killed someone else and ran off?"

"Dan didn't do this," said Sarah.

"How do you know?"

Sarah pointed above Julie's head. "Because he wouldn't have written that."

Julie's gaze followed her finger up to the ceiling and she said, with more calm than she felt:

"Oh, fuck."

There was a message there in what did not look like blood but some kind of thoroughly chewed bolus, a lumpy smear of grayish paste meticulously sculpted into raised lettering:

BLESS THE MOTHER
FOR THIS DOOR

"What the fuck does that mean?" said Dead Air.

"I have no idea," said St. Joan.

Sarah sat rigid in her chair.

St. Joan patted her hand sympathetically. The kindness blew out something in Sarah, who slumped forward, bunting St. Joan's head with her own.

"Could this mean that Dan's dead?" said St. Joan, gently stroking Sarah's hair. "There, there. Death is messy, sometimes, but such is the price some of us pay for life. It won't be your ending if we have anything to say about it."

"Maybe," said Dead Air, his pupils illuminated again by pinpricks of cathode green. "The police have him labeled a missing person. And there's one victim in their records. Guy named Sebastian Hunter. DNA reports say—" He cocked his head, eyes flashing again. "—he's the one smeared all over the crime scene."

"Oh god, they're going to come looking at me," said Sarah. Julie hadn't thought it was possible for her to pale even more, but she did, her complexion waxen and sweat-sheened. "What am I going to say? I have to tell them something—"

"We'll worry about that when it happens," said Julie, coming to kneel before Sarah. St. Joan, forever the astute socialite, backed away to give them space. "Sarah, I'm so sorry about all this. This is unfair and a terrible fucking thing to endure. You've been magnificent about not hurking—"

This earned a tiny fluttering laugh.

"—all over the carpet at this mess, but if you want to leave, no one's going to stop you."

Sarah shook her head. "No. I've come this far. I'm not running out now."

"I really wish you would, though," said Julie.

"Tough shit."

"I wish the cops hadn't fucked up the scene," said Dead Air, pacing up and down the perimeter of the living area, hands at the small of his back. After his third circuit, he gave the sofa an irritated kick. "We could have done spirit scans or death regression on the bodies. Maybe even had a good old-fashioned seance. But they've mucked it up with their bio-signatures."

"We have the tooth, though," said Julie. "That's not nothing."

Sarah raised her head. "What are you going to do with it?"

"Dan's probably a victim. It wouldn't make sense that he'd done something like this. If he was the type, he'd have turned me into Christmas tree decorations when he had the chance. Besides, this shit—" Julie looked delicately around the abattoir. "—kinda involves a lot of special effort. A special kind of crazy, and I think Dan's too boring for that."

Julie held the tooth up to the light: it was a molar, its surface pitted with silver filling. The root was cracked but whole, revealing a pane of nerves. Gingerly, she scratched at the gap, peeling flakes of enamel away. When she had removed as much as she could, Julie rubbed her thumb over the base. Smooth enough, she thought.

"The tooth, regardless of who it belongs to, probably has enough sympathetic resonance to at least give us a direction to point ourselves at."

"Okay?"

"Anyway, to answer your question," said Julie. "I was going to do this."

With a wink and more devilry in her expression, Julie popped the tooth into her mouth and swallowed. Her eyes rolled up in her head before she collapsed tidily atop Sarah's lap.

She woke up with Sarah holding her head in her lap, angling it so St. Joan could funnel into her mouth something that tasted like warm tea brewed from rotten fish. Julie sputtered, shoving back and away from everyone else before jerking herself unsteadily onto her feet.

"Welcome back," said St. Joan.

"Are you all right?" said Sarah.

All Julie could muster was a terse, "We have to get out of here."

"What's wrong? What happened?"

Louder, Julie said, "We have to get out of here."

No one resisted, either shaken by the panic emblazoned on Julie's face or aware enough of Julie's physical capabilities to know they'd be sacked over a shoulder and hauled off whether consent was given or not. Dead Air opened the door a second before Julie charged stiff-limbed through the exit, looking for all the world like a tin soldier on the run. The other three alternately jogged and power walked after. No one spoke: not as they clanked down to the ground floor, Julie the focal point of three identical looks of worry; not in the lobby. Not even after they were in the open and charging through the streets, not until St. Joan performed a beautifully acrobatic, open-palm slap.

It rocked Julie to a standstill, her head still curdled with the vision.

"The hell is going on?" said St. Joan, crossing her arms as she placed herself between Julie and the rest of her death march down Manhattan Island.

"I know what went on up there. That was Dan's tooth. Sorry, Sarah. He's dead. At least, I really hope he is. Holy fuck, I hope he's dead."

Before Sarah could comment, before any of them could interject, Julie said:

"It's my angel."

"What?" said St. Joan, sharply.

"Akrasiel?" said Dead Air.

Sarah said nothing at all, her face that of a woman subjected to too fucking much in too short a time: it held no expression save for a faint, thoughtful pursing of her mouth. She was a taxidermized version of herself, a horrible parody, and even though Julie was half feral with her revelations, she lumbered toward Sarah and folded her in an awkward hug.

"I'm sorry, I'm sorry, I'm so sorry," she murmured.

"Did he suffer?" was all Sarah said.

"No. It was quick," lied Julie.

A hand lightly brushed the crook of her right elbow. Julie glanced over her shoulder to see St. Joan, her expression oblique, and Julie was glad, truly if shamefully, glad for her friend's decorum, because if St. Joan had panicked, Julie would have lost the damn plot. "We need to know more about your vision. I'm sorry, but the aftercare needs to be for later. I need you to focus."

Julie drew a shuddering breath. "It—it—" *It* had been a they previously, amorphous in its gender presentation, but the *thing* that had made dioramas of a waiter's body, had squeezed bile from Dan's entrails to finger-paint the walls, was as far from personhood as Julie could picture. "—killed Dan, and a guy named Sebastian. Poor dude. He was just a waiter. It was wearing—please cover your ears, Sarah."

"How much worse can it get?"

"Please."

"No."

"—fine. It was wearing Dan's skin."

Sarah started to say something, but couldn't find the words. Any words.

"And it's going to keep killing. I don't know who or when or how, but I could feel it as bright as day. It has an agenda. It—there was something about a Mother? About her protectors? I don't know," Julie shook her head like a dog with an earache. "I don't. I know it's going to be bad. I know a lot of people are going to die before it's happy. It's going to murder its way through New York until it gets what it wants."

"What did that message on the ceiling mean?" said Dead Air.

"That one was for me. I know because—" Julie rallied against a wave of nausea. "—it said so. It said my name. My name was one of the first things out of that horror's mouth. I'm never going to be clean again. I heard it—I—"

"Julie, focus," said St. Joan.

"Yeah. You're right. Anyway, fuck. That message was for me. It was a thank-you and a fuck-you note all in one."

"We're really screwed," said Dead Air.

"There's something else."

"Tell us," said St. Joan.

"When I was out, for a minute I was somewhere else. High up in a building. Not a skyscraper, but tall. The walls and ceiling were made of muscle and sinew. The building was alive. The floor shivered and I could feel a heartbeat under my feet. I walked to a window and looked out. I was in New York. Not far from here, I think. I don't know anything else. When I turned, it saw me, and I had to—I had to run."

"What does it mean?" said Sarah.

"I don't know. But the angel is headed there for something. There'll be more killing, but the building is what it wants. And then me."

"I think we should go home," said Sarah, shrugging away from Julie. Some light had returned to her face, for all that it was cold and foreign in its chill. "We're not going to figure this out here."

"Sarah is right," said St. Joan. "We can't talk properly out here. I'll get us a cab."

While St. Joan went into the street to hail a ride, Julie and Sarah waited together, neither able to look the other in the eye.

After a tortured minute, Julie said raggedly: "This is my fault. I brought the thing here. Dan is dead because of me. I'm sorry."

Sarah pressed the heel of a palm to an eye and said, "Could be mine. I can't tell you how many fantasies I've had of Dan just dropping dead. Dan having an aneurysm in his sleep. Dan getting hit by a bus. Or keeling over from a heart attack while he's cheating on me for the fiftieth time . . ."

"That's over. He's over. Forget him. No one is ever cheating on or hurting you again," said Julie, and Sarah gave her a look that was absolutely, one hundred percent worth getting shot for.

Back in Julie's apartment, the Bellocq grimoire laid splayed on the coffee table, ignored by all four of them, for which Julie was glad. She was grateful too for their comfortable banter, and how easily Sarah slotted into the group dynamics, as at home trading jibes with Dead Air as she was interrogating St. Joan for fashion tips. It was wholesome, and it was quiet, and just what their badly frayed nerves needed. Julie would have signed herself into a nunnery if it would mean this would be her forever.

Eventually, St. Joan rose, declaring it time for her beauty sleep, and Julie winced at the thought of the uneasy dreams she knew they would both have that night.

"I'm sorry," she said.

St. Joan only kissed her cheek and smiled, sphinxlike, taking an oblivious Dead Air with her to leave the women alone.

At that point, Sarah was curled asleep in a corner of the sofa, knees tucked to her chest, her hand for a pillow. The kittenish pose was cute, but it made Julie wonder how much of it was from living with Dan, how she'd been trained to be small, to take up as little space as she could, and a wet red fury grew roots in her again. Maybe, when this was over, she would bring his spirit back and stuff him into a snow globe for Sarah.

She cleared the coffee table as noiselessly as she could and brought in a pressure cooker from the kitchen. From her armoire, she took ingredients: powdered rib from a dead thief, a pigeon foot, and more esoteric things still, things she hadn't a name for and would not name for fear it would stir whatever slept in them. These, she plunged into her pressure cooker with chicken broth and frozen trotters, the collagen a bribe. Julie replaced the lid and sat back to wait.

It smelled . . . *good,* which was in part the point: tracking spells were best when built on the back of a lure. Sarah woke as the contents burbled under their glass lid, a drowsy smile on her lips. She stretched like a cat, yawned.

"Are you making dinner?"

Julie shook her head sadly. "Sorry, no such luck. I'm trying to track down the an—Akrasiel with a spell."

Sarah swung bare feet onto the floor. "How does it work?"

"Well, now that everything is cooking right . . ."

"Wait. Is that your pressure cooker?"

"Uh-huh? It's not like I use it much."

"*I* use it," said Sarah, sleep losing its hold on her. "I—what did you put in there? Do I want to know? Wait, I don't think I want to know."

Her head twitched back, as if grazed by a passing bee.

"Shouldn't you be using a cauldron?"

"That's quite an assumption."

"Well?"

"I'll have you know that you're making me relive terrible

memories of pawning my cauldron. My poor beloved cauldron. Handed down to me from—"

Making a face, Sarah said, "Fine. But leave it in the sink when you're done and I'll sandblast it to hell and back."

Julie freed a silver teaspoon from a pocket and waggled it at Sarah, unnerved by the domesticity. It wasn't that she had developed a sudden dislike for it. But after what happened with Dan, she felt like a cuckoo, gorging herself on warmth she had cheated her way into. "Do you want me to tell you about the spell?"

"Yes," said Sarah, propping her elbows on her knees, chin in the open bowl of her palms, every inch the attentive and bright-eyed student, despite the drinks they'd had earlier.

"Now that everything is boiling, it's simple." Julie removed the lid and stirred the spoon into the broth until the silver melted into a concoction: a brief freckling of light, quickly cataracted by fat. "I drink it."

"That can't be sanitary."

"You've seen me put weirder things in my mouth."

Sarah's mouth fell open. Julie, for lack of more eloquent follow-ups, shook jazz hands at her friend, which led to first a disbelieving little snort and then, when her brain caught up, loud braying laughter.

"No comment."

"True though."

And that got Sarah laughing for a solid thirty seconds again.

When Sarah finally subsided, Julie looked back to the pressure cooker. A metallic tang now undercut the rich, meaty smell. With care, Julie went back to the kitchen and found and rinsed a ladle, before she returned to sit cross-legged on the floor. A greasy lather had formed over the surface. It was time.

"Are you really going to drink that?"

"Bottoms up," said Julie.

The elixir tasted very much like raw meat, pureed and forgotten at the back of a fridge. It reeked of decay, a coppery unpleasantness that had Julie gagging within the minute. But Julie would have gargled daily with the potion if it meant any result but the one she was given:

"Fuck fuck fuck."

"What happened?"

"What happened was I saw my own face." Julie blinked. The recursive effect of staring into versions of herself was giving her a migraine. "My tracking spell is showing my own damn face in my own damn apartment."

"Wait, but that doesn't make any sense—"

"No, it does. I gave my blood to bring Akrasiel into the world. It must still have some of my DNA in—"

Julie kept her eyes shut. The endlessly caroming echoes of her thoughts made it nearly impossible to focus. She gnawed her lower lip in frustration, the spike of pain thankfully enough to recalibrate her for coherent speech.

"—It's part of me, I guess? Which isn't a surprise. But still."

"Does this mean you can't track it?"

"I don't know," admitted Julie as arms came to encircle her shoulders, and she hated how much comfort she took in it, and in the fall of Sarah's hair over her face, the sandalwood scent of her. *Someone who wasn't trash would have set boundaries*, she thought wretchedly. "But it's too late to figure out anything right now. How about we get something from the bodega? I'm starving."

"Me too," said Sarah running a slow hand through the other woman's hair. Julie tried to hide the silly smile it elicited, but gave up and just beamed at her.

❧

At Esoteric Unlimited, Billy Starkweather—a lean man in cowboy boots, a crimson checkered shirt, a denim jacket, and back-brushed black hair he kept in place with so much pomade the air around him practically shimmered with the smell—went over the book inventory, hoping that the store had moved more stock than the sales numbers suggested. He found no such pleasing discrepancies as Eric was stacking boxes in the storeroom, but something did catch his eye. Billy checked the shelves twice, discovering what he sought close to the end of the second inspection, hidden behind a stack of rotting Satanic Bible paperbacks kept there for tourists.

"Eric?" he bellowed, sliding his find into his jacket.

"Are you talking to me?" was the response, and a short crash, a muttered curse.

"Can you come out here for a minute?"

"But you said—"

"I know, I know. But I need you to come out here."

"Fine, okay. Just give me a minute."

Billy did not, in fact, give Eric the requested minute. He was on his feet, at the curtained doorway, a hand raised to brush aside the beaded tassels when Eric appeared.

"What?"

He tacked on his broadest, sunshine-iest smile, a smile that would have sent wiser and more informed men sprinting for the hills. "I was just going over the inventory and noticed that the Bellocq grimoire is gone, but I can't find a sales ticket for it. Do you know anything about this?"

Billy had to hand it to Eric. He *almost* got away with it.

"We're going to play a game," said Billy. "You know how much I love games. Card games. Games of dice. Board games. Remember how much I love Catan? Of course you do. Today, because the day is slow, we're going to play a nice game of 'Eric gets five lies to convince me, Billy Starkweather, that he did well by the grimoire.' Are you ready?"

"Billy—"

"Where's the grimoire?"

"I sold it."

"You didn't write down the sale, though."

"I didn't? Could have sworn I did."

"First lie," Billy tilted his head. It was a slow day, and he was bored: no harm seeing how much of a rope Eric wanted to hang himself with.

"I remember the sale now," said Eric, rubbing his flylike grippers together. "No, yeah. I forgot. I had meant to write it down but the client had a civilian with her, and I got distracted by that."

Eric spoke with the easy confidence of a small-time con man, his timbre and swagger such that Billy couldn't help but admire him a little. Really, it took guts to try to put one over on someone like Billy, especially in the face of an undisguised threat.

"Uh-huh."

"Because she was a human. You know they make me squeamish."

"Uh-huh," said Billy, and smiled as he watched Eric tighten the proverbial noose.

"Yeah, well." Eric flicked his gaze to the rectangular bulge under Billy's jacket. "But you're different. I meant regular humans—"

"Uh-huh."

"Anyway, it was Tyler's ex who bought the book."

"Tyler's ex?" said Billy, who very much delighted in other people squirming.

"Yeah, the loud one."

"Uh-huh."

"Uhm, her name was Julie. Julie Crews?"

"Uh-huh."

The minute shift in Eric's voice told Billy that Eric had finally cottoned on the fact he had let himself be walked to the site of his own execution.

"*She* bought the grimoire?" said Billy, still with his placid smile and unperturbed tone.

"Uh-huh." Eric's eyes went again to Billy's jacket.

"How much did you get for it?"

"I just let her take it on credit. You said she was good on that."

"I do say things sometimes." Billy paused. "Did you get a down payment?"

"N-no. I think that might be why I didn't record the sale. Whoops."

Billy ran one hand through his thick hair and held some shredded pages in the other. "Well, that's terrible. No deposit, and a Bellocq torn up like a dead bunny on my shelves."

Eric hung his head.

"What the hell is going on?" said Billy.

"I—I—"

Billy turned the book over. A couple of chewed up pages floated miserably to the floor. "It's the real Bellocq. I can smell that. But why destroy it unless you were in a panic?"

"No. I—"

"You palmed off a fake Bellocq, didn't you? And you were going to sell the real one yourself. Isn't that right?"

"It's not!"

"Fake grimoires can be dangerous things. Especially for me. Whoever faked it could leave out some spells and fuck around with others. People get bad results from my books, they come asking questions. Selling that fake one and destroying the real one fucks with my reputation and soon, no one wants to buy their books from Esoteric Unlimited and that pisses me off. You know why?"

"No?"

Billy grabbed Eric by his shoulder.

"Because I can't die, I can't be free of this shop, until I sell every single book in here and if no one buys books anymore then I'm fucked. Truly fucked. Can you grasp how fucked that would be for me? And how it is for you right now?"

"I'm sorry—"

"I've been selling books here for fifty years," said Billy, thirty-five years old in every feature save for those terrifically ancient eyes. "I don't want to be doing this for another hundred years just because the customers have gone gunshy. Am I making myself clear?"

Eric said nothing.

Brightly, Billy said, "Hey. It's almost your lunch break. Want to play another game? Winner gets the bookstore *and* the bar."

It was here that Eric's nerve, stretched to a garrote tightness, went *twang*. He lurched drunkenly past Billy, shouldering his boss aside with neither excuse nor grace, an animal with the death of its pack in its nose, all instinct as he fled into the street outside. Billy watched him stumble over the pedestrian crossing and down Bowery, accelerating as he went. He waited until he could no longer see Eric's back before he went to the old-fashioned rotary at the counter and dialed a number.

"My darlings," he said when the person on the other end of the line picked up. "How do you feel about a hunt?"

CHAPTER EIGHTEEN

Albert Winterson was learning to bake the day he died. The bay windows of the kitchen broke the light into thick golden slabs, quartering the dark wood table on which Albert had meticulously laid a medley of pastel bowls and measuring cups, a caravan of ingredients still in their packaging. Like his wife Clarice, Albert never jumped before he was prepared. He needed to know the whys, the hows, the whens, every variable that might contribute to the outcome of his decisions. As the old aphorism went, knowledge was power. The Winterson family saw this almost as their motto.

He frowned at the decrepit recipe book and the crabbed handwriting spilling over the page.

His mother had been a prolific baker while she was alive, and an accomplished one at that. Often, Albert joked it was his mother Clarice had wanted to wed, their early courtship having orbited around those weekends when Albert's mother would fill the old house with chiffon cakes and cupcakes and trays of dense fudge. After her death and the onset of middle age, the sweets in the household tapered to the occasional shortbread.

But Albert wanted to make the upcoming anniversary special.

Part of this was because he had been married to Clarice for twenty years. To Albert, this was one hell of a milestone, worthy of substantial celebration. The other reason, the more important one, was he wanted to have ammunition for when he popped a question he'd wanted to ask for two decades.

Albert wanted to know what his wife did for money.

He knew Clarice worked at the legal department of a firm called Thorne & Dirk, but that was the extent of it. He had no idea if she was a lawyer, a paralegal, an accountant, a director of human resources. When he proposed to her, Clarice gave him a conditional yes: she would agree to marriage if he vowed never to ask questions about her work. Albert agreed. It had seemed like such a small fee for the future they would have.

Twenty years later, the question, which had been like an infinitesimal splinter lodged in his flesh, an irritation to languidly ignore, had gone septic. Each time he kissed her goodbye in the morning, greeted her as the owl-light silvered the bright glass of their home, he felt the necrosis spread. Why didn't she want to tell him what she did for a living? Was she embarrassed by it? Was she ashamed? Honesty was a cardinal feature in their relationship. They told each other everything.

Except this.

Twenty years, and Albert still had no idea what his wife did eight hours a day, five days a week.

Absently, he plucked an apple from the stainless-steel mesh hammock holding their fruit, and raised it to the light. Its skin carried a heavily shellacked gleam. Albert grimaced. In this, he and Clarice were eternally divided. Albert hated mass-market produce, both because of its effect on the planet and because of how toxic it was to the human body. Years ago, he'd read a study on how the shine Clarice found so pleasing in her fruit was, quite literally, a resinous insect by-product. Albert brought his research to her, hoping she'd see his point. Clarice laughed in his face.

Because they were husband and wife, the two arrived inevitably at a compromise. They would each buy their produce and keep their acquisitions separated. In a house as big as the one they owned, this was easy, a solution that had functioned perfectly up until now. It bewildered Albert to see one of Clarice's apples in *his* bowl, the fruit red as meat on a bone, obscene in its plasticky luster.

He set the apple down, frowning, worried this might be the first sign of dementia in his wife. They were both getting up in years. As much the idea dismayed him, it wasn't an impossibility. He would bring up the topic with her. Not now, not on their anniversary, but soon.

Deep in his own thoughts, Albert almost didn't notice the apple move. It was only when it smashed itself on the floor, a noise like an infant skull concaving, wet and sudden, that Albert jolted a look in its direction. Half a beetle dragged itself from the mess of pulp. Albert watched, dazed, as the insect tottered along, its antennae warbling erratically, first in one direction then another, and it wasn't until it turned its back on Albert that he saw how the beetle's carapace had been emptied, like someone had reached into its chitin and scooped out what they'd found there.

Albert shuddered. He had heard of ants in Southeast Asia that would live on for minutes on end despite decapitation, but this didn't feel like that. This felt like torture, like he was bearing witness to an insect's private hell, a conjecture so utterly ludicrous he laughed nervously into the quiet.

The beetle continued to move as if under some strange influence. Albert continued to watch.

It took another minute before it dawned on him that the beetle was drawing something—a door.

"Jesus Christ," said Albert, meaning it for the first time since he was eight and still awed by the hope for grace. Disgust poured through him. Almost unthinkingly, he lashed out with a foot, slamming his heel down into the insect. It crunched to a warm paste and Albert, panting heavily, found himself scrabbling to peel the defiled sock from his flesh, flinging the scrap of cloth across his kitchen. He'd killed bugs before. Hundreds of them. Spiders, wasps, beetles galore, that whole milieu of common household pests. Never once had the act or the consequences of such an act repulsed him.

He looked down at the door at his feet and thought to himself, with the dispassionate lucidity of the terminally ill: *I am going to die today.*

Before Albert could interrogate the origin of that macabre notion, the doorbell rang, startling him. Were they expecting a delivery? There was no chance it was a neighbor, a family member, dropping by to pass on a casserole and some gossip. The Wintersons were fiercely protective of their privacy, Clarice especially, and anyone who had their address knew far better than to show up unannounced.

Albert peeled himself from his stool and padded quietly to the front door, illogically afraid of being too loud, of divulging his presence before he could ascertain who was waiting to enter his home. His heart pounded so loudly he could feel its reverberations in the soft flesh bridging throat and jaw. Albert swallowed. This was absurd. He was a fifty-one-year-old man, whose only underlying condition was mildly raised cholesterol levels, and one who'd spent a good thirty years steeped in the physicality of martial arts. He averaged a five-minute mile. Albert was fit and if there was a vagrant looking for trouble on his doorstep, he absolutely could handle it.

The doorbell rang a second time.

Suddenly, Albert felt every year he had lived, every broken bone, every arthritic joint, all the ways in which time had diminished him. He felt old and fragile, like a tenuously placed ceramic, one on the brink of shatter. And he felt foolish. Foolish for having the temerity to believe he could overpower whatever waited on the opposite side of his front door. But Albert was too old, too much of his own person, to be governed by self-doubt. So, he opened the door.

"Hello. You are, ah, *involved* with someone from Thorne & Dirk, correct?"

A tall white man stood at his doorstep, a black New York Yankees baseball cap doffed and held to his chest, his posture slightly apologetic. He was grinning.

"That depends on who is asking."

The stranger clucked at Albert. "Bravado. I loathe it. So much. I don't know why your species insists on it when truth would be easier. *I can smell her cunt on your breath.*"

Whatever other faults Albert possessed, a lack of loyalty to his wife was not one of them. He was a husband first and foremost. When he vowed to love and honor her until death did they part, Albert had meant it, and would stay true to this vow until his dying day. The great irony of Albert's life, however, was that Clarice would never know any of this.

"Get the fuck off my property."

The man laughed. "No. I don't think I will."

Four miles from her house in the suburbs, Clarice Winterson realized her husband was dead. *Dead* dead. Not dead like when she'd discovered him on the floor six years ago, his heart stopped, his spirit caught in the beartrap of her wards. Not dead like he was in the car accident they'd suffered on a road trip through Tuscany, when a fallen telephone pole bored a hole through his skull. Dead as in beyond any capacity of being retrieved. Dead as in irreparably gone. As in erased, eaten, elided from the cosmos. Even as Clarice wrestled with this revelation, she could feel his memory eroding, becoming fine-grained, becoming nothing. His face, the bones of his hands, how they'd felt under hers, the leather of his woodworker palms. It was fading.

Clarice bayed her grief until her voice broke.

This was not fair. She was promised different. When she auctioned her soul, it was for the guarantee that her natural lifespan would never endure disaster. What was the point of *any* of this if the things that mattered to her could be so easily destroyed? She screamed again: convulsively, a torrent of noise so loud and so anguished the windows should have splintered from their fury. It was pointless, she knew. But it was something to do that wasn't crying her heart out.

When she was done, Clarice left her car and stepped into the chill, sweet-smelling night. She raised her gaze to what little sky she could see through the dense canopy, the firmament still that livid indigo of a heaven straddling the city. The moon was nowhere to be seen. If it had been, Clarice would have wanted words.

She breathed the cold deep.

Reality bent around Clarice, belling outward first, before spasming tight around the woman, so for a second it might have looked to a passerby as if Clarice was corseted by reflective silk; couture at its most experimental. Then, as malleable, as molten as it initially appeared, what had wrapped itself around Clarice lost its oiled gloss, calcifying instead into a material so brittle it began to disintegrate even as it formed. Where the cracks formed: a venous maelstrom, furcating and multiplying, going up, up. Where they flowered, light bled through, a grayish-green effulgence, grim and terrible and gorgeous, like the dawn of the last day of creation.

Home, thought Clarice to the brilliance. *Bring me home.*

And snapped her fingers.

The world shattered.

When it re-formed, Clarice stood in the vestibule that connected her living room and kitchen, a narrow hallway looping out of view to the stairs leading to the second floor. Her wards were gone. She could hear their ruin—strobic, glimpses of a slaughterhouse, of eager hands rending them, mouths feeding, a miasma of rust—in her mind.

In another timeline, Clarice might have been incensed at the vandalism, but all she felt was exhausted, almost dizzied by her own fatigue, her debility a bone-deep, broken-backed, bitter, bilious weight pushing her down, compelling her to huddle on the floor and weep. But Clarice would not allow herself that yet. There was time later to hurt.

She fisted a lean hand, the only outward sign of her distress.

Clarice strode then into her living room, chin raised in defiance, determined she would document everything she saw there without embellishment, that she would make an inventory of the wrongs committed against her and hers before she outlined a plan for retaliation. She would treat this as a work assignment; she would not care. She would be as her namesake. She would not *break*.

What Clarice saw made her scream anyway.

Her Albert, her husband, her beloved of twenty years, her compass, her everything, dangled from the ceiling fan there. Clarice knew it to be him because his face was intact, innocent of even the mildest stains. He gawked eyelessly at his wife, his widow, while a many-legged thing, like a silverfish, if silverfish had plumage spun from red tongues, crawled out from a vacated socket and into Albert's slackly open mouth.

His torso, though, was nearly unrecognizable: honeycombed, eaten to a papery transparency, nothing but skin and eggs, pill-shaped and nacreous, snug in their chambers; Albert resembled a hive, a wasp nest soldered to a dismembered mannequin, his lower half excised and discarded atop the sofa, leaking fluids over the amaretto-colored velvet. The hyphen of his spine, licked clean of the blood which soaked everything else in the living room, shone like a taunt.

A message sprawled over a wall:

BLESS THE MOTHER
FOR THIS DOOR

Brautigan was slowly dissolving in a nutrient bath at work when his family burned to death. He had two sisters (one he liked, the other he did not), a brother with a feeble constitution (of their extended clan, he was the only one who shied from the bucolic work of the abattoir), one living parent (his mother), aunts by the dozen, their brood in tow; no uncles. The men of his lineage rarely survived to old age.

Were there an afterlife where they all could converge, they might have come together with Brautigan to discuss how gentle his death was compared to their own, how painless in its efficiency, so very different from being cooked alive. It took seven hours for Brautigan's family to die, slow-roasted in their skins, when it should have been a quick death after their nerves were charred black and their lungs soaked through with carbon monoxide; it should have hurt *less,* at any rate, given none of them had any receptors after the fourth hour.

But it didn't and it was Brautigan's fault.

"There you are," said Lansdale, voice chilly, his grip on the anathema tightened until the horn grip ate into his skin, pressed against bone. "I've been waiting."

The figure, a cut-out silhouette framed against the glitter of New York, cocked its head. Neon haloed the frayed rags that its flesh had become, dangling flags of skin trailing from wrist and jaw. Lansdale saw a flash of bloodstained molars, gleaming from the hole canyoning its cheek. It touched fingers—these were stripped entirely of muscle, gnawed to their ivory phalanges—to the gaping wound, and trilled an ingenue's champagne-fizz laugh.

"Have you?"

"You killed Winterson's husband."

"Did I? Ah. I suppose I did. Hahaha. To be honest, I didn't want him to die. He slipped out while I wasn't—do *not* fight me, I have told you, it does nothing but make you feel pain—paying attention. But that's alright. That is—in the past? Yes. The past. Time is slippery for me. Shall we talk about your *siiiiiiissster*?" The figure glided across his apartment, its grace inconstant; it reminded Lansdale of footage from a damaged VHS tape, seamless when it wasn't stuttering forward, always start-stopping in bursts, a stop-motion nightmare. "She's a very nice girl, isn't she? She knows nothing of this, of you. This life of yours. How you'd let The Mother Who Eats devour her if she asked."

"What have you done with my sister?"

By way of answer, the creature merely tittered.

Lansdale did not flinch. Another man might have, but Lansdale spent sixty-eight years in Afflictions, a department prone to the cannibalization of the weak-stomached. Still, what a strange choice of tools on Winterson's part. He'd never known her to favor ugly things such as this. Then again, Lansdale had never known her as a widow. He understood intimately how transformative death could be, how turbulent those initial days were, and it'd only been hours—the clandestine enchantments he'd stitched into the masonry of her house were sadly imprecise; it might have been less time than that, it might have been more, he would never know for certain—since her husband's tortured end. Winterson was deep in the well of her grief.

"If you're here for Winterson's pound of flesh, I wasn't responsible for his death."

"I'm not—I'm not—hahaha, *her* creature."

"Then what are you?"

The figure halted atop a fingernail sliver of moonlight, its face obscured, the rest of it bared in the sodium glow. Lansdale studied his adversary. Scab-crusted, necrotic, whatever blood it had remaining cooled to a sludge-like black under its decaying skin. It seemed to totter on fawn legs. A brackish, curd-like fluid trailed down its right thigh, smearing over Lansdale's floors. It was dragging something.

"Forgotten," it said. "Empty. Starved. I am so hungry. I waited, and I waited, but she wouldn't die. She was supposed to die, and I was to feed on her carrion. This was the promise. But she would not die, and I'm starving. I've been hungry for eons."

The figure twitched closer.

"What in the holy fuck are you on about?"

When Lansdale was a boy, his mother flung herself from the roof of the high rise they'd lived in—him, his parents, the woman his father had married in secret, Lansdale's half sister from that union. Their home had been a cramped one-bedroom, with the two adult women sleeping on the creaky futon Lansdale's father scavenged from the nearby landfill, and Lansdale and his sibling on bedrolls beside the couch. How such a bizarre arrangement came to pass was a mystery his parents dragged to their respective graves. But it was unlikely to have involved his mother's consent. Though she left no note, no palliative message to assure her son that her death wasn't ever his fault, Lansdale knew, even then, it had to do with the other woman, who was prettier, sweeter, more eager to demean herself for their shared mate.

Either way, his mother had screamed as she plummeted to the asphalt below, and every night after that, Lansdale would hear it in his sleep.

The figure, who Lansdale had thought would advance upon him, was alone and, however hideous, all talk so far. The figure reached into a shadow beside the sofa and lifted a bundle. A vaguely person-shape bundle held in one outstretched hand.

"What is that?" Lansdale said. An intake of breath. "Is that—"

At that, the figure spun abruptly and flung the bundle out of the window, shattering the glass. And as the shadowed object began to fall, he heard again his mother's scream tearing out of his sister's throat.

For a fleeting heartbeat, Lansdale was nine again, in the parking lot, a red ball in his hands, and he was watching as his mother hurtled toward the blacktop, watching as she hit the ground, watching as her head *burst,* and the sun was warm on his shoulders, and it seemed impossible this was his mother, dead on impact, demolished so thoroughly the mortician wouldn't touch what was left and Lansdale's father had to incinerate her remains himself, and—

He ran for her. He ran for the window even though he knew that there was no point and there would be no way to stop his sibling from plunging through the twenty-third-story window to her death. Lansdale almost did not care as the thing in his home grabbed him and flung him after her, the pavement barreling to meet him, like a mother rushing to hold her long-lost child.

CHAPTER NINETEEN

Julie woke up screaming.

She did not stop until Sarah rushed into the bedroom and gathered her into her arms, and Julie could press her face into her collarbone, and she kept screaming for a few more minutes anyway, because terror of this magnitude had too much momentum to be stopped on a dime.

"What happened? Jesus, Julie. Breathe. Talk to me."

"Akrasiel," said Julie when she could finally speak again. "I saw it. I saw Akrasiel kill—an old man? A family; it burned all of them. They didn't *die,* Sarah. It kept them alive. Then a man, a young girl. Thrown from a building. I saw their skulls burst. It made sure I was watching. I think—I think—"

"It wanted you to know?"

Julie levered herself reluctantly from Sarah's embrace, using her arms as barriers: she needed the distance. Otherwise, she would embed herself in Sarah's lap and never move again. If they survived this—when emotions had tempered, and there wasn't the convenient aphrodisiac of a high-risk situation—the two of them would need to talk about how what Julie did led to Dan's death. Sarah was clearly still processing; it wouldn't be fair to either of them if they got any closer under these circumstances.

The raw abandonment that flashed over Sarah's expression almost made her change her mind, though.

"I don't think so," said Julie after Sarah had returned with a glass of water. "I think it's a little bit because of the fact the bastard's got some of my DNA, and a little bit because—" She searched for the phrase and gave up. It was either too early or too late for that. "Woo woo stuff."

"Honestly, Julie."

"Give me a break. I just woke up from watching people die."

"That's fair." Sarah sat on the edge of the bed, smiling with indifferent warmth, a slim leg brought to her chest so the knee could serve as a rest for her cheek. It killed Julie to see her so withdrawn, so poised in her hurt. "So, what now?"

"You think I can get one of those painkillers?" Julie would never air a complaint about St. Joan's potions. If someone had asked, she would have proselytized their infallibility, their enormous capacity for charming a life from Death's needy arms, until someone else came to haul her from the podium. Torture couldn't have wrung a critique from Julie. But they weren't perfect. For all that they could reverse the ministrations of, say, an industrial grinder, they couldn't do anything about the aches and twinges of muscles too quickly regrown, or the pain of fresh nerves compressed by off-center bone, or the agony of new intestines branching from the stitched-up old. The only consolation Julie had was this wasn't new. "It feels like a steam-powered horse kicked me in the gut."

Instantly, Sarah was re-illuminated by an anxious warmth, and more guilt came to lay in the silt of Julie's soul. "I'll get them."

She came back a couple of minutes later with a pill and another glass of water, but it was long enough for Julie, scowling at the wall opposite her bed, to Frankenstein a plan together.

"You thought of something," said Sarah, not a question in her voice. Her gaze was steady.

"Not entirely. It didn't feel like Akrasiel was just arbitrarily choosing its victims. There's some kind of connection. If I can figure out what maybe I can get a jump on the thing. I'm going to go hit up each of the crime scenes."

In the tired elegiac light of the early morning, Sarah could have been another corpse, long dead but tethered by unfinished business: a wraith of herself. "Is that smart? The last time you tried that, the angel knocked you unconscious. You're already hurt. What if you give yourself a concussion?"

"I have a hard skull—" Julie tried.

"No," said Sarah and she didn't shout because she wasn't that kind of person, but the cold in her voice might as well have been the cold of a blade raised in warning. "There has to be a better way. What about the book? Maybe there are footnotes."

Unused to being so sternly yet compassionately berated, Julie could only manage a very intelligent, "Footnotes?"

"Like, user manuals always have a section detailing all the ways you might die from use of the products—"

"Do they?" said Julie, who was in pain and feeling existential, and therefore was self-soothing by being willfully an idiot.

Sarah continued like she hadn't spoken. "It's always buried somewhere. In the margins. At the back. In the footnotes. We might be able to reverse engineer what's going on, maybe."

"Sarah—"

"What?"

"That's possible but it's also very much a maybe and it will take time," said Julie, with all the gentleness she could extend. "Whatever answers we can find in the murder scenes? Those are going to be definitive answers. We need those. I need those."

She hesitated.

"Please. Just let me go do this."

Again, something ballooned between them, dangerous and beautiful and inexorable, that sense of something waiting to be spoken into existence. It felt like a clenched breath, or the split second when a doctor has stepped into a room and it is anyone's guess what the diagnosis will be: Schrodinger's future in its increasingly transparent box.

"I tell you what," said Julie. "You can come with me, but only as a lookout. You absolutely will not follow me into where the murders took place, but you can let me know if any cops are on the way. Deal?"

"Deal."

"Great. Now help me get dressed and let's see how we can

murder an angel. I think I hurt something trying to put on pants the other day."

Outside, New York was cool and damp from an early shower, the pavement still water-stained. Moisture pearled in Sarah's hair. It was, Julie realized, drizzling a little, as Sarah started toward the A train station. Julie pulled her back and hailed a passing cab for them instead.

"Where to, ma'am?" said the cabbie, a thin, brown-skinned man with red-rimmed eyes too old and too exhausted for his boyish face.

"I'm not sure," said Julie. "But I'll know it when I see it. Head downtown."

His accent was ironed flat of any origin that couldn't be described as Midwestern. It wasn't even a New York accent. It was just methodically generic American. "You mean just drive around until you scream stop?"

"That's the idea."

"Okay," said the cab driver. His eyes, despite the fatigue and the bags hammocking them, were sharp and wary in the rearview mirror. "This isn't some kind of drug thing, is it? Or, you know, the other thing."

Julie leaned forward to the partition. "We're not prostitutes and only one of us is a drug aficionado but I'm not allowed to partake or I'll lose my allowance."

"Damn right," said Sarah.

The cabbie started up the fare counter with a long-suffering sigh. "Just, please, don't stiff me on the ride. It's been a long day."

"Drive nice and I'll double your tip."

"You got it," he said as he pulled into traffic.

Julie had him drive them down the Henry Hudson Parkway, nervous the whole way. They wandered—one street at a time to the consternation of their driver—the entire lattice of roads making up the Financial District, even dipping into the side alleys, Julie scowling ferociously out the window throughout. It was when they were a few blocks north of Zuccotti Park and the inside of the taxi was bathed in pink light, patches of glass along the high rises smoldering amber, that Julie mouthed a terse, "Stop."

The cab driver complied with near-preternatural immediacy.

"Are you sure this is it?"

Soft hair tickled the side of Julie's neck. She resisted the reflex to turn, to kiss the smooth cheek she knew would be there less than a breath's distance from her mouth.

"Yep."

The building they were parked beside was identical to every modern skyscraper in New York: a blade of glass windows upon which shone an aureate reflection of Brooklyn, the East River buffed to a satin gleam.

"How can you tell it from all the other high rises around here?"

"I'll tell you when we get out." To the driver she said, "How much?"

When he told her the fare, Julie handed over her credit card, which earned her another sigh, and she thought gloomily about the speed with which money vanished in New York. Quietly, she mouthed a hopeful prayer to every god and demon she could think of, offering some fealty, asking for reprieve from continued poverty. Nothing numinous answered, but even tipping him double, the transaction cleared, which was good enough as far as Julie was concerned. Next month's Julie could worry about what she'd have to mortgage for their bills.

"You ladies enjoy your morning or something," said the driver, very much done with their bullshit.

"If this is the right place, I doubt we will," Julie said.

"In that case, good luck. I'm going to class," said the cabbie, the word *class* drawled at them with lordly impatience.

With that, he rejoined the increasing traffic and vanished into a mass of cars.

"Focus. *Please,*" said Sarah. "We're outside the cab now. Tell me why you're so sure this is the place."

"You see up there?" Julie pointed at the summit.

"Yeah?"

"I can see the ghost of the man Akrasiel killed. He's still falling."

❧

The elevator, a mirror-faced cubicle with a band of steel for a handrail, took seconds to reach the twenty-third floor. The doors opened with a whispered hiss. Outside was a steel-gray carpet that ran up to the beveled frame of a massive door. Black walls with foliate gold hemmed the broad corridor.

"There are no other apartments," said Sarah.

"Rich fucker," muttered Julie. "Anyway, this is where we split up."

Sarah went a little pale. "You sure?"

"A hundred percent."

"Maybe we should wait and call the others."

"They'll be in bed," said Julie. "If we wait, we might have to mess with the police. Someone's going to notice the splattered corpse soon."

"Eww."

"Totally."

Thank god, Julie thought to herself, that Sarah had not pressed. If she had, Julie would need to add more lies to her conscience. Neither Dead Air nor St. Joan would have hesitated to make their way downtown. Julie wasn't even sure if either of them slept, what with one being most likely a small god of rent control and the other a fucking nerd with a new PS5 console. But she didn't want them there.

Just in case.

"Anyway, I'm going to look around inside, but I'll be out in like five minutes. Promise you'll wait here and not come inside."

Sighing, Sarah said, "Fine."

"That isn't a promise."

"Never knew you to be a rules lawyer," said Sarah with acid sweetness.

"You have to say it back. Sarah. Say: I'm going to wait here and not come inside."

"I'm going to wait here and not come inside," said Sarah reluctantly.

"And you'll bang on the door if anyone shows up?"

"Yes. What do I do if it's an angel, though?"

"Ask it for a puppy?"

Sarah sighed again with greater depth of feeling.

"Seriously, if you see anything you even think might be an angel, run. Don't worry about me."

"And what about you?"

"I'll hide until I can get past the thing," said Julie, not sure if it was just reassuring bullshit or if she really could escape Akrasiel.

"Please be careful," Sarah said.

"Always."

Sarah did not call her on the blatant lie, choosing instead to slump against the wall, a certain stubbornness in her eyes and mouth. Julie went up to try the bronze door handle. To her surprise, it turned with a quiet *click*. She let herself inside and shut the door behind her, locking it. If Akrasiel returned for an encore, Julie didn't want Sarah as a third wheel.

The apartment was spectacular, if you liked the chilly minimalism of Scandinavian design theories: white and gray throughout save where it was wrought iron, expensively austere, beautifully monastic. You had to have money to maintain a place like this, or a psychopath's attention to detail. Julie couldn't understand how it could be so clean. No mote of dust could be seen in the jagged light slanting from the broken window in the living room.

She got closer to the ruined glass. Julie corrected her initial surveil of the apartment. It wasn't completely pristine. At the edge of the window, invisible from where she had stood in the vestibule, was a faint brackish stain: human waste comingled with blood. Mercifully, there was no stench.

But there was a ghost.

He blurred into view as Julie neared the window: he had been running when he died, both arms outstretched, a hopeless grief on what had been a weathered but congenial face. As he raced past her, he was picked up bodily and flung through the open air. A too-bright flash of splintering light: the moment of shatter. Julie followed the apparition to the edge, watching as he plummeted, still with his arms reached out. He melted as he fell, like oil washed from a canvas. Below, atop the secluded roof of another building, what Julie would have thought was guerilla artwork if not for the specter of the man, the dead man so thoroughly exploded from the impact the complicated smear he became a thing wholly unidentifiable as human.

A quiet gurgle rose from behind Julie: it was the ghost again, sprinting from the dark toward the cold sky.

Julie stepped away as the wraith was thrown over the edge once more. There was nothing she could do for the dead man. "I'll try to fix this," said Julie very gently, as the ghost passed her for the third time. Turning from the window, she began a cautious walk through the apartment, careful to keep from touching anything. Framed photos trailed along one chalk-white wall: in all of them were the man and a younger woman with similar features. Though the man seemed incapable of smiling, his counterpart practically glowed with warmth. She grinned at the camera with the abandon of someone who decided early on that a pretty face wasn't worth a perfect moment.

Someone's going to have to tell her they died, Julie thought. The idea made her irremediably sad. Whoever she was, whether cousin or sister or some overgrown niece, she'd clearly loved the dead man. She would never see him again.

Nor would Sarah ever see Dan.

No matter what Sarah insisted she felt for Dan now, she had

loved him once. Loved him enough to give up her own life and Julie for years and years. The body remembered love like that, had to. *Don't think about that now,* Julie told herself. She went through each room in turn.

The kitchen was large and immaculate, full of designer cookware that cost as much as a car. The bedroom was much the same—clean lines, austere beauty, and not much else. The monk-like minimalism of the place told Julie very little about the man. She needed more, damnit. And in the living room by a leather and wood Eames chair with a cashmere throw over it she found it.

It was a picture of the dead man in the company of suited peers, the whole monochromatic herd of them pomaded and starched and pressed to shining, sharp-creased douchebaggery. The man was being presented with a certificate by an older white woman, both of them equally grave, whatever recognition was extended being treated like a sentencing. Julie squinted closer. There was signage in the far back, distorted by lens depth and obstructed by a crowd, but it was almost intelligible. It—

"Thorne & Dirk," said Julie aloud to the silent apartment. But someone from Thorne & Dirk, someone who could reap such glory from the company, should have been able to take Akrasiel easy. Right?

Cold snaked up Julie's neck, pebbling her skin. The apartment should have rung with wards, she realized. Even if it had failed at protecting its owner from Akrasiel, it should have had juice enough to punt Julie straight back into the hall. But the walls were only concrete, the floors insensate marble. If there'd been magic here, it was as dead as its maker.

Julie backed away from the photo and heard a snapped-pencil *crack.* She looked down at her feet. Under her right boot was a white feather so utterly pure in its absence of color, it compelled the eye, a negative void like the burning heart of a noonday sun, brilliant and annihilating. She picked the feather from the ground.

Except where she had dislocated the quill and the tiniest freckle of brown at the tip of its barbs, it was perfect, its symmetry as improbable as true love. Julie held the feather up to the light streaming from the window, hoping to augur more clues. Nothing. She brought it close to her nose and took an investigative sniff: sure enough, it had Akrasiel's seaside stink, but nothing more than that.

Fuck. Only one avenue of divination left. Julie touched her tongue to the very tip of the feather. It was like tonguing a live wire. Her vision sparked and fizzed. The edges corroded to white, then more and more of her sight went away, until at last all Julie could see was glare.

Then—

Not Akrasiel's memories but a peculiar second cousin to such; less memory than the residual echo, the sense of having been somewhere: what remains after Alzheimer's had cored out the specifics, the ghost left behind.

Julie saw other rooms, another victim. A house: not quite a mansion but close enough, overrun with sunlight, a place to grow old. An old man in a pale blue apron, sleeves rolled up to show arms still wiry with muscle, standing at the door, full of impatience and a tragic courage. She could no longer smell the worst of the city and its exhaust fumes, breathed instead the cold perfume of deep woods and water.

Yonkers, she thought. A house in the northwest. But why there?

Her visions lost their cohesion. Now she floated through bloody rooms in which were heaped torn-up bodies. Steepled bones and organs. Ankle-deep pools of charnel. None of it caught her interest. What did was a message on a wall, one she had seen before:

BLESS THE MOTHER
FOR THIS DOOR

Julie emerged from the dead man's apartment sick with dread, half-drowned from the visions. She was damp with sweat, her clothes welded to her skin. Despite this, she was freezing.

Sarah said, "Are you all right? You're pale as hell."

Julie wiped her brow with a sleeve and forced a smile onto her face. "Dealt with worse. Got a souvenir, though."

As she said this, she raised the feather and twirled it down the length of her thumb, hoping the distraction of her find would supplant any concern for her personal health. Julie did not want to talk about what had happened.

Her strategy worked—but only to the most perfunctory degree. Sarah pursed her mouth into a hard moue of disbelief, as if shocked and rather disappointed that Julie even thought she had the means to pull one over on her. Lucky for them both, Sarah allowed Julie her slyness, sighing as she did, and focused all attention on the feather.

"That—" Though artificial at first, the wonder in Sarah's voice became genuine. "Is that what I think it is?"

"A real-life angel feather," said Julie before she amended with a nonchalant shrug. "Or as close as we're going to get, I guess. Either way, it's something for me to work with."

"Did you find anything else?"

"I'm not sure. There was the ghost. And a photo of the guy. He worked at Tyler's firm."

"That sounds like a clue, right? It has to mean something."

Julie nodded.

"It does. It means we should get the hell out of here."

Not for the first time in her life, Julie was glad she didn't crave food, abhorred it even during stressful periods. She pecked on whatever Sarah brought her—bread, olives, a prehistoric Tupperware of kimchi—but otherwise focused on her investigation to the exclusion of all else. Had she her barbed wire still, this would have been a less arduous task. A little bit of pain, some blood, and an answer would be gored out in record time.

But in her condition more barbed wire magic could mean weeks of being bedridden, writhing as her skin callused and healed around the steel. Julie didn't have that time. None of them did. Akrasiel was still out there, killing, and killing, and killing, with the glee of a kid told to wreck every sandcastle on the shore. She had felt its joy. She had felt the hunger of the thing, looked upon its bloody work and known from the first vision that it wouldn't stop.

"Don't you want to rest a while? You've been going at this all day."

Julie stretched her arms above her head, hard and high enough for every joint from wrist to shoulder to pop. The stiffness, that was new. Five years ago, she could have gargoyled over the coffee table for a week straight without so much as a twinge in her back.

"If you got me some uppers—"

"No."

"I was actually talking about coffee," said Julie, an elbow on the table, her chin in palm, looking up at Sarah. "I'm allowed that, aren't I? Pleeeease."

"You've been working for twelve hours," came the po-faced response.

"Another twelve won't kill me."

"You're still healing, so no."

Julie unfolded from the floor. "Ordinarily, I would capitulate and let you boss me to bed. But I really think I'm onto something here and I need to work on it."

Sarah glared. Her attempt at sternness might have been more impactful were she not wearing her unicorn slippers and a shirt that said, "Satan Cat Loves You," complete with a devil-eared kitten pulling faces at the world.

"I will wrestle you into bed."

"This is not the threat you think it is," said Julie, leaving that open to whatever interpretation Sarah wanted.

"At least tell me you're getting somewhere—"

"I am—" Julie started to say, but her brain caught up before her fugitive mouth could get too far. "I've been reading these old religious texts and angel lore," she said, which sounded more convincing, "and eliminated most of the wrong options."

"What's left?"

"Same as last time. Taking a bite out of this," said Julie, waving a hand on the feather. It had stopped being a feather about three hours after they'd staggered through the apartment, becoming something more like the arms of a sea lily, the barbs miniscule tubes that stuck to the finger when brushed, the rachis what Julie suspected was a primitive throat. When squeezed, it expunged something that Julie would have sworn in the Supreme Court was phlegm.

"There has to be a better way."

"I've been working for twelve hours. I really don't think there is. I—"

"The book?"

"What book?" said Julie, utterly lost at that moment. Maybe Sarah was right. Sleep could not be the worst idea.

"The Bellocq grimoire."

Julie cast a worried look around. The living room was a landfill of ingredients, some used, some still in their wrappings, others pulled halfway out of their containers and then forgotten. Every bowl and basin in the apartment had been taken out and filled with one bilious concoction or another, which were now either on the floor, the seat cushions of the sofa, its armrests, or the coffee table, both under and atop of.

But no book.

"Where—"

Sarah brought it out from behind her back. "Here. While you were working, I did some of my own reading."

Julie studied her, startled by revelation. Even in the bad lighting, even overly tired, even here and now, in the pigsty of Julie's apartment, scrubbed of makeup, her hair an unruly bouffant clumping to the right of her face, she was the most beautiful woman Julie had ever known.

And she was afraid.

Is she afraid of me? Julie winced at the possibility.

"Did you find anything good?" said Julie. She had wanted so badly for Sarah to stay, and now she would: she needed to be here because god fucking knew what'd happen if she went out on her own.

Some of the tension faded. "I don't know if I found anything good, but I found *something*. It talked about a species of—I'm not sure if an equivalent exists in our world. But let's just say a species of cryptid, maybe?"

"Sure." Julie pushed down on her guilt, her grief.

"You had to summon them in pairs. Because what you wanted to do was make sure there was a fight, and they'd try to eat each other."

"I remember that. But that was for something that looked way different from Akrasiel."

"That was what I thought at first," said Sarah, thumbing through the grimoire. She tapped a finger on a page, causing emerald particulates to plume from the cover. Julie made a mental note to check if she could get Sarah warded against arsenic poisoning. "But I started reading and it said that this species of whatever is a type of carrion eater, and that their ultimate prey is something called The Mother Who Eats?"

"The message on the ceiling," said Julie, suddenly excited. "The one we saw when we went to Dan's hotel—"

Sarah flinched.

"Sorry."

"I'm not sorry he's dead. I don't know why you'd be."

Julie let it go. "What now? Do we summon another Akrasiel and tell it to kill the one we have?"

"We could. You could, at least." Sarah offered an anemic smile. "I can hold your jacket."

"I'd take you up on that. Except . . ." said Julie, glad for the smile however threadbare it was, glad Sarah still trusted her with it. She picked her way through several foul-smelling buckets to stare at the indicated page. On it were linocut illustrations of what looked like worms cowled by a multitude of feathers, if worms could smile like a used car salesman. "Except that if we're wrong, it's going to be a whole group of Akrasiels and we'd be fucked to hell and back."

"It seems safer than the alternative."

"You mean it gets worse?"

"The alternative is—" Sarah tapped the page. "You remember that old Russian story? About a king named Koschei who hid his heart in an egg that was in a duck, and on and on?"

"Uh-huh."

"Akrasiel kind of did the same thing. Except it hid whatever it has that passes for a soul inside some horrible dimension that you'd have to physically go to."

"Great," said Julie. "Sounds like the vacation I needed."

"We won't need to do that, I'm sure. I believe in you," said Sarah, grazing Julie's brow with her own, the barest touch, like a shy cat.

"Thank you?"

"For what?" said Sarah.

"I've been trying to protect you from all of this and you proved me wrong. You found something, something important, that sailed right by me. You did great. You saved me time and probably some people's lives. So, thank you for being you and for all of the rest."

Sarah's smile went from shy to beaming in a few seconds.

"Really?"

Julie had the urge to hug her, but simply said, "Yeah. Really. I'm the loud one, but you're the smart member of the team."

"I'm part of the team now?" said Sarah brightly.

"Yeah. You are. But only for research and being look out. Okay? Sorry, but I still don't want you strolling through hauntings or charnel houses."

"Yet."

"We'll see."

"I'll take that as a yet."

Julie knew arguing would spoil Sarah's buoyant mood, so she just smiled and said, "Yet."

Sarah gave her a little "Yay."

❧

A few hours later, Dead Air and St. Joan were in Julie's apartment. The former arrived schlepping four pizza boxes and his freshly acquired console, the latter in a caftan sleeping robe, already smoking a cigarette as she glided inside.

"What you did was dangerous," said St. Joan, seating herself on the couch.

"Which part?" said Julie.

"All of it." St. Joan thought on this. "Particularly you eating random pieces of the dead."

"You eat one dead man's tooth—"

"I am told cannibalism is habit-forming."

"Also prions," said Dead Air.

Julie glanced at where Dead Air and Sarah hunched over the controllers, bickering over whose turn it was to yank virtual bread out of a cartoon oven in a game about overworked chefs.

"I thought that was just in the brain."

"Bacteria is sneaky," said Dead Air.

"Not," said Sarah, lightly punching him in the shoulder, "helping."

"It can't be worse than some of the stuff I've done before, either way," said Julie.

"No," said St. Joan. "You're right. It isn't worse than some of the things you've done before. You've always been a reckless dolt."

Julie pried a slice from one of the pizza boxes. Babbalucci wasn't high dining, but it didn't try to be, which she appreciated. The Harlem institution knew its demographic and it knew it well.

"Comes with the job," said Julie, biting off the end of her slice. Still hot; the bacon was even still crispy. "Or came from the job. Either way—"

"Either way," said St. Joan, "Akrasiel isn't something for you to face alone. We don't know what it is."

"It's an asshole," said Dead Air, attention on the screen.

St. Joan sighed. "It's like you don't *like* helping."

"In every group, there is one designated peanut gallery."

"We do know what it is, though," said Julie, slightly louder than before. "While I was off being a dolt, Sarah read through the grimoire and figured out a few things. Including the fact that Akrasiel, the lying piece of shit, isn't an angel."

"It's some kind of celestial scavenger," said Sarah, looking over to the pair, her spherical avatar careening off a ledge and into the magma. "They're made to devour the remains of The Mother Who Eats."

Julie nodded. "What she said," she said through another mouthful of cheese.

"The Mother Who Eats," repeated St. Joan. "Why does that sound so familiar?"

"Sounds a lot more end of the worldy than I like," said Dead Air.

"Is that real?" asked Sarah as a mustached onion with stick-thin legs came on screen.

"Yeah. Like old-school cosmic horrors and gods that no one wants to think about anymore. But I've only ever seen them in books. In all the years I've been doing this stuff I've never met a single soul who's encountered Them. They're just—folktales. I think."

"Don't be so sure," said St. Joan very softly. "Dead Air's gods—"

"They're not really gods," said Dead Air with the patient tones of someone long resigned to repeating himself on the topic. He hit pause and swiveled to regard the women on the couch. "They have a similar essence, but calling Them gods is a gross flattening of Their identities."

"What would you call Them, then?" said St. Joan, clearly hoping to stave off a lecture.

"Them," said Dead Air with great innocence.

"You walked into that," said Julie.

"You did," agreed Sarah.

Most of St. Joan's hair was in a gray satin turban, a corsage of jewels holding the folds in place, but a few wisps escaped as she shook her head. Another cigarette was lit, puffed, and studied for a long minute before St. Joan resumed talking. "I remember now. There was a defrocked priest I once lived with. When he took up with the sprites and the fae folk, the English church kicked him out."

"And into your arms. Sleeping with the clergy. Gosh, Joan, isn't that a little blasphemous?" said Julie with a little scandalized gasp. "Whatever happened to him?"

"He died, obviously. As mortals always do. But I will always resent the how of it. The local farmers knew of us, and when their crops failed one season, they decided he—he—" St. Joan *flickered*, like an old television jumping between channels. "—he needed to suffer for the land to give them what they needed. They were wrong, of course. Sacrifice must always be willing. Bad things happen otherwise."

"What kind of bad things?" said Sarah, very carefully. "If it's okay to ask. You don't have to rehash old trauma just for us."

"I wouldn't be telling you the story if it still troubled me, I promise," said St. Joan. "Nonetheless, thank you for that kindness. To answer your question, though, the bad thing was me. *I* happened to them. The fae came to me as I wept over his bones in the ruins of our cottage—the farmers had locked him in and burned him alive, you see."

"Jesus," said Sarah, hand over her mouth.

"—and they told me then that it was not right, what happened to the priest. Hookland wasn't his native home, but they'd claimed him for their own and the county does not forgive cruelties like this. So, they asked if I'd help, and I did. We made sure the farmers regretted it. Their fields burned. Their cattle vanished—"

"Didn't see you as a cow murderer," said Dead Air as he stood to meander to the fridge, earning a prodigious eyeroll from St. Joan.

"—it was mostly goats and sheep, and I didn't *murder* them, thank you. We simply made sure they were rehomed in better flocks far, far away. Anyway, in the end, we drove them out. I found a book much like that one." St. Joan nodded toward the grimoire, which stood propped against the kettle in the kitchen. "It talked about a Mother who slept in the dark, always hungry, always in need of feeding or the end would come bursting from her corpse."

"That's so metal," said Dead Air.

"Do you think they were referencing The Mother Who Eats?" asked Julie.

"Who knows? But there were rituals in the little book that allowed the worshipper to keep away the mother's death. To close the door so the carrion hunters would not be able to make use of her carcass."

"It's definitely possible," said Dead Air, returning with a bottle of off-brand soda. "Sarah and I could start looking into that."

"I really am part of the team!" said Sarah.

"I never thought of a simple ritual," murmured Julie, fingers webbed with strands of cheese. She flicked her hands a few times in vain hope of dislodging the cheese, but they stayed resolutely gummed. "I was set on figuring out a way to murder the shit out of Akrasiel, but maybe I can just banish him."

"It's an idea," agreed St. Joan, unclasping one of the many necklaces she wore. It was a simple thing: a loop of gold strung with a plain golden locket. "For you," she said as she hooked the chain around Julie's throat.

"Is this an anti-angel ward?"

"I wish," said St. Joan with a thin smile. "It's for luck. *My* luck, specifically. It's kept me alive and well for all these years. Hopefully, it'll keep you safe too."

Julie swallowed against a welter of emotion. Most days, St. Joan did not look more than a few years older than her, if that. But she looked ancient then. Her eyes, most especially. Positively antediluvian in her grief and her pain. For the first time since she met St. Joan, it occurred to Julie just how many friends and lovers the woman had had to bury, and how many more she would come to say goodbye to.

"This so you can see me at an open casket funeral some day?" said Julie, her voice thick.

"Yes. Some day. Some decades later."

"Not this one?"

"No," said St. Joan, her head touched to Julie's. "Not this one." And she added, in a whisper low enough that no one but the two of them would hear, "Come back to Sarah."

"I will."

"Good. And promise me you won't do anything on your own until we've learned more."

"I promise."

St. Joan smiled even though they both knew Julie was lying.

CHAPTER TWENTY

It was almost one in the morning and the subway car was mostly empty. It was Julie, two drunken white guys who were palpably finance creeps with their suits and slicked-back hair, a fortysomething white woman with a yoga mat mounted like a rifle on her shoulder, three teenage East Asian boys giggling at their phones, and a homeless person, oblivious to the weather and so mummified in layers of coats Julie couldn't begin to guess their age, gender, or ethnic background, sprawled over a plastic orange bench.

Julie twirled the "feather" between her fingers. One of the lights in the car was struggling to stay lit: it buzzed and died before convulsing back into life, failed again and repeated the cycle anew. Under that guttering luminance, it seemed ludicrous that she could mistake the wetly shining thing in her grip for a feather, and Akrasiel for an angel.

Then again, she'd been fooled by less.

She laughed so forcefully at the thought that the two finance guys relocated to a distant bench. Julie slouched an amused look at them. Newcomers, maybe. No *real* New Yorker would have even registered Julie's baying laugh.

She did often wonder what strangers thought of her, what they saw and concluded from her thrift-store clothing, the self-inflicted haircut. If they thought kind things about her, or if they dismissed her as one of those derelicts who'd die in a ditch one day. Why she cared so much about something so trivial was a mystery to her, but Julie suspected it had to do with her encroaching birthday.

Thirty was a big year. Thirty was when shit allegedly came together and you knew, you just *knew,* what you were supposed to do with the rest of your life. When this was over, Julie would have to go back to piecing together a game plan for the future, one without Sarah. Her world was simply too dangerous to allow a civilian in that deep. Except the moment the thought came to her, she couldn't process the vacuum of Sarah's absence. It felt impossible. They said all roads led to Rome but in Julie's experience, where they really went was to Sarah.

"Fuck," she said aloud.

No, it wouldn't do anyone good if she sat around pining for Sarah. She had things to do. Notably, killing that fucking angel.

Angel thing.

Whatever.

Exhausted, Julie ran a hand through her hair. She would eat a shotgun first before admitting it to any of her friends, but she was beginning to worry that she'd fucked up so badly that she'd already lost and all this was a lead-up to God coming out from behind the clouds to boom stentoriously at her, "You really should have realized sooner." In her heart of hearts, Julie was convinced the entity *meant* for her to spectate its victories, and when it was done with whatever it was doing, when it was tired of this world and bored with its offerings, it would slit her and all her friends' throats, then flutter back where it came from. All she could do was see if Akrasiel would call it even and leave the rest alone if Julie splattered herself over the front of a bus for its amusement.

The only thing keeping her from proactively offering was the acute possibility she was wrong and all her death would accomplish was Sarah's eternal sorrow.

And well, fuck *that*.

She stared at the feather. Under the sterile white-blue fluorescents overhead, it looked gaudy, not so much an artifact from a celestial being—or infernal, hell if Julie knew, she certainly didn't care—as a stage prop from a high-school production. Kitschy or otherwise, the feather remained her one lead and really, hadn't Julie trusted in worse? Tyler's face flitted to the forefront of her thoughts before she pushed it down. Yes, she'd definitely put her trust in even less reliable things.

Sacrifice must always be willing.

She had offered Akrasiel her blood once, and it had crawled up from the void to take her gift. Surely, its cast-offs would do the same. With a sigh, Julie slipped a punch dagger from a jacket pocket. St. Joan had gifted her the weapon several years ago, a limited edition special from an artist she adored; Julie had laughed when she freed it from its crinkly lavender bed of tissue. The dagger was made to resemble a pointy witch's hat, its edges gilded, a cartoon cat staring saucer-eyed from under its brim. Julie thought it was ridiculous. St. Joan pointed out no one would ask questions if she attached a key to the ring dangling from its chain. Julie shut up quickly after.

She ran its bladed end over her tongue, a neat hyphen of a wound, like a papercut, both in size and in substance, so delicate it wouldn't bleed until Julie squeezed her tongue between her teeth. Blood pearled the muscle. Julie combed the feather over her tongue, her posture confrontational. No one in the car questioned her eccentricities. One of the boys stared, as if deliberating on the cost-benefits of filming her for TikTok. He met Julie's eyes, held them for longer than most adults could, which impressed Julie, then dropped them, having clearly decided no, it wasn't worth risking whatever Julie's brand of crazy was.

Her gaze ran another circuit across the faces of her fellow commuters before she closed her eyes. Almost before her lids could fully shutter, the vision came: Dan strutting up to a mirror, more emaciated than he was even hours ago, his hair tugged and torn down to a blood-matted bristle. His mustache was gone, ripped from his upper lip, only a few dark tufts still attached to the denuded muscle, most of his skin there gone the way of his facial hair.

But he was still grinning.

"Julie." Dan-Akrasiel-whatever-the-fuck they/it was said her name with a new husband's lust, and Julie's skin nearly crawled off her shoulders to escape. "Julie, Julie, Julie, what *am* I going to do with you?"

Julie froze. Before, it'd mostly ignored her. But now it was *talking* to her. Questions pounded through her head but what she said was: "You should be worried about what I'll do to you, asshole."

"Oh?" said Akrasiel.

"Yeah," said Julie in lieu of a better comeback. "You just wait."

"I don't think I want to," said Akrasiel, tugging at its temple, pinching at the skin, pulling, torquing it so hard Julie could almost feel the bite of its grime-encrusted nails. With a wet noise, a wad of muscle tore loose. Tears gouted from those sunken eyes as Akrasiel daintily stuffed the meaty clot into its mouth. "I'd rather do as I want. But you're welcome to come try me."

"Fuck. You."

"Bless the Mother for this door."

"I know what you are," said Julie, with as much threat as she could imbue in her voice. "You're a parasite. You're a vampire worm needing permission into the world. I'm going to find you, and I'm going to break every single one of your bones."

Akrasiel grinned. Through the gash of its parted mouth, the lips worried down to scar tissue, something moved: something like a tongue, something worse. Then the subway train rocked to a shrill halt, rubbering Julie back to her body, and she opened her eyes to find herself alone in the car.

❧

There it was.

The house from her visions. Julie stood at the end of its driveway, thumbs hooked in her jean pockets just staring at it, trying to process the thing, but knowing that nothing would reveal itself that way. She had to move to get answers.

She loped across the winding road alone, hoodie pulled up,

praying the whole while that her face hadn't already been captured on some asshole's security camera.

She raked a long look over the house. Julie could see the skeleton of an imposing three-story Queen Anne house, an edifice the Addams Family might have gleefully adopted as a second home: she saw it in its dollhouse roofs, the wraparound porch with its many details, flourishes St. Joan would have waxed ecstatic over. Pretty, and perhaps even prettier before some architect went over it with their own designs, butchering the homestead, gutting it of everything but the bones. In place of wood and glazed brick, there was now glass, so much glass. Shame. Julie wasn't exactly a real estate connoisseur, but even she knew this was a tawdry case of gentrification.

Nervously, she scanned the green lawn, trying and failing to identify the presence of any covert security measures or wards. The fact there wasn't even a *gate* separating the house from the outside world unnerved her. Was this what happened when you have so much money the zeros stop making sense? You just assumed everything was replaceable, and thus unnecessary to protect? Julie looked it over again, memorizing exit points, the positioning of windows. The hard part, she decided, would be explaining why she was here to the rich fucks inside. Would there even be anyone in here? With luck, there wouldn't. But unfortunately, it was the only plan she had.

She went up to the house, swagger on full display, hoping her confidence would compensate for the batshit story she was about to lay at—hopefully—*someone's* front door. Julie rang the doorbell, rehearsing her spiel as she did. *Hi, I know this sounds crazy, but I need you to get out of your home, thanks. Hi, lovely home, I need you to evacuate while I murder God.*

No one answered.

Good. Maybe this didn't need to be messy. Julie gave the front door an experimental push, expecting resistance and finding none. It creaked open instead, allowing Julie a peep into a house as ostentatiously minimalist as its exterior.

White wooden floors. White walls. White rugs, real fur, likely stripped from an animal on the endangered species list. Mirrors everywhere, the largest measuring eight feet in height and wide enough for three men to primp and pose without ever knocking elbows. The only thing to show the vestibule led to a house occupied by real people and wasn't, say, an elaborately detailed film set was a single thickly framed Polaroid. Old enough to be mostly faded, it showed a young white couple standing hand-in-hand in front of a harbor, a wreath of flowers atop the woman's pale head. Her counterpart's smile was more muted than hers, but his eyes flashed with a feral joy.

Julie turned the corner and stopped.

She was in a massive living room, one whose ceiling was about eighteen feet in height. Unlike the entry hall, it had color to balance the oppressive pallor of the general aesthetic: furniture in the orange-red liqueur hues, some deeper in shade, closer to the glass of an old whisky bottle, indicating great value. A single painting dominated one wall, an abstract piece, gold and clarets swirled together, making Julie think of phoenixes or houses being razed to the ground, a few thin lines of gilt punctuating the texture—even from where Julie stood, she could see where the paint dried, the myriad bumps pimpling its surface, the crenellations, even the little filaments where the artist flicked the brush at the canvas and didn't bother smoothing it down. It probably cost the owners millions.

In the center of the room was what looked like a snow globe, the largest ever manufactured. Only it had been preserved at the instant of detonation, all its pieces suspended in the air. Inside each onionskin curl was a segment of human flesh: an inch-thick segment of a man's wrist, an elbow with its knob of bone exposed on both ends, his fingers divided by sixths. The macabre art installation orbited an invisible—

No, that wasn't right.

The fulcrum was right there: a fiftysomething woman, icy in

her beauty, her calm hauteur, white hair stark against the dove gray of her trim pantsuit, sitting atop an ottoman with her hands rested on her thighs.

"I keep trying to call him back," said the woman softly, her voice low, toneless, deep as mountains, deep as grief. "But all I get are the ephemera, the cast-offs. I keep looking, and I keep looking, but he's gone. I can't find my Albert. He's just *gone.*"

"I think—"

The woman fixed Julie with a miserable stare. "What did you do to him?"

Though spoken quietly, Julie recognized the kindling threat in the woman's voice, the aural equivalent of someone picking up a knife and adjusting their grip on its hilt. Too late, she clocked the whole situation for what it was: a setup. Akrasiel had lured her into the vicinity of someone it had royally pissed off, and who had every cause to believe Julie was, if not entirely culpable, then at minimum complicit in creating the recent horror show of their life.

Shit.

"I swear, I know it looks bad but you have to believe me, I didn't hurt your husband. I'm here to stop what did."

The woman rose to her feet. "You know, when Communications insisted we get a haruspex department, I fought so hard against the idea. The future is so unpredictable, after all. And the idea of that much meat in the office felt so, so . . . unsanitary."

She laughed convulsively and without rhythm. The sound made Julie's skin want to crawl off her bones and go hide.

"Do you know how *hard* it is to get blood out of velvet?"

"Jesus fuck a goat, lady. I really need you to snap out of this. I'm here to help."

"They said you'd come back," said the woman, beginning to walk toward Julie, her face hollowing of its initial emotion. As she got closer, Julie could see the proverbial lights were still on but whoever called it home had since skipped town. Saying someone looked dead inside was common phrasing, but never had Julie ever seen such a literal actualization of the metaphor.

That didn't stop the waterworks, though.

Julie's heart tightened at the tears rolling down the corners of the woman's eyes, lacquering her face. Some trick of the light made them shine cartoonishly, almost as if—

No, Julie corrected herself. Those weren't tears.

It was glass.

Before Julie could finish computing what she'd witnessed, her amygdala had sent her dancing back a few steps, two or three for each of the woman's plodding own, her stance transitioning from innocuous to battle-ready. She raised her fists into a boxer's pose, aware it was more than likely to be pointless as the woman didn't look like she had any intention of physically brawling with Julie. Still, the thought is what counts and Julie needed her to recognize that Julie, come hell or glass, was ready to fight.

And from the small, distracted smile that flashed across the woman's lined face, it seemed she did.

"I didn't believe them when they said you'd come back. I mean, come on, everyone knows that a killer—"

"I didn't do it," Julie snapped fruitlessly.

"—should never return to the scene of the crime, even if they're desperate to see how badly they've hurt the people their victim left behind. It's a rookie mistake, I said. I was so sure that anyone devious enough to get past my wards would be smarter than this." Her eyes held Julie's. They'd been celadon initially, more gray than green, nearly an ancient pewter, but whatever it was that was making her cry glass had invigorated the green and now, her gaze was the irradiated, tumbled malachite of a cat's. The glass filmed her throat, glazed the bony rise of her shoulders. It was dripping from her fingertips, a fortune of crystals.

"But I guess not," said the woman. "I know nothing will bring Albert back, but it will still give me great pleasure to hurt you."

"For the last time, I'm here to—"

The air went cold and brassy, Julie's only warning before a blue-white light roared from the ceiling. She leapt aside at the last second, almost too late, the skin of her upper arm scorched black where the light brushed her. Julie swallowed a cry, pushed the pain down, held it there, held it as tightly as she could, ready for later. Her problem right now, though, was she couldn't *see.* As if she'd been surprised with a point-blank camera flash, the woman's first volley had left Julie's vision mottled with dark spots.

"I don't want to hurt you, lady. Listen, my name is Julie Crews. And it's my job to put bad things to rest. Like whatever did this."

"Julie," said the woman, voice still the flat of a polished blade. "You're Tyler's little friend."

"How do you know Tyler?" Julie paused. "Oh, fuck. You work for Thorne & Dirk. You're—"

"Clarice Winterson."

Now, Julie remembered. Tyler, the night before his interview, had pleaded with Julie to review the people he'd be meeting. There were three. Clarice, and . . . Julie couldn't recall the names of the other two. What she remembered was the overdressed pizza and prowling through bluebooks and celestial apparitions of New York's elite in the magical business world, hypothesizing about what interviewers would be like based on things like their academic backgrounds and the quality of their haircuts. Clarice. God, Clarice, of course. How could she have forgotten? Even then, even as a shrunken-down headshot and a laundry list of accomplishments, Clarice had seemed intimidating.

And the photo in the man's apartment, the grave-looking older woman who'd handed him the certificate. That was Clarice too. Julie was sure of that now. But why them?

"I guess when you're committing violent crimes, there's no reason to think about fine details," said Clarice, with a disgusted curl to her lips.

Julie was working on a question about Thorne & Dirk when the woman lowered her hands, palms facing the ground, as if reaching to gather something from the floor. Julie's vision cleared in time to see Clarice's fingers twist, calling an animal to heel, the strings of glass knotted in fractal patterns about her spidery fingers.

And so beckoned, something came—

Oozing up through the floorboards, translucent as Vaseline, little more than blobs in the beginning, but as Julie watched they coalesced into human bodies: shoulders, the laddered rungs of a broad ribcage, hipbones, and to Julie's surprise, the soft paunches of middle age, a thin thatch of grayish hair. Seconds later, two Alberts stood naked, one to each side of Clarice, their flaccid dicks brown and circumcised.

"What the fuck."

"I thought it'd be funny," said Clarice, smiling without the expression even nicking her eyes.

"Wait, please. Jesus. Before you sic—" Julie stared wildly at the twin Alberts again. They were perfect re-creations of the dead man save for the eyes, theirs being smoked glass. "—old guys on me, I need you to listen. There's something targeting your firm. It's an angel—no, it looks like an angel. But it's not actually an angel. It calls itself Akrasiel. It's basically seven tapeworms in a skin suit. And it wants your people dead. I just want to help."

It was babble. Julie knew it to be such, but it had the effect of making Clarice gesture at Julie to continue, so it was *something*: it was time, at the very least, to collect her thoughts and assess her options, few as those were. She and Clarice weren't the same weight class. Julie wasn't sure they were playing the same game. For all her creased skin and gray hair and friable old ladyness, Clarice radiated power. She burned with it like a star in its last hour.

"Is this Tyler's doing?" said Clarice with quiet rage.

Julie froze. She hadn't thought of that. "I don't know."

"But you work for him."

"I do odd jobs for him, sometimes. When I need to. When I need extra cash. But that's it."

"And wouldn't he pay to see his competition obliterated?" said Clarice dreamily. "People keep dying at the firm. But you already know that."

Had Julie been less paranoid and Clarice less injured by her despair, had any of the variables been infinitesimally different, Julie would have been vaporized into a pile of ash. The blue-white light roared down again but this time Julie was ready, spitting a plate of golden energy into the air to meet the blast. It smashed through her measly shield but in doing so, it was refracted, howling past Julie to incinerate a chest of drawers. As it blazed, it rendered the world bluely aflame, making bruises of the gorgeous furniture.

"Tyler's such a little prick."

"I know—" said Julie, attention shuttling between the Alberts and Clarice. The old woman's expression hadn't changed.

"I told them that we shouldn't have hired him. But they insisted. They were so taken by his ridiculous simpering. I *warned* them."

"Please," said Julie. "I really want to help. I want to stop Akrasiel before it can hurt the . . . the Mother?"

She hadn't meant to pose it like a question or have it sound so much like wheedling, but it didn't matter. At the word *Mother*, Clarice's expression lost its glazed distance, sharpened as her eyes narrowed.

"Who told you about that?"

"Akrasiel has been leaving messages at its crime scenes."

"Like with Albert," said Clarice, almost to herself. She shook her head. "If something is truly threatening The Mother Who Eats, it needs to be stopped. It cannot be allowed to hurt her. I—"

"Yes?"

Clarice stared at Julie as if only seeing her for the first time.

"You didn't kill Albert, did you?" said Clarice, each word weighed before it was spoken, placed down with the care a priest might give her votives. "But you're the reason Akrasiel is here, aren't you? That's why my wards responded to you. You weren't his killer, but your blood—*your* blood was used to bring it into this world."

"Something I am deeply and truly sorry about," said Julie, inching back toward the exit. "You have no idea."

"It's alright," said Clarice as she raised a hand and slowly tipped it forward so that two fingers pointed at Julie. She twitched her wrist, miming the recoil of a firing gun. "All this means is we have to remove you from this world, and all shall be well."

The two Alberts threw their heads back, mouths open, going wider, wider, until their heads opened into needle-toothed crowns, radials of them, spoked with even more teeth. They charged Julie, limbs flapping at their sides, dicks jouncing as they ran. Julie punched an arm out, grabbing the first by its skull. A scream tore from her as her palm was minced into hamburger meat.

Between impact and the draw of her next breath, Julie pumped the homunculus full of magic and every drop of pain she'd locked up in her bones. The Albert-thing began to thrash, and Julie hissed a sound like the death of continents.

It exploded.

Gore washed over Clarice Winterson's tidy living room, over her tidy white floors, all over her tidy gray pantsuit. The eruption was so strong it knocked the other Albert-thing back, and it fell ass over head. Julie wheezed for air as molars rained down, *clack-clack-clack.* Clarice *gawked.*

"Sorry," said Julie, a tooth bouncing off her nose. "Nothing personal."

And fled.

CHAPTER TWENTY-ONE

The corridor outside Clarice Winterson's office at Thorne & Dirk was covered in meat. Hearts torn from bulls. Brains carefully excised from large but unidentifiable mammals. Whale spines, elephant livers, and gray ropes of intestine ornated the walkway and the walls of the usually pristine corridor. Clarice—or whoever it was that was brazen enough to defile her office so—had even set a little arch of eyeballs over the top of her door. However, the charnel house decorator who had set up the room hadn't bothered with fixing it so it wouldn't be descended upon by vermin.

As a result, by the time Tyler got there, the air iridesced with blowflies. It was all he could *hear.* He considered wading into the swarm to knock on Clarice's door, mostly so she would step out and see the utter mess she had made of the office. But the eyeballs, he realized, had lids and lashes, and they moved to follow him as he took an apprehensive step toward the blood-splattered door. Tyler retreated again, taking in the charnel. It was hard to say how many eyes there were, given the surrounding carnage, but Tyler spotted enough to make him decide he'd call Clarice from the safety of his own office.

"What do you want, Tyler?"

"I was just calling about the charcuterie platter outside your door. The smell is fucking going all over this floor."

She laughed a bone-dry, tinder-strike laugh. "This you have problems with? I'm learning so much about you."

He goosepimpled at her reply. Tyler liked Clarice because alone of the directors, Clarice preferred the bludgeon to the scalpel: she said what she meant and did what she said and if some of her methods were bloody, it was simply the nature of their vocation.

This talking around the subject was unlike her, and Tyler had long since learned that change was rarely for the better.

He said, "Exactly what does that mean?"

"You know exactly what I mean."

"I damn well fucking do not. Otherwise, I wouldn't be asking." Tyler cleared his throat and tamed the irritation in his voice, couching it as warm concern. "Sorry, it's just that there are a lot of flies, and I'm a little stressed. I didn't mean to be so rude."

"I don't care."

He counted to ten. "Clarice, I'm just trying to help."

"Your girlfriend said the same thing."

Tyler stared at his door as they spoke, watching as a vein of flies crawled up from under the wood and dispersed through his office. "Julie? She's absolutely not my girlfriend. We've spoken about this."

She *tutted* at him. The bitch actually tutted at him. "I know what you both did. You summoned that thing. You called Albert's murderer to this world. And for what? For power? If you had only waited a few more decades, you could have had what you wanted. But no, you had to bring that thing here to kill your superiors. You put The Mother Who Eats at risk—"

"Clarice, I swear."

"Albert has died twice before this, you know?" said Clarice conversationally, with jarring pleasantness, like the two were sat at brunch somewhere and Clarice had at last decided he was worthy of being a confidant. Her voice was warm and intimate, velveted as she spoke. "I brought him back both times and made sure he remembered nothing of the trauma. It was a considerable amount of work, but such is marriage. There was a certain joy in knowing I could protect him. But then your creature—" Her voice lost its gentility. "—tore him out of the world. I can't find my Albert. No matter how I look, he's nowhere. He's even fading from my memories and there's *nothing I can do.*"

"Clarice, you have my condolences—"

"I'll have your head," said Clarice with poisonous sweetness. "I'll use your skull as a fucking urn for poor Albert."

The line went dead.

This was bad. No, Tyler corrected himself, sitting back in his chair. This wasn't bad. This was an ineradicable disaster. Clarice had Upper Management's ear and it wouldn't take much, in fact, it would take nothing at all, for her to convince them that Tyler had to be gotten rid of.

Thank god Lansdale was dead. He had purportedly fallen out of his twenty-third story apartment at a velocity and angle so vicious, there wasn't a corpse to collect, only offal to scrape off a roof before anyone else noticed. Afflictions would be too busy jockeying to take over his post to pay any attention to Tyler yet. So, he had a small window before he was stuffed into a meat locker.

But was what Clarice said true? He chewed at his thumbnail until it broke between his teeth. If old Winterson wasn't lying, maybe he could use this complication to his advantage. It would take some strategizing, a little care in terms of timing, but such logistics could be easily outsourced. All he needed to do was stay ahead of Clarice.

Fuck fuck fuck fuck fuck.

His phone rang as he was midway through preparing himself a cappuccino. Tyler waited until the coffee maker stopped its groaning before he checked the caller ID and picked up the receiver.

"Hello Annabeth," said Tyler with all the cheer he could put into that much-hated name. This was her fault for going incommunicado these last few eventful days. "I was just thinking about you. How are things? Been busy? I hear knitting is a nice way to relax."

An in-drawn breath before: "Just shut up and listen. As you must have guessed, the company is stuck in a blender making a shit milkshake."

"What a way with words you have."

"You've *seen* Clarice's office."

His heart dodged a few beats. Tyler made himself smile as he replied, careful to keep his voice even, restrained. "The outside? Yes. It's a fucking slaughterhouse. I don't even want to think about what it looks like on the inside. But I don't think you're bringing her up because you have an opinion on her new aesthetic directions."

"Correct. I bring Clarice up because she's gone batshit, telling anyone who'll listen that there's someone in the office trying to get a leg up by killing their bosses. She isn't rational and that makes her dangerous."

"Oh hell."

"The good news is that no one is listening to her after she rubbed brisket all over the doorknobs. No one listened except me."

Shit. "You hear everything, Fall."

"She told me that you had Julie summon up, what was it, a fucking nightmare angel—her words, not mine—to kill her husband and everyone else?"

"Damnit! I didn't do it!"

"Clarice certainly thinks you did. Phoebe in HR would have authorized an investigation if not for me."

"Well, thank you for that."

"Wanna know what I did to her?"

Tyler leaned back in his chair. "Would it make you happy to share?"

"Immensely," said Fall. "She's being immolated right now. And next is your girlfriend, Julie."

"Julie *is not* my girlfriend. You know that's bullshit, right?"

"I really don't care about who old people fuck. I just want to get that out there."

"Fine, okay. What now?"

"I've already set the dogs on Crews, which will tie up more of the firm's resources. As the heads of Excision and Internal Security, that puts us in the position to make a few strategic hits and maybe carve up some deals."

"And then what?"

"Then we see if you're worth keeping alive. Clarice had opinions about you."

"I'm sure she did," said Tyler, reaching for his cappuccino for lack of anything better to do with his hands. He looked down and grimaced. There were flies drowning in the foam. "I thought we were in this together."

"We are," said Fall. "Until you disappoint me."

She laughed into Tyler's sullen quiet.

"Like you wouldn't do the same to me if our situations were reversed."

Fall had him there. Tyler nudged his polluted coffee aside and sighed. Tomorrow, he would have to see if the janitorial crew could do *something* about the situation in his office. At this rate, the flies wouldn't need to wait for him to die. He would suffocate on them.

"Fair enough," said Tyler. "Did you hear about Holger Liebezeit and the Moseley brothers?"

"I have no idea who you're talking about."

"They are—or were—two of our biggest clients. But I heard from a contact in Client Relations that they gave the firm the boot this morning. Holger said something along the lines of 'If you shitheels even can't protect yourselves, how are you going to take care of us?' I suspect the Moseleys had something similar to say."

Tyler could hear the smile in Fall's voice when she said, "Happy days. We're losing clients on top of everything else. That's perfect. They'll be going ballistic upstairs. And it'll be chaos everywhere else."

"I'm sure they will. But hey, Fall, are you sure Clarice isn't going to ask someone else to off me while you're busy hunting Julie?"

"No one crosses Internal Security," said Fall, and Tyler could now *hear* each tooth in her smile. "Besides, I've got my hit teams taking down everybody who's even looked cross-eyed at the idea."

"That's going to be a lot of bodies," said Tyler.

"Money makes the world go round. And capitalism will find us new bodies."

Tyler thought things over for a minute. "I have another idea."

"Good for you. For a minute, I thought I was partnered with a trained seal."

He let that slide and said: "I think we need to make Clarice follow Albert into the great beyond."

"You really are that scared of her, huh?"

"I'm not," said Tyler. "I just think that we absolutely need someone big to take a fall. It'll freak out the staff beyond where they are now. Make them utterly pliable."

"That's not a bad idea," said Fall slowly, as if thinking things over. "But I have my hands full right now."

"I can do it."

"You think you can get through all her wards?"

"What do you think Excisions does? You think when we go after a spirit or an off the rails witch we stop at the door, clutch our pearls, and say 'Oh gracious. Wards.' Getting through wards is Excisions 101."

"All right," drawled Fall. "Put your dick away. If you think you can do it, be my guest. I have plenty on my plate already. But take out Clarice off company ground. It's better optics that way."

"I was thinking the same thing."

"Do it quick before she causes too much more trouble," said Fall and hung up.

"Goodbye to you too," said Tyler to the dial tone. He put down the phone and ran through the conversation in his head. Everything mostly lined up—even Fall's posturing about keeping him alive until his value was determined. But there was one thing. What Fall called him.

A trained seal.

Tyler didn't like the ring of that. It sounded cheap, and worse, it sounded disposable. In that offhand comment, had Fall let it slip that she was going to kill him before this was all over with? It certainly sounded possible. He'd have to be on guard. For all that she claimed they were partners in this, Fall had never treated him as an equal. She might even think she was the only one of them fit for a seat at the Upper Management table.

But fine.

Two could play at this game.

He took a bottle of Aberlour from the bottom drawer of his desk and poured himself a large drink. It wouldn't hurt to have some liquid courage for when he went to see what Fall had done to good old Phoebe.

CHAPTER TWENTY-TWO

The firm knew her name.

Fuck, the firm was going to think she was responsible for all the murders. Julie punched her temple several more times and sank her face into her hands. Lucky for her, twenty-four-hour Midtown diners saw weirdos seven days a week. No one paid any attention to Julie's despair. If they did, they kept all comments to themselves.

"Fuuuuuuuuuuck."

A crackly voice radiated from her earbuds. Dead Air. "What's going on?"

"I fucked up," said Julie. "I told them my name."

"Told who?"

"The woman."

"What woman?"

Julie folded her arms on the sticky countertop and laid her head down. Despite the late hour, the establishment was packed, its clientele a mix of strung-out college students, wannabe bikers, drunk tourists, and starry-eyed first daters. "Clarice. From the firm. It was a setup. Akrasiel wanted to get me killed."

"Hold on, hold on," said Dead Air, voice fritzing in and out of comprehensibility. Instinctively, Julie thumbed at her phone before remembering there wasn't a point. Dead Air hadn't called through typical means, not that he ever did. "From the top."

"I was following the visions I got from the—" Julie almost said angel but caught herself. "—Akrasiel. And I went to the site of one of its murders, hoping I'd be able to get more leads."

"I distinctively remember St. Joan saying not to do that."

Julie nodded. "Well, I'm really bad listener. Anyway, as it turns out, one of the murder sites was the house of this woman, Clarice Winterson—"

"Wait, googling her." A second later: "Oh, fuck. She's one scary mother."

"Akrasiel killed her husband. I didn't realize. Not at first. I was trying to tell her that my job is helping people, so I blurted out my name."

"Why?" demanded Dead Air.

"I don't know. Remember? I'm a fucking dolt. Anyway, she ended up going on about how all the dead people were from the law firm, and Tyler."

"Ugh."

"And I don't know. She summoned versions of her husband to kill me and I had to explode one of them. Then I ran the hell away while she was staring at me like Carrie at prom."

"I'm guessing you want us to drag Sarah as far away as humanly possible."

"If you can scrape together inhumanly possible, I wouldn't say no," said Julie, sitting up straight again. A young waitress with massive hoop earrings wafted past, coffee pot in hand. She angled it meaningfully at Julie, who nodded, holding up her off-white mug. "I just don't know what I'd do if Sarah gets hurt."

Julie liked diner coffee more than almost anyone she knew. She'd met purists who turned up their nose at the substance, but Julie unironically adored the taste of watered-down, mass-produced, slightly burnt Folgers light roast. It made her think of college, that first year when everyone including her was under the impression she might make it big.

Instead, she'd made off with a hell of a lot of oxy.

"Julie, you should have waited like you said you would," Dead Air began. "We're—this is like going into a raid with gray gear. This is taking your level one hero to the end-boss. You can't have thought this would have gone well."

"I thought you were on the side of eh-fuck-it, Dead Boy."

"I'm on the side of you not dying."

"Yeah, well that's my side too."

The waitress finished pouring the coffee. Julie mouthed a *thank you* and was rewarded with a brilliant smile as she sashayed off to finish her rounds.

"Good. That's the smartest thing you've said in a while," said Dead Air. "Just—I'd hate to have to start a new co-op game with someone else, so don't fucking die on me."

"I get it."

"And it'd suck to have to do doubles in the arena with a newbie."

"Totally."

Dead Air sighed. "Anyway, we'll see what we can do. St. Joan says she has a house in Buffalo. We could see about getting her there."

"Sure. Buffalo could work," said Julie, scanning the laminated menu again. Breakfast potatoes and maybe an omelet. The mathematics could be made to make sense, especially since there was leftover pizza in the fridge now. "I just want Sarah safe. I'm honestly scared now. It was one thing to have a quasi-angel-whatever-the-hell-that-is after me, but Thorne & Dirk as well?"

"I can max out their credit cards, if that helps?" Dead Air waited for the requisite laugh, which Julie provided, happy for the excuse to groan at her best friend's ridiculousness and not think about why he was supplying the distraction.

"Get Sarah a house or something with the money."

"Will do, Julie." A beat of silence. "What's your game plan? Like, Thorne & Dirk will probably most definitely come after you. And, if you keep rolling up to murder sites, the NYPD is going to have questions too."

"I know."

"So, what are you going to do?"

"The answer depends," said Julie, flagging down the waitress and tapping her order out against the plastic menu.

"On what?"

"Whether you want me to lie or tell you the truth."

"The truth, Julie." There was an unsettling bleakness to his voice, an intensity of emotion uncharacteristic of the man. In the tense statement, Julie thought she heard other things too: whispering in the background static.

"I don't know," said Julie honestly. She thought about the succession of events. When she first touched the blood on the walls, she received a vision of Akrasiel's past activities. Pricking her fingertip and making contact with the feather reduced the latency of her visions. Slicing her tongue? That gave immediate active access to Akrasiel. Maybe the key was a deeper cut. "I'll think of something. You just focus on keeping Sarah safe."

Julie stared at her forearm, crisscrossed with scars from her barbed wire magic and other mementos from the last decade: a patch of poorly healed road rash, scratch marks, a few cigarette burns, the floral tattoo—more spikes than rose—winding around most of the limb. She grimaced. The thought of cutting herself open for Akrasiel annoyed Julie. One thing to self-harm of your own volition, another to risk emptying your arteries for a fucking monster.

But she didn't have a choice, did she?

"Not like I ever had one," said Julie, ducking into an alley. She freed the witchy knife again and wedged the blade deep into her forearm, her vision whiting out along the periphery as she dug, and dug, and dug, peeling back muscle and carving aside skin until she saw the glow of yellowed bone. She was careful to gouge around the arteries but there was only so much she could do. Blood sheeted from her arm, pooling under her sneakers. It was starting to hurt less, which scared her. She hoped it wasn't her brain extricating itself from the knowledge she'd cut too much, too deeply, and that the blood loss was actually fatal. She had heard the stories. Disassociation happened.

A little light-headed, Julie fished out the feather again and carefully wiggled it into the gash. She watched as the veins blushed pink, warmed to carmine, darkened to wine. The barbules stiffened: Julie felt them pierce muscle, felt them anchor, felt them drink the oblation of her exposed flesh. She watched the feather contract and expand, as if matching the pace of her breathing, a tertiary lung incubating inside her arm. It occurred to her then it was entirely possible that Akrasiel might simply grow out of the feather, suck her dry, then climb out of her withered husk. The imagery was so vivid, so unsettlingly plausible, Julie nearly forcefully excised the feather. She was reaching for it, in fact, when—

—glass, and the taste of green in her mouth, a ravenous verdancy like the ascendancy of moss, climbing over her tongue, silking her throat. Green like the ivy, greedy as the ivy too, and Julie was succumbing to the lushness, feeling it entwine with entrails, and if there was a death that could be said to be good, it might be this one, this quiet end in the hungry—

Julie shook her head. *Not yet,* she thought. *Not until Sarah is safe.*

—skin being pulled, being pulled, being tugged on, until it sheared away from the back of a gaunt hand. Julie wasn't looking through Akrasiel's eyes, she realized. She was embedded this time in the hindbrain, buried so far down in Dan's rotting cerebellum, the thing took no notice of her even though she was there, right there, at this very second, in its head, spying myopically through a keyhole connection. Before, all she had were visuals. Now it was multisensorial, and Julie had, to her dismay, ringside seats to Akrasiel's gastronomic experiences.

The gristly skin tasted awful, bitter from having undergone advanced decomposition. Akrasiel kept chewing until the tissue macerated to paste. Then, humming tunelessly, it spat the pulp onto its palm and patted it over a wound on Dan's right calf, the injury syrupy with maggots. The larvae, somnolent before, tore into the mash—

LetmediejustletmediefuckfuckpleasegodJULIEsomeoneJUSTKILLMEPLEASEOHGODLETMEDIEthishurts

Dan's voice, keening despairingly. Julie wasn't surprised by this development—or sympathetic, if she wanted to be honest with herself. Even if everything else went pear-shaped, she would at least know Dan was in untenable amounts of agony: it was one small and collateral good in this fucked-up narrative, the only good thing in this whole ordeal, but she'd fucking take it.

Julie ignored Dan, focused instead on the environment around him/them/it. She needed to see the surrounding landscape, but it was hard. Akrasiel was entirely focused on cannibalizing what little was left of Dan and using the remains to create—no, Julie refused to even speculate. That was a road she wasn't ready for. Instead, she pictured the dial on one of those old cathode ray televisions and adjusted the knob, tweaking it in one direction or another while the image on the screen fritzed between high-definition clarity and static. Then shrinking the motions, tightening them. She saw—

—glass, so much glass, shattered in so many places, vandalized, spray-painted, furred with mold; thick glass doming a wild overgrowth, every planter conquered by vegetal life; glass through which she could see the well-coiffed landscape of Central Park overlaid with something else, a scent-memory almost, of stars burning themselves to dust and brine, an odor that called up, of all places, Coney Island putting on its best show—

Sure that she could find her way once she got there, Julie walked quickly back to the street.

⁂

Of all the obstacles Julie expected to confront getting into Central Park, a good-hearted old man intent on getting medical attention for her wasn't one of them.

"Seriously, man. It's fine."

"I used to be a cop," he said. "This isn't fine. Your shirt is completely soaked in blood."

The stooped little Korean man, pot-bellied, owl-eyed behind his enormous round glasses and bald save for a few wisps of white hair combed lovingly over his forehead, looked so much like Julie's long-dead grandfather it pissed her off. Anyone else, and she'd have told him to shove it or pushed past him to her destination. She had no idea what his age was: Julie placed him anywhere between seventy-five and ninety-two.

"It's not mine—" Julie said, trying to pass off the comment as a joke. But the man's concern bordered on religiosity and for the first time in a very long time, Julie felt again like a teenager trying to break the news of her queerness to her well-meaning but unapologetically traditional family. "Okay, it's mine. But it's no big deal."

She raised her arm, rolling the sleeve back for emphasis: a mistake.

"Who hurt you?"

"Samchon—" Julie tried.

"I said *who hurt you*?"

This was becoming a problem. The old man waved his torchlight for emphasis, its beam hopping along the bare black branches of the park's trees. A few more weeks, and they'd put on their coat of leaves, but not yet. Now, they reminded Julie of fingers chewed down to the bloodied bone.

"Well," said Julie, evaluating her words. "Myself, technically."

"You self-harm?" demanded the old man, his voice losing its dusting of New Yorker, its original inflections pushing to the surface. "I don't judge. But you know that's not a good thing. We can get you help, figure out how to—"

He reached for her wrist. Julie snapped her arm back, at a loss as to how to proceed. She'd been right back in the alley. She could smell Akrasiel, that seaside rot of its presence. A faint little whiff, rather than a full-on miasma, but it was enough to signal what Julie feared. Akrasiel was close, and if she wasn't careful, the old man's life might be forfeit in the upcoming conflict.

"Samchon, *please*. I don't need to be helped! I need you to get away from here."

"I had a daughter," he said, lapsing into Korean. "She was the most wonderful girl."

The use of past tenses wasn't lost on Julie.

"Goddamnit," she said, torn between her irritation at being turned into a proxy for someone's need to redeem himself in the eyes of a daughter figure and her sympathy. "Now's not the best time."

"She said that too. She always told me we'd talk when she was ready. And I let her. I said to myself, 'it's alright, your daughter is a grown woman. She will know not to let things go bad.'" His voice wobbled. "I was such a fool."

"You trusted in your daughter's autonomy, blah, blah, blah. Please. I need to go now."

"No, you—"

Julie was ready for it when Akrasiel's hand—she couldn't think of it as Dan's appendage anymore, not with the flesh grated away, and the phalanges doubled, tripled, every segment of bone fletched with spurs—groped out of the night air, dull knife sawing through cold butter. She rammed a shoulder into the old man's chest, knocking him away, although not before Akrasiel gouged a half-moon from the man's side. Gore splattered. Intestine boiled up to the wound. Fortunately for him and for Julie, the angle and the dimensions of the injury were such that his entrails made a cork of their own coils, and nothing fell, only bulged lasciviously from his ribs.

The samchon staggered like a drunk, stopped, breathing hard. With an expression of academic bepuzzlement, he tenderly patted his mangled side. His touch was light, almost delicate, jolting away from every contact with the protruding organ, as if it stung him that time.

"Run," he said, to Julie's surprise. "Before you get hurt too."

"Go to a—" Julie stopped herself. This was, if not entirely, at least tangentially Julie's fault. And it didn't matter if this meant she was "going soft," Julie felt an obligation to at least try to make sure the old man got home to whatever brood of grandchildren he might have. "Goddamnit."

She trotted toward him even as the man's legs gave out, limbs splaying in all directions as he sank onto the cobbled path, a puppet freed involuntarily from its strings. The look he wore was ill-matched for his face: a child's expression, full of hope that an adult would relieve him of its fear.

"It'll be okay, it'll be fine, don't worry," Julie murmured hurriedly, nonsense words, platitudes, little soothing noises meant to reassure rather than provide explanation.

Julie gashed open her thumb with her teeth and swiped the blood across the old man's face, scrawling a sigil she prayed wasn't too messy to work. A fever-heat shimmered down her spine and through her bones, indicating that yes, she had indeed pulled it off. Julie allowed herself one feral smirk. The old man's eyes rolled up to the whites as he tried to sit up, then thudded onto his back, vernixed in a mucusy slate-colored glow, snoring softly. A Band-Aid solution if there ever was one but it'd keep him from bleeding out.

One problem solved, Julie turned to the other, teeth bared in a snarl.

"Hey, Akrasiel. Didn't anyone teach you not to bully old people?"

It rasped a laugh in answer, crooking a finger at Julie before the rest of it withdrew languidly into nonexistence, like the air was a curtain to slink behind. The spectacle of it ticked her off. Everything about Akrasiel did. Julie fleetingly mused about how much of it was the parasite and how much of it was Dan seeping through. Dan, based on first- and second-hand experience, was a bit of a dick all unto himself.

"That how you want to do it?" said Julie to the salt-pungent noise. "Fine."

From a deep inside pocket in her coat Julie pulled out a different weapon that she rarely needed to use—a boline thrice blessed by a Wiccan high priestess, who would swear up and down her faith was about ritualizing her approach to life, unwilling and unable to see the little worm-gods who loved her. Julie raked the sickle-blade down through the air, a slit in reality fluttering open, disgorging emerald light. Beyond it: her quarry. Julie swallowed her last breath of this world and plunged through.

She landed on damp grass seconds, centuries, hours, weeks, epochs, and eternities after she leapt, disoriented by the temporal inconsistencies of the substance ligamenting worlds. Some magic practitioners made the jaunt regularly, treating it as banal, but Julie could never figure out how to. It weirded her out each time.

Julie stood up. It was colder here, the air sharper. There was precipitation of a kind, a soupy ouroborosian drizzle with fat raindrops that seemed to do nothing but circle the air lazily. What Julie could see of New York reminded her of the painting in the Wintersons' abode, the brushstrokes chunky and impressionistic, more color and concept than factual representation. Almost everything here was similarly hazy, and Julie had to fight to keep from checking to see if she too was devolving to abstractness. The only landmark that wasn't was the Victorian conservatory garden sprawling over the hillock in front of Julie.

She walked up to its ornate, brass-framed entryway, looked it over with a distrustful eye, taking in the oxidized curlicues and the rusted grins of the few gargoyle heads embedded among the decorations. Anything this pretty was invariably dangerous. The glass was milky with residue, constellated with moss. Julie reached out a hand to touch the doorway. Immediately, she was besieged by the green hunger she'd sensed while delving into Akrasiel's head earlier, except this time, well, Julie had originally filed away the experience as "overwhelming" but she was revising her opinion now. What she experienced was a flimsy joke compared to the intensity of her current communion.

This was the waking dream of Central Park, she realized, its disgust at being dolled up because the city elites couldn't bear the faces of the working-class as it was, couldn't stand to look at their churches and their communities, couldn't dream of a world where they didn't hold the leash and thus, needed to civilize it under the excuse of collective betterment; this was Seneca Village's rage, its anger at being made refugees in their own city, marched from their homes when they'd already been running for hundreds of years.

Julie felt its hunger ripple over her, listened:

It was waiting for the city to die. It would wait forever. It did not need this to come to pass now. It was used to waiting. It knew, in the way of green things and deep earth, that a day would come when humanity's heart stuttered to a halt, and then, it would eat. It would sink its roots into Man's bones; it would eat and it would grow and it would spread until even the memory of what it had become was engulfed in green.

Until then, it would dream of that slow apocalypse.

Given all the newfound context, Julie thought, its choice of appearances really did make sense. The green—there'd have been the shape of something like a name in those visions, a quiver of electrons that might jigsaw into a coherent moniker if only Julie stayed, and listened, and slept under the grass—released her, its point made. Julie blinked hard. Though freed, she still felt slow, her blood thickened to sap. She wanted to lie down, let this place enfold her, bury her in ferns. If she did, she wouldn't have cause to be anxious again. Nothing would matter. Myelin would enrobe her ribs like so much lace. She would, she would—

Julie tossed her head like a horse ridding itself of flies.

"No," she said sternly. "Not yet."

The green—how ravenous it was, how thoughtless its hunger—receded further, as if chastised.

Julie nodded and entered the conservatory.

She found Akrasiel under a slant of otherworldly light, the luminance faintly opaline, rainbowed at the margins. It no longer looked like Dan. The mostly eaten scarecrow was gone and Julie discovered she was unutterably thankful for that small mercy. Her hate for Dan had bordered on an inferno. It had burned through her, its smoke choking any thought that didn't involve protecting Sarah, killing Akrasiel, and curb-stomping Dan so hard he would need a fresh jaw transplanted in order to even sip coffee.

Julie still wanted to bleach her eyes after seeing what he'd been molded into.

Given that, she was glad for this new horror, glad for the weird treelike figure he'd metamorphosed into. Dan's body looked like it'd been plastered with bark. Even his face was gone, hidden under a mask of a stiff, scabrous substance.

LetmediejesusfuckingletmedieJULIEPLEASESHOOTME-BREAKMYNECKDOSOMEthingGodithurts

Dan's shriek echoed through the space, better than any alarm. So much for the element of surprise. Akrasiel turned dreamily to her, raising its head, its eyes half-lidded under a coating of grayish purple.

"The Door comes to see what it has let out into the world, I see," it said with an almost carnal pleasure. "But does it regret what it has done? Is it proud?"

"Enough with that eldritch bullshit. You know my name."

"But the trappings of myth are so fun," it said in Dan's voice, with Dan's drawling cadences.

"So is kicking your ass."

"Can it wait?" it said, again in Dan's voice.

She closed her eyes and rummaged around in her head for spells. Finding what she wanted, she silently recited a rhyme as old as Sumeria, and said one word aloud.

Now.

The green burst through her, eager to swallow the ocean that was Akrasiel, its pelagic nature. Eager to welcome Dan, who Julie could feel straining toward the promise of dreaming under the soil, of being still and silent and blessed while the worms churned him into something beautiful.

LetmediepleasetakemeletmedieletmedieletmesleeppleasePLEASE

Akrasiel roared its fury while ivy helixed up along Julie's legs, up over her arms, trellising her. Jasmine rushed up after the ivy, knotting itself around its stems, armoring Julie. She felt a surge of joy, uplifted by the wild world, by the sight of Akrasiel's rage. It wasn't invulnerable. Julie was sure of that now.

Weighted down by the green, she ran toward Akrasiel, palms out, like a girl reaching for a lover. The green wanted them both, wanted her, but it'd settle for the pair, one who was begging to be enfolded into its roots, one who could keep it watered and fed for epochs to come. Yes, it wanted Akrasiel.

Roses tore through the glass, their blooms the largest Julie had ever seen, every one of them the midnight claret of a heart cooled in death.

"What a piteous offense," snarled Akrasiel in Dan's voice, swatting at the greenery, at the blackberry brambles crawling across the floor. "Flowers and berry bushes. I was old before the earth dreamt of its leaf, older than the water. I am—"

"—Really bad at seeing the obvious."

There were three things in the world that Julie Crews was known for. The first was an appetite for vices. The next was her aptitude for magnification. The third was having a right hook so vicious it could stop a bull in its tracks.

Julie swung.

And the world exploded into light.

CHAPTER TWENTY-THREE

It was almost ten p.m. when Tyler convinced himself to head to Clarice's office. Neither the eyeballs nor the wards on the door had survived an afternoon with what felt like the entire continent's population of blowflies. Thankfully, most of the insects had either dispersed through the ventilation system or surrendered to sated comas. Tyler went inside the darkened office without event. Clarice sat like rubble at her desk, staring miserably down at a framed wedding photo. She was filigreed with sleeping insects—what parts of her weren't coated in shining glass.

"What do you want?" she croaked, not bothering to look up. She sounded like she hadn't had a sip of water in days. "Too impatient to wait for your girlfriend to do me in?"

"I'll let that slide because I know you're grieving."

"Fuck you."

Tyler inched closer, sparing the light switch his attention. The office was unilluminated save for the floor lamp right behind Clarice's rolling chair, and while the bulb wasn't of any notable potency, it was bright enough to hint at the outline of what laid in the penumbral shadows. Tyler had no need to see it in glorious detail. "Clarice—"

"I want you to die. Slowly," said Clarice, with more force this time. "I want everyone to die. I would lock everyone in this godforsaken building in this office and set it all on fire if it'd bring him back."

"It won't, though," said Tyler, very gently, sliding to sit atop a clean corner of Clarice's desk. He suffered a brief fit of envy. The desk was upsettingly gorgeous, replete with the kind of embellishments that he just knew were included to add extra zeros to the price tag. Absolutely no one needed diamond inlays. "You know that."

Clarice jerked her face away from view instead of snarling at him.

Good. He had scored a hit. Tyler now needed to press his advantage while Clarice was vulnerable and her grief was too raw to be put away where it wouldn't risk her. He shrugged on his best smile, reaching out a hand to rest it audaciously on her fly-specked shoulder. Clarice tensed under his touch but did not otherwise respond.

Tyler said, "What I don't know is why you're here instead of out there looking for him—"

"I've tried." Glass crawled up Tyler's fingers, trailing over his sleeve. It took everything for him to stay put, to keep smiling. "I've tried fucking everything to get Albert back."

"From this side of the equation."

Though he had practiced relentlessly in front of the mirror in his office, Tyler's heart nonetheless sped as he said those words. Clarice jolted her attention back to him, her face devoid of any expression, gray and cadaverous amid the half-shadows. She'd been thin before; her madness had eaten at what little fat she possessed still: Clarice was bone in a drape of skin, and her eyes burned like a fever.

"What," said Clarice, "are you talking about?"

"Energy doesn't just disappear. That's the first law of thermodynamics. Even if the thing Julie set loose on the world had pulled Albert out of this universe, he has to be *somewhere.* And we both know that the veil between the living and dead can, how shall we say, distort things. If you were on the other side, however, you'd have more clarity—"

Clarice was smarter than he gave her credit for. Before he was done with his speech, she brayed with sudden mocking laughter, lips pulling back from teeth as gray as the rest of her.

"You idiot child. You're trying to get me to kill myself."

"Is it really death for someone like you?"

"What?" said Clarice, a cruel humor animating her features. "Someone old, you mean?"

"Someone *powerful*. You've been on the other side a thousand times. For meetings. For lunch dates with—with—whatever you want to call our clients. Death isn't new to you. I bet it doesn't have to be permanent. You'd find a way to come back with Albert. Someday. But—"

He leaned in. The glass stopped its ascent along his shoulder. But he could *feel* Clarice in his mind: an ice-rain of glass shards beating at Tyler's defenses. Stupid woman, he thought. As if he couldn't tell. As if he'd let her.

He'd learned a trick during his time at Excisions: if you were smart enough and powerful enough, or confident enough to pretend you had those first two qualities in spades, you could often just *talk* things into doing what you wanted. You needed the words too, of course. And Tyler had those as well.

He pushed back against Clarice, murmuring the words in his head in time with what he spoke aloud: "—if you don't do something now, you're going to lose Albert's trail. A month from now, ten years, who knows where he'd be when you finally decide you can't do anything from here."

Clarice said nothing.

Love, Tyler thought, *was such a bastard.* Contrary to what everyone else said about him, he didn't have the ego to believe he would have had a shot if Clarice wasn't so wrecked by misery.

"This is a trick," she said after several long minutes passed.

"I have ulterior motives," Tyler agreed, keeping his voice low and murmuring. "But it isn't a trick. I guess you could call it a wager instead. I am gambling that you know you've tried everything. Except this. Except this one last thing. And who cares if an asshole like me gets a better job out of it? This is about you and your husband."

"You're not going to stop until I'm dead, are you?"

"Actually, I'm done," said Tyler amiably. "From now, it's your decision as to whether you're going to go after your Albert and hope for the best. Or stay here, ordering hits on younger folk until you're too old and decrepit to do anything but wheeze in a hospital bed, unable to die because Thorne & Dirk never lets management die. Alone for the rest of your life. Because *you* worried I was trying to take your job."

He cocked his head. "What is it going to be, Clarice?"

⁂

Tyler sat at his favorite table at Club La Pegre, the club behind the bookstore. The table allowed him to keep his back to the wall but still gave him an unobstructed view of the entire room.

It was a typical after-work crowd, a mix of humans, semi-humans, and the patrons he considered monsters even when he drank with them and hired them for clandestine jobs. Their twisted bodies, sporting feathers, tentacles, or horns, had made him uneasy since he'd stumbled into the place as a boy, after wandering into Esoteric Unlimited and learning he was special. Billy had been behind the counter then and had barely changed a bit since the first time Tyler saw him.

What a loser, surrounded by moth-eaten old books for all those years. Tyler laughed to himself, a hysterical little burble of noise. He was so amped on cortisol, it felt like he would shiver apart. He could not stop shaking. The tumbler of amber whisky sat untouched on his table after he'd nearly spilled it on himself twice while trying to take the inaugural sip.

He'd convinced Clarice Winterson to kill herself.

He actually *talked* someone into taking a knife to their own throat.

It had been touch and go for a while, and she had looked at him with those furnaces for eyes, with that half smile on her lineated face. The air was bright spears of glass, all of them pointed at Tyler. He remembered thinking *oh fuck,* and bracing for his transformation into a human sieve. Only it never happened. The glass withdrew. Clarice took an athame and she cut her throat. She ran it from one ear to the next, holding his gaze throughout, holding it even as the blood began to pour and she began to slump, her eyes never losing their pyretic brilliance, not until the last moment when the light in them simply winked out.

He'd been lucky. When he was sure Clarice was dead, he called Fall, mostly to gloat over his success, but also to ensure that Winterson's suicide was recorded for what it was. He didn't need people looking sideways at him for a murder he didn't commit.

Fall, of course, rose to the occasion. She and her team ran Tyler through a stripped-down version of the necessary procedures before he was declared witness to an unfortunate tragedy. Internal Security descended then on Clarice's house, as did the janitorial staff, and everyone else was sent home to mourn.

Tyler took his half day to the club. He deserved a celebratory drink.

With Clarice taken care of, Tyler had one last problem to solve: Julie. He still wasn't sure he could trust Fall with the job.

What the hell is really going on with you, Julie?

Was she on some depraved murder spree? That didn't seem like Julie. She had her problems, sure. Her temper. The absolute dearth of impulse control. Her truly concerning drug habit. But she wasn't a murderer.

Tyler ran through the possibilities as he swirled his scotch. Maybe Julie had snapped. He discarded the notion as quickly as he conjured it. She had too much spite to break. No, the worst-case scenario was that Julie and whatever infernal thing she summoned were in cahoots, murdering their way through Thorne & Dirk planning revenge on him.

And that doomsday scenario wasn't *bad,* per se. Inconvenient in how it implicated his involvement, but if he could just figure out how to steer the messaging, how to direct Julie's wrath even, this could work out amazingly for his career advancement.

He watched the new cocktail waitress flounce up to his table, her ruffled skirt umbrellaed by the quills radiating from her ass and, really, everywhere else. Those on her abdomen must have been softer or long enough to be flattened down: he could see the outline of them under her uniform, frothing out and up through her sleeves and the expansive cleavage. Her smile might have been pretty if the lower half of her face didn't open into segments.

"Here you go, sir," she said with a slight lisp. Tyler had to suppress a giggle. A monster who lisped.

Sure. Why not? This is New York.

The waitress set down his second scotch of the night but lingered at the table in clear hope of starting a dialogue. He raised his eyes to hers and flashed a blandly professional smile. "Is there something I can help you with?"

Getting closer, the waitress said, "You're Mister Tyler, aren't you? Julie Crews's *friend*?"

Tyler pushed his chair back a little closer to the wall. Suddenly, she was no longer a curiosity. His eyes narrowed as he gauged the count and reach of her spines.

"I'm not sure *friend* is the word," he said.

"But you know her." She had a gaspy but pleasant voice, like an out-of-breath Marilyn Monroe.

"That was a lifetime ago."

The waitress closed the distance between them even more. Tyler could feel the prick of the quills fletching her elbow. Instinctively, he tried to withdraw, only to bump against the wall he was already sitting flush against.

"I'm only asking because we have a bet going," said the waitress.

"A bet?"

"Do you think she really got shot, or was it a trick so she could pretend to be sick and kill all those people?"

The news had gotten out, then. He wasn't surprised. Recruitment at Thorne & Dirk hired for power, not personal discretion.

With an Internal Security team as rabid as theirs, there wasn't any need to fear the notion of nondisclosure agreements being violated. The department could be ruthlessly thorough about tamping down on leaks. So, Recruitment hired who they wanted, and trusted Internal Security to winnow out the gossips.

But with Fall intent on having Julie take the heat, small wonder that the rumors had spread so thoroughly. He beamed at the waitress, and gestured her just a little nearer before leaning forward to murmur conspiratorially. "Between you and me, I've been thinking the same thing. It would be good cover for a murder spree, don't you think?"

"I do," said the waitress excitedly. Her eyes were chemical shades of blue: the sclera a little paler, the irises darker.

"But hey, let's just keep it between the two of us. It's only speculation. I was close to Julie for a few years, but not that close. So, I'm sure I'm wrong." He winked at her, touching a finger to his mouth. "Anyway. We don't want to go spreading rumors, right?"

The waitress stood up with a little bounce, clapping her hands. "No. Of course not. I won't say a word to anyone."

Liar, he thought. You just said you had a bet going. By the time I leave, you'll have told everybody in here. And they'll tell their friends. Tyler sipped at his scotch. It was wonderful how gossip transcended species. Everyone loved other people's filthy laundry.

"Enjoy your drink," said the waitress, and swaggered back to the bar.

Tyler held up his glass to her retreating back.

He hadn't accounted for the possibility that information about Julie's alleged kills would have already disseminated through the public. But yeah, this worked. There were precious few people in New York who would cross Thorne & Dirk, and those who could survive a feud with the company wouldn't have any interest in taking Julie's side. She was problematic. Julie was good in parties, and great in a fight, but you kept your distance if you were gunning for respectability.

If the scuttlebutt kept making its rounds, Julie would be ostracized, hopefully leaving her desperate enough to come to him so he could—finally, if a bit sadly—finish her himself. There was, of course, the chance that Fall's goon squad would catch up to her first, and that too was an acceptable outcome, a tidy bow on a loose end.

Tyler emptied his drink with a grin.

Things were definitely coming together.

CHAPTER TWENTY-FOUR

It was common belief that the Barghest Sisters had no names. This was false. The Barghest Sisters did indeed have names, but like all their kind, they were possessive of them, aware of how the immoral could melt down the syllables to make collars like iron. Only the Barghest Sisters knew their true names, the twins having devoured their parents early in their childhood, and that suited them fine.

"Good job with hunting down Eric," said Billy Starkweather, counting out their share of the evening's tips in his office. "Really showed him why he shouldn't fuck with me or my shop."

The two women exchanged looks but said nothing at first.

The sibling on the right, who was inappreciably taller than her counterpart but taller nonetheless, a distinction earned by the fact she was the first to gnaw out of their mother's belly, looked to her sister and then said, very mildly, "Why did you send us after him, Billy?"

Billy stopped his counting. The rest of the staff peeled away. None of them had ever had unpleasant personal encounters with the Barghests, but all of them had seen the damage the pair could do.

"I thought you two could use the exercise. You seemed bored."

"We don't get bored," said the rightmost twin.

"Fine, fine," said Billy, chuckling like a father caught stashing Christmas presents under the tree: a little guilty, a little abashed at having been surprised, but otherwise unmoved by his discovery. "It's because he fucked with one of my books."

"Which book, Billy?"

"The Bellocq." Billy's voice losing its humor, his face giving up on its smile. He stared at them with chilly indifference, hip cocked, a thumb hooked in a pocket of his jeans. "But you already know that."

"Oh, you're having problems with books? How sad," said the woman, upper lip raised into a dog's curling smile. "That's good to know."

"The Bellocq? Eric destroyed the original when he tried covering up what he'd done. It's not going to give anyone any problems, least of all me."

The Barghest on the left, younger, a little less attached to the veneer of humanity, shook out her dark hair. One of Billy's most recent hires, a scrawny Black kid who wanted nothing more than to be a librarian and was coming to terms with how interning at Esoteric Unlimited wasn't at all the experience it was advertised to be, stood far away enough from the rest of the crew to have a ringside view of the Barghest Sisters' shadows, and how they were changing, doubling in volume, tripling, swallowing the breadth of that dimly lit wall.

"The —," the rightmost Barghest said. "It's out in the world again."

"That's impossible."

"Actually, it's really fucking possible," said the younger Barghest finally, voice Barry White deep, so whiskey-scratched and cigarette-roughened every word slid out as a growl.

The Barghests smelled the fear dampening his shirt, his natural musk seeping through the cedar and sandalwood of his cologne. The Sisters grinned as they took notice. He could posture all he wanted but they could smell his terror.

"No. Shit. Goddamnit. I just didn't think he'd put something that dangerous out into the world. I mean, most fakes have the most powerful spells left out, right? You pay full price and get watered down nothing. But someone put something *into* the Bellocq Crews took? Why?"

The Barghests shrugged in unison.

"Well, —" Billy tried to say the entity's true name only to choke, blood speckling the curve of his lower lip. He dabbed his tongue over the corners of his mouth and frowned, as if displeased by this reminder that, despite everything, he was still mortal in the ways that mattered most. "Akrasiel being released—" This was the thing's other name, as valid as its true one, as far as anyone in the know was concerned, for after a number of millennia, any distinction between host and parasite becomes purely semantical. "It shouldn't be a big deal, right? A few more killings and then it'll get bored and be done with things."

The younger Barghest laughed. The older one did not. By the time the sound died away, the only people in the cramped back-room office were Billy and the Sisters.

"No. —" the older sibling said its name again and Billy flinched once more at the sound. " —isn't just a killer. It has been hungry for epochs."

"It is starving," said her sibling.

"The Mother Who Eats comes, and —" That word again. Like an icepick wiggled through Billy's brainpan. "—is desperate to devour her. From her corpse, it will grow the end of days. But that isn't your problem."

"You should be worrying about how you messed up with your laziness and assumptions," rasped the other Barghest, eyes rolled up in her wolfish face. Her tongue, too long for a human mouth, brindled with gray, the muscle so athletic it curled like a ladle at the tip, lolled out of her grin. "But that's how you ended up saddled with Esoteric Unlimited in the first place, isn't it?"

"Fuck," said Billy. "Fucking Escamotage. I told him I didn't want the book in the store. But he insisted. I thought it was just one more book I had to sell to pay off my debt to him. It was too dangerous. I told him so."

"We don't care," said the taller sister. "The fact is that the situation exists."

"And it's as much your fault as it is Eric's. Was Eric's," said the other sister.

"No. It's not like that."

"We can do what we want, Billy Starkweather," said the Barghests in chorus as they stretched their arms overhead and rolled their shoulders, limbering themselves, and Billy tried not to think about what might constitute a warm-up for them, if a quick chase in a small office was how they readied themselves for bigger prey. "You're not our master."

"Don't forget why we're here in the first place," purred the younger Barghest.

"Yes," said her sister. "We're here to keep count of the number of times you fuck up. Can't wait to see you hit that magic number."

"Because when you do, we—" said the other Barghest, knuckling onto Billy's desk, more concept now than person, the filaments of her hair pooled along the walls, the particleboard under all of Billy's many ledgers, spreading everywhere, melting into the shadows. If Billy forced himself, he could see a canine structure to the dark: the points of ears, the long feathery bow of a tail wagging in its contentment. He didn't try very hard, preoccupied instead with the lambent white gaze, a color the purity and brilliance of the hottest flame, pinning him to his chair. "—get to hunt *you*."

A taloned finger rapped his nose.

"Boop."

Billy jerked away from the touch. He prided himself on always being in control. He had a poker face someone once described as hall of fame worthy. But it broke down, his lizard brain happy to chuck whatever it could at the big predator to convince it to go elsewhere.

"What do I got to do to fix it?"

The rightmost Barghest cocked its head.

"Let's start with you letting us eat Eric," it said.

"Eric," chuffed the leftmost Barghest, dragging itself closer to Billy.

He hated the Barghest Sisters then. Hated the smell of them. Hated the ease with which they had driven him into a literal corner. Hated, more than anything else, their brazen awareness of how they were better, stronger, faster, much scarier than him.

No, that was a lie.

What he hated most was his past self for believing he could keep them leashed. Hand to chest, that was the worst part of wild animals: the way they lulled you into thinking you'd domesticated them. Billy remembered a story from the early 2000s, when a chimpanzee brutalized a woman over a Tickle Me Elmo. As punishment for daring to fuck with the beloved toy, the chimp, Travis, had torn away her eyelids, her nose, her jaw, her lips, broken the bones of her face. He'd ripped off her arms.

The Barghest Sisters reminded him of the psychotic ape.

For years, they played the good bouncers, never asking for much. And though Billy had been wary in the beginning, he was soon lulled into complacency. The Barghests didn't seem to care about money. He paid them peanuts and they said nothing. It was every club owner's dream. So, like an absolute shmuck, he let his guard down, trusting in their easygoing veneer when what he should have done was stay alert. The worst thing about all of this was there really wasn't anyone to blame but himself, a situation he loathed more than the grinning twins themselves.

"Well?" said the rightmost Barghest.

"Take him if it'd make you happy," said Billy. That was the thing with entities like the Barghests. They always needed permission from their master or employer. "I don't fucking care."

"You sure?" rumbled the other sister.

"You ladies are my first priority. Eric is replaceable."

"Good," said one of the Barghests. Billy wasn't sure which. "Because if you had said no—"

"We have standing permission to eat *you*."

Billy paced his office, noise-canceling headphones over his ears, while the Barghest sisters made a meal of poor Eric. The devices were top-shelf quality. Billy had spared no expense in their acquisition. There were nights, after all, when he needed to deal with accounting while music blared from his bar. *Karaoke nights are the worst,* he thought exasperatedly, as a wail knifed into his attention.

Fucking technology. It so rarely worked as advertised. There were always some caveats, always a flaw in the system. Billy couldn't understand how Dead Air could tolerate their manifestations.

He also wished to hell that the Barghests would stop playing with their fucking food.

"Animals," he muttered.

Billy was worried. He was worried about what else he might have failed to give due consideration. The Barghests had also left his office with a hell of a non sequitur: we have standing permission to eat you. Who had given them permission? Was it the Escamotage? Someone else? He could deal with some external power being the authorizing party. As long as it wasn't the Escamotage. Although why would he, of all the things that lived in this world and the next, give the Barghests the option to eat Billy?

Maybe he's found someone else.

The idea turned his stomach. It wasn't an impossibility. He hadn't been promised forever, only this ridiculous bookstore. Billy leafed through his accounts again. It was less progress than even he would have liked. The books kept coming back. No matter what he did, no matter how earnestly he screened his clientele, how he worked to match tome with customer, too many came back. Way too fucking many.

Maybe the Escamotage had noticed.

For the first time in a great many years, Billy was well and truly terrified, a situation which he resented to no small degree.

His fear made him feel powerless and Billy Starkweather hadn't come this far in life to do powerless. Not now. Not ever again.

The noises outside his office ebbed for a moment. Through the drywall, he heard Eric choking out a few last words.

"Tyler. Tyler gave me the fake Bellocq. He did it."

"Where did he get it?"

"From that company where he works. He paid me to give it to Julie."

Billy exited his office and what he saw unzipped over the hallway outside his door sickened him, though he took care to show nothing but bored indifference. He nodded to the Barghests, who met his nod with a slight bob of their respective heads: one sister nearly human, the other—well, there wasn't a word for what she was but looking at her was like blinking through glass shards.

He went to Eric—what was left of him—and said, "Why did Tyler want her to have it?"

"He just wanted to fuck with her. Teach her a lesson."

"Fuck. Did he want this to happen? Let Akrasiel loose?"

Eric stopped talking, so Billy slapped him a couple of times to bring him back around.

"I don't know," Eric slurred.

Billy thought about it.

No, Tyler was a moneyed prick and that's all he was. He wouldn't have any reason to let something as awful as Akrasiel into the world. But he could be a fuck-up. That's why he kept Crews around to clean up his messes. Was this whole thing some kind of joke, or worse, a lovers' spat that got out of hand?

It's possible Tyler is that stupid.

Billy looked from the sisters down to Eric.

"For what it's worth, I'm genuinely sorry, Eric."

"Please I—"

For a fleeting moment, Billy considered begging the Barghests for mercy. Eric was young; Eric had overstepped; Eric would learn if he was given the chance to learn. The defenses floated up in his mind. But then he looked into the Sisters' eyes, fluorescing in the shadows where they stood, waiting for Billy to be done so they could resume their game, and he knew such an attempt would be ridiculous. Worse, it might have them think he was bloody fool. He patted Eric on the jaw, like the dying man was a stranger's frightened child, and went back to his office, leaving the Sisters to finish their grisly work.

When it was done and the Sisters again loomed at his desk, Billy said, "What now?"

The sister on the left picked at her teeth with a sliver of bone, grinning as she worked it. Most of her had been stuffed back into human shape except for the dentition. These were still visibly canine teeth, much too large for even her broad face. Their presence engorged her cheeks; the Barghest looked like she was nursing an infection. "What do you mean 'what now?'"

Billy gritted his teeth. "My inventory is a mess. The fake Bellocq is still out there. I'm down one very good employee. Akrasiel is running loose. I said what I said: what the hell now?"

The other sister laughed throatily. "Not our problem."

"No, no, no. Fuck that. You can't just wash your hands clean of this. You need to do something about one of those things. Any of those things," said Billy, trying hard not to shout. "I don't care. Pick one. It's all the same to me. You *owe* me. After what you did to my store—" He gestured stiffly at the charnel. The floor was strewn with entrails. There were patches of carpet that would never be the same again. "—you owe me."

The Barghests' gazes followed his arm and Billy was reminded of a wolfdog an old acquaintance had kept until the beast ate the face off a teenager whose only sin was jumping the fence to say hello to the doggie. Every time Billy's friend had thrown a ball, the dog had looked at it the same way the Barghests were looking at Billy's arm, with the same distinctive indecision, as if weighing the value of going after the ball or the body that had flung it and being unable to decide if either warranted the energy.

"No," said one sister.

"None of that matters at all to us."

"Way below our paygrade," grinned her sibling.

Billy wanted to scream. "Then why are you even here?" he said.

"We told you already," said the Barghests in easy symphony.

"We're here to track how many times you mess up."

Angry enough to feel a bit defiant, Billy said, "Tell the Escamotage I can't get rid of his books if he keeps letting assholes like Tyler stuff the store full of their bullshit."

Neither Barghest answered. Instead, they stared at him with expressions that were kissing-close to amused pity. Billy realized he wasn't going to get any traction this way. He needed a different tactic. He gathered himself while the Barghests playfully fought each other over Eric's femur, their growling carrying the resonance of an airplane engine. He smoothed his anger down, slicked it behind his salesman smile, and drew a harsh breath.

"Look, ladies—"

At this, one of the Barghests shrieked with a coyote's laughter, her grip on the much-contested bone slackening for a split second: enough time for her twin to yank it howling from her possession.

"—far be it from me to comment on what you find amusing in life, but if Akrasiel brings about the death of the universe, we're all going to be in purgatory together, with me trying to sell books to ghosts. I don't think any of us want that."

The sister on the left chuckled. "Won't happen."

He was getting nowhere.

"You're not making sense," said Billy sweetly, sensing that the Barghests were actively trying to anger him. He wasn't going to let them win. "You said that thing is out there trying to bring about the goddamned apocalypse or whatever."

"This is not the first time—" The Barghest said the thing's

name again, driving Billy to slam his fist on his desk over and over until the pain of his bleeding knuckles drowned out the agony of the sound. "—has tried. It won't be the last. But the door is easy enough to close. Kill the summoner." Billy gnawed open his tongue. "Kill the parasite."

Her sister grinned. "Good thing we're always hungry."

CHAPTER TWENTY-FIVE

Tyler sat back and watched Thorne & Dirk disintegrate into an immediate and bloody chaos following news of Clarice's suicide. Though viewed at first as the weak-minded consequence of her widowing, it quickly metastasized. There were fraudulent claims that Clarice had foreseen her death at Julie's hands and wanted no more than to escape it on her terms, then tense gossip about a planned culling, which then resolved into vicious and unshakeable folklore about how, every century, Thorne & Dirk went about slaughtering junior staff to ensure the longevity of its board, and that absolutely killed any remaining sense of decorum the firm possessed.

The next few days became a bloodbath, one Tyler only eluded because Fall made it clear that messing with Excisions meant screwing with Internal Security, and even in the throes of homicidal terror, no one wanted that. Tyler stopped counting the dead after the second afternoon of interdepartmental bloodshed. Enough staff members and their families had been reduced to decentralized studies of the human anatomy that it was getting boring. So boring, Tyler was beginning to idly toy with the idea of joining the massacre. It'd be something to do other than wait in his office while the corridors rang with screams.

Then, on the morning of the third day, Todd Cranston from Upper Management called to request Tyler's presence at precisely two in the afternoon. Fall, he said peppily, would be in attendance too.

"Should I bring flowers?" said Tyler.

"Only if you'd like to die," came the sugary response before the call was cut.

Tyler was outside Cranston's office at exactly one fifty-six, wondering where the hell exactly Fall could be. She wasn't the type to ever be late: the young Head of Internal Security was too aggressively New York for that. For one panicked moment, Tyler wondered if she might have died—killed by a motivated subordinate. He was surreptitiously checking his jacket to make sure he was suitably armed when Fall swaggered out of the elevator, dressed bewilderingly in a mustard silk ensemble.

"Always the early bird," she said.

"What does that mean?"

"It means you're a bit of a teacher's pet."

"Teacher's pet?" He was still processing the gauche amount of color Fall was wearing. "I—This is Cranston. You don't want to fuck around with him. He's Upper Management and takes that shit seriously."

"Yeah and that's exactly why we're going to be ninety seconds late."

"Do you want us to get killed?"

"Follow my lead, you coward, and all will be well," said Fall. "It's about making an entrance."

Tyler knew about making entrances—or at least, he thought he did. But under Fall's caustic regard, he felt out of his depth. He had no idea what Fall was angling for, and that, more than the growing sense he was entering obsolescence, unnerved him. The opaqueness of Fall's intentions was going to be a problem.

He glanced down at his watch. "We're already one minute late," said Tyler as he reached for the doorknob.

"Not yet, shithead."

"When?"

Fall looked at *her* watch—a rose gold–framed Panerai Tyler would have sold a kidney to own—and counted down under her breath.

"Now."

Tyler swung the door open. As was traditional for Upper Management, Cranston's office was disproportionally large on the inside, its walls floor-to-ceiling glass, exposing a vertiginous two-hundred-and-seventy-degree view of the Financial District. The centerpiece was Cranston's desk: a behemoth of a thing, sculpted from a single chunk of polished black obsidian. The lower half of the desk held the image of a man mid-evisceration, a harpy perched over him. His countenance was as ghastly as his tormentor's face was beautiful, the horror in his expression so exquisitely detailed that the terror in his eyes were palpable. They'd even sculpted his tears.

Tyler was midway to being impressed with the craftmanship when the man twitched. It was just a fraction of an inch, if that—but his head *turned.* And as though galvanized by the man's retreat, the harpy's claws moved too, slipping just a fraction deeper into the froth of entrails. Tyler understood now that the desk *wasn't* carved. The figures on the front had been alive once, but were imprisoned now in igneous rock. He wondered how long the man had spent dying like this. At the rate the two figures moved, it could have been decades. Perhaps even centuries.

"I see you admiring my desk," said Cranston. He was impressively statured, his honed physique at odds with the unnatural translucency of his skin, its weirdly diaphanous nature not helped at all by the pale suit he wore. His chalk-colored hair was unbound today, flowing over his shoulders, combed to a satin finish. Cranston, who'd been writing a note with a gold Montblanc fountain pen, finally looked up at the two of them and gave them a sour smile.

"You're—" Cranston's eyes flicked to the ornate mahogany hourglass on his desk. "—two minutes late. I hope you enjoyed your afternoon tea."

Fall strolled forward with an unrepentant smile, Tyler shuffling a step behind. She affected a curtsy, which raised Tyler's brows high enough that the skin of his forehead should have wrinkled off his skull.

"Sorry, sir. There was an altercation downstairs. Banks and I decided to handle it before we came to see you."

The perfect mask of Cranston's face *wobbled,* and for the hinge of a second, Tyler thought he glimpsed fear there under the metaphorical ice floes. "Was it Crews again?"

"No, not Crews. We're still working on identifying her exact location. No, I'm afraid this was simply a disagreement between HR and several discontented employees. The latter wanted protection. The former needed fresh hearts." Fall giggled, proving to Tyler his capacity for astonishment was without limit. "It was messy."

Cranston stroked a hand over his gleaming hair, destroying its unearthly finish. "The Subsumation event is so close. The Mother Who Eats is almost here, and we're bickering like idiots over nothing. There will be no forgiveness for any of us if this comes apart."

"I understand, sir," said Fall. "Know that Banks and I are entirely committed to ensuring the success of the coming ritual."

"Absolutely," said Tyler. "One hundred percent."

"If you were as committed as you claim to be, you'd have already dealt with Crews."

"We will," assured Fall. She was like a flare in the massive room, a tongue of flame, the only color in an expanse of glass and black stone. Tyler couldn't help but stare, and in doing so, notice how even Cranston stared, riveted by the spectacle that was Fall. "I assure you we'll have Crews soon."

With that bit of propulsive news, Cranston nodded, his face resettling into apathy. "Kill her on sight. I don't care if it happens in Times Square at high noon in front of a busload of vestal virgins. I want her dead yesterday."

"Just need HR to clear use of time magic," said Tyler, and both Fall and Cranston judiciously ignored him.

"No," said Cranston once Tyler had lapsed into an embarrassed quiet. "I take it back. Bring her in alive. I want her to be made an example of. I want to see her *burn.*"

He paused, then added with grandfatherly brightness, a sudden tone shift so repellent Tyler felt his gorge rise at the joviality, "And I want cameras there. Video footage. From every angle. I want sound too. Good sound. So I can hear her beg when she burns."

"Yes, sir," said Fall, as if Cranston had done nothing more than put in a lunch order. "Is there anything else?"

Steepling his long pale fingers, the old man said, "How is Garland doing?"

"She still burns, sir. Would you like us to complete immolation?"

"No. Not yet."

Tyler had to subdue the urge to wince. The last time he saw Phoebe, she had been cooked down to a patina of charred skin over bone, a marionette figure with surreally white teeth suspended in a column of blue flame, one room down from where the fifth floor ate lunch.

"Understood, sir," said Fall piously.

"Stupid woman," mumbled Cranston. "Still can't believe she set a formalus loose on our clients. Small wonder her department is made of fucking miscreants. You know what?"

"What, sir?" said Fall before Tyler could jump in.

"Kill them all."

"Sir?" said Tyler, starting at the words. "Kill who?"

"The HR department. All of them. They should have done damage control when Clarice died. Instead of allowing for this absurd insurrection. Useless idiots, all of them. I told the Board we didn't need them. But they insisted. Because it was the human thing to do. Fucking idiots," said Cranston, succumbing to memory, his voice trailing to a low, impatient murmur.

"All of HR?" said Tyler.

"Of course. I mean, it's somewhat irrelevant given the current climate—" On cue, someone wailed outside Cranston's office, a high-pitched shrill quickly ending in a damp burble. "—but we don't exactly have authority to kill other staff members without just cause. *Tyler* doesn't have authority to do that ever, not unless the personnel is compromised."

"Correct, sir," said Fall before Tyler could speak.

"Well, right now that changes. I'm promoting you from department leads to full management. This will give you free rein over the firm. Do whatever you have to do. Arrest whoever tries to stop you. Kill whoever gets in your way. Just get things done."

The enormity of what Cranston had said hit Tyler like a car crash. He was reeling. It seemed impossible that he and Fall would have earned a promotion like this so casually, their ascension to near godhood brought about by what? Sheer impatient whim? The infinitesimal mote of him that still gave a shit about earning his place in the world was aghast, but the rest of him brightened with rapidly compounding glee.

"That's all I have to say to you right now. Congratulations on your promotion and remember that I'll personally kill both of you if you fuck up."

"Of course. We wouldn't have it any other way," said Fall breezily, genuflecting as she backed out of the office.

"You can count on us," Tyler said, wondering if he and Fall would end up in Cranston's desk if they didn't satisfy the old bastard.

"Out."

Tyler got to the door first and held it for Fall. Despite his nervousness over the looming possibility he and Fall would be petrified and made into ornate office furniture, he was grinning the moment they returned to the hall, the corridor thankfully bare of screams for the time being.

"Damn," said Tyler. "We're *management*."

Fall, who he had expected to be demanding praises for her machinations, stared expressionlessly at the opposite wall. She breathed in shuddering gasps, both hands clenched into fists at her sides: her entire frame was rigid enough to be used as a measuring tool. As Tyler reached a hand to touch her, she jerked her attention to him, her eyes entirely pupil. The incredulity on her face startled him. She looked terrifically young then, like a girl scarcely out of her freshman year. All her brazenness, the caustic arrogance, the cruelty was gone, washed away by an expression like someone being told yes, they were special.

"I did it," she whispered, blinking hard at him. "I fucking did it. I'm the youngest manager in Thorne & Dirk history."

"Goddamn right."

"I did that," said Fall, jabbing a finger at her breastbone. "Me. I did it. They said I was going to die before the year was out. But I made it. I did it. I outlived those motherfuckers."

"And now you get their ghosts to dance for you, if you want."

Fall raised her hands to her face. Her shoulders began to rock and quake, and Tyler could not tell if the sounds emitting through her fingers were sobs or laughter.

"I did it," she whispered, barely loud enough to be heard.

"Yeah."

When Fall lunged for him and dragged him close, he did not stop her, nor did he recoil when she kissed him, or wince when her teeth tore into his lower lip. So very few things were better aphrodisiacs than triumph—and there was nothing like sex to lower a person's guard. He circled an arm around the small of her back and pulled Fall closer when she did not resist. It was possible Fall wasn't planning his murder, that her remarks about Tyler being past his best-by date were bravado, spoken without forethought. That she was just acting out because she was dreadfully frightened by being an ingenue in this house of wolves.

But Fall looked like she would be a freak in bed, and the thought of her waking up the next day and going *blech* at the revelation that she'd fucked an alleged old person was too good to pass up.

CHAPTER TWENTY-SIX

Sleep wasn't in the cards for Sarah. She lay on the sofa, head pillowed on her folded arms, staring up through the skylight embedded in the ceiling. Sarah was glad for the orangey-purple sky, and how it never truly darkened to the deep black of a rural night here in New York. At heart, she was always a city girl, finding comfort in the light pollution, the sense the city would always be awake with her, listening sympathetically. Not that she'd ever admit this to anyone, aware it likely represented something that was damaging the environment. As Dan said, "there is no ethical consumption under capitalism."

At the thought of her ex, Sarah made a face. She hated how Dan occasionally bubbled up out of nowhere with his idiot observations and his smug little philosophies. In hindsight, she should have broken up with him after he clambered down into the r/incel subreddit, but she'd trusted him when he said the curiosity was entirely scholastic, born out of the obligation to understand what the other side was pursuing. Understanding your enemy is half the battle won and all that.

A definite red flag. Unfortunately, those were never raised until one's back was turned.

Still, that was in the past. Dan was in her past. With luck, he would stay there, and Julie—

Sarah rolled over onto her side, knees curled to her chest. She hadn't been able to sleep since Dan shot Julie. Despite the sedatives, magical or otherwise, all Sarah had been able to do was scrape together a few hours of fitful drowsing. The exhaustion was starting to whittle at her ability to hold it together.

Blearily, she reached for the clock on the dresser. After Julie had wanted to charge ahead and deal with Akrasiel, St. Joan had insisted that Sarah migrate to the older woman's residence instead, a penthouse apartment sprawling over the summit of the building. Unlike Julie's accommodations, it was gorgeous, immaculately kept, styled like it was home to some Russian oligarch. When Sarah exclaimed as much to St. Joan, the latter smiled enigmatically and asked if her new guest had a preference in teas. And then when Sarah observed the spatial impossibility of there being a skylight in Julie's apartment and a penthouse here, St. Joan coaxed her into listening to a lecture on why water temperature mattered for tea.

3:30 a.m., read the numbers on the electronic clock face.

That's it. Sarah kicked her way out of the tangle of her duvet and sat upright. Despite her tiredness, she felt what was almost like a buzzing in her marrow, a skittish energy that hummed and skipped and trilled erratically through her, wholly independent of her fatigued brain. A sigh gusted out of her as she pressed the heel of a palm against an eye, wishing for, well, she wasn't sure what. What she wanted was to be at Julie's side, except she understood she would be a liability. Sarah was athletic, even impressively so, but calisthenics and rock-climbing only did so much for the body, and absolutely nothing to arm her against a rogue angel-but-not-actually.

Nonetheless, she could still be useful. She was part of the team now, had pledged Julie research help, and that's exactly what she was going to give her.

Sarah padded out into the hallway toward the kitchen, evaluating the bookshelves she passed. St. Joan's place was replete with ancient texts and old movie posters; the apartment smelled of them, something Sarah loved. Surely, an answer was in one of these tomes, she thought, running a finger along their spines.

"You'd help me, right?" whispered Sarah into the books, and she was almost sure she heard the library carol adoringly in answer.

The kitchen, alone of the rooms in the dwelling, was sleekly minimalist: white marble tiles, mahogany countertops, a massive island that might have accommodated an entire cast of reality show chefs. St. Joan only had cast-iron cookware, each one expertly seasoned, several of which hung from the hooks on the walls. Sitting alone on a barstool at the kitchen island, flipping through a book, a dented Bialetti and a cup that might have been white once in accompaniment, was Dead Air.

He shocked Sarah with how young he looked with his usual veneer of insouciance laid aside. Looking at him like this, it dawned on Sarah that she'd never once heard him discuss parents or siblings, a family, an epiphany that left Sarah melancholy.

"Hey," she said from the doorway.

Dead Air startled at her voice. "Shit, hey, hi—god, you should be asleep. Do I have to get Them to send elephant tranquilizers?"

Sarah walked over and hopped up to perch on the counter, legs crossed at the ankles.

"Couldn't sleep. Too busy being worried about my—"

"Girlfriend?"

"—best friend," said Sarah, hoping her cheeks weren't burning. "It's definitely cause for insomnia, thanks."

"I didn't say it wasn't. I just said you need to sleep."

She laughed. "Fair. I—"

"You two really should just kiss already."

"It's not like that between us."

"I can see your search histories," said Dead Air, far too casually.

This time, Sarah knew she went beet red. More than one sleepless night had been spent browsing Quora for topics like *how do I tell my best friend I like her.*

"Anyway, yeah. I get it. It's hard."

"I'd be asleep if I knew how to be, honestly. I *feel* tired," said Sarah, the humor wicking from her voice. She stared at the walls as she spoke. "But every time I lie down and try to close my eyes, I'm thinking about Julie again. She wouldn't have gotten in all this trouble if it wasn't for me. She wouldn't have been *shot* if it wasn't for me. And now she's out there again, chasing down god knows what that angel thing really is, and it's—it's—"

"Coffee?"

She nodded. It would, at the very least, be something to do with her hands.

Conversation faded to an amiable silence as Dead Air prepared them both a fresh pot of coffee. He set the timers on the base of a goose-necked kettle; ground fresh beans; extracted a whisk and a fat-bottomed glass from the cabinets. He spooned the pulverized coffee into the Bialetti after which he filled the dull iron canister with boiling water. When the espresso had finished brewing, he heaped brown sugar into the glass, adding a minimal quantity of coffee, before whipping both into sepia froth. Then and only then did he serve them both small cups of the coffee, which smelled of caramel.

Sarah took an investigative sip. It was very good, sweet yet earthy, and for some reason it drove her to tears.

"Hey, hey. It's cool. There's nothing wrong with being scared." Dead Air crawled onto the island beside her, a finger timidly rubbing circles over her second knuckle.

The absurdity of the gesture, combined with the earnest worry in his expression, brought a choking laugh to Sarah. "I so regret asking Julie to be my knight in shining armor."

"For what it's worth, I think she doesn't."

Sarah said nothing, embarrassed to have broken down like this, once again someone to rescue. She kept her eyes on the floor tiles, studied the subtle differences between each enameled surface. So focused was she on the tilework, on keeping contained the sobs burbling in her lungs, that she only noticed Dead Air placing a book in her hands after he'd curled her fingers over its dusty cover.

"Here."

She looked down. "It's Julie's book."

"Yeah," said Dead Air. "I was reading through it tonight, trying to cross-reference it with existing information. It's—it's not good."

Reflexively, Sarah began leafing through the book, mesmerized by the crackling pages, how they crumbled to ash along the edges as she flipped through the volume. There were grotesque drawings she'd somehow missed on her first dozen reads: linocut-like renditions of the ocean, of deep-water horrors that nonetheless smiled like a drunk on his twentieth beer, needle-toothed things, things that weren't really anything but constellations of entrails, worms crawling up from the bottom of a page toward what looked like a sleeping angel.

"With Cthulhu, it's never good," said Sarah, venturing a smile.

"I wish it was Cthulhu. Cthulhu, we could handle. We'd just need to lure him into the salt mines and *blam,* calamari for everyone." Dead Air raked thin fingers through his dark lank hair. "The Mother Who Eats—there are rumors . . . actually, let's walk that back a bit. So, all of Wall Street has its own patrons. Some of them are old and common knowledge. Inari is shared between way more companies than you'd believe. But then there are places like Thorne & Dirk. They worship things like The Mother Who Eats."

"This isn't going to be good, is it?"

"No," said Dead Air. His worn-through youth was excruciating to see, his face precociously lined. Sarah wondered again about how lonely it must be to be the only priest to a sea of gods. "The Mother Who Eats is—I guess the best way to put it is, uhm, think of her as a whale."

"A whale."

"Yes. A great eldritch monster whale."

"*Eldritch monster whale.*" Sarah giggled. The alternative was to give in to her tears again and no one wanted that.

"Uh huh." Dead Air paused. "Do you have a problem with my analogies?"

"With eldritch monster whale? Yes. What do you think?"

Dead Air flapped his hands over his head. "Okay, I am not good at analogies. But humor me, okay? Think of The Mother Who Eats as a great eldritch monster of a whale swimming through the cosmos, bumping heads against other great eldritch monsters—"

"Are these also whales?"

"You are the absolute worst. Anyway, the point is eldritch monster whales eventually die, and when they do, they sink through creation, and the great carrion beasts of the dark come out to eat. Akrasiel, we think, is one of them. Akrasiel, as far as They know, is the larval form of whatever it is that will eventually devour The Mother Who Eats."

"Okay, I'm with you."

"But right now, because it's essentially a helpless grub—"

Sarah thought of the first illustrations she had found. "It needs a host body until it can crawl inside the Mother—well, that's some Oedipus bullshit."

"Nerd," said the veritable pope of nerds. "But yeah, far as I could figure, Akrasiel needs a host to survive, but it can't just be excised from the host. We can't just gouge it out. There are no spells for it. Nothing I've seen. The summoning that Julie did—it's basically a spiritual umbilical."

Sarah continued rifling through the book, not wanting to look up. She could hear in Dead Air's voice what he wouldn't say, the dreadful thing he'd unearthed in his research and hoped to kill through sleepless observation: they'd both known this was coming, for all their procrastinating with stupid jokes.

"No," said Sarah, very quietly, after several more minutes had passed.

"Akrasiel can only be banished with the death of the host who called it into the world."

"No. There has to be another way—"

"Nothing I could find."

"No," said Sarah again, setting her coffee cup down with a definitive clank.

"I'm sorry."

"I'll look."

"Sarah—"

"I'll look," said Sarah as she glowered at her trembling hands. "I'll keep looking. There has to be something we've missed."

"There is."

"What?" said Sarah excitedly. "Tell me."

"The book is a fake. I cross-referenced some of the information with other sources I have, and, well, nothing added up. This isn't a real Bellocq. Someone sold Julie a fake."

Sarah's stomach knotted, but she tried not to show her shock. "Who would do that? And why?"

"I don't know. Billy Starkweather wouldn't knowingly sell a forgery."

"What if he didn't?" said Sarah, her mind racing. "What if someone wanted this? Maybe not all the murder and chaos, but for Akrasiel to be let loose and for Julie to be blamed for it."

"Who would do that?"

Sarah thought back over the time she and Julie had been together and finally said, "Tyler Banks."

"What? Are you sure?"

"Reasonably. He told her he wasn't her guardian angel anymore. It planted something in Julie's head. I don't know if it was magic or him simply manipulating someone he knew, but Julie talked about a guardian angel after that. I'm sure of it."

Dead Air sat back and looked around. "If Tyler did this and someone finds out, holy shit for him."

"Fuck him. This is good news. If the book is fake and the information tampered with, then maybe the stuff about Akrasiel is too," said Sarah excitedly.

"It isn't. Believe me, I checked a dozen sources. Whatever else might have been wrong with the book, once Akrasiel enters the Earthly realm the information is real."

"No."

"I'm sorry."

"I'll look again. And again," said Sarah, and Dead Air said nothing else, only reached over to hold her. She all but crawled close to him, face buried in his thin chest, no shame left to her, every pretense shed: she wept like a widow, like someone who knew their heart would be shattered so utterly, there wouldn't even be pieces to mourn.

And the two sat together at the counter until dawn slit open the night, spilling gold onto the world, neither acknowledging that Julie was going to be dead soon.

CHAPTER TWENTY-SEVEN

The first word that Fall said to Tyler when she rolled over was indeed *yuck,* an epithet quickly tailed by *what the fuck* and *Jesus Christ, how drunk was I?* Tyler sprawled contentedly under Fall's sheets as the woman screeched out of her bedroom, swearing with increasing volume and creativity. When she returned an hour later, Fall bawled an irate, "*Fuck* me," to which Tyler replied grinningly, "Already did. Twice," and that led to the woman slamming out of the room again, howling a torrent of profanities in flawless Spanish.

Tyler beamed as he heard the front door bang shut.

He had been right about Fall. She did indeed fuck like a tiger; his back was striped with weals. In places, she'd even broken skin—but so had he. Their lovemaking made a ruin of Fall's bedroom and there was still debris from when they shattered a heinously expensive–looking table lamp on the parquet. But it was good. Very good.

As was what had happened while Fall slept.

Thirty minutes after she stormed out, the woman returned to sit very rigidly on the corner of her bed dressed in a three-piece woolen suit. Each time Tyler moved, Fall flinched as if someone had shouted in her ear.

Tyler quelled a chuckle. Really, it was such an easy joy to piss off his recent bedmate. "So, what's the plan for today?"

"Buying new sheets, for one," said Fall, sotto voce.

"I wonder if—No. It's insane."

"What is?"

"The ultimate power in this company comes from the Proctor. Could we get him on our side?"

Fall shot him a suspicious look.

"I swear to god, Banks. If I find that you've been going through my records, I'll eat your guts for lunch."

"What are you talking about?" said Tyler, a little shriller than he'd intended.

"Security has been studying the Proctor too, but purely on a defensive basis. But what if we could get him on our side?"

"I just said that."

"Yes, but you'll fuck it up. I could do it, though. I talked us into management, I know enough about the Proctor to do this too."

"Are you sure?" said Tyler quietly. "I was just thinking out loud."

Fall warmed to her topic. "Look, he's coming down from whatever shithole dimension he lives in to fuck the building senseless, right?"

"Yeah?"

"We need to first make sure he thinks the firm is incompetent and run by idiots, and that we're the only people here both ready and capable of attending to him without any risks to his personal safety. Not the firm. Just us."

"You want him to make us Upper Management?"

"Exactly."

"It would be nice not to wait centuries for the chance," said Tyler. "But how do we call him? Don't we need a quorum or something?"

Fall stood up. "Nope. And I know the ritual by heart. We pull this off and the firm is ours."

He watched as Fall gathered his clothes, chucking each article at him in turn. Fall had said *ours*. But had she meant it really? She was a killer through and through, and not the sharing type. There was no way she wasn't waiting to drive a knife into his back.

Maybe, just for laughs, she'd even make him look like Julie's final victim.

But he already had contingencies for that.

❧

They made it to the penthouse together without incident, meaning that if Fall was intending something, it very likely had to do with the Proctor. Would she sell him out to the monstrosity? Maybe there was some obscure component of the summoning ritual that he was missing? Something that required a sacrifice. Maybe her human allies—who? Tyler checked a mental ledger of who they'd pissed off: there were none left—were already in the rooftop office, waiting to run him through with knives.

I need to get my shit together, thought Tyler grimly. *This is do or die time.*

Once Fall closed them into the room, they put on the requisite paraphernalia: disposable booties, gas masks, industrial earmuffs. The interior was empty of adversaries. One of the meat lockers in the shadowed corners thumped like a brief and desperate heartbeat before its inhabitant gave in to despair again. If Tyler concentrated, he could almost convince himself he could hear whispering.

Above them hung the pointlessly baroque gold and glass vessel in which the Proctor made his manifestations. Tyler felt his pulse speed to a chattering intensity.

Despite Tyler's skepticism, Fall had been right. The ritual could be satisfactorily performed by just two people, so long as one of them was someone like Fall. She bullied him in the brisk and impersonal manner of a drill sergeant, barking corrections whenever Tyler faltered in even the most infinitesimal manner.

The door to the room opened unexpectedly. They both turned to look and saw a surprised janitor standing with a mop and bucket. "I'm so sorry. I didn't know anyone—"

Fall cut off the apology by pulling a pistol and shooting the man in the head. Tyler stared at the swiftness of it all.

"Should one of us close the door?" he said quietly.

"Fuck that. We're too far into the ritual. If any other dummy walks in here, the Proctor will deal with them."

But no one came, and soon enough, the Proctor was returned

to the world, bigger than Tyler remembered. Its flesh slopped over the vessel, toothed tendrils meandering over the slick tiles.

Confronted with the terrible spectacle of the Proctor, Tyler almost forgot his reservations about Fall, and the plan he'd been working on, idiotically glad to have another human in the room, his lizard brain clinging to the idea that two meant a herd and a herd meant safety.

"Proctor," said Fall. "We come bearing unfortunate news."

"There is a law and you do not follow it. You are not to summon me without being given permission." It was trying, Tyler realized, to peel itself out of the vessel, but the cancerous mass of itself acted as a cork. Had he been less terrified, he might have laughed at the revelation.

Fall said grimly, "It was an emergency, Your Grace."

"And who are you, zygote?"

"I'm Annabeth Fall, previously Internal Security lead and now Security Manager," said Fall before Tyler could collect his thoughts enough to speak. "And this is Tyler Banks. He works here too."

A hot spike of rage speared through Tyler. *What the fuck is she doing?* thought Tyler, shooting Fall a venomous stare. "Works here too" made him sound like a secretary, like he was an extraneous limb. Like he was fodder.

Fall deserved what was coming to her.

"Actually, I'm Manager of Excisions," said Tyler.

"*You,*" said the Proctor, straining in his direction. It was coming perilously close to escaping the vessel. "You are familiar to me. You, yes, you're Tyler Banks. I gave you an order. Was it fulfilled?"

"Yes. Our clients are safe."

This was it. The time to move.

"But—" said Tyler, his attention on the Proctor and only the Proctor, that ziggurat of flesh and embryonic hands, all of which flailed now in his direction. He swallowed any fear he might have had, what dim and misplaced guilt he suffered, stored them away. "—you're not," he said and he heard Fall gasp.

"Fall was the one to release the formalus among the clients. She's also the one who sowed so much dissent in the company. She dreams of power, Your Grace. Your power."

"Tyler, I swear to god—"

He spared her a glance then. A strange peach-colored smoke roared from her eyes, wrapping about features rictused in anger, melting into her hair. No, not melting *into* her hair. She was becoming smoke. Fall's head was dissolving into a brilliant titian fog, rising into the gloom of the ceiling.

"I'm going to kill you," she snarled in a madrigal of voices. "I'm going to make you regret you were ever born. You fucking bastard."

"I give you the traitor. I offer you her blood and flesh. I give you the wet of her body and the fibers of her hair."

Tyler inhaled and stepped into the sigil with the Proctor, both palms extended, as Fall began to lunge, too late to stop him, too late to save herself.

"The contract is met. The offering is taken," said the Proctor.

For all that Tyler was a grade A piece of shit, unrepentant as a tyrannical infant, he did flinch as the Proctor broke from its containment: a nightmare of gristle, and teeth budding on lengths of swelling cartilage, and so much venous filaments, so much marrow spun into garotte-fine wire. There was so much *pink*. The Proctor slammed into a now-screaming Fall like a truck into a pedestrian, and she crumpled almost souffle-like, concaving as though there'd never been any bone in her small frame, like she was only ever sugar-glass.

Tyler held his breath as Fall screamed.

Would it work? It very well might not. Never mind the fact that no one in the history of Thorne & Dirk had ever allowed the Proctor unfettered access to the world outside of its vessel. Always, they'd used proxies to fulfill its will. The firm had been so careful to keep the Proctor contained. But Tyler wanted—needed—to deal with Fall and make it someone else's fault. The question was: would *he* survive the aftermath?

His answer came as the Proctor shattered Fall's bloodied skull between his teeth. As brain matter welled from expanding cracks in the bone, the Proctor began to shriek, in perfect imitation of Fall's shrilling from seconds before.

"What have you done?" It turned on Tyler. The eye sockets were no longer empty, their circumference growingly lined with a pale, gore-tinged mucus. Tiny abscesses formed as the substance lost its translucence, becoming opaque: these scabbed over excessively, blackening pustules that then hatched into—

Eyes.

"They took something out of your world and stuffed it into my head when all this began," said Tyler, almost meditatively, as the eyes boiled out of the Proctor's sockets, seed-pearls in a dribble of phlegm. The Proctor screamed again: a killing noise, a warning. "A little parasite that was supposed to hatch if I didn't behave. Fall dug it out of my brain. But I kept it. I kept it until I could put it inside Fall. Because I figured while there might not be anything in this universe that can hurt you—"

The Proctor thrashed in Tyler's direction but it was getting bogged down by the nascent, still-growing parasite. New growths—pale, where the Proctor was very much the pink of flayed muscle—erupted through each joint, anchoring it further. It was being eaten alive.

"I was pretty sure there's something in yours."

When he was sure the Proctor was dead, Tyler looked over the pitiful leavings that comprised Fall. What he saw could be identified as human: there was a curve of pelvic bone, a bracelet of jaw; her spine was miraculously intact. But everything else had been pulled apart, mashed into a sort of bloody oatmeal.

"You were a good fuck," he declared to the silence, his only eulogy for his one-time conspirator before going to look for a shovel.

Stuffing everything into the disposal chutes was going to take work.

CHAPTER TWENTY-EIGHT

Sarah knew when she was being treated like rare porcelain, something to coddle in satin and put away on a shelf, high above the reach of the world. Her parents had done it to her first. Then Dan, when he wasn't screaming at her for wanting to be more than decorative. She recalled friends who sighed in envy over her situation, who said to her face how much they wanted to be like her: loved without exception, prized beyond reason. Sarah had smiled when they said that, even though what she really wanted to do was scream. A trapped bird was still trapped, no matter how pretty its cage.

So, when St. Joan gently suggested a trip to Gatineau, Canada, languorously extolling the virtues of her cabin there, how peaceful it would be, how rejuvenating the experience, Sarah cleared her throat and said:

"Thank you very much, but fuck that."

The room went immediately silent.

"Well," said St. Joan after a long minute. "That's that, then."

The group was sitting in what St. Joan had named her parlor, a rectangular hall with eighteen-foot ceilings, domed with what Sarah decided was a satire of the paintings roofing the Sistine Chapel. Instead of biblical figures, it had stars from the Golden Age of Hollywood. Judy Garland instead of Noah. Marlon Brando and James Dean substituting for God and David. Cary Grant as Goliath, brought down by Errol Flynn's David.

St. Joan leaned back in her chair, a gorgeous high-backed leather wonder that dwarfed her five-feet-ten frame. In the dim light, Sarah thought her eyes glowed.

"Sorry," said Sarah. "I just—I'm not going."

Dead Air shook his head. "Look, there's nothing we can do. You checked the book. So did I."

"I can help," said Sarah, aware on some level that she likely sounded like a petulant child. *Well, kids throw tantrums for a reason,* she thought to herself. Sometimes, they worked. And so long as she didn't resort to being overdramatic, no one would have cause to discount her wishes.

"You *have* helped. You figured out that whole thing with the Bellocq and Akrasiel. We can take it from here," said Dead Air.

"And?"

"What do you mean, 'and'?"

"You haven't gotten to the part about *why* I need to stop helping and go hide out in goddamn Quebec." Sarah straightened her posture. "Julie said I'm part of the team, so I'm going to help."

"How?"

"Well. Research. I'm not good at magic like you, but apparently I'm pretty good at finding obscure pieces of information."

St. Joan and Dead Air exchanged looks. Sarah tensed for the inevitable reply that while they appreciated her enthusiasm, her mundanity meant she would be more a liability than anything else and now that she'd helped with the research, she needed to listen to St. Joan and go away.

"Fine," said St. Joan.

"Wait, what?" said Dead Air and Sarah in unison.

"Fine," said St. Joan. "You have proven yourself decent in that area. We could use help on that front. And we can use help with the ritual."

"You can't be serious."

"Deadly."

"Julie is going to lose her shit if she knows."

"Julie has bigger problems."

"It's going to take years off Sarah's life," said Dead Air.

Sarah didn't hesitate. "I'll do it. If you two are willing to make that sacrifice, I am too."

"That's the thing. We're not like you."

"A regular mortal person, you mean."

"Sort of. What I mean is that we might lose a few months, you'll lose—perhaps ten years."

"I don't care. Anything to help Julie."

Another set of looks were passed between the other two, Dead Air's expression losing its usual nonchalance, becoming brittle and unhappy.

"Aren't you even going to ask what it is?" said Dead Air.

"Nope," said Sarah. And when Dead Air opened his mouth to protest, she said more gently, "It'll be worth it."

"He wasn't joking about the decade that'd be taken in payment—"

"You two aren't fully human, are you?" said Sarah slowly.

"Yes and no," St. Joan said softly. "I have all the years that my name should have had in history and judging from the fact I'm nowhere near dead yet, those were a great many."

At Sarah's puzzled expression, St. Joan continued.

"I was . . . very respected once as an actor. The kind that might have been spoken of in the same breath as Homer. The type whose name might have been turned into an adjective," St. Joan's smile was nostalgic and careful, the smile of someone who'd lived long enough with a hurt to find its beauty. "Those names were traded away. Year for a year."

Her murmuring drifted into a breathy *hmm.* St. Joan toasted the pair with a martini glass Sarah was sure she hadn't been holding before, the olive gleaming like a peridot, or a wolf's eye in the dark, and looked out of the atelier windows curving along one exposed-brick wall.

"And They don't mind wrecking a few Nokia phones for me," said Dead Air, a little too loudly, evidently trying to steer the conversation back to less troubled country, which Sarah was grateful for. "You'll be amazed how much of what we now consider obsolete technology will outlive us." In sotto voce, he added grumblingly: "Unlike the nonsense you get today."

"Magic is about equivalent exchange. Always has been," said St. Joan.

Sarah thought on this for a minute. "Well, they say if you wanna leave a pretty corpse, you gotta die young. So, let's get going."

The ritual itself was simple: a few drops of blood dripped on the red glass of an ornate mirror and the words "I consent to making a gift of my life" spoken in French. There was no pain, unlike what Sarah had feared. There were no pyrotechnics either, nothing to say that Sarah had tithed away a decade of her lifespan.

"Jean-Aimé de Chavigny was the alchemist who came up with the Miroir de Sang," said St. Joan abruptly, lofting the mirror for inspection. "Charming man. Intense lover. Overdramatic in all aspects of his life except for his work. I sometimes wish it was the other way around."

"Why is that?" asked Sarah as she applied a Hello Kitty Band-Aid to her fingertip. It pleased her to find she wasn't even shocked to learn that St. Joan had been intimate with de Chavigny. Sarah was becoming acclimated to the weirdness surrounding her.

"Because he's the reason that stupid Bloody Mary thing exists. Idiot made such a fuss about how he'd summon the witch who held the keys to his future that people stuck to his damn sales pitch, and took no notice of the fact he was just trying to call his goddamned girlfriend," said St. Joan, voice rising in volume with every word spoken, until the last word—girlfriend, hissed somehow, despite the term's lack of sibilance—thundered through the air.

"Geez," said Dead Air.

"There are a lot of unflattering renditions of Bloody Mary," said St. Joan with a little sniff. "It just kills a girl to see it."

"I shouldn't have taught you how to get on Twitter."

"It let me find Archive of Our Own. Hush."

"What does the Miroir—" Sarah stumbled over the pronunciation and stopped herself. She had no desire to be *that* kind of American, who'd stampede over languages, flattening them to fit in their monolingual jaws. "—blood mirror thing do?"

"It's . . ." St. Joan looked at Dead Air.

The three were huddled in St. Joan's absolutely palatial bathroom. St. Joan perched on the lip of her bathtub, while Dead Air and Sarah stood. Dead Air pushed away from the wall, gesturing animatedly and Sarah tried not to pay too much attention to how the cut along the back of his hand glittered.

"Think texting, except actually secure and you don't need to recharge your phone, and Julie can answer from anywhere so long as she bleeds herself a little on a piece of glass somewhere. And before you ask, They wanted to help but couldn't, not really. You can still hack Them. With the Miroir de Sang, anyone trying to tap into our frequencies will end up getting stuck in thirty years of futures. All of the futures. The ones we will live if we continue down the paths we've taken. The ones we'll have if we change our minds at one juncture or another. All the deaths we might have too." Dead Air grinned broadly. "Which is a cool security feature."

"Nerd," said Sarah.

Dead Air cracked up. Sarah loved the sound. Dead Air laughed the way Julie did: with the entirety of his body, without shame, with a commitment to personal expression that bordered on religious ecstasy. No surprise the two were such close friends.

"What now, though?" said Sarah as Dead Air's laugh ebbed to chuckles.

"We tell Julie to go into hiding until we figure out how to do this without getting her killed," said St. Joan.

"And hope," said Dead Air, "that she doesn't decide to get *herself* killed."

Again, Sarah saw the luciferin glow in St. Joan's eyes, saw her eyes brighten until the green swallowed the black of her pupils. The bathroom's pale clinical light was soon replaced by the same marine lambency as St. Joan's eyes.

"Is—is it okay if I do this on my own?" said Sarah, very softly. "This might be the last time I talk to her."

St. Joan nodded gently, rising to move to the door, Dead Air following after.

"Say her name," said St. Joan kindly.

"Three times. It might help if you prefaced it with Bloody. You know, like—"

"I will sew your mouth shut, I swear to god," hissed St. Joan as she shut the door behind the two.

Sarah closed her eyes and murmured Julie's name under her breath. No one had given her any further instruction than that, but she decided it would help if she focused on Julie, if she offered whatever spell she'd watered with her blood her best memories of Julie. Julie, at sixteen, grinning like she'd run a race against the sun and won. Julie on the couch with her, a bag of popcorn in hand, wearing an oversized Joan Jett T-shirt and neon-pink bicycle shorts. Julie, softly promising the one-eyed tom that hung around their fire escape a neutering, while feeding the cat a better meal than the one she'd have. Julie on the hospital bed, with all the light in her extinguished, haggard and smiling and holding Sarah's hand.

"Julie," she said again, louder. "Julie."

"Sarah?" came Julie's voice through the mirror, as if from a long way off, and through a hissing ocean of static. "What the hell is going on?"

Sarah took a deep breath and told her what she'd learned—but not everything.

CHAPTER TWENTY-NINE

Julie mulled over the information Sarah had shared. So much of what happened made sense now in context, and it annoyed Julie to have missed the signs, to have mistaken the grimoire for gospel and predicated everything on that belief. A fake Bellocq? Of course it was. Counterfeiting wasn't foreign to magical circles. She had trusted Billy to be an honest professional, but she really shouldn't have assumed Eric was cut from the same cloth. When this was over, she and he would have words in the colloquial meaning of the phrase.

But that was for later.

Now, she had to get answers.

Being blasted out of Central Park's subconscious had left her shocked and disoriented, the feel of Akrasiel's nose splintering under her knuckles still a fresh pleasure, but it wasn't without benefits. She landed twenty feet from where she sawed reality apart, and sat up to the sight of an EMT scrambling over toward her, wanting to know if she too was the victim of whatever had taken out the old samchon and if she needed medical assistance as well. Julie might have accepted their offer if not for two things: the fact she could see suited representatives from Thorne & Dirk milling amid the tableau, and that Sarah's face was staring out at her in the reflection of the man's cat-eye glasses. A quick incantation later, she was free, and rushing into an alley to convene with her friend.

The information Sarah gave her was limited but helpful: Akrasiel was like Koschei, hiding its heart in the oceanic dimension where it'd come from. Getting there, according to the fake grimoire, was slightly harder than calling a being from its depths, requiring a sacrifice from the original Doorway and more blood, of course.

Julie had nodded, said her goodbyes, and then wrenched the pinkie finger of her left hand out of socket, a white pop of agony blinding her for a second as she swallowed the ensuing scream, gripping the wall so hard her fingernails almost split.

Finger dangling uselessly, breath shallowed to hummingbird speeds, Julie then cut the back of her forearm again, dipped the feather into the stream of blood, and painted a door onto a wall, hoping she knew what she was doing and that she wasn't making the situation worse.

But how much worse could it get? Akrasiel was going to eat the world. Only if he dipped each of us in Sriracha sauce first could she imagine a worse fate.

Immediately after she connected the first line of the door to the last, the drawing went from a bloodied scrawling to a pitch-black opening in the dirty brick. A whiff of briny decay seeped from the doorway, and Julie grinned like a wolf into the dark: she would know that scent anywhere.

"I'm coming for you."

❧

Between one breath and its sister, Julie arrived on a pale pebbled shore. There was no sky overhead. Instead, a negative space her mind insisted on reading as darkness, and was happy to assert it was darkness so long as Julie didn't think too much on the subject. Similarly, though she could smell the water, could feel a light wind traveling over its surface toward her, Julie saw no ocean but allowed herself the fiction of its existence. It seemed easier and safer that way.

Julie tore the sleeve from her shirt and carefully pinioned her broken finger to its neighbor, wincing as she did.

Her blood continued to drip, a fluorescent swirl of red, the only color in the void.

"As we live and breathe, it's Julie Crews," came a half-familiar voice from behind her, a rich contralto more growl than bass, every 'r' reverberating darkly. "I would've expected you to choose elsewhere to die."

"Maybe she's trying to avoid collateral damage for once," said another voice, half an octave lighter than the first, this one nearly human, close enough to human that it lit up a memory in the recesses of Julie's exhausted brain, conjuring a face edged in neon colors, dark hair that had always reminded Julie of a pelt, of a wolf-skin worn in place of a wig—

"Oh, fuck me. You two. What the hell? Is Billy expanding his business to other dimensions?"

She turned, expecting to see the Barghest Sisters, and what she laid eyes on instead was, while not what she expected, in a peculiar way, truer to her subconscious understanding of them. Though the sight of them made her eyes water, there was an odd comfort in finally seeing them for what they were.

"Hey," Julie said. "New haircut?" Julie thought she saw a flash of lupine teeth in the roiling shadows.

"What are you doing here, Julie?"

"Well, as it turns out, Eric sold me a fake—"

"We know," interrupted one of the Sisters. "We dealt with that."

"You—" Julie made the connection. "I assume he's pretty dead."

"Not pretty," said one of the Barghests and they both laughed as if they'd pulled a harmless prank on an old friend.

Julie did not pursue the topic further. "What is this?"

"A waiting area, I suppose," said a Barghest.

"A nursery," growled the other.

Repulsion frissoned over Julie's skin. "A nursery for what?"

The Barghests chuckled but said nothing further. In their silence, however, Julie felt an impression of something: bones, bones everywhere, bones and bodies, some of which still shivered and groaned, only half-eaten, unable to die; bodies as large as continents, as faith; bodies still capable of locomotion, and those were the most tragic: they shambled through the dark pregnant with slugs, with wreaths of antlered coral, with great grinning and terrible life.

She shuddered.

"So," said Julie when the silence dragged into something uncomfortable. "You've dealt with Eric. But what about Akrasiel? I don't know if you've realized, but it is raising hell out there. Also, on that topic, the fuck is that thing anyway?"

"Hungry," said the Barghests. Julie was no longer sure which of them was speaking and if the distinction mattered. As they spoke, Julie felt again the impression of a memory: a winged, wailing thing—this was Akrasiel as they were, Akrasiel hunted from the heavens, chased into this eternal nothing—crawling away from a surge of lamprey-like bodies. It stumbles and is caught. It is perforated at the throat first and then the skull, then where the column of the breastbone yields to the cathedral roof of its ribs, then everywhere, until it is blanketed by them, its weeping suffocated under their bodies.

"I'd be too, if I had to feed a heart long-distance."

"Heart?" said the Barghests.

"Never mind. What do you two assholes know about the heart?"

"It tastes good," said one and they both chuckled as if it had been the funniest thing ever.

Julie squatted down, pinching her nose bridge between her fingers. The salt air prickled at her skin. She thought of Sarah and wondered if Sarah had ever visited Coney Island, and what she would have thought of the Mermaid Parade held there annually, if she'd have asked Julie to dress up with her so the two could ride a float with the other prismatic celebrants.

"Well. Whatever. What I need to know is how the fuck do I kill Akrasiel?"

"Kill yourself."

"Haha, very funny," said Julie. "How do I kill it?"

"You cannot."

"Okay, fine, how do I get it to fuck off out of this plane of existence?"

"There has only ever been one way to remove Akrasiel from this world. The Doorway must close; the summoner must die by their own hand."

"Not Akrasiel's."

"No, no," purred a Barghest. "If Akrasiel kills the Doorway, it wins."

"What happens if the Doorway doesn't close?"

"Everything dies."

Julie thought of Sarah as an old woman, surrounded by grandchildren, by the children of whomever she had helped and their children too, so adored by the world that Sarah would be sick for solitude. In her brief fantasy, she imagined Sarah as someone who gravitated toward charitable work in her later years, and being very good at that, having a natural aptitude for organization and a heart big enough to care for fuck-ups like Julie. Sarah could be happy.

All it meant was Julie not being there.

She thought on this. She thought of Sarah growing old and fat and happy. Julie laughed dizzily, raking a hand through her hair, no longer caring how the blood there would mat the strands because in a little while, none of it would matter. To her surprise, she was exhilarated by her resolve, both startled and pleased by the ease with which she arrived at her decision. It was so obvious, even if a little bleak.

"Akrasiel goes away if I die?"

"Until someone else makes a doorway for it."

"Good enough." Julie paused. If she could do one thing over, she would have kissed Sarah. "I've got one last ask here."

"Mrrrfrrrm?" rumbled the Barghests.

"Can you drop me off right on Akrasiel's head? I want to see the surprise in its eyes when I tear its head off."

⁂

To Julie's mild disappointment, the Barghests offloaded her right outside the entrance to Grand Central Terminal. As she stood there, stunned and more than slightly disoriented from being shuttled so rapidly between dimensions, people bustled around her, pushing her this way and that, sometimes brusquely, sometimes gently, almost always with complaints. Finally, she centered herself enough to follow the crowd inside.

She wasn't sure what she'd expected, but Grand Central looked exactly as it always had, with its gold-leaf stars on its distant ceiling and the four-faced clock atop the information booth, its arched windows and towering pillars, and its restless hive of commuters.

She hadn't a clue as to where to start, but the Barghests wouldn't have dumped her here without reason. Even they must give a shit about whether the world was going to end. Julie prowled through the station, looking for anything out of place, and headed down to the dining concourse. She spotted a kid pickpocket, about eight or nine, with a missing tooth and a frenzy of auburn curls—a good one too, given he nabbed two wallets from two different businessmen in the span of thirty seconds. There was a young woman in saffron robes going table to table handing out religious literature. A couple of undercover cops loitering beside the Shake Shack. In their ill-fitting suits and cheap ties, they looked as out of place as a couple of killer whales at a quinceañera. Then, she turned, just so, as a gaggle of leggy models spilled out of the Oyster Bar, and spotted something.

Two somethings.

One was Akrasiel in the last tattered remains of Dan, the skinsuit buttoned precariously together by eschar and layers of dirty fabric. It tottered with each step; it swayed, and dripped, and shivered.

The other was Sarah.

Sarah had an arm offered to Akrasiel, the skin there laced with blood, too much blood, and Julie wanted to scream at the incurious onlookers who barely glanced at the pair. Julie crept closer, but kept out of sight.

"Dan dreams of you," hissed Akrasiel. "He wept for you so many times. His Sarah, beloved betrayer."

"Then you know I'd be perfect for you," said Sarah, lofting her arm even higher.

Her face held a terrible dignity, the look of a woman setting clear terms with her own Death, and there was no fear in Sarah's eyes or in her voice, only a fatal calm, and Julie's heart broke at the perfect strength in her expression. She wanted to scream. She was only ten meters away, not even, the length of a sprint, but it felt overwhelmingly too far, and what even the fuck was Sarah doing here?

"Your body for his, then," said Akrasiel.

"No, my soul for hers."

Oh.

Oh, that's what.

Julie knew then, Jesus fuck, she understood at once and too late what Sarah had done, why the goose chase into the dark. The paralytic surprise dissipated. All her fucking talk about how ignorant the men in Sarah's life had been, how stupid they were to dismiss her as a pretty face and an accommodating heart, and as it turned out, Julie wasn't any better than they'd been. So obsessed was she with protecting Sarah, it never occurred to her to treat her like a fucking equal. She should have never left Sarah on the sidelines.

Should have, could have, would have.

Mantra of her life, wasn't it? Same shit from cradle to college to this current moment, the only person she'd ever really loved about to let a suit of worms wear her like a fucking coat.

"Hey!" she bellowed at the top of her lungs.

Akrasiel did not turn, although Sarah jerked a startled glance in Julie's direction, mouthing her name.

The not-angel dropped the pretense of Dan's ragged body and the clothes it wore and bared itself to the Grand Central mob.

There were a few screams and then more, mounting into shrieks. People began to run as Akrasiel laughed and laughed. At the sound of the commotion, two cops appeared inside of the terminal, their guns drawn. When Akrasiel turned to them and a cop caught sight of the creature's true face, he panic-fired his gun. The bullets hit Akrasiel in the chest, dislodging a few squirming maggots. Then it turned its full attention to the men. The second cop fired, dislodging more maggots. The not-angel's expression didn't change for an instant. It merely waved a delicate arm barely clothed in meat in their direction.

The cops froze where they were, looking absurd in their shooting poses. Then they screamed as the flesh began to wind off their bodies like someone peeling an orange. When the surface flesh was gone, their muscles unwound. They screamed and screamed but didn't fall.

The few remaining people in the terminal ran for the exits until the place was virtually empty.

"I love you, Sarah!" called Julie. She freed a tiny sliver of steel from inside the hem of her sleeve. It wasn't anything much, a little disposable razor with not a thread of enchantment on it, but it was enough. "I have always loved you. And I'll love you until the wheels come off. And I should have told you that at the goddamned clock and not here, not in this stupid dining concourse."

"Julie, what are you—"

Whatever Sarah was going to say next was lost in Julie's mouth as she ran up to her old friend, her first love, the only fucking person she ever wanted to grow old with, and kissed her. Hard. Hard enough, Julie hoped, that Sarah would never forget her. That Sarah would kiss her back in the afterlife. Because god knew that Julie would wait for her on the other side. She'd wait centuries to see Sarah again.

You should have kissed her sooner, hissed that familiar little voice.

Yeah, well, she thought right back. *Fuck you.*

"I'm so sorry," Julie said.

"What?"

Then she did it. Right in the circle of Sarah's arms, the taste of Sarah's mouth still on her tongue. The most stupid, most obvious thing she could do. For the first and the only and the final time in this life of hers, Julie chose the route she'd been told to take. She set the razor in the soft place right under the lobe of her right ear, drawing the blade across her throat.

She cut deep.

And as the world spiraled away, she heard Sarah scream.

CHAPTER THIRTY

Tyler went into Esoteric Unlimited with more cash in his pocket than he'd ever carried in his life. It was a special day, and he wasn't going to let a little thing like haggling ruin it. Whatever price Eric would quote, he'd pay it. A few thousand dollars next to the prospect of advancing into the hallowed halls of Upper Management.

There was no one inside the shop when he entered, so Tyler went to the bell and rung it between each shouted word. "Eric," he said, "are you back there? Get your ass out here. It's payday again."

Instead of Eric, it was Billy, in his red Pendleton shirt and shiny boots, who strolled out from behind the beaded curtains, a baseball bat propped on his shoulder. His voice was congenial, but his expression was not.

"Hello, Tyler."

"Hey, Billy. I didn't expect to see you here this time of day. I was looking for Eric."

"Yeah, I know. You were howling his name not ten seconds ago, Tyler."

"Is he around?"

"No, Tyler. He's mostly not."

Tyler didn't like how Billy was saying his name over and over again. There was something disrespectful about it. Maybe even—and this was hard to imagine—threatening. He kept an eye on the baseball bat, taking note of how the bookstore owner lightly bounced it against his collarbone as he stood there. Nonetheless, he replied with his most corporate smile, "Will Eric be around later?"

"No, he won't, Tyler. Because the itty little pieces of him are being melted down by the stomach acids inside the Barghest Sisters' bellies. In a day or so, they're going to shit him out into the toilet back in the club and flush him down the sewers, and that will be the sum total of his stupid life. Isn't that funny, Tyler?"

Billy was trying to rattle him. He wasn't going to let it work. "Okay. Stop saying my name. It's getting really annoying."

In reply, Billy slammed the bat down on the counter and punched it forward into Tyler's midsection. He gasped at the impact. The end of the bat had hit him in the solar plexus, and for a second, all Tyler saw was white. It took him a few seconds to catch his breath and by then Billy had come around the counter toward him, the bat held high, ready for another swing.

Emboldened by his recent success with Clarice, Tyler stared straight into Billy's gaze. Billy, with his stupid red shirt and his ridiculous cowboy boots, was a lesser being. He was smaller than small. He was worse than the meanest imp, more pathetic even than those infernal ticks which sometimes got into the corners after a long summoning.

Vermin.

Just as he expected, Billy stopped in his tracks. He looked around for a moment, rested the end of the baseball bat on the floor, and leaned on it. With an expression of considerable unhappiness, Billy touched his palm to his forehead. Then he cocked his head and stared at Tyler. After a moment, he said rather incredulously, "Are you trying to hypnotize me, you dickless little bug?"

Tyler hesitated, stumbling over the chant in his head before he redoubled his efforts.

Billy laughed, a sound that had jack shit to do with humor, and picked up the bat. "You *are.* You're trying to get inside my skull and to do what, exactly? Make me your Renfield? Give you my books? Maybe let you replace my stock with fakes? Yeah. I know all about what you did."

"I didn't do anything of the kind," said Tyler, still trying to recover his breath.

"I was looking for a copy of—"

"Wait. You fuck with my inventory and then come in to actually buy something legit?"

"I didn't fuck with anything!" shouted Tyler.

"Eric told me everything, shitbird. A deathbed confession, so I'll take his word over yours any day."

Now Tyler was mad at this mere *clerk* giving him a hard time.

"Yeah? What are you going to do about it? You don't have any proof—"

Before Tyler could say anything more, Billy took a hop-step forward and, with a stance so perfect he would have been signed onto Major League Baseball on the spot if a coach threw even a passing glance at him, he swung, driving the bat straight into Tyler's balls.

Tyler went down.

As Tyler sprawled there, both hands over his crotch, his lizard brain absorbed with the nightmarish worry his testicles had splattered from that hit, his vision gyring from pain, mottled with welts of light, Billy set the bat under Tyler's chin and raised his head, so the two were looking at each other mostly in the eye.

"The customer isn't always right, you know? That Wall Street privilege and those thousand-dollar loafers mean nothing here. This is *my* shop, fucker," Billy said. "You have no idea of the things I've done and seen. You think someone like you could ever scare me? If it wouldn't result in weeks of annoying conversation, I'd twist you into a pretzel right now and squeeze until your fucking head popped off. But because I have better things to do, I'm going to let you crawl out of my door on the condition you never, ever come back here again. Got it? You're banned from the store and from the club."

He kicked Tyler in the ribs. "Get the fuck out."

Billy nudged him with a toe again, knee slightly bent. He was thinking about kicking Tyler again, which the latter could see even through the haze of his agony. With a shake of his head,

Billy traded that idea for raising the bat over his head. Tyler flung his arms up protectively, knees tucked to his chest.

The sight of Tyler curled up so pathetically surprised a boisterous laugh from Billy, the man throwing his head back as the store thundered with his amusement. Tyler saw his advantage then. He pulled the 9mm from where it was strapped to his ankle and shot. His aim was true. Billy went down as Tyler emptied most of the cartridge into his right shoulder, the swoop of muscle and bone erupting in a spray of red.

Billy collapsed onto the floor. Impossibly, Tyler found the will to crawl up onto his feet and limp to where Billy laid prone, kicking him until the world steadied enough for him to grab the baseball bat, utter a spell to vanish the protective wards, and smash the glass doors of the cabinet behind Billy.

Pawing through the debris, Tyler groped through the collection of books inside. These were Billy's most powerful tomes: strictly for display only, a testament to the man's arrogance and purported power.

And now they would be Tyler's.

Except—

It wasn't until he was a quarter inch from the floor that he actually noticed his feet no longer touched the wooden paneling. He twisted in the air to see Billy with a hand raised in his direction. Blood pooled around him and his shoulder was mangled, but neither of these things seemed to have affected his power. As Billy closed his hand into a fist, Tyler felt a pressure build along his spine, his back arching. In a few excruciating seconds, it would be snapped.

But Tyler still held the gun.

He shot Billy twice more, hitting him in both legs: one in the knee, the other in the inner thigh. Billy crumpled again and Tyler was dropped onto the floor. Luck alone kept him on his feet. Billy's hand dropped and so did Tyler, who barely caught himself from falling over. Truly panicked now, he scanned the books in the cabinet. When he spotted the one he wanted on the bottom shelf, he grabbed it and fled the store.

⁂

Back home in his sprawling flat high above Fifth Avenue, Tyler placed the book on his dining room table. Though he'd caught a cab just a couple of blocks from Esoteric Unlimited and had taken the elevator up to his apartment, he was still breathing like he'd run a marathon.

The fight with Billy had hurt, much more than he ever expected from someone who was essentially a glorified retail worker. He had no idea how Billy had been able to withstand his hexes, but it was over now even if his balls still ached from being flattened with a bat. Billy would need to be dealt with, but that could be done later and with company resources. He could absolutely requisition a hit squad for his purposes. Get them to stage a fatal mugging.

The book he'd stolen was by Louis de Vanens, a seventeenth-century alchemist, poisoner, and secret sorcerer. It was an emaciated volume bound in worn, burgundy-colored leather. The deckled pages were yellowed along the edges. What was really interesting about the book was that there was nothing printed on its front, back, or spine: that was how he knew it for what it was.

Valens kept his most important works deliberately untitled—it was his little wink to the like-minded. There was just one problem. The book was in a steel cage so tight Tyler couldn't open the damn thing more than a few millimeters.

Tyler had enjoyed picking locks when he was a teenager. It made him feel smart and powerful, like a genuine criminal, but he knew that trying something as crude as an ordinary lockpicking wouldn't work and, more importantly, might piss off the cage or the book itself, rendering it useless. No, he needed something more subtle.

He ran mentally through his options: there had to be a good

lock-breaking curse somewhere. Something powerful, but not so strong that it might damage the book. Eventually, he arrived at a likely candidate. The last time he'd used it was in the penthouse apartment of a member of Congress. The man's maternal grandmother, dead for fifty years, had taken possession of the top floor of the place, and locked the door behind her using a combination of fiendishly intricate spells. It had taken Tyler two solid hours of spell work to break through the crone's defenses and send her back to the void where she belonged.

That scored the firm a whole tray of brownie points with the government, which subsequently became one of the reasons Tyler went from Excision functionary to head of the whole damn department.

He poured himself a glass of scotch to relax and rolled his shoulders, limbering for the spell. When he was ready, Tyler began to murmur the incantation and as he did, the lock began to glitter with pinpricks of light. Then, with a hissing noise like a cartoon fuse lit and on the race to detonation, the entirety of the cage lit up like a giant sparkler, growing brighter and brighter. Tyler eased up on the spell at the last minute so he wouldn't hurt the book: the white motes of light paused and then coalesced into a miniature sun behind the lock, before exploding outward with enough force to knock Tyler backward off his chair and onto the floor.

When he sat up again, the book was still in its cage, the steel undented.

Getting to his feet, he got a hammer from the tool chest and—fuck it—began smashing the lock with all his strength. This did nothing but gouge deep holes into his desk as the book reverberated in its cage. Still Tyler refused to give up. He continued pounding at the book until his wrist ached and his fingers cramped and he was tired enough to worry about losing control of the hammer and crushing his fingers. Sweating, furious, embarrassed that an inanimate object was getting the better of him, he discarded the hammer and reseated himself in his chair.

He picked up the book in both hands. There wasn't a single mark on the cage anywhere. No sign at all that he'd been abusing the thing for several minutes. It was time to think and regroup. He had tried violence. He could give a shot at diplomacy.

Tyler stroked the cage with the back of his fingers and said gently, "Hello. I'm Tyler and I know who you are, darling. How ancient, great, and powerful you are. You're not going to give up your secrets to just anyone. You know what a find you are. I get that. Sorry for being so rude earlier." He velveted his voice. "How about this? I pledge you my fealty and my protection if you will reveal yourself to me." On instinct, he picked up the broken pick from the floor and drove the ruined end through the tip of his right thumb. Several fat drops of blood fell upon the lock.

A few seconds later, it popped open.

Slowly, warily, tensed still for a trick, Tyler slid the book from its cage and opened the cover. It was indeed a Louis de Vanens manuscript: no title on the interior, no copyright jargon, no signature, nothing but de Vanens' blood thumbprint on the inside of the front cover to verify it as authentic.

Though it lacked a table of contents, Tyler had a pretty good idea of what he was looking for. He went through its pages, crooning to the book, flattering each illustration and span of paragraphs. His medieval French was rusty, but it was enough for him to navigate through the text. And besides, he was confident the book would give him what he wanted.

Halfway through his reading, it did.

Le Parasite Glorieux.

That had been the name Cranston mentioned, the horror rivalling his own. Tyler stared down at the meticulously shaded drawing on the page. The parasite resembled, for all intents and purposes, an undersea butterfly: gelatinous, fletched with spines. There was a face there in the illustration though he couldn't make out the details, smeared by what looked like something spilled on the page how many centuries ago?

Fucking idiot, thought Tyler. No wonder the book was so reluctant to open itself up for him. It'd been so neglected, so abused by its previous owners. "I'll take care of you," he said aloud and he swore that he could feel the tome vibrate minusculely in joy.

To his surprise, manifesting *Le Parasite Glorieux* was a relatively simple affair. He'd worked harder at conjuring much weaker creatures, which told him something important: the creature wanted to be born. There was no test. There were no complex incantations to sift through and decipher, no traps to dodge, no need to endure days of vigil. Looking over the process for a fourth time, Tyler was sure he would be holding the little miracle in his hands in under an hour.

He set to work quickly: measuring, cutting, burning, drowning the necessary ingredients. When he had mopped up the blood and ridded himself of the effluvium, he began the ritual itself. To his surprise, the spell required him to drink the concoction he'd brewed. Which, after a few minutes of thought, made a kind of magic sense to him: it was, as it said on the box, a *parasite.* Why would it want to appear in the world, vulnerable and without the sanctuary of a host's flesh? Increasingly excited, Tyler renewed his focus and concentrated on each step of the process until he reached the end.

What resulted was a multicolored sludge that clung to the bottom of his beaker: a milky swirl of greens, oranges, and purples that reminded Tyler of the photos of Jupiter he'd seen as a boy. Thinking of it that way—as swallowing a whole world—made the potion much more palatable.

When the colors had settled, Tyler raised the beaker to his

mouth, saluting the quiet expanse of his apartment, and drank the emulsion in a single gulp.

The experience, short as it was, was beyond horrific. It smelled awful—months-old takeout and sour bile—and tasted equally rancid. For a moment he was afraid he would vomit, but he held everything down through sheer force of will.

His discipline paid off. A moment later, he felt a faint tickle in his throat. It moved up and up, just thick enough to stretch out his esophagus. He retched instinctively, and that helped whatever was in him, was already squirming into his mouth, exit.

A thumb-size slug plopped wetly onto the table in front of him.

As he watched, one end of the infant parasite split in half and through the dark gap in its pearly body, something else emerged: a thing like a sprout, like a seedling. It grew in bursts and leaps, expanding as the parasite torqued and wormed across his desk. Soon enough, an angelic face on an elongated neck was staring at him.

What is your name, you who conjured me?

"I'm Tyler." It was beautiful. Stunning, even. A face for magazine covers and Rembrandt paintings if one could forgive the absence of a torso, and the fact that the neck extended from the body of an oversized maggot. "Tyler Banks, and I'm your servant."

Tyler! Tyler Banks! We saw that name when we were inside you! We taste you! Yes! Yes! We will love you forever.

"And what will you give me for my love?"

What is your deepest desire?

"Power. I want to be Upper Management at my place of work. I want to run the place. I want immortality. To be untouchable."

Yes! Yes! Forever! Love us and we shall love you!

"Always and forever."

Always, always.

The parasite was still growing as they spoke, only stopping when its face was the size of Tyler's own, and its body so large it threatened to spill from his desk. It was staring at him with rapt and slavish adoration, the idiot worship of a hound for its master. More tendrils peeled then from its body, and from those sprouted copies of the first head.

Are you ready, mortal?

The rational part of Tyler's brain howled in objection, only to be drowned out by his ruthlessness. "Yes."

Yes! Ours now! At last! At last!

All at once, he was beset by kisses from the parasite. The initial barrage was almost chaste: shy pecks on his cheek, his brow, the curve of his lower lip. But soon the parasite was jostling with itself to press hungry kisses to his mouth, its tongues between his lips, tasting of molasses. Tyler was beginning to take a confused pleasure in the attention when the parasite deepened a kiss, its tongue worming up to the back of his mouth. As Tyler gagged, it pushed, filling his mouth, his throat: it stretched him until he thought he would tear.

At least I'll be unconscious for that, thought Tyler as his vision mottled with black, graying. He struggled in his seat, discipline forgotten, unable to resist the animal need to thrash and push against the invasion.

Tyler lost his balance and fell back in his chair.

The world went black.

CHAPTER THIRTY-ONE

The next afternoon, and only after Dead Air had succeeded into securing them all passes, he, Sarah, and St. Joan went to the downtown morgue, ostensibly to identify Julie's body but really, to bring her home. Her death had been almost instantaneous, something Sarah would always be thankful for. Still she was cold and numb at the same time. It was bad enough that she had to watch Julie die before her eyes. If it had been less immediate, more protracted—well, Sarah had no idea if she would be sitting on that hard metal bench. More likely, St. Joan and Dead Air would be looking sadly at her through the bars of a psychiatric ward as she shrieked herself unconscious.

"Sorry it took so long," said an older Filipino woman in a lab coat, a kindly fretwork of lines bracketing her mouth and the underside of her eyes. This was someone who smiled a lot, and Sarah liked her on sight. Julie, though, would have been suspicious of someone who radiated so much nice and Sarah throttled any other thought she might have had of Julie before she could start crying again. "I'll take you to the body."

The body. Not Julie. Not anything but a slab of frozen bone and deteriorating meat. As gently as she said the words, Sarah still flinched from them. The woman's smile faded.

"Sorry." The woman wrung her graceful hands. "It's just—"

Sarah swallowed. "I get it."

The woman let the trio into the morgue. A row of metal gurneys stretched from the door to the back of the room, which smelled far more sterile than Sarah could have expected: antiseptic and chilly.

"You understand that this isn't an official identification procedure, right?" said the woman in the lab coat. She had told them her name when they entered the facility but the memory fled from Sarah each time she stretched for it. "That needs to be done by family or a spouse."

"I'm the spouse," said Sarah before she knew the words had come out of her mouth.

"But—" The woman pursed her lips and then nodded. "I see."

Sarah tensed.

The woman's expression softened. "I'll leave you three to the task, then," and it was a kindness, Sarah knew, an act of trust: the woman made as if to pat Sarah on the shoulder but thought better and left.

"Do you know how many deaths I've seen since this all began?" said St. Joan, and Sarah said nothing because she was weeping like a child who'd had their heart broken too many times for it to ever be put together again. "Thousands. Thousands and thousands of deaths. I've been to so many funerals, the world feels haunted these days. And every time—" Here at last, St. Joan's voice cracked. "—I feel so helpless and stupid. Words always fail me when I should have something to say."

It killed Sarah to see Julie so still. She had been—Sarah wanted to scream at the ease with which she too shifted Julie from present to past tense, an artifact instead of a woman, and god, how many memories would she lose by the time she was old?—a hurricane of a human being prone to restless movement. How small and fragile she looked laid out on the gleaming metal gurney. St Joan dabbed an embroidered handkerchief to her eyes and Dead Air looked away so that no one could see his face.

"She never gave me shit for being weird," he said finally.

Sarah was beyond words, beyond even simple grief. She felt hollow, just a cheap paper toy propped up by matchsticks, ready to drop at any minute. She'd had a plan, one she'd kept to herself since learning that Julie needed to die to stop Akrasiel. When the time came, as Akrasiel took over, she would have used the monkey's paw she'd taken from Julie's cupboard to deliver them elsewhere, wherever the relic thought fit to send them, just her and Akrasiel forever, separated from anything the latter could have hurt. Julie would have been safe.

"Julie can't go," said Sarah. To her amazement, her voice was steady. She drew several deep breaths to steady herself before she opened her handbag and removed the monkey's paw, setting it atop Julie's chest. "Bring her back. No matter what the cost."

"Sarah," shouted St. Joan. "You can't—"

"Why not? Because there are consequences? It'll take more years off my life or damn my soul? I've hidden from consequences my whole life. No more. I'll burn down this whole city for Julie."

"Listen to me. It's against every law of magic. And the monkey's paw is a cursed object. It doesn't grant wishes, it *twists* them."

"I don't care."

"Think, Sarah—"

"I. Don't. Care. It can have my fucking soul if it wants. I—I can't lose her. Not again. Not like this. I won't."

"Sarah, please—"

"It's too late," said Dead Air quietly. "Look."

True enough, the last mummified finger on the relic curled.

It was done.

So, they waited. And waited more, but Julie didn't move. When their breath began to mist, St. Joan put her arm around Sarah's shoulder and said, "It was a good try, dear. Maybe it took Julie to make the paw work. Or it could have run out of power. Sometimes, they do that. Wherever she is, she knows you love her and that you made such a wild attempt to bring her back. She loves you too."

Sarah broke down then, her grief at last too much to hold up, and she sank with the weight of it, going to her knees as she screamed without apology into the chilly silence. St. Joan held her, while Dead Air gently pulled the sheet over Julie's body. After he was done, they both helped her up and the three headed from the door.

There was a sudden rush of freezing air.

From somewhere behind them came a loud clang as a body sat bolt upright and yelled, “Motherfucker!”

CHAPTER THIRTY-TWO

Despite the healer's best efforts, Billy's shoulder throbbed like a son of a bitch. Each time he convinced himself he was fine and reached to pick a book from its shelf, a shock of pain reminded him otherwise. His only consolation was the memory of kicking the shit out of Tyler and seeing him laid low. That never failed to bring a smile to his face.

But he still had a problem.

He had to get the damn book back.

Or did he? He was pondering the question when the front door of Esoteric Unlimited opened and a man Billy hadn't seen in fifty years walked in.

The Escamotage hadn't changed a bit. His skin was still the bluish gray of a drowned corpse, marbled with veins, and he was dressed exactly as Billy remembered him: a shiny snakeskin sports jacket, embroidered black shirt, thin red tie, and black trousers Billy suspected were intentionally a size too small. His feet were bare and rosy, miraculously clean of street grime.

"Hello Billy. Long time no see."

"A long goddamn time."

The Escamotage looked over the bookshelves, his expression irritatingly paternalistic. "I see you've moved quite a lot of merchandise. What a pleasant sight."

Billy made a face. "Not enough. Not nearly enough for half a century."

"Still. Keep at it. You'll get there."

"That's what you said when you first brought me here."

The Escamotage smiled and spread his hands like he could hold the entirety of the shop in his arms. "And look how well you've done. The store chugging away. The club a mecca for one and all."

Working his thumb in the crevice of his shoulder blade, the muscle, Billy said, "What brings you here after all this time? You're not here to pay me compliments."

The Escamotage studied him for an endless moment before he touched a hand to where a heart would beat in a normal man and gestured to the counter. "Lean on the counter for me, Billy," he said, his voice the gravelly voice of a preacher who'd spent thirty years at the pulpit, telling his flock of the apocalypse to come. It even carried a lithe Arkansas lilt, which made Billy want to laugh. He couldn't picture the Escomotage in a church, not unless it involved some flames. "So I might lay hands upon you."

In all the years he'd known the Escamotage, Billy had never touched him, would not touch him. With his drowned man's skin and otherworldly air, there was something slightly obscene about the idea. Unclean. Still Billy did as he was told, wincing as he braced himself.

Gently, the Escamotage set a hand on Billy's sore shoulder: his touch was cool through the fabric but otherwise human. When he removed his hand a moment later, the pain was gone. Billy rolled his shoulder in an experimental circle then lifted the arm and did the same, rotating it several times with a look of burgeoning suspicion.

"What's it going to cost me?" he said.

"Billy!" said the Escamotage, aghast. "How could you say that? It will cost you nothing. You are my best salesman and I can't have my best salesman in such a sorry state," His mouth twitched into a faint smile. "It might affect business."

"Well, thank you," Billy said, no less suspicious than he was before. "I mean it. But you couldn't have come all the way over to the store just to fix me up. Why are you really here?"

The Escamotage propped his elbows on the counter and stretched like a cat, his eyes glinting red under the brim of his pinched-front cowboy hat. "I'm here because you had a burning question: Do you or do you not collect the stolen book from one Tyler 'shit for brains' Banks? The answer, I'm afraid, is *yes*."

"Why? In all the years I've been here, you've only ever wanted me to get rid of them. Why do I have to get this one back?"

The Escamotage studied his manicured matte-black nails. "I want that book back because it's mine, and what I might do—or not do—with it is my business. You know this, Billy. Don't get sloppy on me."

"We played a game and I lost. I had to take on your burden—this shop—and I won't be free until I empty it. But you won't let me do that!" shouted Billy.

"Did you think this would be like selling cupcakes to children and tourists? Books, knowledge, these are serious things and must be handled in serious ways," said the Escamotage. "I thought you would have learned that by now."

Putting a hand to his forehead, Billy feigned the beginning of a swoon, his accent shifted back to its native Texan. "I just get so tired sometimes. I didn't think the burden would be this heavy."

"You came to me. Chased me across the world because you wanted to play a game. Because I am the best. So, we played. And you lost, fair and square."

"I know. Don't remind me."

"I know what will make you feel better," purred the Escamotage. "How about we play another game? Winner takes all—including the responsibility of returning that book to the store."

He already had a fan of gold-edged cards in his hand.

Billy closed his eyes. He was a gambler and it had cost him so much more than it was worth. Still, he loved it. He routinely challenged people to games of chance, just for the joy of them flinching at the invitation, knowing full well they would demur.

The Escamotage did not wait for Billy to answer, instead laying out three cards face down on the counter. He flipped up the one in the middle, revealing the Queen of Diamonds for a second, before he returned it to the triptych and began to shuffle. "All of your troubles are just one play away, Billy. This time, your luck might change. And if it doesn't, why, we can always play another game."

"Games are how I got into this mess in the first place."

"Come on. Just pick a card. You're so good at this. You'll have no trouble at all finding your queen. She's calling to you. Can't you hear her?"

Billy hesitated, which was foolish. Because he already knew what he was going to do, down to which card he would choose.

After a few more passes, the Escamotage stopped and rested his hands at his sides. He said, "Your move, Billy. As the young punks say, death or glory."

Billy chose the card on the far right.

"I tell you what," said the Escamotage as he made a low *hrmm*-ing noise deep in his chest. "I'll do something I never do. I'll give you a second chance. If you have any doubts about that card, any slight doubt at all, you may choose again."

Billy clenched his jaw, shook his head. He trusted the Escamotage as far as he could throw the man. "No. That's my card. I can feel it."

With those long dexterous fingers, the Escamotage flipped the card.

It was the four of spades.

The error was with him. Billy knew it. His fault for having hope, for believing the cards might side with him over the Escamotage even though it'd never happened before and never would. Though he knew this with wrenching clarity, it still felt as if the wind had been knocked out of him.

The Escamotage patted Billy on his now uninjured shoulder. "It was a good play. You were so close."

"Not close enough. Never close enough."

"Try to enjoy yourself more. You never go to the club anymore. Have a drink with friends. Relax. This isn't a bad life if you have the right mindset."

"Sometimes, I think you cheat."

The Escamotage laughed in that warm way he did, folksy and kind. "That's loser talk, Billy. And I'd appreciate it if you kept from saying such foolish things again. We're friends and friends do not speak to each other like that."

"Sorry. I know you don't cheat," said Billy, trying so hard to keep his voice even. "It would just make me feel better if I could believe you did. I never lost before you, you know? I used to win every game I played."

"Maybe someday you'll beat me," said the Escamotage. "And then the burden will be mine again. But until that day—" Here that Southern kindness slicked out of his voice. "—get back my book. Do whatever you have to, but it must be returned."

"How am I supposed to empty the shelves if books keep coming back?" He was whining but he couldn't help himself. The thought of those fifty years stretching to fifty more, and then another fifty, and god knows how many more: it made him dig his eyes out.

The Escamotage straightened his tie. "That's not my problem. I'll see you around, Billy."

"In another fifty years?"

Shrugging, the Escamotage said, "Who knows? The universe spins. Worlds whirl in the great void. Most of all, things change. It might be fifty years, but it might be next week. These things are so hard to predict. Take care of that shoulder, Billy."

"I will," he said, but the Escamotage was gone.

Depression speared him through, and Billy sank heavily onto the counter, panting with aborted hope. He'd been one card away from a new life. Just one fucking card. The Escamotage had even offered him a second chance, which he should have realized never happened among gamblers. It'd been a gift: an unsubtle one too, a little nudge in the right direction. Pity Billy had been too arrogant to pick up on the hint.

Next time, he thought when he was done feeling sorry for himself. *Next time, I'll win. I can feel it.*

He opened the cash register and freed the battered deck of cards he always kept in the change drawer. Shoving it shut again, he made his way into the club. Though it was late and clamorous with drunks, every eye turned to regard him with wary respect. There wasn't a soul here that didn't know him by sight. Billy relaxed under the attention. Why had he practiced such unneeded hermitage? This was home. The music. The smoke. The smell of food being grilled in the kitchen.

Billy found an unoccupied table slightly removed from the rest of the crowd. He held up his deck of cards and with one hand cut them, and then cut them again, moving among variations of the Charlier cut until he was bored. Then he pulled out the ace of spades, tossed it in the air, caught it, held up the deck of cards and with one hand cut them, then cut them again. He moved the ace of spades from the top of his deck to the bottom, counted out four cards, turned them over to find all the aces in a tidy queue.

He still had it.

Billy strolled over to the nearest table. A group of young bank executives, each of them blazing with marks from their patrons, looked up from their drinks, uncertain how to react. In response to their confusion, Billy set his deck on their table and with a finger spread them into a perfect arc.

He said, "Want to play a game, gentlemen?"

A thin young man with an even thinner head of blond hair looked up. He wore sunglasses even in the dim bar, and a houndstooth suit he was likely still paying off in installments. It had such a Savile Row shine to it.

"I'm always ready, old man," said the idiot, pulling out a fat wallet.

Billy swept the deck back together and nudged the cards over for him to cut.

This was going to be fun.

❧

Tyler's new office was much nicer than his old one, not that the last had been shabby. But this one, god, this one was gorgeous. Caravaggios on the walls. A fifteenth-century Persian carpet in the center of the room. He had a desk the size of a Cadillac to sit behind and a new leather chair he could adjust thirty-six different ways.

All that was worth nothing next to the new privileges he had been granted, the control he had always wanted. He could have impromptu firm-wide meetings, hire and fire people—and worse. Plus, with the murders having stopped, and Julie off the hook for them after the Grand Central Station theatrics, there was no one to answer to anymore but Upper Management. He went to a corner of his office to gently feel the sculpted arm of the marble Grecian goddess that stood in the corner. As he did, the parasite spoke:

You are happy, beloved?

"For the moment. There's still so much more to do."

Yes! The work continues!

"You still haven't told me what you want."

Not yet! Let us love you first, Tyler! Let us court you. You asked us for power! We will give it. We will give all of it. And when you are happy, we will tell you what we want!

"That sounds good to me."

However, we want the eggs in the mother gone! They are an affront. We hate them! Remove them for us!

"With fucking pleasure."

Exhausted by the last few days of dying and coming back, but determined, Julie crossed her fingers as she returned to the gorgeous Arturia Estate high rise, hoping that Greg, the doorman she and Brad had tormented during their fight with the formalus, would still be working there. With the mess they'd left upstairs, there was every chance that he wasn't just fired, but in jail for gross something or other—an obscure law or two that rich people could always find and twist to their favor.

To Julie's delight and relief, she entered the lobby to find Greg was there, still in his tacky B-movie red velvet uniform and just as bored as ever. Julie waved to him from the door, wary of spooking him. She had, after all, punched him in the face.

"Hi," she called from the door.

Greg's pale features drained completely of color as he jabbed a finger at her. "No."

"Nice to see you too."

"Get out."

"I swear I have a good reason for being here."

"Get out or I'm calling the cops."

"Come on, man. It's not like you got fired."

"Get. *Out.*"

"I know I didn't apologize halfway near enough when we parted ways last time—"

"Apologize? *Apologize?*" The doorman's voice wobbled with fury. "You and your asshole friend wrecked almost an entire floor of the building. Like, oh my god. What did you even do there?"

Julie took a couple of tentative steps toward him. Greg backed away in simpatico, hands held out before him. "No, no, no. Just leave." He added after a moment, "And don't hurt me."

"Why would I hurt you? I said I'd make things up to you. Give me a chance."

Greg shook his head. "You don't have to. Pleeeeease just go."

Julie inched up to the doorman's desk and set a white plastic card on top before retreating back to the door, shouting out, "I just wanted to give you a little thank-you present."

Greg stared at the card like it was a snake. "What is it?"

"A prepaid ATM card. But a real special one."

"Special how?"

"It gives you free money."

Now the doorman approached the card. He picked it up tentatively and turned it over in his hands. "It doesn't have a number or a bank ID."

"I said it was special."

"Don't be an asshole to someone you're apologizing to."

"Sorry, true. Okay. You don't need any of that with this card. You can put it into any ATM anywhere in the world and get a thousand dollars a day for as long as you want."

The doorman's eyes narrowed. "No one gives away something like this for free."

"I do. When I owe a friend a debt. And I like to think that we're friends."

"We're definitely not friends."

"Okay. But close acquaintances."

The doorman looked at Julie and back at the card. "How do I know if what you're saying is legit?"

Julie nodded toward the ATM by the lobby door. "Take it out for a test drive."

Keeping his distance from her, Greg came out from behind the counter and went to the ATM. Julie backed away by a few respectful steps.

"What do I do with it?" he said.

"Put it in the machine. It's just like a regular ATM card."

The doorman slid the card into the slot on the front of the machine.

"It wants a password."

"Here. I wrote it down for you," said Julie and she handed him a business card. On the back in big block letters she'd written FUCKYOUTYLER.

The doorman didn't comment on the password. Instead, he stared at the card once more and then punched in the pass code. He went through several screens before noting, in a suspicious voice, "This machine will only give out two hundred dollars at a time."

"Try it anyway," said Julie.

Still looking skeptical, the doorman pushed the two-hundred-dollar button.

Twenty-dollar bills began to cascade from the machine onto the floor. Fifty of them, fluttering to the floor. The doorman got down on his knees and stuffed the money into his pockets as quickly as the bills fell.

"Holy shit. Holy shit," he murmured, eyes wide and unfocused.

When the bills finally stopped flowing, he looked up at Julie, his expression halfway between worship and terror. The doorman held up a fistful of twenties and said, "How . . . ?"

"Don't worry about it. From now on, you can do that once a day for as long as you like."

Greg squinted at her. "Is this illegal?"

Julie batted her lashes. "Me? Do something illegal? Do I look like the type? You won't get into trouble over the card. I promise."

Shoving the rest of the money into his already overstuffed pockets, Greg said, "Thank you. Thank you so much."

"We friends now?" said Julie.

Greg returned to the counter just as a couple of businessmen entered the lobby. He saluted them crisply as they went to the elevators, all without acknowledging him. When they were gone, he grinned at Julie. "Fuck yeah, we're friends. Best friends."

"That's what I thought," said Julie. "Take care of yourself and think about how you're going to tell your bosses to fuck off. I suggest tossing bills at their faces."

Putting out his hand, Greg said, "Thank you—"

They shook. He had a solid grip: firm, without being crushing. There was less pretense there than Julie had expected. Maybe his insouciance had been an act, a defense mechanism. "Julie. Julie Crews. It's on the card. If you ever need help with demons, insurance, or divorce, I'm your girl."

"Thanks, Julie."

"You're very welcome."

With that, she left the Arturia Estate and walked to the subway. It was nice seeing Greg so happy, nicer still to know she'd done good at Tyler's expense. The card was rigged to draw funds from one of Tyler's offshore accounts and was just small enough that he would never notice. Dead Air was far too good at what he did.

On the way home, she stopped by a liquor store to restock her supply of vodka and gin. But for some reason that she couldn't quite put her finger on, she went down the block to a bodega and bought a Butterfinger bar instead.

CHAPTER THIRTY-THREE

Julie counted all of her fingers and her toes, wiggling each digit in turn, disproportionately concerned about whether they were correctly attached. She'd been checking them every day since Sarah resurrected her. The broken pinkie raced a jolt of pain up her arm, as if irritated by her cajoling, but she could only smile. The pain meant she was alive.

She was alive, still here.

"Are you trying to piss off your physiotherapist?"

Sarah sat down beside her on the sofa, lipstick a little smudged. Her eyeliner had run so much, her eyes resembled a hasty charcoal sketch, the edges blurred to smoke. Julie'd never seen anyone so beautiful.

"It's still weird to be here. I wasn't supposed to be here."

"I disagree," said Sarah, passing her a sandwich.

Julie took a bite. It was simple but pleasing: good sourdough, a few slices of tomato, far too much lettuce for her liking, and a meager layer of bacon. What dazzled Julie, however, was that it was a sandwich made in *her* kitchen, with ingredients stored in *her* pantry. Under Sarah's care, her apartment was becoming more than a halfway house for empty vodka bottles and takeout containers.

"This is exactly where you should be, actually. With me," said Sarah.

Julie opened her mouth to answer and was quieted by a kiss, Sarah's lips tasting of the bacon she'd sneaked while preparing their lunch. The taste was delightful, but the feeling was a pleasant electric shock bouncing up and down Julie's spine. She had more to say, but it took her a moment to find her voice. Sarah just smiled at her breathlessness.

Finally, Julie went on. "You were supposed to be married to a nice accountant and have six kids, all of whom would give you grandkids. Then you'd hit the lottery and buy a villa in Norway and a cottage in Calgary. Live a long life and die in your sleep, and after that, I find you." Her voice hushed. "Then I say hi, and maybe we get our story then, but this wasn't how it was supposed to go."

Sarah gazed sternly at her.

"I have a question."

Julie raised an eyebrow.

"Why an accountant? Accountants are boring."

Julie laughed and took another bite of her sandwich, unable to repress the upsurge of happiness. Her joy wasn't without guilt. Julie knew what Sarah had done. New Yorkers no longer dreamed normally. They woke up screaming instead, shrieking about water and smiling mouths in the abyss. The luckier ones insisted they were being visited by God, who promised them everything so long as they opened the way.

"Accountants are safe, though. And stable."

"Fuck safe," said Sarah, with the relish of someone savoring their favorite guilty pleasure. "Also, fuck stable."

"You're going to sing a different tune when we're broke again and St. Joan's trying to throw us out," said Julie, laughing knowing that would never happen. Not after the past few weeks.

"This is why you're going to let me be your apprentice," said Sarah brightly.

Julie was seized by a vision of Sarah in Brad's clothes, in the suit and skinny tie getup all her interns seemed to prefer, uniforms that inevitably proved dismal protection against all the blood. She caught herself before her catastrophizing led her down a worse route, one with Sarah on the table, gutted, Julie's hands buried in her abdominal cavity, the formalus squirming out of reach.

"Hell. No."

"We'll be a two-income household if you let me."

"No. Absolutely not."

"Why?" demanded Sarah, cheeks puffed, so adorable in that instant that Julie almost caved.

"Because I love you," she said.

Sarah's expression cleared, the half-hearted petulance whittled to a fragile joy. Hearing herself say it here, softly, in the perfect banality of what was now their shared home, Julie was struck by the weight of the phrase and by how much she meant it.

"I love you," she said with more force, as if trying to undo the years they'd spent apart because Julie was made of too many sharp corners to let anyone safely in. "I love you, I love you—"

Sarah kissed her.

"I love you too," said Sarah, a hand nestled in Julie's hair. "You're still not becoming my apprentice."

"Damnit."

Soon they would have to deal with the fallout from when Sarah used the monkey's paw, what it meant that New York now dreamed of those dark waters. Later, there'd be a fee, Julie was sure. Something large and dramatic, because that's what curses—the damned drama queens—always demanded. But for now, there was Sarah, warm in her arms, her hand in Julie's hair, her forehead touched to hers, and she was alive.

As their lips touched in a kiss, someone knocked on the door.

"Are you expecting anyone?" said Sarah.

"No. You?"

"Not a soul."

"I suppose I should go see who it is."

Sarah frowned.

"But we're so comfy here."

The knocking came again.

"Don't worry. I'll get rid of whoever it is quick."

Julie got up and padded across the apartment in bare feet.

When she opened the door, she knew immediately that answering the knock had been a mistake.

There was a male corpse standing in the hallway. It didn't look bad as far as corpses went, but its sallow color and dull eyes immediately marked it as the living dead.

"Hello," said the dead man. "I understand that you take unusual jobs."

"Sorry. I don't work for zombies."

Without hesitation, the dead man used both hands to pull back his head and yank down his jaw so that his mouth elongated unnaturally. To her great surprise, a small red fox head looked at Julie from where the corpse's throat should be.

"But I'm not a zombie. See? Hi!" said the fox happily.

"Hi," said Julie slowly.

Sarah came up behind her.

"Who's your friend?" Then, "Oh. Are you—?"

"A fox? Yes!"

Julie sighed.

"Here's the thing, little fox. I don't work for zombies or, now that I think of it, animals, because, and don't take this personally, they don't have money."

"I can pay in gold. Would that do?"

"Absolutely," said Sarah, standing aside to let the fox in. "Come inside."

The fox yipped happily and walked its human body into the apartment. "Do you have tea, by chance?"

"Uh, Sarah—"

"Don't worry. Look. It's a cute little fox and it needs our help."

On the one hand, Julie was delighted by how quickly Sarah had become accustomed to her world and her eagerness about learning the basics of magic. On the other hand, there was a talking fox in a dead man's body in her apartment.

"Julie. Are you coming? The fox wants tea and I don't want to leave our guest alone."

"Coming," said Julie, falling in love with Sarah all over again as she sat on the sofa chatting with the fox like it was something she did every Sunday at brunch.

"Sure," said Julie. "Why the hell not?"

ACKNOWLEDGMENTS

I'd like to thank my wonderful agent, Ginger Clark, who's stuck with me through so many ups and downs. I also want to thank our terrific editors, Kelly Lonesome and Kristin Temple, who made the book much more than I ever imagined. Thanks also to David Southwell and the Hookland Guide for their constant inspiration. And, of course, thanks to Aces, who sleeps by my desk and eats my Post-its whenever I turn my back.

—Richard

I'd like to also thank Kelly Lonesome and Kristin Temple for their heroic efforts in getting the book into shape. We couldn't do it without you two; my agent, Michael, for tolerating every shenanigan I throw at him; thanks especially to Ann Lemay, Ceri Young, Gabrielle Marshall Goulet, Mitch Dyer, Dedie Kanda, and everyone else at WB Montreal, who showed me what home was like when I was nothing but raw nerves. So much of what is good and stable in my life wouldn't exist now if it weren't for these wonderful people, their kindness, and their patience with me as I picked myself up after a terrible year.

Thank you as always to Mouse. Let's be fucking hooligans in the old folks home one day, and make nurses decide if they're going to separate best friends for the sanity of the rest of the institution.

—Cassandra

Turn the page for a sneak peek at
the next Carrion City novel
from Cassandra Khaw and Richard Kadrey

A DEMON IN THE BRONX

Coming soon from Tor Nightfire

NIGHTFIRE

CHAPTER ONE

"Two months of rent," snarled Julie as a many-eyed horror carried her across the ceiling. "No, fucking *three* months of rent. St. Joan, do you hear me? I get three months rent-free when I get out of here."

Her only consolation was that *it* had taken her instead of Sarah, who for some reason was still in the room instead of hotfooting it for St. Joan like she promised she would. Julie might have roared for Sarah to leave, but that might have the spirit switching targets.

It should have been a straightforward contract. St. Joan had promised Julie a month's rent free for clearing out the empty apartment on the sixth floor. Well, *almost* empty apartment. *Something* had taken residence up there after the previous tenants vacated. St. Joan thought it might be an addled domovoi. Dead Air, to Sarah's horror, insisted it was probably the spirit of a dead rat king. Either way, it had presented itself as a rather trivial specter.

"Why don't *you* deal with it, then?" Julie had gloomily demanded.

"Because I'd rather not consider what the situation might do to my wardrobe," said St. Joan airily, setting a cigarette in its holder. "Eternity is far more entertaining when you're not worrying about your laundry."

Were St. Joan anyone else, Julie would have argued the point further, but even she knew better than to antagonize her landlord, who was prompt about building maintenance and exceedingly generous about Julie's delinquency when it came to rent payment. So when St. Joan capped the sentence with a cold look of expectation, Julie grunted and slunk home to prepare for the exorcism.

When she was ready, she and Sarah went upstairs, the latter armed with a small iron urn. The late-evening light bloodied the shadows that seemed to grow with every floor until they were thick enough to swallow the women's footsteps, to chew their conversation down to whispers.

"Remember," Julie said when they'd first entered the apartment. "This should be a quick in-and-out job—"

Sarah stared at her. "Was that—"

"—entirely unintentional. Unless you're into it."

"I want to leave all that crassness in the grave with Dan."

Julie felt a soft heat clamber over her face. "I never said I was good at flirting. Look, we can discuss that later. You remember what to do, right? This should be easy but if anything goes sideways—"

"I run out and call St. Joan for backup," Sarah said. "I know. We've gone over it a dozen times."

"You promise you're going to go straight to St. Joan?"

"I promise."

"No heroics whatsoever."

"None."

"No trying to save me."

"I will let whatever we meet eat your toes instead of helping." Sarah gave a Girl Scout salute, expression grave. "Cross my heart and hope to die."

Julie didn't believe for a second that Sarah would leave if shit hit the fan, but all their reconnaissance suggested this would be a straightforward affair. In and out, as she told Sarah. Besides, she couldn't imagine St. Joan setting them up for ruin. Forcing a smile to her face, Julie took Sarah's head in her hands and pecked her on the lips before setting a hand on the apartment door, its wood so old and worn it couldn't be called any color but ancient.

"Ready?"

"Yes."

"Here we go."

If the corridor outside was quiet, the apartment was where sound went to die. Nothing moved. The anechoic silence seemed to dull even the thump of Julie's heartbeat in her ears. There were tombs she'd been in that were more alive, filled with the soft subterranean noises of worms and beetles at their work. A chill slicked down Julie's back. This didn't feel right. Some simian corner of her brain shivered with ancestral memory of deep jungle and hungry mouths waiting in the dark.

But Sarah was there next to her, her hand in Julie's like this was a date in a haunted house. She smiled with such ferocious trust.

"In and out," Julie muttered to herself.

St. Joan said the haunting was centered in the main bedroom, but Julie made them do a circuit of all the other rooms. To her immense relief, there was no sign of abrupt departure, no indication the tenants had skedaddled with only their luggage and their lives in hand. If there had been any indication of such, she'd have sent Sarah back down.

Still, that faint chill remained.

Nerves, Julie told herself, freeing a vial of holy water and a handful of black salt from a pocket in her jacket. Or more likely, she was picking up on Sarah's own fraying confidence.

"You okay?" Julie hissed, fingers brushing her—girlfriend? Lover? She couldn't bring herself to use any of those terms yet, not when things were new, their love so frangible—companion's forearm. "You don't have to stay for the whole thing, you know? This one seems shy."

"You kidding?" A feverish excitement kindled in Sarah's face, burning away any signs of fear. "You couldn't pry me out of here with a crowbar."

"I'm just saying—"

Belatedly, it dawned on Julie that she did not actually want

Sarah here, for all that the two had fantasized about how, after a period of apprenticeship, they'd be equal partners, the pair of them against the world. No, Julie wanted Sarah at home, tucked under a blanket on the couch, in pink slippers with her hair in curlers and bored stiff of being safe. Nothing in the apartment *screamed* danger but still there was that lingering chill, that unease laving down Julie's spine like a tongue.

"Shh," said Sarah before Julie could articulate anything further, pointing to the mattress in the center of the master bedroom (Julie's first thought was *squatters*, but surely St. Joan would have said something). A pink duvet lay over the mattress, and where Sarah was pointing, there was a raised bump like a kitten had hidden itself there.

"Here, little ghosty ghost," said Sarah, face bright as a lamp. "Come out so we can take you uptown to a much nicer building."

"Sarah, stay here," said Julie, moving to impose herself between the other woman and the now-alerted shape, the mound on the bed rippling a few inches in the direction of the far wall. The moment Julie's foot creaked on a loose floorboard, however, the entity blurred away from under the duvet to behind a dressing table—*had that always been there?* Julie couldn't tell, wasn't sure, and the fact she could not turned her unease into a spike of cold—that stood heaped with makeup containers and half-empty bottles of perfume. She heard clicking under the baseboards as she stomped up to the dresser.

"Where is it?" said Sarah.

"I don't know. Do me a favor, stay right the hell—"

"*There,*" bellowed Sarah, pointing.

Julie whirled in time to see the wall on the opposite end of the room swell wetly as something wormed its way to the electric socket.

"Fuck," said Julie, kicking the wall where the ghost had disappeared. She thought she heard a woman's faint laughter graze the air. "If it can move through the wiring, who the hell knows where it's going to end up. St. Joan is going to be pissed. I swear to god, every time someone tells me it's going to be an easy gig, it always turns into a *thing*."

"But supernatural entities don't like the Hum, right?" said Sarah.

"You *remembered*," said Julie.

"I was always a bit of a teacher's pet," said Sarah, urn held to her chest like it was a child, a half smile anointing her lips. "Besides, the Hookland books were really well-written. Anyway, it'd probably take a minute before it can get anywhere else."

"Let's take advantage of that then," said Julie. "Be ready with the urn. You're going to want to slam the lid shut the moment I get the fucker in that."

"Got it," said Sarah, uncorking the urn.

Catholic magic always felt to Julie like being drunk. Godliness was apparently next to good vodka. Her head swam as she chanted the words. In her vision, every surface grew limned with a golden light and Julie thought deliriously to herself that God, as the Catholics knew them, probably should give their publicity department a raise. She splashed holy water into the electric socket, hoping to the hells and back it wouldn't start a fire. "Princeps gloriosissime caelestis militiae, sancte Michael Archangele—"

Someone—some*thing*?—made a low displeased noise, like some well-bred Midwestern woman at brunch sighting a mispositioned canape.

"Uh, Julie?" said Sarah.

Really, her problem with Abrahamic traditions was how they necessitated follow-through. Exorcisms couldn't be truncated. Blessings couldn't be abbreviated to a quick, "Hope it's all gravy from here on." You had to walk the road from start to finish or you'd stay there forever in the glare of that distant divine power.

"Julie?"

Except Sarah's voice was a half-octave higher than it was before.

"Hm?" said Julie, a little dreamily, inebriated on God.

"Julie, I think—"

Something exploded out of the wall, scattering plaster and bits of rotten wood, smelling of perfume and mold. It wasn't the tiny apparition Julie had anticipated. The creature that now stood quaking before them was twice her size: a matte-black skull fronded with an excess of jawbones, like feathers trailing from its brow and its cheeks. Barbed insect legs extended from where a spine should have lolled.

"Sarah, *get out now.*"

There wasn't time to see if Sarah would take her word as gospel. Julie had to keep the thing distracted, keep its attention on her as long as she could and she'd deliberate on the rest later. Julie spat a word at the chittering monstrosity, felt something tear in her mouth as the magic lifted the horror and flung it across the room. Except as it lurched away, the thing vomited a string of lymph-yellow silk straight at her.

Too late, Julie tried to scramble away; it had her cocooned in seconds, the yellow strands blistering her naked skin. Then before Julie could think about escape, the world inverted itself as she was hoisted upwards and carried upside down along the ceiling.

"St. Joan owes me so fucking bad for this—"

"Hey, asshole!"

Sarah.

"What the fuck? *I told you to run–*"

Julie stared with a mix of horror and uncut awe, the kind of wonder she thought she had left behind with her innocence at age eight, as Sarah *springboarded* from a wall to smash a chair over the monster. It was a glancing blow, only enough to cause a few vestigial jawbones to spray across the air, but holy shit, Julie thought giddily, did Sarah just do *parkour*?

"Over here, fucker," shouted Sarah, landing with only a mild wobble. Julie would have applauded if she wasn't strung up like a slab of ham and terrified for Sarah's continued good health. "I'm over here!"

In answer to Sarah's attempt at intervention, the thing simply dropped Julie onto the floor below. Again, Julie heard that sound of a woman expressing her displeasure, a pettish *mmmm* bristling with undertones of I-want-to-speak-with-your-manager, almost eclipsed by the shock of hitting the ground shoulder-first. Something tore.

"Oh fuck," said Sarah, backing into a wall. "Julie, I think I made a mistake."

"The urn. Get the urn ready," panted Julie.

Sarah dove for the urn as Julie screamed a spell as foul and grisly as anything she'd ever used. She could feel the magic scrape ten years from the tail of her life and staple a promise to what was left: when the time came, it wouldn't be easy. Julie would go out screaming. But that was for a future version for her to worry about. Here and now, all she cared about was keeping Sarah out of that monster's reach.

The spell detonated through the air, corkscrewing into the monster and Julie could see bone boil away into liquid, a growing helix of ivory arrowing straight for the open urn now in Sarah's arms. If Sarah faltered, the spell would take her too, condensing her into a fatty emulsion. Julie held her breath, not wanting to watch, unable to look away.

But Sarah rose to the task like a dead woman's wrath, face bright with resolve. The thing let out one last *mmmmmrm* before it vanished entirely into the urn. Sarah slammed the lid down half a second later, and the room went silent save for Julie's agonized panting.

Setting the urn on the floor, Sarah ran to Julie to help disentangle her from the webbing. Whatever made the silk burn like acid was gone with the creature, but Julie's skin blazed with furious red welts.

"Do they hurt?"

"Like hell."

Sarah withdrew, palms held up and toward Julie. "I won't touch you then."

"That's worse," Julie threw her arms around the woman. With their cheeks pressed together, she said, "You were supposed to run."

"And this was supposed to be an in-and-out job. I guess we're both liars."

"I thought you hated the phrase."

"Not right now, Julie."

"What about after some fried chicken?"

"That's bribery."

"Sure, but would it work?"

"Maybe," said Sarah, helping Julie to her feet. "You okay?"

Julie was objectively *not* okay, but her throat was uncut and her ribs unbroken. At least this time, she didn't have her bowels in her arms. Compared to some of her previous injuries, this barely qualified as a scratch. It was a mosquito bite, a stubbed toe. And Sarah looked too worried already.

"I'm a little sore," said Julie because lying outright felt like blasphemy.

"Let's get downstairs to fix you up then," said Sarah, hooking an arm around Julie.

Together, they limped to where the urn lay on its side. Julie, wincing, bent to scoop it into her arm. If she had even an inkling of how the night was going to go down, Julie would have had Sarah stay far, far away.

"What are you going to do with that?" said Sarah as they inched down the stairs.

"Seal it with a million wards and witch's wax, then throw the fucker in the East River."

"I thought we were going to take it to a nicer apartment uptown?"

"That was before—" *Before I was scared shitless you were going to die.* Julie swallowed the rest of the sentence as she stared into Sarah's face, smudged with dirt and sweat, her expression still bright despite it all. "Look, I'm covered in hives. Fuck that thing in its bony ass."

Back downstairs in their—the word *their* felt as precarious as *love*—apartment, a corpse sprawled over their sofa. The cadaver, along with the small red fox entombed in its throat, had been sleeping for three days straight, waking only occasionally to eat whatever meat they brought into its proximity. The women tiptoed past their guest into the bedroom and shut the door.

"Take off all those burned-up clothes," said Sarah, heading to the bathroom.

"Uh, I'm not sure if my cardio's—"

Sarah emerged again, stripped down to her sports bra with her hair smoothed into a businesslike ponytail. She had Bactine in one hand, bandages in another. "I'm *not* trying to have sex with you."

"Tyler used to—"

"I'm not Tyler," said Sarah, seating herself beside Julie. "I don't need you to do anything for me. I just want to make you feel okay."

"What if making me feel okay meant sex?"

Sarah daubed the weals spread over Julie's arms with antiseptic. "Would it?"

"No."

"Then what would?"

"A nap," said Julie, a little aghast at how her voice shook as she spoke the word, how thin it'd become, how infinitely more fragile than she ever recognized it to be. "With you in my arms."

"Okay," said Sarah. "We can absolutely do that."

❦

When they emerged from the bedroom a couple of hours later, the corpse was upright, hands on its lap, head lolled back. Its jaw was hideously distended, stretched such that it barely hung on to the skull by a hinge of skin. Peering from the abyss of its throat was the head of a small red fox, its snout barely jutting past the dead man's tonsils.

"Hi!" it said happily. "What were you two doing in there?"

"Uh—" said Julie, who in her storied life had never been required to explain her bedroom activities to a woodland creature. "Um."

"You made a lot of noises," said the fox with such rabid cheer, Julie found herself wondering how much of the interrogation was actual curiosity, and how much was just raw mischief. "Some of it sounded quite strenuous."

"Listen here. Even if we *were* having sex—"

"You *weren't*?" The fox bared its teeth in what looked almost like a smile. "But why not? I'm told it's so much fun."

Sarah sat down heavily on the sofa beside their guest, her tone conciliatory as she said, "I was wondering if any of your memories might have returned."

The damn thing looks like a tumor, Julie thought, slouching a hip against the armrest closest to Sarah, arms folded over her chest. "I just want to know why you're stuck in a dead body."

The fox shook its head with considerable gusto, which in turn caused its host cadaver to flop alarmingly. "Sadly, all I know is that I'm not from around here."

"Could have told you that," grumbled Julie.

"And that I did not agree to be put in a corpse."

"How *illuminating*," said Julie, rolling her eyes.

Sarah hushed her.

"And," said the fox, "there's a bad man."

"A bad man?"

"A terrible one, really." The body sagged forward so the fox could stare at the hands of the corpse in which it was penned. "I think he did this to me."

"My condolences," said Julie. "Sorry for your loss and all that. Too bad—"

"Julie."

"It ate," said Julie, jabbing at the air with an arm, "my filet mignon. My dry-aged perfect steak. Whole. While it was frozen."

"The ice crystals add flavor!"

"I will throw you out—"

"You could," said the fox, grinning again. "But I just remembered something else."

"What?" growled Julie.

"That bad man? He kills everyone who is nice to me."

ABOUT THE AUTHORS

CASSANDRA KHAW is a Bram Stoker Award–winning game writer and former scriptwriter at Ubisoft Montreal. Khaw's work can be found in places such as *The Magazine of Fantasy & Science Fiction*, *Lightspeed*, and *Reactor*. Khaw's first original novella, *Hammers on Bone*, was a British Fantasy and Locus Award finalist, and their novella *Nothing But Blackened Teeth* was a *USA Today* bestseller; a Bram Stoker, Shirley Jackson, World Fantasy, and British Fantasy Award nominee; and an Indie Next Pick.

Twitter: @casskhaw
Instagram: @casskhaw

ABOUT THE AUTHORS

Allan Amato

Richard Kadrey is the *New York Times* bestselling author of the Sandman Slim supernatural noir series. Sandman Slim was included in Amazon's "100 Science Fiction & Fantasy Books to Read in a Lifetime" and is in production as a feature film. Some of Kadrey's other books include *The Grand Dark, The Everything Box, King Bullet*, and *Butcher Bird*. In comics, he's written for *Heavy Metal, Lucifer,* and *Hellblazer.*

richardkadrey.me
Twitter: @Richard_Kadrey
Instagram: @rkadrey